FREE TO REUNITE

AMARYLLIS SERIES
BOOK 10

TRACEY JERALD

ISBN: 978-1-7358129-9-1 (eBook)

ISBN: 978-1-959299-00-4 (Paperback)

Editor: Melissa Borucki

Proof Edits: Comma Sutra Editing

Cover Design: Deborah Bradseth—DB Cover Design

This book is a work of fiction. Names, characters, places, and incidents are either products of the author's imagination or are used fictitiously. Any resemblance to actual persons, living or dead, events, or locales is entirely coincidental. The author acknowledges the trademarked status and trademark owners of various products referenced in this work of fiction, which have been used without permission. The publication/use of these trademarks is not authorized, associated with, or sponsored by the trademark owners.

DEDICATION

This book is dedicated to the people who asked me to stand up and speak.

I never would have had the courage otherwise.

RE80

PLAYLIST

Linkin Park: "Numb"
Kygo, OneRepublic: "Lose Somebody"
Dave Matthews Band: "Grey Street"
Switchfoot: "Meant to Live"
Fall Out Boy: "Centuries"
Taylor Swift: "Mean"
Luke Bryan: "What She Wants Tonight"
Nickelback: "Far Away"
Hozier: "Almost"
Taylor Swift, Chris Stapleton: "I Bet You Think About Me"
Dave Matthews Band: "Everyday"
The All-American Rejects: "Move Along"
Annie Lennox: "Why"
Switchfoot: "Dare You to Move"
ICEHOUSE: "Electric Blue"
Adele: "Easy On Me"

ALSO BY TRACEY JERALD

Amaryllis Series

Free (Phil's story) - newsletter subscribers only!

Free to Dream

Free to Run

Free to Rejoice

Free to Breathe

Free to Believe

Free to Live

Free to Dance

Free to Wish

Free to Protect

Free to Reunite

Free to Fall (Winter 2023)

Devotion Series

Ripple Effect

Flood Tide

Troubled Water (Coming Soon! Expected 2023)

Midas Series

Perfect Proposal

Perfect Assumption

Perfect Composition

Perfect Order

Perfect Satisfaction (Coming Soon! Fall 2022)

Glacier Adventure Series

Return by Air

Return by Land

Return by Sea

Standalones

Close Match

Go to https://www.traceyjerald.com/ for all buy links!

THE LEGEND OF AMARYLLIS

There are variations regarding the legend of how amaryllis flowers came to be. Generally, the tale is told like this:

Amaryllis, a shy nymph, fell deeply in love with Alteo, a shepherd with great strength and beauty, but her love was not returned. He was too obsessed with his gardens to pay much attention to her.

Amaryllis hoped to win Alteo over by giving him the one thing he wanted most, a flower so unique it had never existed in the world before. She sought advice from the oracle Delphi and carefully followed his instructions. She dressed in white, and for thirty nights, appeared on Alteo's doorstep, piercing her heart with a golden arrow.

When Alteo finally opened his eyes to what was before him, he saw only a striking crimson flower that sprung from the blood of Amaryllis's heart.

It's not surprising the amaryllis has come to be the symbol of pride, determination, and radiant beauty. What's also not surprising is somehow, someway, we all bleed a little bit while we're falling in love.

PRESENT DAY

PRESENT DAY

Kelsey

"And then what happened?" I clutch my stomach to hold back my laughter.

Val delivers a pointed stare in my direction. "I stepped outside, calm as you please, then I walked over, turned the valve on the tank, and pressed the button. They all stood there gaping at the flames."

The words pop out of my mouth before I can stop them. "Are you telling me that none of them—not even my cousin-in-law who owns a restaurant?—checked to see if the gas was turned on before attempting to start it?"

"Kels, I swear it was the finest example of male bonding I've ever seen," she declares, her eyes gleaming.

"Oh? What makes you say that?"

"They all did this." Val immediately crosses her arms in front of her chest and points in opposite directions. I snicker at the imagery. "You should have seen them blaming one another."

"I wish you had taken pictures," I complain.

Val takes a sip of her drink before declaring boldly, "This is what happens when you—how did you phrase it—take some time away to decompress." She gives me a head to toe once-over. "For what it's worth, when you stumbled in the next day, you didn't fool anyone. Despite pulling it back, I hate to tell you, but your sex hair was obvious."

My lips curve up in a private smile as I recount the hands that slid through it, tugged and pulled it that night. All I admit to Val is, "I was too worn out to try to fight with it before checkout."

"Who would have ever thought you would have a cat-that-ate-the-canary look on your face after talking about a trip to Savannah?" she muses.

"Right?"

Sitting at Café Du Monde in New Orleans, my best friend Val Macando and I catch up for the first time after the most important speaking engagement of my life. Despite the teasing, I knew my emotions would be close to the surface.

So would my love.

After which I spent the night closing a circle that began five years ago.

I learned the hard way memories are portable and long-lasting but so are love and family. And for this event, I stacked my deck with both when I flew my support system in from all around the United States to meet me as I conquered something I never truly wrote the ending to.

The high school years I endured.

"You know that old joke about how many men it takes to screw in a light bulb?" Val asks, snapping my attention back to her.

I cautiously take another sip of my iced coffee before replying, "Yes."

"The answer is no longer mysterious. It's obvious the men must have called a woman for help—just like Darin when he hollered asking for matches. Every man who tried to start that grill deserved to turn beet red."

I try not to let my hair fall into the pile of powdered sugar coating the plate of beignets as I howl in response to the disdain in Val's voice.

"I shit you not, Kels, there they stood. Four grown men pushing the ignite button over and over. Muttering something was broken. Not one of them thinking to turn. On. The. Gas."

"Stop. Please." I can't catch my breath.

"It was like Chevy Chase reprised his role for a new movie—*National Lampoon's Graduation*. You didn't mention eighties late-night comedy as a side benefit to flying to Savannah."

"I had no idea. Now, I wish I was there to see it."

The wicked look she flings at me is all-knowing. "There is no way you would have traded your night just to watch your extended family demonstrate—again—that distinguished looks and sharp minds do not equal common sense."

I lift my drink and salute her. "Amen to that." Our plastic cups tap against one another with a thud. I pinch off a piece of the cooling beignet and pop it into my mouth. Something niggles at my subconscious. I mention offhandedly, "You never told me what you thought about it."

Confusion flits across her brow. "Thought about what?"

I pin her with a glare. "Um, hello? The speech? The whole reason we all uprooted our lives and families to head to Savannah in the first place."

Her lips tighten and her head jerks to the side. "You don't want me to tell you what I thought."

I rear back. "Excuse me."

Val reaches for a paper napkin from the dispenser and starts to tear it with her fingers.

The tiny bite of sweetness I just nibbled on churns in my stomach. Shock holds my voice to a whisper as I say, "You didn't think it was okay?"

"Okay?" A jagged laugh escapes her lips, shredding my soul. That is before she declares, "I think you should have recorded it. Professionally, not just by cell phones. It should be curated for the archives of the Library of Congress."

My chest immediately aches with the pressure Val's words cause.

"The words you spoke—the message you imparted—should become mandatory for every man, woman, and child in this world to hear."

The first tear spills over my lashes.

"You bared yourself fearlessly. I've been waiting for that moment since the night you first told me about the hell you endured within the hallowed halls of prep school."

My voice is raspy. "You have?"

She nods decisively. "Oh, yes. So, no, I didn't think it was okay"—air quoting for emphasis—"you surpassed okay when you stood up behind the podium. You entered the realm of stratospheric when you introduced yourself as Kee Long before admitting you chose your pen name due to the awful nickname bestowed upon you by your classmates."

A sob escapes me. "It was time to let the past go."

"No, it was time you accepted it made you a crazy, brave, strong woman who can handle whatever life throws at you. You set out to incinerate the evil living within your high school using nothing but your mind, your heart, and your voice. I've never been prouder to call you the sister of my heart than when I watched you toss the match to start the flame."

"It's been building up for a long time."

"That it has. How do you feel now that you have half the world talking about it since it's been posted all over social media?"

I consider her question before answering, "Humbled. For years, I hid behind a mask so I wouldn't be hurt again, but all I did was keep myself shut off from the rest of the world."

Val gives a derisive snort. She doesn't need to lecture me again on that misconception. I know better. Now. Instead, I try to put the emotions shooting off inside me like fireworks into words. "Every day, I wake up blessed. I know I deserve this life, love, and happiness."

Val wipes her damp eyes with the shredded napkin. "I am so damn proud of you."

"I couldn't have become the person I am without you." Reaching for another napkin, I slap it into her hand.

"That may be true"—her eyes widen fractionally before pleasure wipes away the emotional rawness threatening to overtake her—"but I think someone else may have been a bit more influential."

Just as I'm about to ask who, a shadow drifts over the table. I twist my head and fall headlong into cool blue pools.

After I manage to drag my eyes away from his, I meet Val's amused ones. Her smirk tells me she knows exactly what inspired my speech.

What's inspired me from the very beginning.

CHAPTER ONE

FIFTEEN YEARS AGO

Kelsey

I'M SO COLD.

Even as the nurse lays another heated blanket over me to stop my shivering, I can't get warm.

It's not nerves. Nope. It's an unusual fear that what I'm about to subject myself to isn't going to change a thing—that no matter what, I'll always be what they taunted me with all through school.

Gross. Disgusting. Fat.

King Kong.

It may be a whisper only through my mind, but it's like someone shouted it in the pre-op room. I'm more grateful than ever for the anti-nausea medicine that's pumping through my system as my stomach roils. Tears well up in my eyes as I recall the last person to call me that. I'd just had my high school diploma placed in my hand. I was so eager to be done with Forsyth Academy that I never expected the attack.

Not from him.

Never from him.

He'd always protected me as much as he could from the bullies who thought nothing of shoving me to my knees, making me eat something, anything, before they'd let me stand again. There was the time I caught him out of the corner of my eye slapping someone's hand away before they could slip another note into my bag commenting on my weight.

I began to think he looked inside and saw me. Maybe he didn't care for me the way I did him, but Benedict Rierson Perrault was my first love. It wasn't because his smile made my stomach clench or the way his dark hair would fall across his forehead when it was drying after he got out of the pool. It was because he had something everyone else at that school didn't have.

A heart.

Then I made a fatal mistake. I was shown there's no mercy for someone like me, only different levels of hell to endure. God, why was I so stupid to leave my bag with my journal in it after the cheerleaders cornered me in the library that day?

It wasn't long before posters of King Kong holding a miniaturized Benedict were strewn around campus. Sections of my handwriting blown up and slapped in every bathroom stall.

And the cafeteria? I groan aloud, drawing the attention of a nurse.

"Are you all right, Miss Kennedy? It won't be long now." She reaches over and pats my hand kindly.

"I'm fine," I murmur.

No, it won't be long until every wish I've ever made comes true. By working at a job I never wanted to for years, I've saved up enough money for what's about to happen. Soon the past will be erased. And maybe, just maybe, one day, the pain inside will heal as well as I'm told the incisions will.

There's a flurry of movement as one of the physician assistants comes in. Josh, a handsome man in blue scrubs, leans over me. "Are you ready, Kelsey?"

He's been kind over the few years I've known him. I know he's trying to reassure me, but I can barely nod. I'm too overwhelmed to speak.

"Then let's get you to the surgical suite." Whistling a tune, he walks alongside as they wheel my bed down the corridor. "Dr. Toli is getting scrubbed in. While we're en route, can you tell me your full name, date of birth, and what we're doing today?"

I rattle off the first two. When it comes to the third, I flush hard. "A vertical gastric bypass with a full panniculectomy." I wait for the attractive assistant to make some cutting remark, but all he does is smile.

"Excellent. Are you excited? Nervous?"

I chew on my lip before I answer, "Anxious to get started."

By this point, we've reached the OR suite. Josh lowers the bedside rail and helps me to sit up. The anti-anxiety medicine they pumped into my IV earlier makes me a bit woozy. "Kelsey, do you remember what they said you'd have to do at this point in your pre-op appointment?"

I nod. I weigh so much, the doctors and nurses can't lift me onto the table to begin my procedure. "Yes." I start to swing my legs over the side.

"Take it easy," he warns. Soon, I'm standing next to the surgical table where, for the next nine hours, I'm going to trust Dr. Toli and his team to change my life.

"Okay, Kelsey. Are you ready to climb up? If it makes you more comfortable, you can wait to take off your gown until you're up there."

I shake my head. With a determination I didn't realize I possessed, I reach behind me. It takes a quick flick of my wrist to undo the bow holding the enormous surgical gown. It pools near my feet. Josh kicks it out of the way so no one trips on the tent of material.

Naked, with folds of fat falling over one another, I stand proudly for the room to see. This is the last time I'll be like this—exposed, ready to be brutalized either by strength or words. When none come, I use the specialized step stool to climb onto the surgical table.

After getting me centered on the narrow space, the anesthesiologist comes behind my head. I blink up at him hazily due to the drugs. "Kelsey, I'm going to lower this mask on your face. When I do, I want you to tell me about the first thing you're going to buy when you're out of surgery."

"Wait!" Everyone seems to pause their frantic activity to listen. "Will you promise me something?" I feel tears I haven't shed in years well in my eyes.

Dabbing at them with a tissue, he asks, "If I can."

"Will you make me beautiful?" I choke out.

He shakes his head. "We don't have to because you already are. All we're doing is enhancing what's already there." That's sweet of him to say. I find myself relaxing. "Now are you ready?"

I nod. The mask makes a hissing noise as it approaches my face.

"What's the first thing you want to treat yourself to?" he reminds me to answer.

"Clothes," I mumble as lethargy settles over me. "Really expensive, super-sexy lingerie. The kind I can't fit . . ."

And as the medicine knocks me out, I know I'll eventually fit into the kind of lingerie models wear. I plan on buying the custom-made sexy bits of nothing not because I need them due to my size but because of their exquisiteness. I'll buy them, wear them, and luxuriate in them even if I'm just wearing jeans and a T-shirt. I'll do it even if it's to silently gloat in the face of every person who hurt me after I take on the world and conquer it.

Because from this moment on, there's no looking back.

CHAPTER TWO

FIVE YEARS AGO

Benedict

"Hello?" comes the alert voice on the other end of the line.

My voice is shaky when I ask, "Am I interrupting anything?"

My best friend, Cade Miller, snorts. "I just got home from work."

I frown. "I thought you were working days?"

"I'm a resident, Perrault. I go where they tell me to go. So, for the next few months, I'm covering the overnight surgical rotation." I start to question why when he interrupts, "But that's not why you called, is it?"

I swallow past the melon that's taken up space in my throat. "No. It isn't."

"Nightmare or memory?" he asks with the directness I've come to appreciate.

I choke out a laugh around a sob. "Aren't they one and the same?"

"Some nights, they are. And some, even our minds find places we never were forced to go."

There's a long stretch of silence between us before I admit, "I got the invite to my class reunion today."

Cade lets out a sigh. "Well, that will do it. Are you going to go?"

As easily as I can dredge up the nightmare that I endured, I pull up the memory of her soft, round face with tears tracking down it. I say, "I have to. You know that."

"Yeah. I do." Through the phone, I hear a cabinet door open and close. Then the sound of glass touching crystal—as a distinctive ping rings through the air. "Okay. Since neither one of us is getting back to sleep, tell me what woke you."

Before I start enumerating the hellacious details—many of which are factual recounts of both our pasts—I give thanks for the fact that Cade's working nights.

I have a feeling the nightmares are just beginning. Again.

All due to a fucking invitation to return to Savannah to mingle with my former classmates.

CHAPTER THREE

Kelsey

You are cordially invited . . .

Those words—when they appeared in my email box for the third time since I graduated from high school—produce immediate, violent emotions to course through my body. I knock the cup of cooling black coffee my cousin Ava had casually dropped by my elbow onto the floor with a crash, causing my face to burst into flames as all the eyes in the Coffee Shop turn my way. When Ava rushes over to help me mop it up, she frowns in concern as she whispers, "Is everything all right, Kelsey?"

I lie without hesitation. "Fine. I was just clumsy."

Her brow furrows as she pauses wiping up my mess to study my face. "I don't think so. You look like you've seen a ghost."

I open my mouth to deny it, but what comes out is, "Can we talk about it later?" *Maybe when half the town isn't here to witness me having a breakdown when we do?*

As if by divine intervention, a jingle sounds above the door. Ava's, my, as well as a majority of the patrons' heads swivel in the newcomer's direction. My closest friend in the small town of Collyer, Connecticut, Jillian Beale—fiancée of our new fire chief—comes rushing through the door with a beaming smile on her face.

And why shouldn't she be happy? Jillian's lived through the tests of fire and come out of them with a future so bright, people around her can't help but absorb her energy and react accordingly. Me included.

I shove my embarrassment aside and help Ava to her feet. "Besides, I don't have time right now."

Ava's lips curve into a knowing smile. "It's the big day?"

"Absolutely. Are you sure you don't want to have Matt watch the Coffee Shop and come with us? You know Jillian asked. We're swinging by to pick up her grandmother." I slap the lid down on my laptop and shove it carelessly into my oversized handbag. I'll deal with the evite and what it means later. I have much more important things to do than worry about a past I'd sooner forget than relive.

Ava flaps her hand before reminding me, "We've already discussed this. I want to be surprised when Jillian walks down the aisle."

I laugh as Jillian joins us. I can't help but tease my cousin, "Now you sound like the groom."

Ava considers my words for just a moment before she does a fair impression of Jillian's fiancé while he's barking at one of his probies. "If you can't run faster than that up a single flight of stairs with a hose over your shoulder, what makes you think you're going to outrun me at the 5K in full turnout gear?"

"We have to swing by to get your grandmother. We don't want to be late," I remind Jillian over both her and Ava's laughter.

Jillian's cheeks flush with pleasure. "I'm so ready."

Ava shoos us both away. "Go buy something beautiful."

I call over my shoulder, "We're heading to Amaryllis Designs to shop for Jilly's wedding dress. Is there a possibility of anything else?"

"Remember, Amaryllis Designs won't be right around the corner if you move."

Not but a few minutes later, Ava's words ricochet through my head as I flip through Emily's sketchbook of formalwear—an honor afforded to those she considers cherished clients and friends—while waiting for Jillian to emerge from the dressing room.

Somewhere along the way, my relationship with Ava and Matt has brought me into the close-knit circle of the Amaryllis Events family. Since I moved here, I've been invited to events on their immense farm property ranging from semi-formal events to haphazard barbeques. The enormous family keeps expanding by leaps and bounds, testing my comfort level. Though I know they adore Ava and Matt, other than my bond with Emily through her designs, I find it hard to connect to the rest of the multifaceted family. Maybe I'm inhibited by my natural shyness combined with the image I still see in the mirror, but spending time with the Freemans leaves me with a hunger for something more.

My eyes land on a powerful drawing of a V-neck gown that's intended to skim the floor. I regretfully trade off the ease of snatching up my semi and formalwear originals directly from the famed designer for something much more enticing.

A chance at experiencing happiness in a city that knows next to nothing about me.

Jillian's grandmother is calmly crocheting next to me while we patiently wait for Jillian to come out in her first dress. My fingernail taps absentmindedly on the page, wondering if I have an upcoming occasion to wear the gown Emily drew that has me intrigued when I hear the designer herself call out, "Grandma? Kee, what do you both think?"

My eyes shoot upward and meet Jillian's wet ones, happiness turning the normally stormy gray color into liquid silver. Seeing the joy emanating from her face as she tries on her first wedding dress, the last knot inside me loosens. I can leave Collyer knowing everyone I care for is going to be fine because they've found their happiness.

Now, it's my turn.

After all these years.

CHAPTER FOUR

Kelsey

As I ENJOY A GLASS OF WINE WITH AVA AT HER AND MATT'S LATER that night, I explain about receiving the evite to my reunion.

Ava, predictably, explodes. "No. You shouldn't go. Of course not. Why would you go back and relive that nightmarish experience?"

"I bet that you would say something like that."

"This is why you didn't tell me when I was working?" Ava guesses.

Not saying anything, I smile down into my glass before taking a sip. The fruity blend explodes on my tongue. "You do realize no one except those closest to me would understand why I feel this way. If I were to tell my publicist about it, he'd be salivating for me to go." I do a fair impersonation of the man. "Kee, *so* glorious. It's like your character has come to life. The media would eat it up. You just *have* to do it."

Ava says in no uncertain terms what her opinion is. The foul words coming from my normally mild-mannered cousin have an unexpected burst of laughter falling from my lips. I tease her, "I wouldn't use such words at the Coffee Shop. You might drive customers away."

"Or bring them in. You'd never believe the drama we've overheard," she retorts.

I stretch out and balance the stem of my wineglass on my stomach before asking, "Have either of you actually ever stepped in during customer arguments?" My mind drifts back to some of the doozies my parents had no qualms about having in public in front of me and how I wish someone—anyone—would have saved me.

Saved them.

It's Matt—a former VA psychologist—who answers. "Once or twice. Generally, it's enough for someone to approach a table to help tempers diffuse."

"Unless Matt's feeling overprotective. Then all bets are off." Ava aims a loving glance at her husband, who flushes slightly.

"I know. I've been a recipient of it. It's one of the things I'm going to miss when I move." I recall how many times I've been in my favorite booth at the Coffee Shop and Matt's come out of the kitchen to guard my person from people unwilling to respect my privacy.

"Why New Orleans?" Matt asks.

I grin before reminding him, "Val."

Matt chortles as I expected he would. "How could I forget?"

Ava snickers. "The two of you got into so many shenanigans during college. I swear Pop-pop called me every day."

My best friend since college has convinced me to do more than a few things that have led me outside my comfort zone over the years. The most recent was to sell my small home. I take a quick swallow of wine and wave my glass in the air before declaring, "She reminded me my job was portable."

"Which it is," Ava concedes.

"Therefore, it was time to 'haul my booty to New Orleans to be closer to her.' I believe were her exact words."

Ava shrieks with laughter. "That is something I can picture Val saying."

Matt, more pragmatic, asks, "But have you found a house to live in?"

I shake my head. "She knows I'm not entirely sold on the idea yet."

"You're not?" The hope in Ava's heart makes my own twist. Since I moved to Collyer a few years ago, we've become closer than ever. It's with her love and support I've been able to accept so much about who I was. Who I'm meant to be.

Who I'll never become.

Shoving those thoughts out of my mind, I smirk. "I called her and said, 'I must love you if I'm willing to learn to live with having alpaca hair the minute humidity touches it.' "

Ava chokes on her wine. Matt roars with laughter. Once he has himself under control, he asks, "To which she said?"

"I'm putting some special hair product onto the vanity in the guest bath. You won't care after the first week anyway. You know you've secretly been lusting to move near me for years."

Ava and Matt have fallen onto each other; they're laughing so hard. I finish the story. "Val hung up on me laughing when I asked, 'Does your husband know you have these delusions? Maybe he should do something about it before your child arrives.' "

Val's my best friend for more than one reason, the least of which is because she's never let me get away with any shit from the time she met me in college to now.

"What does she think about this whole reunion business?" Matt asks suddenly.

Uncomfortably, I shift so I'm sitting upright. Setting my glass aside, I twine my fingers together before admitting, "I haven't told her."

"Why not?" No accusation, just curiosity.

Wryly, I inform Matt, "Because she'll want me to go."

Sagely, he informs me, "Reunions represent more than a marker of time; they represent a resurgence of anxiety. Despite the passage of adult years, those feelings resurface even if they've been buried so deeply."

"Or you could try my method and try to never think of it at all."

His eyes twinkle at me. "That's not normally a recommended method for dealing with trauma, Kelsey. It's not healthy to bury your emotions."

"I left that life, and the person I was forced to be, long behind me when I graduated."

"A version of it. None of us can eliminate our past."

"Thanks for the pep talk, Matt," I drawl.

"Kelsey," he begins patiently, "reunions are no longer what they were once intended to be—a chance for contemporaries to visit with one another. Instead, they're a pageant of sorts—a parade of people trying to demonstrate the high school hierarchy they established is still in full force. In so many ways, they're inappropriate and appalling."

"Then why attend?" I challenge him.

"Maybe it's time for you to lay your own ghosts to rest. Move on, bury the past," Ava says.

Pray to God, I don't see him.

On the surface, it's a simple concept. Return to my high school reunion, mingle socially for a few hours, then leave. But the idea of attending my class reunion feeling the way I do is intimidating and daunting.

Bluffing, I declare, "Frankly, I feel nothing but pity for the people who attend, who only try to gain some kind of social acceptance with their accomplishments while shielding their insecurity."

"I went with fear coursing through my body," Matt remembers.

I gape at him. "You?"

His fingers twine with his wife's. "Kelsey, no matter whether a person was the most popular individual at school, the shyest, the smartest, the exiled, or the class clown, reunions bring up issues from our past we long to forget.

But as Thornton Wilder said, 'The past and the future are always present with us.' It's up to each person as to how they choose to liberate themselves from the vulnerabilities holding them tied to the need to be accepted."

I'm considering his words when Ava reminds me of something important. "Kelsey, none of us are the same person we were in high school. We don't look the same or act the same. We don't have the same hopes or dreams. We're not as joyful nor as cruel. And every person there is in the same boat you are—they all remember."

"You know what they did to me, Ava." My voice is low but thick with heat.

"I do." Her voice fills with telltale signs of bubbling fury. "I could never forget it, but I want you to be happy more than I want you to hold on to this anger. I want you to let go and move on."

I squirm uncomfortably. "I thought I had."

Matt goes in for the kill. "Sometimes, the only place you have the chance to do that is at a reunion."

CHAPTER FIVE

Kelsey

SAVANNAH, GEORGIA. I FEEL THE FAMILIAR CHURN BEGIN IN MY stomach that used to happen every time I'd drive to school each day. After all these years, the idea of facing my classmates causes my stomach to drop almost as severely as the last altitude bump did.

Jesus, what the hell am I thinking?

There isn't a single person in the two hundred people I graduated with fifteen years ago that I would consider an acquaintance, let alone a friend. My family doesn't even live here anymore, and I have no need to be here. So why am I? To prove I am beyond their taunts, the mental and sometimes physical pain I suffered for four years while I buried my head and pretended to not exist in the cruel, often vicious halls of Forsyth Academy?

The reality is this weekend is nothing more than my chance to walk in bolstered by my success, not weighed down by the world as I once knew it.

Through my headphones, I hear the flight attendant announce, "Please stow your laptops and other portable storage devices." Quickly saving the chapter of the newest book I've been writing, I slip my Mac into my oversized purse. I snag my phone, making a few notes on the next section of the plot before tossing that aside as well. I just stare blankly at the ground quickly approaching below, trying to gather my strength for the next few days.

Savannah, the oldest city in Georgia, the birthplace of the Girl Scouts, and the cause of every fear I have to this day when it comes to self-perception.

My publicist might make my public image one of strength, but the reality is I'm still just the terrified girl who ran away as soon as high school graduation was over.

"You're checked in okay?" Nana worries over the phone from her home in North Florida. Since leaving Georgia the morning after high school graduation, I've never been back. My grandparents, who raised me when my parents were killed in an accident in my early teens, never questioned why. They would fly out to see me wherever I happened to be living, or I'd visit them in their retirement community.

Lord knows that place could keep me well stocked in characters to write about for the next decade.

Smiling, I lean back against the arm of the couch in the suite of the Westin Savannah Harbor Golf Resort & Spa I'm relaxing in. "Yes, Nana. I'm fine. I'm going to work out, do some writing, and answer some emails from my agent. Then tomorrow, I'm treating myself to a day of pampering at the spa."

"Good," she says forcefully, surprising me. "I want you to look stunning on the night of that stupid party."

I snort. "Doubt that's possible."

"Do we need to have this talk again, Kelsey? Just because the people at that horrid place hurt you doesn't mean they define you."

"I know." And intellectually, I do. But the scars I wear are both mental as well as physical. And they lacerate my heart and soul.

Nana continues to grumble. "I don't even know why you're bothering to give them your time."

"Ask Ava and Matt. Or Val. Something about walking in with my head high and closing the chapter on my life—that was Matt, for what it's worth. Val thinks I should just go in and gloat about my success in a gorgeous dress and heels to regain my pride."

"Oh, I'll ask them something. I'll ask them what the sweet tea they were thinking," Nana declares.

I can't help but chuckle even as my mind thinks back to the whirlwind past few months—packing and moving to New Orleans, writing my next book, a nonstop press tour, and allowing myself to be convinced flying to Savannah was the right decision. "But not without a kickass dress," Val avowed.

Which, of course, meant flying back to Collyer twice—once for my own dress fitting and once to be there for Jillian's bridal shower.

"I was going to ignore it like I did when I got it in years five and ten," I confess to my grandmother.

"And you let yourself be talked out of it."

"Let's just say Val once again made me see reason." Not even Ava or Matt could convince me to put myself forward the way the conversation with my best friend did.

"Walk in there proud of who you are, and tell them all to go to hell, Kels," she argued. "You rose above what they did to you, even what happened at your high school graduation. Get unstuck from the loop of whatever it is they have you trapped in so you can move on with your life."

"I'd hardly call my life stuck in a loop," I drawled, thinking of the crazy whirlwind—especially the last ten years.

"Don't you want to have the chance to put those feelings behind you?"

Chewing on a piece of celery, I swallowed and answered, "I thought I had."

"For the most part, you have. Except for one thing," she reminded me gently, just as I was about to take another bite.

Since I knew how damn dangerous it was to try to eat the stringy food on a good day, I threw it on the plate in front of me. "You mean Benedict," I declared flatly.

She nodded before walking around the island to lay her hand on my arm. "There's still so much hurt inside you, Kels."

I shook off her arm. "I'm fine."

Val snorted. "About this—about him—you're more fragile than NOLA fans seeing our beloved quarterback take a hit on the field. Honey, what was done to the girl that lives in you is just wrong. You know this." Val took both my hands in hers.

Breathing hard, I nodded.

"But I've read your books, Kelsey. You are so *angry* at the others. But you're still *hurt* by *him*. Don't you want the opportunity to look him in the eye and finally purge those emotions?"

"Even though I disagree I'm 'trapped' in anything"—I use her own word—"I do feel a certain interest in shoving who and what I've become down the throats of the people who made my life hell for years."

"That's my girl." Giving me a swift hug, she moved away, and I was on the website accepting the invitation.

That was months ago, and other than flying back to Collyer for my dress, until this week, I didn't think twice about it.

Now that I'm standing here, I'm not so sure I've made the right decision in coming. I have no idea how to handle the swirl of emotions I've never settled in my soul for him. Because there was both the care that Benedict Perrault showed me for almost a year versus the viciousness he demonstrated at the end—that's what I can't seem to forget.

I'm snapped back to the here and now when Nana declares, "Well, as much as we love Val, Pop-pop and I don't like it."

A flood of warmth rushes over me. After everything I dealt with at Forsyth—so close on the heels of the death of my parents—my grandparents became everything to me. They've supported every personal and business decision I ever made wholeheartedly. When I was looking to cover the remains of my surgical scar, I did so with a chain of shockingly pink gerbera daisies, Nana's favorite flower. Despite everything that's happened to me, Nana never lost her belief that everything would turn out all right in my life. She never had any doubt in me, despite the ones I still have in myself.

I shove to my feet and walk over to the window to study the muddy green waters of the Savannah River. "What are you and Pop-pop doing today?" I ask—anything to distract her from venturing further down the path of emotions I don't quite understand.

"Oh, we've got ping-pong tonight, darlin'. I tell you, that man is going to throw out a hip diving for a little white ball, I swear." I grin, thinking of my eighty-one-year-old grandfather.

"It could be worse, Nana."

"How's that?"

"He could be trying to play golf again," I remind her.

"Ain't that the truth." Her heartfelt statement makes laughter explode from me. "Remember what Dr. Royster said the last time?"

"I'm not quite certain if it's possible to recreate the torture chamber from *The Princess Bride*, Nana." I'm wiping tears of mirth from my eyes.

"You know she'll try, gosh darn it! If he messes up his back and hip like that again, she'll figure out a way, honey," she declares firmly.

"I'm sure she will," I console her, my smile evident.

She hesitates, and I wonder why before she asks, "Are you going to be all right there alone? Pop-pop and I can be on an airplane in a few hours if you want us with you." I hear a note of concern for me being here in her voice.

"You know I appreciate the offer," I begin.

"Then let us—"

"But I need to confront my past on my own," I interrupt. This time, I'll be armed with the skills and strength that I learned over the last fifteen years. I won't be weaponless like I was the day I drove away with tears blinding my sight as I headed west into a future even I couldn't have imagined.

Nana's ranting in her loving way about finding a way to drive her car over the people who brought me to my knees—much like in the movie *Fried Green Tomatoes*—but I'm only half listening as the tranquil view tries to lure me into believing what's outside the sanctity of the hotel in the city beyond can't hurt me.

But I know better.

Taking a deep breath, I turn away and concentrate on the first task at hand for the long weekend ahead.

Setting my grandmother at ease before I make my way downstairs to burn off some energy.

"Nana, listen. Tomorrow night, I plan on going in late, making a sweep of the room, and leaving. Does that make you feel any better?" I admit, exasperated.

"Immensely. Are you getting ready to go work out now?"

And at my "yes" response, Nana's concern changes to reminding me how humid it is in Savannah. *Like I don't appreciate that living in New Orleans? Alpaca hair wasn't the only thing I sacrificed to be near Val,* I think wryly. I haven't inhaled a breath that hasn't been laden with swampy heat.

My lips curve at the corners. In the end, if these small steps reunite me with the parts of my soul the city I'm presently standing in stripped, it will be worth it.

After hanging up on Nana, I throw on some workout gear and some well-worn sneakers. Tying my hair back away from my face, I slide my key card, credit card, and cellphone into my lower back zipper pocket and slip a pair of wireless buds in as I wait for the elevator to ping, signaling its arrival.

When I get to the main level, I stop at the concierge desk to ask for directions to the gym. Much to my disappointment, I'm told there's not a fully equipped gym at the hotel proper but there's a path around the hotel to the club next door for the use of the guests. I push off at a brisk trot to warm up my muscles with "Centuries" blasting. My mind empties of everything but the heat raining down on me from the sunlight above and the contradiction of feeling from the cold water bottle in my hand given to me by the concierge "Free of charge. It's part of our partnership with the fitness center."

Perfect. Exactly what I was hoping for. I claim one of the treadmills and find my view overlooking the crowded pool filled with families, businessmen, and—I cringe—some of my old classmates. Stepping to the side, I stretch my muscles, warmed up from the walk, so I don't pull anything from the workout I'm about to put my body through. Jumping on, my legs straddle the tread as I program the workout I want—*something rigorous which still gives me a chance to manage to make it back to the hotel,* I think with amusement. I throw the pool a glance of longing before pressing Start. While I much prefer swimming, the resort's pool isn't designed for the kind of laps I usually put my resurrected body through. As the treadmill picks up speed, I start running as the thoughts for my newest plot start creeping in.

Pilar is walking down the hall when suddenly she's shoved up against the floor-to-ceiling windows, books scattering everywhere. Her head slams back against the glass with a hard thud. Two sets of strong arms pin her there while a group of people start to lift her shirt, exposing her stomach to the crowd that's gathered, the crowd that's doing nothing to help her. Again. What feels like a million fingers poke and prod at the fleshier part of her stomach. "Jesus, Martell, what did you eat for dinner last night?" one boy taunts.

"Must have been that missing animal from science lab they mentioned over the loudspeaker. Didn't you notice? She's even more of a dog than she was yesterday." All the students surrounding her collapse in laughter.

Pilar's face is almost purple in humiliation. Tears scald hot tracks down as she tries to break free. It isn't until an authoritative voice calls out, "What's going on here?" that the students flee leaving Pilar to pick up not only her books but the pieces of her broken heart.

My legs pump harder as I increase the treadmill speed. I use my motion to try to burn out my fury of that memory. I relive so much of my life at Forsyth through my character "Pilar." Quickly, I pull up an ongoing text I have with myself and send a breathless voice message so I don't forget this next section of my current book, *Humility*. My young adult series about a girl at a private boarding school living through much of the same hell I endured at Forsyth is making waves all over the world. As Kee Long, I've been able to purge myself of the pain, no, the fucking shame I endured.

Maybe this weekend, I'll be able to bury it and finally move on with my life.

At least, that's the plan.

About forty minutes and a few more dictations later, I finish three-and-a-half miles on the treadmill and have staggered back to the Westin. After stepping into the cool lobby, the same concierge greets me. "Welcome back! How did you enjoy your run?"

I smile ruefully as I accept a fresh towel to blot the sweat off my face. "Enjoy is a subjective turn of phrase, Renaldo."

His chuckle is as warm as the Savannah air. "True, but now you can say you're done and indulge in something from Escape or Aqua Grill."

I shake my head. "Too much work to do. I'm more likely to order something from room service."

He does a quick check around before easing his way closer. "You know, there's a few places downtown that are pretty fantastic." His tone opens the door if I want to cross through it for some company.

Completely flattered by the attention of the darkly handsome man, I politely decline. After all, he's likely flirty with most of the guests. I know I'm nothing special when I'm measured up against many of the women out there.

I'm just me.

CHAPTER SIX

Benedict

My fingers are flying across the keyboard as I take notes about the contract I downloaded to work on during the three-hour flight from New Orleans to Savannah. I need something to distract me from my thoughts of coming back for this high school reunion.

I endured both of the previous ones. Once the nightmares started again, Cade tried to convince me to bail on this one. "You're not a superhero, damn it. Accept what happened and move on," he insisted.

I had just about come to that same conclusion until I saw the online acceptance list. She's planning on attending.

Kelsey Kennedy.

Unable to focus now that my mind went to the one place I wasn't ready for it to go, I toss my wire-rimmed reading glasses aside. Relaxing back against the plush leather seats in the first-class cabin, my thoughts wander to what she's been doing for the last fifteen years. Is she married? Does she have kids? Do her gray eyes still darken to storm clouds when she talks about writing?

Above all, is she finally happy?

Shoving a hand through my hair, I realize it's learning the answer to the last question that got me on a plane. Because this really isn't a reunion as much as it's an ongoing prison sentence I can't ever escape from despite the years and distance I put between myself and the people of Forsyth. But as much as I hold hatred for that place, it is nothing to what Kelsey must feel—for it and for me.

Was it worth it? I ask myself the question for the millionth time and answer it the same way I did fifteen years ago. Yes. But being the person to destroy the last part of Kelsey Kennedy's strength has weighed on my soul every day. There hasn't been a single morning I've woken up where she hasn't been on my mind.

I even went so far as to have her investigated, but the investigations firm couldn't provide any information of use. After running down a litany of general information, they brought me in to discuss what they found. The owners of Hudson Investigations—one happens to be my boss's older brother—told me in no uncertain terms, "What we can disclose is Ms. Kennedy is still alive. However, there are some serious blocks around her profession. Do you want us to breach them?"

"Is this common?" I asked.

Caleb Lockwood shrugged. "It's not unusual."

One of Hudson's other owners, Keene Marshall, argued, "These are the types of privacy screens we see when someone doesn't want to be found. It's a sign they're trying to hide or being hidden professionally."

Startled because I couldn't imagine sweet, shy Kelsey involved in something that required her life to be secured in such a way, I ordered the men, "Back off. It's enough to know she's alive." *Because for a while, I wasn't sure she wouldn't try to take her own life after everything she endured in high school.*

Some of what I thought must have leaked because Caleb tapped a few fingers. The screen in front of him disappeared, sliding neatly into his desk. "Case closed."

"Yeah," I managed. "Case closed."

Except, it wasn't. Not for me. Never for me. Especially not as I fly back toward the scene where my greatest shame and biggest sacrifice occurred.

My fingers pinch the corners of my eyes as true regret wells up inside me. I know if there's one face that haunts Kelsey about being bullied in high school, it's mine. And she has every right to hate me. Even as I recall my last months of high school, the guilt I continue to feel about what happened between us is something I can't let go of.

And subsequently, I've never quite been able to let go of her or the memories high school still has over me.

"Maybe this time," I murmur to myself as the tires screech on the runway as my plane touches down.

About ninety minutes later, the car I hired to get me from the airport to the Westin Savannah Harbor Golf Resort & Spa pulls up to the grand circular entrance. I slide out of the back, nabbing my briefcase while the driver gets my weekender from the trunk.

Looking around at the majestic tower sitting on the bank of the Savannah River, I don't feel the same feeling of home I do when I jump out of my rental at my parents' place on Skidaway Island. Holding up a hand to block the sun, I catch sight of a lithe woman making her way into the lobby. Using the ends of her workout shirt to wipe her face, I can't help but admire her dedication in this humidity. Maybe it's because I've lived in the South for most of my life, but if I can avoid it, there's no way in hell I'll be caught running in the thick soup we call air. Despite the number of times I've debated giving it up, I've always been a swimmer. The weight of the world feels like nothing I can't shoulder while the cool blue water engulfs me.

And there have been a lot of burdens I've carried unwillingly.

Swimming was my salvation in the last fifteen years, through the stress of college, law school, new jobs. I suspect I'll do a lot of it this weekend until I can look Kelsey in the eye and give her a long-overdue apology.

Cade told me over drinks the other night it was "highly probable she's forgotten all about you."

"I've tried to explain it, but you have no idea how bad it was," I muttered.

"It wasn't like you were involved with her," he argued.

"It wasn't involvement. I was protective of her," I said. But it is more than just that. Looking at my relationship with Kelsey with the maturity of a man versus that of a boy who ached to get out of the never-ending hell, the emotional investment between us was almost . . . intimate. Because Kelsey was my tutor in creative writing, she learned a lot about my inner thoughts. And I learned about her deepest pain, her hopes and dreams.

We kept each other's secrets completely private until her journal was discovered one day. And I, along with the rest of Forsyth, found out what I already suspected about her crush on me.

Back then, my heart quickened when I learned the soft-faced, gray-eyed girl had feelings about me. It touched me to realize she didn't categorize me in the same way she did the rest of the student body. The things I got to read—not by her choice—made my heart swell, made me feel special. Purposeful. So, I became Kelsey's champion more than I already was against the bullies, standing up for her, tearing down anyone I could who would harm the gentle girl who'd done so much for me.

Until I couldn't.

Until I ended up being the one causing her final destruction, shattering her in front of hundreds of people.

But I couldn't let them do what they did to me to anyone else.

I just couldn't.

Stomach churning, I collect my room key and make my way to the elevator just in time for the doors to close on the woman I glimpsed running when I first pulled in. Not wanting to be with anything more than my thoughts, I don't make any effort to race for the elevator doors or yell for her to hold them.

Instead, I flip through the reunion pamphlet that was waiting for me at check-in as my thoughts are consumed by all things Kelsey, hoping she's happy. Because no one deserves it more than she does.

Absentmindedly, I wonder if she'll come to the barbecue tonight out by the river. Will she come with a date? Her husband? Maybe she'll bring him to the cocktail hour tomorrow, and by meeting him, the small part of me that felt a flash of something for less than a heartbeat years ago will finally be able to say goodbye.

Maybe I can finally be free from these chains of self-reproach.

Jerking my head, I toss the pamphlet aside. All I know for sure is Kelsey RSVP'd for the main event. And unlike before, I'll proudly stand by her side if she needs me to protect her from the sociopaths we graduated with.

Because now they can't hurt me.

Or the ones I love.

CHAPTER SEVEN

Benedict

"Ben! Oh, it's so good to see you." A sweet Southern accent accompanies a tap on the shoulder that night at the barbecue. I turn around, ready to be immediately hostile, but it's someone I enjoy. "Hey, Molly." I lean down and hug my baby sister's best friend. "What are you doing here? Did you forget you graduated a few years after I did?"

"Cute. I'm one of the event planners here at the resort." She waves her hand to encompass the patio area lit by small Edison bulbs and filled with my obnoxious classmates. "I'm just the one who was blessed to work with Juliette for this event."

"Do I detect a note of sarcasm in your voice?" I tease. Molly and Lisa were more like twins growing up. They were even roommates at the University of Georgia when they both graduated Forsyth, only separating when Lisa ended her engagement a few years ago and moved to New Orleans to start over.

"I could fill the pool with sugar, bury her up to her neck in it, and it still wouldn't make a difference in her disposition," she tells me bluntly. A second later, her face becomes a blank mask. "Mrs. Gaines. How are you enjoying your evening?"

"The bar is out of Maker's Mark. We're low on canapés, and when will the pig be done? I selected this resort because of its impeccable reputation. This kind of inattentiveness will be reported immediately to your supervisor," Juliette Gaines, née Juliette Bernard, snaps behind me.

I roll my eyes at Molly before saying loudly, "Thank you for taking the time to explain the history of the resort, Ms. Roth."

"Not a problem at all, Mr. Perrault. Mrs. Gaines, I'll immediately check on your concerns. Shall I call you or find you directly?" But Juliette's already dismissed Molly from her target since she has a new one in her sights.

Me.

"Well, well, well. If it isn't Benedict Perrault," Juliette purrs. She drags her ringed fingers up my arm. I want to sneer. Instead, I let them reach my forearm before I pluck them off and drop them away from me.

"Where's your husband?" Not that I particularly care, but I sure don't want this python's attention directed at me.

I never did.

She waves her hand. "Around. Where have you been? I haven't heard much about you lately."

"Not around." I don't offer any more than that despite her impatient waiting.

On paper, my life looks picture-perfect. After I graduated from high school, I left for college and hardly looked back. I proceeded on to Harvard Law, where I summer clerked for Watson and Rubenstein. I worked my way up to an associate for Baker McKenzie, where I worked heavily on cross-border deals. One, in particular, attracted the attention of Jared Dalton—newly minted partner of the now Watson Rubenstein and Dalton.

Jared was someone I was an acquaintance with during my time at Watson and Rubenstein, even though he was a well-established member of the firm by the time I clerked there. While I was in court in New York, he contacted me to meet him for drinks. The offer he laid on the table was more than intriguing—but it wasn't to work with him. Over a glass of whiskey, he casually mentioned, "I think you're just what Ryan needs."

"Ryan? Your husband, Ryan?" I clarified, knowing damn well who Ryan Lockwood is. Chairman of the board of Lockwood Industries. This man has planes, trains, and shipping vessels with his company logo emblazoned on the side. Having inherited the empire from his late father, Ryan has grown it even further with his own exceptional business acumen. There isn't a major company in the United States who can't trace back some of their supply chain through Lockwood Industries. I was astounded Jared thought I had the legal chops necessary to work for such a large conglomerate and wasted no time telling him so.

"I've watched your career, Ben. You'd be an asset to his legal team."

"Thanks for the compliment." And I sincerely meant it.

That's when an unfamiliar yet strangely recognizable voice said from behind me, "It wasn't intended as one. Jared wouldn't have arranged for us to meet if he didn't feel you had something to give to me, to bring to Lockwood Industries."

My head snapped around at the mild rebuke. Then my jaw sagged slightly as my eyes roamed over a younger, less craggy version of Caleb Lockwood. "Well, I'll be damned."

Jared stood. Ryan leaned over and kissed his husband hello before admitting, "You might be before this interview is over." He then waived a server over to add his own drink order to ours.

Though Jared kept an eye on my career throughout the years, that first meeting was nerve-racking, to say the least. One drink turned into dinner as I was grilled on every case which could impact Lockwood Industries. I had little doubt Caleb was involved in pulling a list of the pertinent ones for his younger brother, as thorough as he was in searching for Kelsey.

I don't know whether it was my lack of kissing ass, my precise responses—even when Ryan vehemently disagreed with me—or just dumb blind luck that had him reaching out to offer me the assistant general counsel position at Lockwood Industries three years ago.

"Will I have to move to New York?" I recall asking.

"Do you want to?" Ryan returned.

"What are the options?" I asked back.

Ryan ran a finger along the rim of his crystal tumbler. "Recently, I opened another office in New Orleans because of the number of operations we're running out of the Port of New Orleans. We've permanently taken over eight berths out of the forty available."

I let out a low whistle because that's not just some major cash—that's the kind of money kings and queens go to war over.

Ryan's tone sounded frustrated. "I can't be everywhere at once. I need people I trust in each location and frankly, Louisiana law is a pain in my ass."

Absentmindedly, I remarked, "That's because it's based on Napoleonic code."

Ryan's lips curved. "How do you feel about taking the bar again?" At my groan, he incentivized it. "Because if you don't want to move to New York, you'll essentially be my eyes and ears on the ground in New Orleans."

It's been three long years, but amid stolen cargo, customs issues, and trade deals the size of which I might have been in my fifties before I had my hands in at my old firm, I've made my mark at Lockwood Industries. Ryan recently rewarded that when his old general counsel stepped down due to health reasons, promoting me to the head chair.

Even beyond the work, both Ryan and Jared have been added to my short list of trusted friends. But with Ryan, there's a line I don't dare cross. I know how seriously Ryan takes his business. At the level he operates at, friendship doesn't come into play, only hard work.

I should have it all—the job, the lifestyle, the money. But there's a hollowness inside of me that keeps me working in the office for too many hours. And I can't even blame it on Ryan any longer, not since he's started delegating more to his global department heads.

I have a front row seat to Ryan and Jared's relationship, been regaled with stories about the love found within their extended family, and I realize there should be more. I'm just not sure I deserve it. Flickers of shame and guilt wash over me, and my heart begins to race as bile twists my drink in my stomach into something noxious ready to be expunged when I remember what I was forced to do.

And not just to Kelsey.

Juliette harrumphs before pouting in a way I'm sure she thinks is attractive, but all it does is enhance the fact she's spent way too much money on Botox. Slyly, she prods the beast living inside me. "I hear King Kong's going to show her face this year."

"Her name's Kelsey," I bite out harshly. The fist not holding a beer is clenching in the pocket of my dress slacks.

"Oh, that's right. After all, who'd remember after seeing her? Or not being able to unsee her? Then again, you had to spend more time with her than anyone. I'm not sure how you didn't have to have eye surgery or something to repair your vision, Benedict. She was a bea—" Juliette's nasty laugh is cut off when I get into her space as close as I dare.

"Not. Another. Word." My voice is low and vicious. "I'll say now what I should have said then: I won't tolerate another insult or slur against that perfectly sweet woman." *At least not again.*

Juliette leans in, undeterred by my threat. "Aw, poor Ben. Did you come here thinking she was going to offer you forgiveness when she likely sees you as the person that represents all of us?" She laughs in my face before turning and walking away.

I'm frozen stock-still, unable to move, barely able to breathe before finding the wherewithal to move off in the other direction. Finding the nearest trash bin, I toss my beer inside and make my way down the ramp toward the yachts docked at the end of the pier.

Juliette's not wrong. I need to confront Kelsey tomorrow night and publicly beg for her forgiveness the same way I destroyed what was between us. No matter what she does or says, I have to accept that she may never forgive me for an act so hurtful, so heinous, it did turn me into one of her monsters—*the* monster.

And just because I'm scared of the outcome, just like I was on graduation day, doesn't give me the right not to accept the consequences of my actions. It's consuming me, this not knowing. But I owe her the apology face-to-face. Much like I caused her pain fifteen years ago.

CHAPTER EIGHT

Benedict

She isn't here yet.

Propping my shoulder against the far wall, I sip at the drink in my hand. I've been scanning the room as the door opens. Each time, there's a new collective gasp before a feminine squeal or a loud call of "Hey, man!" or "Dude!" bursts out.

I was one of the first people to arrive, hoping to intercept Kelsey, and convince her we should go somewhere to talk before we walked in together —a united front against the vitriol that's waiting in that room.

But she's not here.

My raging disappointment is held in check by the fact I still need to navigate my exit from this farce of an event.

"So, you actually work?" Brayden Pierce asks me, aghast. His third wife is clinging to him desperately. *Better hold on,* I think, with some amusement. Brayden was overheard at the last reunion saying he liked his wives to match his cars. And I think I heard him saying earlier he was on the market for a new one of each.

"I do." Lifting my highball to my lips, I take a sip of the watered-down drink. I didn't want anything impairing a conversation with Kelsey, but if she's not going to show, I might refresh my drink.

Just not here.

"When do you find time to socialize with the right people?" Brayden's wife asks. He squeezes her shoulder to either agree with or hush her, I can't be sure.

"You find the time when you care about the people." At that moment, my cell vibrates in my pocket. Perfect timing. "If you'll excuse me, I've been expecting this call." Slipping my phone out, I frown. There's no reason for Ryan to call unless something's wrong.

Placing my drink on the nearest high top, I slip out the veranda doors. "Talk to me."

"I called your assistant. You're on a flight back for tomorrow." Ryan's tone brooks no argument.

Immediately all business, I demand, "What happened?"

"We've either got a breach or a threat. Information is being sent to your phone."

"Not my corporate email?"

"I don't want anything going across the network until we know what the fuck happened."

I begin to pace back and forth. "Can you read me in now?"

He hesitates. "All I'll say is be glad you're three states away, or you wouldn't be receiving this call," he bites out before hanging up.

Crap. That means whatever it is originated in the legal department. A few seconds later, my new flight information arrives. Quickly, I check in to my flight. I'm stuck in Savannah until tomorrow afternoon, but I can finish the revisions to the contracts off-line.

Recognizing Ryan may not want me to, I shoot him a quick text. *Do you want me to keep working on Project Titan?*

Within seconds I get a reply. *Go ahead and work on it. Keep your computer off the internet.*

Roger that, I send back before sliding my phone back into my pocket.

A million thoughts are flying through my mind about the storm about to erupt at Lockwood Industries, so I'm only half listening when I hear, "So, Kong came, found her badge, and left? How tragic. I really wanted to see her face."

Yeah, that pulls me away from my worries about work. Stalking out of the shadows, I confront Juliette Gaines. "What the hell did you do?"

"I just made sure she recognized her name tag." She lets out a shrill laugh that's immediately echoed by her cohorts.

"Which was?" I step forward into her space, no longer under the threat the power base of Forsyth once held over me.

Defensively, she crosses her arms. "All I did was put her proper name on her badge."

"You mean Kelsey Kennedy?" Juliette squirms, telling me all I need to know. "I hope you have an exceptional lawyer on retainer," I mention offhandedly.

"What? Why?" Her voice holds a note of nervousness she tries to hide.

"Because what you did could be construed as a misdemeanor under Georgia law. You deliberately cultivated feelings of hatred, provoking a breach of peace."

"Really? Who would dare press charges against me?" Her chin juts out pugnaciously.

I smile cruelly before shoving my way past her and her little posse, leaving her to think that maybe somebody was going to hold her accountable for her remorseless behavior. Finally.

Now, I don't just want a drink before I go to my room to work, I need it. Then, maybe I can try to forget when I'll ever have a chance to apologize for my mistakes or if I'll be left to regret them for the rest of my life.

Pushing my way through crowds of partygoers, I feel like I've lost my last chance to say everything I've needed to get off my chest.

I fucked up.

I never wanted to hurt you.

Can you forgive me?

The answer to the last is something I've spent fifteen years waiting for. The problem is, every time I've asked the question in my head, silence is my only answer. Like I suspect it would have been if I'd gotten the chance to talk with Kelsey tonight.

I enter the Aqua Fuego Bar, and the place is packed. Golfers and couples waiting for their spot in the adjoining restaurant are taking up every available seat except one next to a woman who is talking on her cell phone near a modern piece of aqua blue backlit glass. Sighing in relief, I begin to weave my way toward the empty spot at the bar, hoping no one beats me to it.

But as I get closer, I can't help but notice the light catching the highlights in her warm brown hair as she tosses her head back while she laughs. It cascades over the creamy skin of a bared shoulder, reminding me vaguely of someone, but I can't quite put my finger on who.

Maybe she's someone I went to school with? Before I know it, I'm standing right next to her. Her face is in profile while she listens with a smile to the person she's speaking to.

Clearing my throat to interrupt her call politely, I ask, "Is this seat taken?"

Blinking up at me with eyes that are bright gray, I freeze in place. I still don't move when she murmurs into the phone, "I'll text you later. Something's come up." After giving me a full head to toe perusal, she nods as if she's making an internal decision.

Turning her face to the side, she says, "Have a seat."

Sliding my ass onto the stool next to her, I immediately raise my hand to get the bartender's attention before I start to ask her a million questions.

Like how do I feel like I know her when I have no idea who she is?

CHAPTER NINE

Kelsey

THE ONLY THING THAT'S PERFECT ABOUT ME IS MY DRESS. EMILY outdid herself—it's fucking gorgeous. The sharp V-necked gown I spied the drawing of when I went wedding dress shopping with Jillian is perfect for the reunion. Paired with sculpted leather heels covered in pyramid studs, my body appears longer than I ever dreamed it could be after Dr. Toli operated on me all those years ago.

And before I stepped into the lobby in front of the shitshow of a fifteen-year high school reunion, I felt sexy as fuck. I felt like I could walk in and do precisely what Ava, Matt, and Val wanted me to do—stride in with my head held high and walk out with people's souls trailing behind me. I was prepared to be as gloriously distant as possible before sweeping out—leaving Forsyth in my past forever.

Now, as I trace the lone name tag on the table with a perfectly manicured finger, I feel like I'm the one who has been trampled over.

King Kong.

Memories of that being screamed at me from all directions as I walked into class, into the cafeteria, as I walked into that fucking building, swamp me. But none so horrific as the last. Shame sends a burst of heat along my cheeks, brightening their pale blush tone.

"Why did I let myself be talked into this?" I murmur aloud. After casting a look of practiced indifference toward the door, I'm seconds away from snatching up the loathsome, tacky clip when I hear voices behind me.

"Do you think she'll have the guts to show?"

"Please, if her brain works half as well as her mouth did on food, she won't even try to board an airplane. I'm sure the airlines have to charge her double anyway." Juliette Bernard, former head cheerleader, knockout blond, and the leader of my former tormentors, sneers, "I probably wasted the money even having her name printed on the tag. If Kong doesn't understand by now, she should simply . . ." Spotting me, she looks me up and down even as my heart beats erratically in my chest. Does she recognize me even though I'm over two hundred pounds lighter?

Her face transforms with a perky smile I want to punch right off. I could because all those boxing classes taught me a hell of a lot. Instead, I'm momentarily taken aback when she coos, "I adore your dress. Where did you get it?"

Fortunately, I've learned how to deal with my fair share of people just like this. "A designer boutique in Connecticut. It's one of a kind." My voice is calmer than I would have expected under the circumstances. Maybe Val was right—maybe I did need to come here to face my demons.

Thoughtfully, she taps her finger against her lips. "I'll pay you two thousand for it."

My lips fall open. "Excuse me?" I want to laugh not only on my behalf but Emily's. The paltry sum doesn't begin to cover what an original Amaryllis Design costs.

"It's divine. I have to have it. I'll write you a check right now." Juliette reaches for her crystal-encrusted clutch.

"You don't even know what size it is," I say with more than a touch of disbelief.

Giving me the once-over, she declares, "Even though you're a bit wider in the hips than I am, I bet we're close to the same size. An eight, right? So, does that amount work? Listen, I'll even give you my gown to get back to your room." She goes to reach behind her before I hold up my hand to stop her.

"Stop. It's not for sale." I cannot believe the audacity of this woman. A little voice in the back of my mind is nudging me, saying, *Maybe it wasn't just you. Maybe she treats everyone like this.* I silence it as I enter a staring contest with a woman who's been given everything and fears nothing.

Not the least her sanity.

"Everything has a price," she smirks. The women around her nod. I vaguely recognize them as part of her cheerleading posse from fifteen years ago. Then again, she could have said the next president of the United States was about to be hatched from her stomach as a chartreuse alien and they'd have agreed to it.

I was never so glad not to be part of the "in" crowd as I dreamed of so many nights as I am right now. I'm ecstatic I have something more substantial, an ability to think for myself. "No, not everything." I pause before adding, "Breeding and class certainly don't."

I arch a perfectly threaded eyebrow as I saunter past the gasping gaggle of women with two thoughts in my mind: a glass of wine and a call to my best friend.

"I can't believe I wasted good money on this. It was a fucking farce, Val."

"Calm down, Kels. Besides, it gave you an excuse to fly home and see your family when you had your dress fitting," she reminds me.

"True," I concede. And now that I'm not around the toxicity of my high school reunion, I've fallen in love with the gown Emily custom fit to my body all over again. A small smile curves my lips at the feeling of the silk sliding away from my legs as I cross them.

"Remember, your flight takes off early tomorrow morning. Darin will pick you up at the airport and bring you right here."

"I'm so glad I decided not to stay an extra day," I grumble as I take a sip of the full-bodied pinot grigio in front of me.

"What time will you land?"

"Around one because of the layover. You know, why don't I arrange for a car and meet you at the house? This way, Darin won't have to leave work in the middle of the day to get me."

I can practically hear the wheels turning on the other end of the line. "It would help," she agrees. Val and Darin live in a beautifully refurbished home near Audubon Park. Until I find my new place in the Big Easy, they've generously let me move into their guest suite. But I need to find something soon. After all, it won't be long before their baby arrives and Darin's family descends to claim the space I'm currently occupying.

My smile spreads further when I think about how I'm going to spoil this baby from the sister of my heart. Val has no idea of the things I have planned for her precious Lucille. Being a hands-on aunt to this miracle is what pushed me over the edge to make the final decision to move to New Orleans. As she pointed out, "Everything you need is inside of you."

Wryly, I responded, "A good computer and internet connection helps."

That's when she put her hands on either side of where my niece would soon begin to show. "It's not like you couldn't have that here."

This is why all my furniture is locked in a storage unit, and all my clothes are wedged in Val's guest room closet. For now.

"Did anything good happen?" Val's question brings me back out of my reverie.

"Well, my favorite cheerleader offered to buy my dress." I pause for effect. "Off my body."

Val starts to giggle.

"She reached into her clutch to write me a check. Even offered me her gown to get me back to my room. Like it was a disposable robe from the spa next door or some shit." I take another sip of wine as Val erupts into full-out laughter.

"Stop. Right now," she drawls when she can catch her breath. "I'm clutching Lucy so she doesn't make me pee on myself."

I grin. "And thus, my mission of the day has been accomplished."

"What mission? I know it wasn't telling that piece of work to go fuck herself. You have too much class for that."

Sadly, she's right. I wish I'd had the strength to rip that offensive badge off the table and slap it across her nasty face. But that's not my style. At least not in person.

Now when I'm writing, there's where I'll get the retribution I need. Longingly, I wish I was back upstairs in my pajama shorts and the T-shirt Val bought me that says, "Don't piss me off. You'll end up in my book." I know that's where I'll come up with the witty retorts I should have said while I'm transforming this scene for use at a later date. There, my lonely Pilar has evolved to become stronger than the girls who target her from her first day at the private school her well-meaning parents sent her to. *Maybe by her senior year, she'll even have a date,* I muse. Very unlike myself. At least I have some new fodder for my books since nothing about the inspiration behind my prosaic purge has changed. Nothing ever will. Their cruelty is the kind that will continue until something or someone stops them in their tracks.

I thought it could be me who took them down a peg tonight. I was wrong.

Fingering the clip-on badge and my hotel key card in my clutch, I start to answer Val when a vaguely familiar deep voice startles me. "Is this seat taken?" My heart is sputtering in my chest as I turn to meet the bluest eyes I've seen in a long while. Certainly, I've never forgotten them in fifteen years.

Even as the wine churns in my stomach, I murmur, "I'll text you later. Something's come up." Val is still squawking in my ear as I push End on our call.

Val was right when she figured he would be here. After all, unlike me, he had nothing to fear. He was captain of the swim team, the most handsome boy in school, and, ultimately, the final blow that drove me away.

Benedict Rierson Perrault.

I place my phone in my purse, and my fingers brush again against the badge. King Kong. The name seems to ricochet in my head. Does he recognize me? Judging by the smile flirting on his lips, I'd say no, he doesn't. My eyes drift to his fingers resting on the bar next to me. No ring. I'm surprised a man with his kind of charm hasn't been snapped up by some nubile young coed from some prestigious college they likely attended, and they don't have three perfect children waiting for them at home.

Tipping my face aside so maybe he won't recognize me, I say, "Have a seat." Anxiously, I switch the legs I'd just crossed, rearranging my dress. The shimmer of the material catches the overhead light before I swing my legs under the bar.

He slides onto the barstool next to me. "Am I taking someone's spot?" At the negative shake of my head, a look of pervasive relief crosses his face. "I'm surprised to find you alone. It seems everyone here is with someone."

From King Kong to a pickup line. I want to throw my pinot in his face and walk out. But a longing little voice I've suppressed for fifteen years whispers, *This is your chance, Kelsey. There's something you want more.* I shrug. "My plans fell through." Cutting my eyes toward him, I give him a quick perusal. "I could say the same."

Frustration crosses his face. "I was hoping to run into an old . . . friend. I'm supposed to be at a class reunion upstairs."

I cluck my tongue in mock sympathy. "An old girlfriend?" Maybe if I bait him with enough questions, he'll realize who I am.

"It wasn't like that. We were close though. I was really hoping I'd have a chance to . . ." He looks like he wants to say more, but the bartender comes up with a cocktail napkin.

"What can I get you?"

"A manhattan." Benedict reaches into his pocket for his wallet.

I smile and shake my head at the bartender. "I've got it."

Benedict's hand drops away from a lean hip. He opens his mouth, unsure whether to protest or say thank you, but Isaac winks.

"You got it, Kee." He saunters off to make the drink.

"Is that your name? Kee?" Benedict's attention is locked on me fully at this point.

"Kee Long." I pause to see if he makes the connection. But even as I hold out my hand for him to shake, I refuse to think about the fact I picked my pen name from a derivative of the hurtful name hurled at me day after day for four excruciating years.

Still, I find it difficult to swallow as the boy-turned-man I never quite forgot doesn't take my hand to shake but instead lifts it to his lips. "Benedict Perrault. Call me Ben."

Isaac places his drink down next to him, but Benedict doesn't release my hand. "Tell me about yourself, Kee."

There's a kernel of the girl who tutored him who wants to be outraged and offended he doesn't recognize me. It's tempered by the more pragmatic part of me who looks in the mirror every day. I wouldn't know who I was either if I hadn't lived through the transformation myself. Instead of slamming both of my hands in Benedict's chest or dumping my excellent wine over his shirt, I find myself slipping into a character I know well. And within a few minutes, he's looking at me much the same way most people do when they realize who I am—with admiration and respect. After all, I've hit all the major lists with my writing. I'm no longer a little nobody. I'm Somebody, with a capital S. And judging from the admiration on Benedict's face, he's impressed by it.

It's a whole different look than the pained one I last saw on his face, that's for sure.

Shoving aside the voices in my head screaming at me to tell him who I am, I finish my drink and wave for another.

Time passes quickly as we keep talking. It feels like only minutes have passed, so I'm surprised when Isaac quietly approaches to tell me it's the last call.

I feel good—so much more relaxed with Benedict now than when he first approached me. In talking about my life, even if he doesn't know who I am, I realize it doesn't matter if anyone knows. My lips curve. Unbeknownst to him, to even myself until right now, I got the closure I came here for.

I'm about to ask him if he'd like a final drink when he brushes my shoulder-length hair away from my cheek. "How about we get a bottle of whatever you're drinking to go?" His fingers rest on the pulse at the base of my throat.

The invitation is as open and relaxed as our conversation has been. My lips part to ask if he thinks this is too soon after we've reconnected, but the reality I've helped perpetrate sets in. To him, we're just two strangers. Only I know there's so much more that lies between us. That long ago, his hurtful words were my last memory of this city.

If I walk away, we're a chance at what might have been—nothing more, nothing less.

But as I stare into fathomless blue eyes, for once I want to know what it might have been like if I could have had a date with Benedict—if I was "good enough" to have been seen with him, not just smart enough to have helped him as his tutor. I want to know what I should have been able to have felt if I were as beautiful as my grandparents told me I was, as Benedict himself said I was. Even if he only muttered it the one time when he hugged me after getting the grade guaranteeing him entry to his first-choice college.

So, I do what I normally do when I find an attractive man who obviously is interested in me. I turn off the memories of who and what I was. There's no place for Kelsey here. If I didn't know Benedict before tonight, I'd want him. And, my heart taunts me quietly, there's no way I would have been able to have had him before.

Sliding off the stool, I let my hand rest lightly against his chest. "I have an early flight." I'm pleased to see the flash of disappointment cross his face before I whisper, "I don't need any more wine if I'm going to keep my head on straight when I touch you."

His nostrils flare. "Why don't you wait for me by the elevator?" I suggest. I still need to sign the bill, and I don't want him to see the woman he's been flirting with as Kee Long and Kelsey Kennedy are one and the same.

Tipping his head close to mine, I feel my hard-won stomach muscles clench when his lips brush my ear. "Don't be long." He takes a quick nip, then strides off. Quickly, I scribble my real name on the receipt with a hefty tip for Isaac before following him.

I'll give myself a few hours to indulge in my fantasies, the ones Kelsey had that Kee will fulfill. Then my ass will be on a plane back to New Orleans, never to see him again.

Quietly, I slip out of bed where Ben's still sprawled. The bed is a wreck, much like my body. I refuse to delve into what my heart and mind are feeling. The things we did. It almost makes me want to call the airline and reschedule my flight, but I force myself to turn my back to him and tug the silky material over my body.

I hunt for—and find—my shoes. I don't bother with the panties since Ben ripped them off me, and they're lying in shreds on the floor. Sliding my feet back into my heels, I slip out of the bedroom to where I dropped my clutch.

I flick open the clasp and pull out my room key. Holding it tightly in my hand, I pause just before I open the door. Damn, he seems so perfect. If only I didn't know what he's really like. Ruthlessly turning, I slip into the hallway to make my way back up to the penthouse suite. I have only an hour until the car picks me up for my flight.

Later, after I'm settled in the back of a private car on the way to the airport, I turn my phone on. There are half a dozen messages from Val. The only one I answer is, *What the hell is going on?*

Quickly I type, *Too much to tell you in text. I'll catch you up when I get back to your place.*

There are a few floating dots before I get, *Good. I've been up all night worrying.*

You've been up all night because Lucy is giving you heartburn.

Well, that too. I laugh out loud at my bestie's honesty.

The further the driver takes me away from my reunion and Benedict Perrault, the more I can feel myself relaxing back into the secure, self-confident woman I've become.

Content.

I can live with content. Maybe happiness is for fools and dreamers. I stopped being one of those fifteen years ago.

Leaning back against the seat, the quick trip to Savannah/Hilton Head International Airport passes quickly. Within hours, I'm airborne. I refuse to give too much thought to what happened.

After all, I never have to see any of those people ever again.

Including Ben.

By the time we hit 20,000 feet, I'm dozing in my seat to make up for the lack of sleep, knowing I face an inquisition when I touch down in New Orleans. My lips curve just before I fall into a deep sleep.

Everything about how I'm feeling is different from the last time I left Savannah, that's for sure.

CHAPTER TEN

Benedict

The sun streams through the windows when I wake up the next morning. Fuck, that was a hell of a night. *Kee Long is one sexy as hell woman,* I think, as I roll over to my stomach. I can still catch the scent of her perfume on the pillow her head was on. My body tenses as I remember how I drove myself inside her tight body.

What wouldn't I give to see her again? Dropping my head down, I inhale a delicate floral scent that makes my cock immediately hard. Jesus, the thing should be dead after the few hours I subjected it to, but nope. The unique smell of a beautiful woman with a smart mouth and a sexy brain and the damn thing can't help but react. Scrambling, I reach for the bedside phone. Quickly dialing "0," I impatiently wait for the operator.

When they greet me with, "Good morning, Mr. Perrault, how can we assist you?" I wonder at my sanity.

"I'm not sure if it . . . I'm not sure if you can." I let out a harsh sigh. "It was a stupid idea."

The operator can't fully tamp down the chuckle that escapes, and I'm too agreeable to call them on it. "Would you like to order breakfast to be sent up with your messages?"

"I have messages?" I ask dumbly because there's no way Ryan would have left a message. He would have called my cell directly with any updates. A quick check of my cell confirms that. Despite whatever is happening at work, he also knows I was planning on confronting Kelsey last night with a long-overdue apology. Ryan happened to be in New Orleans last year on the anniversary of my high school graduation. When he stormed into my office, he bluntly told me, "You look like shit, Perrault. What's wrong?" Then he sniffed the air before demanding, "Are you drunk?"

I paused in lifting the crystal tumbler to my lips before reaching for a clean glass. Handing it to him, I explained, "I'm trying to get that way." Then the words just fell from my mouth about what I did to Kelsey.

The operator's voice pulls me back to the present when she says, "Yes, the young woman was insistent you receive it upon checkout, but since you're not scheduled to leave until late this afternoon, I don't see why you can't receive it now."

Kee must have left me a message. Maybe she felt the same things I did and left me her contact information. Hopeful, I sit up in bed, the tangled sheets falling to my waist. "Yes, please. Whatever you recommend sounds great. Just lots of coffee."

"Of course, Mr. Perrault. That will be about thirty minutes." The operator disconnects. I want to leave the bed where I took Kee about as much as I want to retake the Louisiana bar exam, but I can't answer the door naked. Scrambling from the bed, I figure I have just enough time for a quick shower before room service arrives. Pulling a T-shirt and basketball shorts from my bag, I head toward the bathroom and think about Kee as the spray hits me all over.

Soft, wavy chestnut-colored hair framed her delicate gray eyes. Beautifully pink-tipped breasts filled my hands more often than not once we got into the room. She has the sexiest tattoo of flowers and vines I've ever seen spanning her lower stomach and hips. When I asked her what it was, she said, "Gerbera daisies," right before she leaned down and took my mouth. Yet, her sass catapulted last night from a great night into something more.

There's something special about her.

Twenty-nine minutes later, I realize I'm starving when there's a knock at my door. Finally. I throw open the door. There's a carafe of coffee and a covered plate that distinctly carries the smell of bacon. Plus, an envelope is propped on the front with my name scrawled in beautiful feminine penmanship.

Benedict

It taunts me more than the overwhelming smell of bacon.

"Thanks for bringing everything up so quickly." I wait to be presented with the bill. Leaving the room service attendant with a fat tip, I usher them to the door. I reach for the envelope and tear it open. My heart quickly plummets when I read what's inside.

Thank you for a truly memorable night. ~K

"That's it?" I wonder aloud. I can't say I haven't indulged in my share of one-night stands with women, but this is the first time I've felt more and wanted to explore it.

Shaking my head, I turn to head over to the sitting area when I stub my bare toe on the table. "Shit. Fuck. Damn!" Then to make matters worse, I step on something hard and metal. Wincing, I bend down to rub my throbbing toe when I pick up a plastic-coated name badge.

Huh. I'm pretty positive mine was in the pocket of my jacket. "Then whose is this?" Flipping it over, I choke.

Suddenly, the sight of the food, the coffee, makes me nauseous.

Because Kelsey Kennedy's sweet face is staring up at me. Only beneath her picture, the fucking bitches we went to school with put the name King Kong.

King Kong? Wait. "How the hell did this get in here?" Then like the tumblers to a lock opening, so does my mind. *Kee Long*.

"Choosing a pen name's a boring process." I can hear Kee's lightly accented voice dismiss my question. "It wasn't the most fun thing I've ever done."

I murmur, "Of course it wasn't." Because for four years, the people who helped her to establish her alter ego made her life a living hell. And I was quite possibly the worst of them.

No wonder there was that moment of recognition when I first saw her. I'm gasping for breath as flashes of Kee—no, Kelsey—rising above me tumble through my mind. Her beautiful face, her smile, her fucking perfect gray eyes.

Eyes I remember shining in excitement as she squealed when I hoisted her under her arms and spun her around the empty classroom the day I told her I got into college. Eyes that took my breath away when her long dark lashes lowered before lifting in shock when I hoarsely told her she was beautiful. A face that looked at me with such devastation when I called out that name, the name she was tormented by her entire high school career.

"Oh my god. What just happened?" I brace my hands, one still clutching the despicable nametag, against the table. The hole I've tried for fifteen years is wide open, and the septic ooze coming from it is burning through my soul. I never got the chance to tell her why I did it. I never got the opportunity to tell her I was sorry before she left Savannah for college herself not long after. I can still hear her grandfather snapping at me, "Get off my land, you nasty son of a bitch."

"But Mr. Barron," I pleaded. My father stood behind me, supportive but silent.

"*She's gone*! And she ain't comin' back—all 'cause of the likes of kids like you. And what's worse? She helped you get your dream. What did you give her but nightmares?" he said right before he slammed the door in our faces.

I don't know what to think about the fact she knew who I was last night without giving me the chance to apologize for fifteen years' worth of misconceptions before sleeping with me.

"Jesus Christ," I mutter as I run my hand through my hair. Leaving the food untouched, I stumble to the couch as I'm lost in painful memories. Ones I never shared with anyone but my father, the president of Forsyth, and Cade. But not before Kelsey left Georgia. She up and left her family behind. Now, it makes sense why my inquiry into her identity was blocked. I laugh aloud bitterly. Of course, the identity of one of the world's most famous authors would be protected at all costs.

No one heard about Kelsey Kennedy ever again until last night when she tried to unite her past with her present and left me in her wake.

Why? Why didn't she tell me? The questions float through my head, but I don't have a chance to ponder the answers. I come out of my stupor when I hear the alarm on my cell ringing. Shit. I have less than three hours to make my flight back to New Orleans.

Clutching both the note and her badge in my hand, I put them on top of my laptop so I don't lose them. Now that I have an idea of how to contact her, I need to think of the right words to say.

Me, the lawyer, trying to think of the right words.

All the pain from the last fifteen years coalesces into a bitter laugh as I begin packing to make my flight.

CHAPTER ELEVEN

Kelsey

"Are you crazy?" Val yells at me. We're sitting around her kitchen drinking coffee—mine fully loaded, while Val's is decaf. "Why didn't you *talk* to him? For Christ's sake, Kels. You could have known instead of always wondering why."

I shrug because her words sting with the bitterness of truth. Instead of an incredible night of sex, I could have had answers to the questions burning deep inside of me. As much as I claim to be living my best life, there's a nest of hurt feelings I allow few to see because few are permitted to get that close. Benedict was the final straw that broke the camel's back. And the woman across from me was my oasis in the desert.

Val knows how deep my scars run, and not just the physical ones left over from my surgery. After all, she helped me to fend off a whole new host of bullying when she became my roommate at Pepperdine.

Only Val understood the emotional wars I fought as I walked next to her in the cafeteria, eventually eschewing it for Styrofoam noodle cups or oatmeal in our room. Val appreciated when I struggled to get to class on time because I was out of breath or covered in sweat.

Val understood how hard it was not to give up on my dreams because of humiliation.

And Val is the only person who ever asked why I weighed so much—if there was some hurt holding me back from being the beautiful person she knew I was inside. "Did something . . . happen, Kelsey?" Before I could answer her, she rushed on, "I learned in psychological counseling this week one in every four women who is deathly overweight may have been sexually assaulted."

Tears flooded my eyes at the betrayal those poor women endured—the loss of themselves far beyond even what I endured. "No, Val, it wasn't like that. It was different."

"Oh, Kelsey," she began.

"It wasn't something that happened just once. It happened over and over for years."

That night, I told her about the car wreck that took my parents' lives where we lived in Florida—how they'd been fighting over my mother's recent discovery about my father's affair. They both assumed I was asleep in the back seat, but I wasn't. "If there's anyone to blame, Anne, it's you. After you had Kelsey, you just don't appeal to me."

"That doesn't give you the right to break your vows!" my mother shrilled.

He laughed cruelly. "You think this is the first time?"

My mother began hitting him, sobbing. "How could you?"

He took his hand off the steering wheel. Twisting his head, his indifference to her rage was apparent. His lofty sneer was unmistakable. Just as he was about to respond, my heart stopped.

Stopped.

There in the middle of the road, was a wild boar—roughly half the size of a large cow. They were as common in our North Florida community as alligators.

I screamed.

I dully informed Val, "My father swerved to avoid hitting it. Instead of avoiding the thing, he overcorrected and hit a tree at high speed, killing them both and leaving me trapped in the back seat."

Val stroked my hand as I explained, "I don't remember anything after that until I woke up at Wolfson Children's Hospital being treated for a severe concussion with those words seared on my brain when my grandparents came to get me."

"Then what happened?"

"Obviously, I moved."

"That must have sucked."

I think back to those early days before admitting, "I was numb. I don't remember that much. At first, I ate because I equated food being a sign of comfort and love from my Nana. Then, I had time to think. Food became a way to hide, you know? I mean, if I wasn't pretty, who would ever hurt me the way my daddy hurt my mama?"

Val just sat there, holding my hand as we both cried. She nodded, waiting for me to go on. Taking a deep breath, I did. "My grandparents wanted to make sure I had the best education, and there was an inheritance from my parents. It was enough to pay for my high school and college." At Val's nod, I continued, "So, they sent me to this private school. Val, it was awful. The things I was called . . ." My face flamed, and the tears flowed over my cheeks in remembrance. "Then I ate to forget. I remember stopping at the local grocery store in the mornings. I'd race up to the deli counter and order pounds of meat and cheese. I'd sneak to my car to wolf it down between classes." I think I broke my own heart a little when I said in a small voice, "Food became the only friend I had. It was so easy. I was never scared of the truths it would tell me."

We both sobbed as I kept talking. "I'd see how the kids would watch me, and I don't know what was worse: the emotional or physical pain."

"They touched you?"

"Oh yeah. Slammed me into lockers, into walls, desks, you name it. I hid the bruises as much as I hid the fat." Even I heard the bitterness in my voice. "That pain almost seemed tolerable in comparison to the words. God, I can still hear them in my nightmares."

"Get rid of them. Give them to me." And so I did. I pulled the box I hastily packed from the closet and described the viciousness of Juliette Bernard to her. I explained how broken my heart would be each time a new folded note would stick out of the locker or slip into my bag, how people would guess at my weight. That someone tried to trap me in the nurse's office to get on a scale before I ran away and started screaming.

And finally, I told her about the razor blades that would occasionally be left with a note telling me to end it all. After all, the letter suggested, it would be better for everyone if I did. I'd take up less space on the planet.

"I won't pretend to understand what you've been through, Kels, but I promise you I won't treat you like that." Val sounded as broken as I felt. "This"—she shoved her hands against the box of stuff we'd sifted through—"doesn't define you. This"—she laid her hand on my heart—"does. It's strong and courageous if it can withstand what you've endured. There's something beautiful waiting to emerge. I can't wait to see it."

I collapsed in her arms, crying. We skipped classes the next day to watch movies like *Sixteen Candles* and *The Breakfast Club*.

It wasn't until weeks later that Val noticed I'd stopped eating. She raised holy hell.

A nutritional science major, my new best friend did her best to help me. That is after she stopped screaming at me for endangering my life. "No! This isn't how you fix what's wrong. I'll help you, but we're going to do this right. I'm not losing you now that I found you."

For years, we ate healthily and worked out regularly. No combination of caloric intake plus exercise seemed to work. I'd lose some weight, but not much for my effort. I was even stumping her professors, who she enlisted to help. Through some research, we determined I had damaged my metabolism as a result of the weight gain. "Great," I lamented. "Nothing's going to work."

That is until Val's senior year when she researched and found a bariatric surgeon in Long Beach who needed part-time help in his billing office. "He has a three-year waiting list, Kels. But maybe he'll make an exception if it's one of his office staff."

I gave it some thought before I applied. The last thing in the world I wanted to do was work in an office—I was a creative writing major, after all. I had dreams of working for a publishing house, maybe being an editor. I certainly didn't fantasize about working in an office where I'd always be reminded of the single thing that could send me spiraling into a severe depression. But after some thought, I figured what did I have to lose? Certainly not my pride. That was long gone. I was both mildly surprised and somewhat disappointed when I was brought in for an in-person interview. I thought they'd throw me out the minute they saw me. Instead, I was blunt when asked why I wanted to work there. "Because I need help, and Dr. Toli is my last hope."

"What makes you think that?" his office manager asked.

"Because I can hear my heart beating too fast every night as I stare out my dorm room window. I'm afraid it's going to stop, and I'm going to die."

I was offered the position the next day.

I worked for the famed surgeon part-time for the rest of my senior year and full-time the following year and a half. Between what I managed to save and the remainder of my parents' estate, I had enough money to cover what insurance wouldn't. A chance for hope. And it worked. I lost and have kept off over two hundred pounds.

Blessed isn't close to how I feel when I think about the miracles I've been given over the last decade between my health, my career, and my true family and friends. My regrets, well, most of those are tied to Forsyth.

"It's not like I'm ever going to see him again, Val," I reiterate calmly.

"You don't think he's not smart enough to realize you're . . . you?"

I snort. "Not hardly. I mean, the man was staring me right in the face while he was . . ." A loud cough comes from behind me. Val grins.

"Hey, baby! You're home from work early." Val starts to edge herself to the end of her chair so she can greet Darin, who's still just as sexy as he was when he was playing basketball for Pepperdine. His huge smile flashes at me, showing the dimples in his cheeks that made coeds everywhere sigh, and Val threaten to shank a few of them more than once.

He squeezes my arm as he makes his way past me to his wife, who he greets with a long kiss. I rest my chin in my hands, watching openly with a grin. I'm so used to their open affection for each other that I have no problem rating their kisses. "I'd give that one a five, Dare," I tease him. He shakes his head before he answers his wife.

"Something told me to wrap up early because trouble was brewing between you two."

"She's the one causing all the trouble," Val announces. Darin raises a brow at me. I flick up my hand as if to say *whatever*.

"I do believe it was your husband who called me the calm in our storm," I remind her of Darin's teasing words when we were still in school.

Val gags even as Darin scoffs, "That was a long time ago, Kels. I've seen the natural disaster you've left in your wake as you've embraced your inner hurricane."

"Me?" The idea is mind-boggling. And not completely unflattering. My smile gets wider as Val falls back in her chair in exasperation.

"Just remember, confidence is great—when you use it in the right way," she scolds me.

"And on that note, how about I go out back and grill up some shrimp for dinner," Darin offers. We both agree. "Let me get changed, and then I'll be out of the way." He leans back down and snags another kiss from his wife before heading through the kitchen toward the back of the house.

We both watch him go. "You're so lucky, Val," I tell her, not for the first time.

"I know it, sister." I lean over, and we clink our glasses of iced coffee against one another. "I just want you to feel this kind of happiness someday." Her hand smooths over her bulging stomach.

"Not all of us are as lucky as you are."

"We make our own luck, Kels."

I tip my head to the side and find her smile waiting for me. It's an argument we've had for years, but I know I've won—or lost, depending on how you look at it. There's not a man out there who wants to deal with the tangled words running through my head day in and day out. He'd have to be crazy to take that on.

Especially when there's always the possibility I could still erupt back into King Kong.

Later, as I'm getting ready for bed, I smooth cocoa butter all over my skin. I remember Ben's whispered, "Your skin's so smooth," as he danced his fingers gently over my shoulder. Brutally shoving last night out of my mind, I lift my nightshirt and rub the lotion all over my stomach, paying careful attention to the scar line that's hidden by my gerbera daisy tattoo.

Some might say I was stupid to get a tattoo when I may get pregnant someday, but since I can't imagine a man ever remaining in my life long enough to consider having a baby, I wasn't worried. "After all, if I ever fell hard enough for that to happen, I'd want a man who understands I'm not perfect." Then I whisper bitterly, "And since perfection seems to be the only thing men want, I'm not worried about falling anytime soon."

Slapping the cap closed, I toss the tube onto my nightstand before climbing into bed. Switching the light off, I let the gentle breeze from the ceiling fan overhead lull me to sleep.

CHAPTER TWELVE

Benedict

"I WANT TO SEE THE DRAFT REVISIONS BY LUNCH." I STAND, CLOSING my laptop as I do. "Is that understood?" Several heads bob up and down rapidly. "You have three hours. I suggest you get to work," I add scathingly.

Chairs can't be slid back fast enough as the inner circle of attorneys and paralegals who directly report to me scurry for the boardroom door. "Christ, I left for two days and the contract with Larruscain has gone to hell." I whirl on Ryan who flew in this morning. He's sitting with his fingers steepled against his lips. "Is this what you were alluding to yesterday? Did you think I'd deliberately fuck up this contract out of all of them?"

He gives me a thoughtful perusal as he rubs his thumb over his lower lip. "What's her name?"

Not caring I could likely write myself up for violating six different corporate policies, I flick him off as I stalk to the windows of the fifty-fourth-floor conference room. I see nothing but Kelsey's gray eyes when the unusually overcast sky reflects back at me. Damn it. Turning, I find a very patient Ryan Lockwood waiting. Knowing he'll wait me out all day if he has to, I bite out, "Kelsey," before I walk back to my seat and fall into it.

"The same woman you went to Savannah apologize to?" His voice is incredulous. I want to punch him, but I'm not an idiot. His brother's investigation firm could likely hide my dead body and make it look like an accident. I recall the way I hired Caleb's expensive investigations firm to find Kelsey Kennedy—Kee Long—I mentally correct myself brutally and can't prevent the bitterness that edges into my voice when I answer, "The one and the same."

Ryan lets out a low whistle that's grating. "Fuck you, Ryan," I tell him bluntly.

"No, thanks. I'm pretty certain you have enough to do fixing the problems you just found in our contract."

Damn, I hate myself even more right now than I thought I did ten minutes ago, if that's even possible. Leaning forward, I brace my forearms on the conference room table. "I swear, those clauses were not in that contract when I left. Look." I swivel my laptop around. I haven't had a chance to connect to the network since I woke up late. The date on my copy is when I last downloaded it.

Two days ago.

Ryan stares at the screen a moment before sighing. "That's what I was afraid of. I want to bring Sam in on this."

It doesn't surprise me in the least when he mentions Sam's name. Sam Akin —one of the partners in Hudson Investigations—is known the world over for being a computer savant. Since his early teens, he has penetrated systems in the name of country, business, and for the sheer enjoyment of it. Now, he specializes in protecting the Hudson Investigations infrastructure and assisting with corporate espionage cases—for the right customer. And Lockwood Industries certainly qualifies.

I scrub my hand over my hair in frustration. "Are you sure? Can't you give me a day to check the other contracts in the hopper?"

He growls low in his throat. "Are you willing to risk it if this isn't a careless mistake?" Before I can respond, he holds up his hand. "You've got until lunch, but you'll let me know if you find anything?"

"Immediately," I assure him.

He nods. "Now, take a breath before you combust. Tell me what happened in Savannah."

I want to do that less than I want to spend time reviewing the multimillion-dollar contracts that are supposed to be locked.

Leaning back in my chair, I wish desperately for a drink. It might wash the bitterness in my voice away as I recount the events of the past weekend. Even Ryan's whiskey-colored eyes widen when I bite out, "I don't know if she left the fucking badge for me to find or if it was an accident."

"Jesus, Ben. Is there a chance she didn't recognize you?"

"Not when I introduced myself." My voice is pure acid.

"I might be able to help you get in contact with her now that you know she's Kee Long. I mean, I actually—" he begins.

I stop him before he continues. "She didn't want me to know who she was, Ryan."

He winces. Before he can say another word, I stand, putting an end to our conversation. "In the meantime, I have about three hundred pages of contracts to review before lunch."

He rises as well. "Let me know what you find out or if you change your mind."

Somehow, I don't think he means about bringing Sam in. And yet, I can't be irritated with the nosy bastard. A wave of affection washes over me as he makes his way out of the executive conference room. Ryan's just too used to the rest of his ever-expanding family poking their noses into each other's business. He can't help himself now that he's more often than not the one poking his nose in first. "It didn't always used to be like that," Jared admitted one night when the three of us were grabbing a quick beer in the Quarter. "Before we got married, our family—such as it is now—was scattered to the winds."

Ryan, who wears his contentment like the finest tailored suit, remarked. "That's because before, I wouldn't have called what we had family." Before I could ask why, he changed the topic to tell me a funny story about his sister-in-law, Cassidy, and how she threatened to straddle her brother and cut off his hair with pinking shears. "Normally it's scissors. She must be really pissed."

Then and now, I find myself envying the older man, the openness he has with his family—and the person he chose to spend his life with. Except for those few moments with Kee—Kelsey!—I've spent the better part of my adulthood disconnected from relationships, even those with my family.

If they knew what I sacrificed, would they ever look at me the same way?

Running a hand through my hair, I know the answer. It's the look I turn from in my father's eyes—a mixture of pride and pain.

Would I see it in Kelsey's?

I spent the whole flight home trying to find the right words so I could contact Kelsey through her publisher. But I stopped myself. I can't violate her privacy by sending the long-overdue message through her publisher. That might make things worse. After all, I owe the apology to Kelsey Kennedy, not Kee Long. And being a damn lawyer, having tried to reach her once, I know the layers of protection she went through to hide any trace of herself.

Fuck, I don't have time for this right now. Snatching up my laptop, I make my way to my office. I feel a perverse pleasure when the heads of my employees sink in their chairs a little as I storm past.

This situation is a monumental disaster that's ready to explode. It would have cost Lockwood Industries millions of dollars to European regulators within the first month. "You all have two hours and forty-five minutes," I bark out just before I slam the door to my office.

Then again, so do I. Flinging myself into a chair, I boot up my desktop, still not connecting my laptop to the network. Pulling up a classified proposal Lockwood Industries is bidding on with the US government, I begin to read. Logically speaking, it's easy to eliminate a large portion of the legal pool as only people with certain levels of clearance have access to this network.

Twenty pages in, I spot the first issue. It's insignificant, but it's enough to keep me reading.

Thirty-two pages in, I scoot closer as I review the list of the key personnel that pops up. "That's not right. Jesus, none of those people are US citizens. They'd laugh us out of the room." I slam a fist against the table in frustration

Thirty-nine pages in, my eyes widen comically when the price sheet scrolls past. "Holy shit," I breathe. Blindly, I reach for my phone.

"Mr. Lockwood's office. How may I help you?" Ryan's secretary, Miss Carter, answers.

"It's Perrault. I need him. Now." I know I'm one of the few people who can call and have Ryan interrupted.

"Certainly, Mr. Perrault. Please stand by." There's a moment of silence before Ryan picks up.

"That was quick."

My anger is far from being under control. So, it's a surprise when my words come out so calmly. "Call Sam. It's a confirmed insider threat."

I hear Ryan's muted curse right before I hang up on him and move on to the next contract. But not before I shut down my laptop.

Sam's going to need it as evidence.

CHAPTER THIRTEEN

Benedict

"I NEED A DRINK. A BIG ONE. MAYBE WITH A LITTLE PARASOL IN IT TO help me forget about this day." A heavy glass is plunked down in front of me. Without even opening my eyes, I lift it to my lips. Smooth bourbon slides down the back of my throat. "Or this. This helps."

"I thought it might." My sister, Lisa, moves around to drop down next to me on the leather sofa in my living room.

I was at work for fifteen hours, and I honestly didn't know how I would make it home before I called her. It's after 11:00 p.m., and I'm finally starting to wind down from the shitshow that's been going on all day.

But it's over.

Sam Akin was able to remote into our office within minutes of the call once we gave him the verbal okay to do so. He tracked down the perpetrator to a paralegal who had access to all the modified files and—under intense questioning—was unable to account for how they paid for their new Audi on the salary that Lockwood Industries provided; while not unsubstantial, it does not account for a new six-figure car.

Once Nancy began to crumble, the entire story came out. "It started as a way to get money for Jimmy," she sobbed. Nancy assumed responsibility for her college-age brother when their parents passed on last year. "I just wanted him to finish school without any worries."

While everyone in the room might have felt sympathy over her plight—look at what I did to protect my sister—we also would have all paid the price. And so did Nancy. First, with her job. Second, by knowing her national security clearance was being revoked and her likelihood of ever working in a position of public trust would never occur again.

And that's if the company decides not to push forward with pressing charges.

"What a fucking mess this week has been." I drain the glass before I set it on the table next to me. Rolling my head to meet my sister's worried eyes head-on, I smile briefly. "Thanks for picking me up."

"Because it's so hard to pick up my big brother who lets me live with him for free while I get my degree at Tulane. A degree he's footing the bill for."

"You say that like it's a bad thing."

"You could let me get a job!"

I frown at my sister. "You know they don't like students to work. Besides, you love volunteering. And didn't you agree that will look better in the long term for your resume?"

Taking a sip of her drink, Lisa makes a snuffing sound into her glass. "What did I ever do to deserve a brother as awesome as you?"

Immediately, my mind flashes back to the moment in Savannah when I realized Kee and Kelsey were the same. "I'm pretty certain there are people out there who would disagree with you."

Lisa finishes before she leans forward and puts her glass down with a sharp clink. "Then, they don't know you—not the way I do."

A faint smile crosses my lips as I tug at the long braid hanging down her back. "Few do."

"I'm serious, Ben."

"So am I. Most people don't know I was ten when I stopped trying to eat my boogers." My voice is bland, even as I'm shaking in an attempt to keep my mirth in. "Let's face it, boys do gross shit. And I did more than my fair share."

Lisa makes a gagging face. "Seriously, I didn't need to be reminded of that. I thought Mom was going to faint when I finally ratted your ass out."

"I appreciate that—now. Back then? Not so much. You forced her to take my on-the-go snack away." We last about point two seconds before we're a heaping mess of hilarity.

And this right here is all the repayment I need—a sister who is happy, healthy, and whole. I was a monumental fuckup at eighteen to help to protect her from the kind of things that would have scarred this loveliness.

Permanently.

I want the chance to thank Kelsey for helping me give her that before I shake her for her duplicity.

CHAPTER FOURTEEN

Benedict

THE SMELL OF CHLORINE PIERCES MY NOSE, SCALDING ITSELF ON MY BRAIN as tears run down my face.

I never want to smell it again.

Never.

I feel my body being shoved forward until my cheek slams against the cold metal locker. There's laughter all around me.

I can't do this.

"Fuck!" I come awake with a roar. My knees lift and my arms brace on them. I feel the coolness of the air conditioner begin to dry the sweat on my skin from having the nightmare again.

Then I flip back the covers and race for the bathroom connected to my en suite. Dropping to my knees, I begin hurling the contents of my stomach into the toilet. With gallows humor, I think, *I guess I should be grateful I didn't have one the night I spent with Kelsey.*

And I never thought I'd have a reason to be grateful for anything related to Forsyth.

Or for the fact Kelsey walked out on me.

CHAPTER FIFTEEN

Kelsey

"It doesn't matter what you say to me," I read aloud. "I know what's inside of me. And one day, you're going to regret everything. Give me enough time, and I will figure out a way to make you pay back every tear." *Good,* I muse. Setting up that inner core of my character Pilar is always such a rush. When I started writing the series based loosely on the emotions I felt at Forsyth, I paid homage to the main character's name from my favorite Hemingway novel, *For Whom the Bell Tolls*, naming Pilar after her.

Fondly, I reach over and stroke the worn copy I've had since my freshman year honor's literature class. Ernest Hemingway's story of war, loyalty, beauty, and love are interspersed with some of the most memorable quotes that have stuck in my mind about the perception of human nature. After all,

Hemingway said it best when he said that if we win here, we win everywhere. And throughout my pages, I have Pilar triumph one brutal day at a time over the bullies that make her life a living hell at the private school her parents sent her to because they don't have time for her in their lives.

Tilting my head left and right, I release the pressure gathering at the base of my neck. As joints pop, I know mentally I could go for another couple of hours, but my body is protesting mightily—like it's going to revolt if I don't step away from the keyboard.

I've been writing nonstop the three days since I got back to Val's from the reunion. I'd be more concerned about things like dehydration, except for the fact Val's house has a full water filtration system, so I can go to any tap to fill my water bottle. It's also why the mad scientist who created protein bars retired long ago on the proceeds from his or her stock sales.

I have a deadline coming up, but I'm well ahead of the curve to meet it. I just fall into these moods where all the words want to vomit out of my head and my heart. I keep going until I run out of juice, or the character's worn the same outfit for a while and is probably pretty rank. Much like I'm beginning to feel.

Saving the file in three separate locations, I strip out of my clothes and head for the shower. I'm too gross even to contemplate working out before I clean up. *That's when you know it's bad. When you're too disgusting to go sweat,* I think ruefully. I scrub my scalp hard, my nails feeling amazing as they cause the suds to get thicker and thicker. I duck my head under the water as days of ick slip away.

A knock at my bathroom door startles me. "Yeah?" I call out.

"You're alive!" Val pokes her head inside the steam-filled room.

Ducking mine around the shower curtain, I give her a wink. "And I'm starving. Do we have any yogurt?"

"Bleeeech! You're coming out of a three-day self-imposed liquid diet, and you're asking for yogurt?"

"That's not entirely true," I protest as I yank the curtain closed while Val shuts the door behind her as she steps inside. After years of living together, I know she's just waiting for me to keep talking. "I had protein bars."

The shower curtain is yanked completely back, exposing my naked body. "Hey!" I protest. I'm not ashamed of my nudity the way I used to be, but seriously? I start giggling.

"I'm pregnant, I'm hangry, and I'm craving sugar. Therefore, as my best friend, you need to be hangry with me, not laughing. And not looking so . . . so . . ."

"Wet?" I suggest. Quickly I turn off the shower that's spraying us both with water. I twist my hair in a towel before reaching for one to wrap around my body. Just as I step out, I hear Val bark out a wicked laugh.

"Certainly not by me. Besides, I thought you had plenty of that kind of stuff in Savannah," she taunts.

I roll my eyes at her before stepping up to the mirror. Val has lowered herself to the toilet to watch while I dry off and quickly blow the dampness out my hair, leaving the rest to air-dry in loose curls around my shoulders. Setting down the dryer, I tease, "Oh, you're still here?"

"I'm needy today. Let's do something. I want to go somewhere." With school out for the summer, if Val's not volunteering, then she's at home.

I reach over and pat her stomach. "Are you okay to walk around with Lucy?"

"Right as rain." She lays her hand on the side of mine. We both jump when her daughter kicks us.

"She's strong," I murmur, smoothing a hand over her stomach, feeling the little ripples under my hand.

"I know. Just a few more months and we can hold her." Val lays her hand on top of my own. Our eyes meet over her blossoming baby belly and we both mist up a little.

"Okay!" I declare. "Enough mush. Let's get out of the house and then let's do something we haven't done in forever."

"What? Clothes shop?" Val says excitedly. Val has found a new addiction—baby clothes. Despite the fact her mother has warned her that Lucy will be living in onesies and bibs, Val doesn't care.

I glare at her. "Bite your damn tongue. I need to buy a house. If I walk into a clothing store—even one for Lucy—I'll end up spending my down payment for sure. No, I was thinking about beignets from Café Du Monde."

"Ooh, honey, that's an even better idea."

My stomach rumbles in complete agreement even as my mind protests consuming the sugary delight.

Maybe I'll have half.

After all, I can't let myself turn into the girl I was ever again. I just can't.

Val and I wander through Jackson Square. Along the way, we laughingly sit for a caricature of the two of us to hang in her daughter's nursery. I'm gasping for breath when the artist cleverly transforms our likeness into Minnie Mouse and Daisy Duck, respectively. Pursing my lips, I try to squeak in a high pitch, "Well, I never!"

Val almost knocks over the artist's easel as she pays him. Tears are falling down her cheeks. "Just don't start singing the song that never ends," she warns me.

Narrowing my eyes at her, I curse. "Great, now that's stuck in my head."

Linking her arm through mine, she says, "Then let's distract it with some sugar."

Thanking the artist, we continue past talented street performers juggling more items than I can hold, let alone toss. Musicians render the air with the blues, everything from the sweet and sad to the haunting and seductive. Finally, we make our way around the square and cross the street to the ever busy Café Du Monde.

"Do you want me to wait in line while you get a table?" I suggest, but Val shakes her head.

"Nope. I figure you can use the time to tell me why you chained yourself in your room for three days." The woman waiting in line in front of us turns around, startled. Val winks. "It's not what you think."

I decide to mess with her. "Maybe it is. You keep telling people you don't like chaining me up, but we both know that's a lie."

"You know there are bars for that kind of stuff here in the Quarter if you were really into that kind of kink," Val snickers.

The pretty brunette smirks. "I can tell y'all get into the right kind of games for women to play."

I tilt my head, intrigued by her assumption. "Really? What kind of games are those?"

"Your shirts. Totally gives your secrets away. I love them." Her smirk turns to a beautiful smile that lightens her deep blue eyes that, unfortunately, remind me of a pair I stared into in great depth just a couple of days ago. Shaking my head in bemusement, I wonder if all blue eyes from now on will remind me of Benedict's. Trembling a bit, I smile when Val proudly displays her "I'd like to think wine misses me too." maternity shirt.

"All women should." I'm wearing a T-shirt that declares I'm the property of Amaryllis Designs that Emily gave me when I had my last fitting for my reunion dress. Touched to be a recipient of one, I immediately made a huge donation to the Collyer Police and Fireman 5K, which I would be missing this year as my next trip back to Connecticut isn't scheduled until Jillian's wedding.

"Amaryllis Designs?" The brunette's brows raise to her hairline. "Do you work for them?"

"Not exactly," I hedge, trying not to say more.

"Well, if you like their designs, you should drop by this amazing store on Royal. There's an Emily Freeman original in the window," the woman mentions casually.

"See, you can't get away from your addiction anywhere," Val teases.

I shake my head vehemently. "No. Just no. I told her"—I stick my thumb out at my laughing best friend—"I need to buy a home. I can't have Emily's work dictating my house. It was bad enough when I lived in the same town as her. I'm not limiting my choice of a forever home because I go shopping for her dresses in another," I declare triumphantly. I whirl on Val to make my intentions clear. "Nor are we going lingerie shopping."

She pouts. "You're no fun."

A curious look flashes across the woman's face. "Why no lingerie shopping?"

"You'd have to know me to get it. I'm obsessed with clothes." And have been since I dropped fourteen sizes with my weight loss.

"This store causes obsessions," the woman assures me. Even as the line surges forward, I remain in place, gaping at the petite brunette with dawning horror.

"Nooo," I whine pathetically. I glare at Val accusingly, who's trying to subdue her laughter. "You! You lured me to move here, knowing I'd fall prey to the demons inside me. I'm trying to behave, damn you."

We've made our way to the counter. The woman quickly places her order and steps aside, shoulders shaking. Val and I order two large iced coffees and an order of beignets. "You two are a stitch. But if I don't get this order to the guy who asked for it, he'll be ready to kill his coworkers with his bare hands—not that he's not all ready to. If you'll excuse me." She turns to accept a to-go order handed to her. Before she leaves, a devilish smile crosses her lips. "But seriously, you really should go visit Easy On Me." With a laugh at the groan that erupts from my chest, she waves, then begins edging toward the fringes of the crowd.

After Val and I get our food and find a table, I take a long drink of my chicory coffee, lightened only with a splash of milk. There's a smile flirting around my mouth. Now, I have it all—Val, my future niece to love, a city filled with a hugely creative vibe, and a place to shop that carries Amaryllis Designs. Who could ask for anything more?

"Listen, it's not like you can't afford to indulge yourself," Val protests with a smile.

Putting my cup down on the white-topped table, I lean in to take a nibble of the flaky square donut heaped in powdered sugar. "So delicious," I moan. *Which is why I'll only allow myself half*, I think determinedly.

I'll never go back to being that beast of a girl, but I can go forward to being more.

"I've been thinking," I say slowly. "Once I'm a little more settled, maybe it's time to stop being so . . . closed off like I was when I lived in Connecticut. I mean, I lived there for years, and I never felt like I got to know anyone outside my circle."

"True, but maybe that's because you have family there? Maybe you didn't have to make an effort?"

Taking another sip of the delicious coffee, I think about Ava, Matt, and the coffee shop that was my haven in Collyer. My lips curve at the edges when I recall the way Jillian and I used to while away the mornings—her with her knitting and me with my words. And after Jillian was injured? I shudder in memory. How many days did I tuck myself away, burying myself in my words, worrying until that day Jillian burst through the door again? My admiration for my friend's capability to face her fears head-on causes doubt to seep into my voice. "Maybe. But since Jilly recuperated, I've felt like there's something I'm missing—some other way I could help."

"From the way she tells it, you were there by her side the whole time—pushing her out into the world when she needed it, Kels. And look what it brought her," Val reminds me.

"That's just it. Yes, I lived in Collyer, but I was on the fringes of it unless I was Kee Long." Val's eyes spark with understanding. "I write books about being bullied, but what do I *do* about it? I feel like there's something I can do—help more."

"Don't belittle what you've done, Kelsey. Even if all you've been able to give is money, that's more than most."

"That's just it. I want to do more, need to. Maybe I can do something at Le Cadeau?" I ask, naming the center where Val volunteers. With a whisper, I add, "Maybe someone out there is waiting for someone like me, but I'm too closed off for them to reach out to?"

Val jerks back in surprise, spilling heaps of sugar down the front of her purple tee. "Are you serious?"

"You don't think it's a good idea?"

"No! I think it's wonderful! I have some ideas we can talk about when you're ready."

"Probably not until after this next book is sent off," I think aloud.

"That makes sense. And you have to balance this with that part of your life."

"True. But I'm blessed, Val. With my health, with you, Darin, Lucy." I reach across the table and squeeze her hand. "I've been fortunate enough to have my words read by people who relate to my stories. And yet, I feel like there's a barrier between me and the world."

"Well," she hedges, but I pick up on it immediately.

"Well, what?"

"I don't know if that's you, the author, holding yourself back, sweets, or you, the woman." Before I can speak, she holds up her hand. "They're not the same. You were devastated by what happened to you. How much have you allowed yourself to heal?"

"I thought more and more with each book. But seeing those people again this weekend . . ." My voice trails off as my fist clenches on the table. "I could have walked in there and held my head up. Instead, I walked away."

"Well, as your best friend, I can tell you all the reasons why or let you figure them out."

Leaning back, I gesture for her to continue.

Val leans back as well. "Part of you decided they weren't worth it. You looked the worst of them in the face and decided letting go was better than holding on to that anger. And you're not the type to jump into the fray to confront someone."

I swirl my cup. "Is that why you encouraged me to go? To get past all of that."

"I'd have been happy if you slapped each one of those assholes across the face for everything they did to make your life a living hell, but no. I just wanted you to see they don't have the power to hurt you. Did you?" she retorts.

I laugh, releasing even more tension. "Maybe? I guess time will tell. But I will say it's yet another reason I love you."

"Because I'm the angel on your shoulder telling you to fight?"

"No, because you're the angel at my back. Always. But, back to what I was saying, it's not solely because of the reunion I'm having these thoughts. Even in Collyer, I kept thinking I should do more. I mean, I participated in local charity events like the ones Amaryllis Events sponsored or ones Ava and Matt ran through the Coffee Shop. Still, I truly believe it's time I did something more substantial about the issues I'm passionate about besides dressing up or writing a check. Besides"—I shake my head ruefully—"it might keep me away from the stores."

"Darlin', ain't nothin' gonna keep you out of that shop. Give it up now," Val drawls. We both laugh because it's true.

"I don't want to turn into one of them." I straighten in my chair. Val does as well—well, as much as her pregnant body will allow. "I want to keep the magic alive inside my books. Show that every day can be a miracle, where castles can be built, and if you close your eyes, Prince Charming will pop up out of thin air."

A shadow passes over our table. "I'm glad to hear you think that, Kelsey," a dark, somber voice says from beside me. Twisting, I gasp when I find myself staring into Benedict Perrault's bright blue eyes.

"What are you doing here?" I whisper. I can hear Val's sharp inhale of breath. After all, it's practically unheard of for a man to call me by my given name. It just never happens.

The real question is, how did he figure it out?

"I've lived here for quite a while. The real question is, what are you doing here?"

"I think I'm going to be sick," I whisper.

A bleak expression crosses his face before it goes carefully neutral. "Then, you now understand how I felt when I woke up in Savannah, realizing who you were."

And just that quickly, I want to throw up the tiny piece of delicious beignet I'd just swallowed. After all, why am I surprised? It's why I never gave him my real name to begin with.

I'll never be able to shed the image I've carried around with me. I'll always be overshadowed by the past, unable to shed the weight of it. I'll never be free from the heartache I ran from fifteen years ago. I'm about to speak when out of nowhere, the brunette from the line slides up next to Ben. She lays her hand comfortably on his arm. "Hey, I've been looking everywhere for you. You're going to be late. Here's your usual." She hands him a white paper bag and a paper cup. "Have a good day. I'll see you at home later."

Oh my god. He's living with someone, maybe even married. What did I do? Shoving away from the table, I grab my purse. "I've . . ." Wildly, I look around.

Like always, Val reads me. "Go. I'll meet you by the car."

I take off without another word, knowing Val will quickly extract herself, and we'll soon be on our way. Then, I can be back behind my computer where nothing can penetrate the barrier I put up between my heart and the world.

CHAPTER SIXTEEN

Benedict

Judging by the look on Kelsey's face, she misconstrued my words and is berating herself about what happened in Savannah. Fuck. Taking the coffee and treats from my sister, I lean down and brush my lips against her cheek. "Thanks, darlin'. Now, don't let Professor Owens scare you in class again."

Lisa shudders. "I don't know what made me decide to do this."

Brushing my hand over hair the same shade as my own, I grin. "I do."

"Yeah, yeah. You're a pain in the ass, but you're my pain in the ass." Lisa wraps an arm around my waist and gives me a brief hug before disappearing into the crowds.

I open my mouth to ask Kelsey's friend where I can find her, but I'm taken aback by her full-on attack.

"You're even more of a piece of shit than she described you over the years. When she got home the other day, I scolded Kelsey for not allowing you to explain what happened all those years ago before she snuck out, for not facing her insecurities. And now I know nothing even comes close to what you did." As she stands, I see Kelsey's friend is ripe with pregnancy. "Now, if you'll excuse me, Mr. Perrault, I have a ride to catch."

Stepping in her way, I block her. "By her not telling me who she was, she never gave me a chance to explain what happened all those years ago. I went to that damn reunion solely to apologize," I snap.

"And instead, you compounded your atrocity by cheating on your wife?" She makes a tsking sound. "So classy."

"Wife? What the hell are you talking about?"

She grabs my arm and jiggles the bag of beignets I'm holding. "Spousal equivalent? Girlfriend? Live-in lover? Whatever you call the woman who brought you these. Kelsey would never cheat," she declares.

"But she'll lie by the sin of omission?" I throw back hotly. "And not for nothing, I call the woman who gave me this sister."

"How dare you, you son of a . . . wait. Did you say sister?" Her head jerks in the direction Kelsey went in.

"Yes." The sudden paling beneath her caramel-colored skin hits me like a ton of bricks. I let out a harsh sigh at what Kelsey must have thought. She didn't recognize Lisa. Crap. "Christ, can one thing go right with Kelsey since that damn day?" And I don't mean the reunion, I mean our graduation day.

A brief flash of empathy crosses her face. "That sums it up beautifully." Turning, she totters off in the same direction Kelsey went in, leaving me holding a bag of almost nauseating-smelling sweets and a full cup of coffee.

The cup's overflowing with sweet richness, but I couldn't swallow it right now if I tried.

Having lost my appetite, I walk over to the nearest trash can and throw away the breakfast my sister bought me while I took a call from the office before heading to Lockwood Industries. I keep searching for a glimpse of Kelsey or her friend as I cross Jackson Square, but of course, I can't be that damn lucky.

Later that night, I'm at my local fitness center, burning off my frustration by swimming lap after lap. I replay my last three encounters with Kelsey in my head. *So much misunderstanding with no resolution,* I think angrily. My arms rotate over and over, hands cupping and pulling back until I reach the wall, execute a turn, and push off again.

The burst of adrenaline I feel when my body sluices through the water leaves my mind blank, and at that moment, I'm weightless and free. Kicking to the surface, I wonder what it must have been like for Kelsey to have lost all that weight, to feel less burdened.

I'm so proud of her for her accomplishments, but is that what I said today? No. Of course not. I immediately went on the attack, giving her more reason to reinforce her fortress walls. While I glide through the water, I recall the creative writing assignment I failed that almost got me thrown off the swim team. Our teacher asked her to work with me. At first, I was resentful a teacher had asked another student to assist me until she handed me a one-page paper. All Mrs. Wiley said was, "Read this," before she walked away. And so I did.

I can't remember every word of Kelsey's essay, but I've never been able to forget a few lines. It made me look at her differently. Her words gave me the window to see her—see beneath her skin, inside her heart. I knew the calm facade she used to ignore the bastards was simply a coping mechanism. She refused to show them she was broken. She would never let them see how she used everything inside her to deal with the trash thrown at her. It's why her words grabbed me by the throat, the guts, and the heart. And they still do. So much so, I had them etched on glass where they rest in my study at home.

"The worst thing that's happening to you is the best thing that will ever happen to someone else. All you can do is move past it. After all, if life were meant to be easy, I'd have already won the game."

My hand slaps the wall a final time. I'm breathing hard when my head breaks the surface. I go to rip off my goggles when I get a glimpse of long legs standing at the edge of the pool next to me. Sinking further beneath the surface, I follow the line of them up, over the hip where the Speedo emblem rests, past the intricate tattoo I touched, tasted, only a few days before. Her body is fit and conditioned but not so skinny that I'd wonder if I was going to break her in bed.

Then again, I already know the answer—I won't.

She swings her arms around in windmills to warm them up. Her dark hair, still loose, doesn't hide the troubled expression on her face. Unlike the dimly lit hotel room, I can make out her tattoo more clearly. My eyes widen when she turns her back to slip on her own cap and goggles. From this angle, it's easy to notice that her skin is discolored outside of the tattoo's delicate lines on one side.

A scar.

The urge to pull Kelsey into the water and to demand what happened is overpowering. But I have no right, particularly after my spectacular display of idiocy at Café Du Monde. She'd likely wrap the lane line around my head and send me into the deep end to sink.

What happened to her? Quickly I think through everything I devoured on the internet about Kee Long after I got back to New Orleans. Nothing mentioned an accident of any kind to cause that kind of scarring.

I stay submerged while she scoots to the edge before letting her legs effortlessly slide out from beneath her into the warm water. Without a look around, she sinks into the deep blue and pushes off.

Her stroke isn't that of a competitive swimmer. I stand to my full height to watch her as she makes her way to the deeper waters. But her kick is surprisingly strong.

Just like the woman herself.

As she touches the far wall, I duck under the water, yanking my cap off as I do so. Hauling myself out, I admire the gracefulness of her glide—not too fast, not too slow.

Much like the way her hands touched my body a few nights ago.

Gritting my teeth against the tingles forming in my lower spine—something I came to the pool to work out—I make my way to the men's locker room and debate if I should approach her or if I should give her the solitude I know the deep blue waters can give to a soul that's in need of some quiet.

CHAPTER SEVENTEEN

Kelsey

Fat. Stroke. *Cow*. Stroke. *Hippo*. Stroke. Each time I swim, my brain does a dump of the names I remember being called, purging them from my soul. Some days, I look in the mirror and still see the reflection of the woman who was so grotesquely overweight. I rarely see the woman whose body can go to any boutique and find an outfit to buy. I shy away from people who compliment me on my looks because I doubt they're telling me the truth. After all, I know what lies underneath.

Me. And the attention I'm worthy of isn't the kind I want to attract.

Wasn't I told by enough people I should do the world a favor and kill myself? And what's worse is I contemplated it. I tried to carve "King Kong" onto my arm. The top of the *I* remains to this day as a scar on my forearm from where I pressed the blade just a little deeper than the other letters as I carved the offensive words in before the sight of all that blood made me sick. As a result, in the summer between my sophomore and junior years of high school, I wore long-sleeved shirts to cover up the mess I made of my heart and my mind.

Of course, I was ridiculed for that too. *What? Are you too fat to want to show your skin in the middle of the heat?* Who does that to another human being and goes unpunished?

That's right, my classmates at Forsyth.

My kick gets more forceful as I remember. I created a barrier around myself when I walked through the not-so-hallowed halls of Forsyth. That is until I met Benedict in the second quarter of my junior year.

My creative writing instructor asked me to assist the popular junior in writing. She explained this would be a safe place for me. With my permission, she provided him with one of my writing samples and me with one of his. Immediately, I could see what the concern was. Benedict was holding back. Technically, his writing was excellent, but he was writing according to a textbook.

Not according to his soul.

When he came in for his first session, I was shocked when the handsome boy immediately said, "Your writing is beautiful. It captivated me from the first word."

I stammered, "Thank . . . thank you." Even now, even as my arms cut through the water, I feel my cheeks redden in memory.

As he dropped onto a desk next to me, he asked me bluntly, "So, what am I doing wrong?"

I blurted out, "You're holding back." Pulling out his essay on swimming, I asked him one question. "Don't tell me the mechanics. What is it you feel when you're in the water?"

His jaw tightening, he refused to meet my eyes. "Escape. That's what I feel."

My stomach bumping hard into the tiny desk, I whispered, "Then write about that." I gathered my backpack. "I'll see you in a few days."

His head shot up. "That's it? That's what your advice is?"

I shrugged. "Creative writing—for me, at least—isn't about perfection. It's about letting loose the emotion boiling over inside of yourself that you can no longer contain. It's about letting out the pain that's suffocating you. It's about finding something to clutch onto before you drown." I let out a bitter laugh as I swing my bag over my shoulder. "Unless the thing you are trying to grasp onto is the very thing trying to drown you."

Benedict's lips parted as if he wanted to comment, but nothing came out. I went on in a rush, "Creative writing is the hardest and most rewarding thing I've ever done, but it's not for everyone. You'll always struggle with it if you don't let yourself feel. You have excellent writing skills. The only thing I can offer is advice on what you're writing about." Without another word, I shuffled my way toward the door.

In my locker a few days later, there was a folded piece of paper. *Great,* I thought, *another note.* There were often notes, cruel, insulting pieces of trash I couldn't bring myself to throw away. But this one was special.

It was a hastily scribbled-out copy of Benedict's revised essay. And it was beautiful.

Of all the things I threw out when I purged myself of my old life, I kept that one-page handwritten note on finding escape in the cool blue water, how the echo of nothing in his ears was more soothing than the waves of the ocean—that there was nothing to interfere with blanking out the pain. How weightless his heart, his mind, his soul could feel when there was something else to support it. Benedict never knew it, but his description of water is what initially drove me to look for colleges near bodies of water. They just happened to be as far away from Georgia as I could get.

I mentally give myself a shake when I turn my head to the side for a breath. Facing back into the void of the water, I'm swept into the memory of our tutoring sessions. After I'd read his revised essay, I met a very nervous Benedict later that same day in Mrs. Wiley's classroom. He was staring out the window when I first walked in and closed the door behind me. Before I could even greet him, he said, "I'm not entirely certain I'm comfortable with writing like that."

"Not many people are. It's a lot easier to read someone else's words and relate to them than to write your own," I replied quietly.

He nodded, his back still to me. "Why do you do it?"

My heart stopped in my chest. There was no way he could know about the volumes of journals I poured my heart into at home, purging the toxic emotions out of my soul. My breathing harsh in the room, I answered, "Because if I didn't, I would fall to my knees under the burden that's shoved down on me."

Finally, he turned to face me. We locked eyes. We were half a room away from each other. "It's wrong what they do to you. I've tried to stop it."

"I know." I'd witnessed Benedict Perrault tell his friends to "knock it off" whenever possible.

"Don't let them break you," he'd said fiercely. And I fanned that flame of strength until it was too late. When one final moment snuffed out all the light—made it so I'd never want to take a shot at trusting another person with that deep core of myself ever again.

It was the moment he'd become one of them and broke me.

I ran off that stage into the waiting arms of my grandparents. Forsaking the lovely dinner out in downtown Savannah, Pop-pop made sure my old car was as fit as it could be for the cross-country trek I blubbered I was making that night. He topped it off with gas while Nana alternately held my heaving body to her breast, then helped me pack all my belongings. I was going to take everything with me to sort through once I hit the opposite coast. While I wanted nothing of Georgia to touch my life in California, I would have no choice but to take it with me and go through it there since I didn't plan on staying any longer than necessary in the humid hell I lived in.

Despite what happened on my graduation day and the campfire grill purge of my past Val and I performed with all the old notes I'd accumulated, I kept that first essay from Ben. There was something so honest in it, more so than anything else he'd ever said or done.

And I found out he was right.

After surgery, the water became my exercise refuge. Surrounded by its weightlessness, I could do more, dream more, be more. I tip my head to the side to get another burst of air, continuing to rotate my arms over again. Finally, sixty laps later, I glide into the wall. "Not bad," I murmur to myself.

Then I hear a voice above me. "No, not bad at all. If you cool down, you'll have swum over a mile. Jesus, Kelsey, I'm impressed."

Tipping my goggle-covered eyes upward, I follow bare feet up to a pair of nylon pants, past a T-shirt, and into the remarkably handsome face of Benedict Perrault.

Dunking under the water, I yank my goggles off over my head. Popping my head back out, I toss the tangled mess on the deck at his feet. "What are you doing here?" I'd only just started coming to this gym at Darin's recommendation. It's centrally located in the areas where I'm looking to buy a home and is a fantastic facility. Darin has been a member for years. Did he know that Ben was a member here too? No, there's no way—I quickly disabuse myself of that notion. Sinking, I let the water's motion pull me slightly back so I can meet his gaze head-on.

"Waiting for you. And I'll keep waiting if you want to cool down."

"That might take another fifteen years." I reach for my goggles and untangle them before slipping them back into position. I start to push off into a slow breaststroke for the last 200 meters when I hear him say, "But at least I'd be around you trying."

Shit. Ducking my head beneath the water, I surround myself with the cool blue to calm my mind.

And my racing heart.

CHAPTER EIGHTEEN

Kelsey

After I push out of the water, I don't look in Benedict's direction even though I catch sight of him out of the corner of my eye, body slung on the low bleachers. Once inside the women's locker room, I shower off the chlorine and slip into a loose sundress. I'm still not used to the humidity of living in the South again. Between my time in Southern California for college and then living in Connecticut, I haven't endured the persistent sweltering heat in longer than I can remember.

Even in an air-conditioned room, it feels tangible on my skin as I swing my purse and workout bag over my shoulder. Opening the door to the locker room, I pull out my keys so I can make a quick break for my car. Not looking where I'm going, I bump into someone. "Excuse me," I offer politely before a warm hand slides up to clench my waist.

"No apologies necessary. I was deliberately trying to get in your way," Benedict tells me.

I go to open my mouth to lambaste him when his phone rings unexpectedly. "Do you mind holding on just a moment? It's my sister, Lisa."

A sister? Vaguely, I remember Benedict mentioning a younger sister years ago, but I can't recall much about her since she was a few years behind us in school and I was very much focused on the world of hurt I was experiencing then.

"Hey, Lisa, what's up?" My head snaps when his voice changes to aggravated. "No, I haven't heard from Mom and Dad today. Did they try my cell? Well, why the hell not?" Agitatedly, he runs his fingers across the scruff of his five o'clock shadow. "Don't tell me Dad tried to change the tire on his own." A short pause. Benedict spins away, pacing. "Oh, for fuck's sake, that's what they have triple A for!" He comes up short, spine straight. "Wait, let me guess, Captain Impatience didn't want to wait?"

A giggle escapes me before I can stop it. He quirks a brow. I slap a hand across my mouth and shake my head, trying to indicate that I'm not laughing at his phone call when it's all I can do to not double over as it's incredibly reminiscent of the calls I've heard Val have with her siblings.

Benedict narrows his brilliant blue eyes on me before he continues, "No, I'm still at the gym. I ran into Kelsey here. I was going to try to convince her to have a drink with me to explain what happened when we ran into her at Café Du Monde this morning, but apparently, my family is a bunch of crazy lunatics who I have to run interference for from three states away." Rubbing the back of his neck, he grumbles, "No, I'll be home in a bit. Tell Mom to keep her cell nearby. Love you too." Pressing a button on the screen, he demands, "Do you need a more creative explanation than that, or were the highlights enough?"

I burst out laughing. I can't help it. The adoring frustration on Benedict's face is priceless. "So, that really was your sister earlier? Not your wife?" I confirm, despite Val's declarations in the car on the way back to her house. I want Benedict's eyes on me when he answers.

The emphatic shake of his head underscores his words. "No. I'm not that kind of man. Though I can forgive you for thinking I might be with the past laying between us the way it is. Still." A slash of pain crosses his face.

Dark silence settles between us as we face one another in the fading sunlight of the hallway between the locker rooms leading to the pool. Stepping back into my personal space, he reaches up and tucks a piece of hair that's escaped my clip behind my ear, and he asks me somberly, "Will you give me a chance to explain what happened all those years ago?"

I nod, albeit reluctantly.

The tips of his fingers remain on the edge of my jaw. "And the reunion?"

I'm not entirely sure I want to open my heart or mind up to the recent past, but Benedict has to be confused by what happened between us in Savannah. I owe him an explanation as well—including why I didn't fess up to who I was before sharing a night so intimate I can still feel the effects between my thighs. I nod again.

The small smile that curves his lips causes an ache inside my chest. I just refuse to acknowledge it. We stand there motionless until he finally breaks the spell. "There's nothing more I'd like to do than to go with you somewhere right now and continue this conversation, but I have to go. Where's your phone? Let me give you my number."

Pulling out my phone, I hand it to him. Benedict quickly programs his number before dialing his own. I smile when his ringtone, a distinctive Dave Matthews song, hits the air. I can't prevent the curve of my lips as he bites down on his lower lip, much as I did the other night, as he concentrates on trying to save the information. Finished, I'm hit with the blast of his brilliant eyes before he promises, "You're now saved as a favorite."

"I made a favorite list?" I purse my lips. "I've never actually been told that before. I feel like this is a new milestone in my life—*New York Times*, *Wall Street Journal*, *USA Today*, and now Benedict Perrault's Favorites. Remind me to call my publicist to notify him of the news."

He barks out a laugh at my mouthful of wiseass. As he leans over to get his gym bag, I get a glimpse of the rippling muscles I ran my hands over repeatedly in the darkened room. My fingers itch with the urge to reach for him again. Benedict straightens to his full height. Our gazes clash. In his eyes, I find heated memories rimmed with leftover pain. And I regret more than ever I didn't put us on even footing that night. "I hope everything works out with your family," I offer.

His lips curve. "I'll call you soon."

"I look forward to it," I tell him honestly.

He hesitates, "Kelsey?"

"Yes?"

He releases a heavy sigh before admitting, "I never meant to hurt you, then or today." With that, Benedict turns and strides down the hall toward the exit.

I'm frozen in place by his words. Does he mean then as in back at Forsyth? How is that possible with what he yelled at graduation? Until then, I'd considered him a friend, even if my feelings went well beyond that. Especially after that one moment where I felt something more. Something that set my heart to dreaming girlish dreams. And the residual effects of those dreams manifested themselves into something much more the other night in the hotel room.

With startling clarity, I realize everyone's been correct. The sooner Benedict and I erase the past between us, the better off we'll both be. "Hey, Ben?" I call out.

He jerks to a stop, hearing his nickname from me for the first time since our senior year. Not even once in our night together did I call him that. I lift both of my hands and I shrug. "I'm glad I ran into you. I hope everything is okay with your dad." Before he can respond, I turn and head in the opposite direction to where my car is parked.

And back to Val's to tell her what just happened.

Four days have passed since I saw Benedict at the pool.

Like a lovesick girl, I keep checking my phone, hoping everything is okay with his family. I hope nothing serious has happened that required him to make a trip back to Georgia. Frustrated, unable to concentrate on writing, I storm out of the bedroom with my phone in my hand. "What the hell was the name of that boutique Lisa mentioned at Café Du Monde?"

"Uh-oh." Val exchanges a worried look with Darin.

"Tell me now, or you know I'll just wander the Quarter and find it anyway," I warn.

"Do I need to call a U-Haul?" Darin jokes.

Val elbows him in the stomach. "This is serious, Dare. Do I need to call Morgan and tell her I won't be in to go with you?" Morgan is the center coordinator at Le Cadeau.

All friends everywhere should be as amazing as Val, I think to myself. Then again, she'd lie and I swear to it just to get us out of trouble of any kind, so her offer isn't as much a surprise as a warm balm that soothes my aching—no, infuriated, damn it—heart. "Nope. I need time with me, clothes, and my credit card."

"Easy On Me. On Royal." When I raise my brow at her in mild surprise, she shrugs. "I knew you'd cave eventually. Now you don't need to look up the address."

Walking over, I wrap my arms around her and hug her. "Thanks for never letting me down," I whisper.

"Never will. Now, go buy something sexy I can only dream of wearing while I'm cooking your niece."

With a wink over her shoulder at Darin, whose expression says that everything Val does is sexy, I murmur, "Will do," before I let her go to grab my purse.

If there's ever a time a girl needs a new outfit for absolutely no reason, it's because she feels like she's either been blown off or helplessly overwhelmed by a new relationship. As much as I wish it was the second, I'm pretty damn sure it's the first.

To hell with Benedict Perrault. To hell with men. To hell with wanting to be a responsible adult, mortgages, deadlines, and shit.

All this girl needs is to forget about a man named Benedict Perrault by buying a new dress made by her favorite designer.

Too bad I won't have a place to wear it. Knowing the kind of designs Emily has in her new line, anything from it will be a showstopper, regardless of the occasion. I can only imagine wearing one for a date.

That would be if Benedict planned on calling.

Which apparently he wasn't.

CHAPTER NINETEEN

THREE DAYS EARLIER

Benedict

"WHAT THE HELL DO YOU MEAN THEY'RE TRYING TO BACK OUT OF THE deal?" I demand. This contract with Larruscain has taken months to negotiate. The revenue from the Barcelona-based imports company will be one of the highest revenue generators for Lockwood Industries for the next twenty years. And I shepherded that baby along since I started at Lockwood years ago, only to be blocked as we get down to the final contract signing. Which is supposed to happen later this month.

"I don't know, Ben. Something about wanting to revisit the marketing permissions one last time before we put pen to ink," Carol, one of the executive vice presidents in marketing, tells me agitatedly.

"Find out what they're looking for. You have"—I lift my wrist—"three days. Otherwise, I'll ask Ryan if he wants to kill the deal." *And likely my job along with it*, I think grimly.

The same thought must pass through Carol's mind because she quickly shuts the top of her laptop and heads for the door.

Jesus, between my father last night trying to change a tire on a two-ton vehicle and now this? I snap up my phone and scroll through my recent calls.

There it is, taunting me from when I used her phone to call mine. Missed Call: Kelsey Kennedy.

I don't want to say everything I have to say to her over text, but I need to let her know I'm going to be out of touch for the immediate future. For far too long, words have been left unspoken between us. I grip the phone harder as I contemplate what to say. Murmuring aloud, "I burned a lot of bridges with what I did on graduation day, but maybe you'll understand I'm not perfect when you understand why I did it."

And the thing is, I know Kelsey's not perfect either. *What was going through her head?* The question still burns through my brain as much as the tantalizing images of the two of us setting fire to the sheets at the hotel in Savannah. I begin to perspire in my dress shirt. *Christ. I never imagined it would be like that between us.*

Relaxing my grip slightly, I wonder if our emotions were always dormant between us—that I didn't recognize them for what they were when we were just kids. My head was so fucked up with wanting nothing more than escaping the hell of Forsyth Academy. I open my mind to a cherished memory—the one of Kelsey and me in Mrs. Wiley's class when that first arc of attraction sparked between us. *If we weren't interrupted, would I have kissed her the way I wanted to in that moment?* I wonder now as the man looking back at the boy who saw beneath the rolls of Kelsey's soft skin, remembering her golden heart pounding against my own chest in a moment that was interrupted too soon.

Yes, my mind answers. Because even as I sit here, the memory of what Kelsey meant to me stirs me as much as the beauty she is today. I recall my thoughts from the plane—I wasn't hoping her outside had changed. I was hoping for her happiness. I'd hope if we'd run into each other at the reunion, she'd have forgiven me. And I knew she'd be what I always knew she was.

Fucking amazing.

Just as I'm about to send her a message, Ryan barges into my office. "Tell me what the hell is going on with Larruscain," he demands.

As I stand, my phone clatters to my desk, forgotten. Snatching up my laptop, I motion him over to the small table in my office. "They're looking for additional permissions in these territories where they feel Lockwood doesn't have a strong presence."

"Bullshit," he says succinctly.

I couldn't agree more.

It takes us up to the last minute to ferret out that someone at Larruscain was trying to nickel-and-dime the contract because they didn't want the appearance that Lockwood Industries was taking them over. "If they want to see a takeover, then we'll put that on the agenda next," Ryan grumbles.

"I just want to see the inside of my eyelids," I moan. I haven't seen my house, my bed, or taken a call not related to this contract in the last seventy-two hours. Even Lisa, who usually can get through in a heartbeat, has been relegated to dealing with my assistant.

He laughs before answering his cell. "Hey, Lynne."

I manage a weary smile hearing Lynne Bradbury's name. I'd offer more, but I'm afraid I might snore if I open my mouth.

"No, I did not forget you and Marco are in town." There's a brief pause. "You're kidding, right? Jenna realizes I run a business of my own? All right. I'll stop at your hotel and then the store on my way home." Hanging up, he drags himself to his feet. Ryan and I look like we've been through a shipwreck. "Come on. I've arranged for a car, but I have to stop by Lynne's hotel on the way home."

"Can sleep here," I mutter into my arms. This is quite possibly the most truthful statement I've ever uttered. I'm already in that Zen-like state right before the drool starts trickling.

"You look like shit. You need to shower and a real bed," he tells me bluntly.

"Asshole." I shove myself to my feet. "I don't smell."

"Yes, you do."

Flipping him the bird, I quickly slip my laptop and a few files into my briefcase. I grab my suit coat and frown down at it. "Didn't I wear this yesterday?"

Ryan lets out a deep laugh. "You've been wearing that suit for three days. This is why I don't trust you behind the wheel of a car."

Three days? "Holy shit? Three days?" Frantically, I shove my hand into my suit pocket and scroll through the multitude of texts I've received. Mom, Dad—letting me know he's all right—Lisa, varying people from the office.

Not a single word from Kelsey.

"I'm fucked," I moan.

Peering over my shoulder, nosy bastard he is, Ryan remarks, "Missing a message?"

I snarl, "Don't you have enough family of various types to avoid meddling in my life?"

"They have Phil to meddle in their shit. They don't need me to add to it." Ryan names his brother-in-law through marriage, a notorious character who I want to meet if only to find out if the stories about him are really true.

Leaving my office, I mutter, "So, you want to get your kicks off mine?"

"It's amusing to watch you squirm on occasion," he admits.

I dig deep to pull up a withering glare when all I want to do is determine if the carpet tiles look as soft as they appear. "I don't want to see Chinese takeout for at least a week. I also need to find a gym."

"If I don't say it often enough, Ben, I appreciate what you do," Ryan tells me somberly as we make our way to the elevator. A few people walk by and acknowledge us with nods, but even I notice they keep their distance. *Do we really smell that bad*? I'm too tired to care.

I slump against the wall near the elevator before asking wearily, "How about giving me some advice then?"

He mirrors my pose. "Like what?"

"How do I get back into the good graces of a woman I was supposed to contact four days ago, with whom I was already on shaky ground?"

A quizzical expression crosses Ryan's face. "I'm sorry. Can you repeat that?"

"Yeah, not offering me any reassurance, buddy." I punch the call button.

"It's not that. It's just I never thought I'd see you twisted up so much about a woman."

"Since I got home from the reunion, I realized I may have been twisted up about her for fifteen years." I'm so exhausted from the last few days I don't realize what I'm saying.

Ryan ushers us both into the waiting elevator. "Well, women are all different. What works for Cass, Em, Ali, Cori, and Holly"—he names his sisters-in-law—"isn't going to work for your Kelsey." At my raised brow, he smoothly continues, "I presume that's who we're talking about, of course."

I don't say another word to him for the entire ride down to the lobby.

The doors to the elevator open, and I shuffle out ahead of his laughter. "Look, come inside while I see Lynne. You know she'll be pissed if she doesn't get to say hello to you while she and Marco are in town. Then you can ask her for her opinion. She sure isn't going to sugarcoat it for you." I can tell he's openly laughing at me right now, but in my exhaustion, the idea holds merit.

Swiveling my head toward his, I nod eagerly. "That's a good idea. Thanks, man."

Both of us descend the steps into the waiting car.

Within moments, we're pulling up to a bed-and-breakfast, and Lynne comes rushing out the door, her arms laden with dress bags. I groan just as her husband emerges from the front door holding an infant in his arms. Marco tucks the tiny girl closer. The hint of his French heritage laces his voice when he teases, "I was going to see if you wanted to hold Danica. Now, I am not so certain."

Having handed off her bundles to our chauffer, Lynne quickly takes the precious burden from her husband. "Gimme. Ryan hasn't seen her since she was born."

"And he filled our home with balloons in celebration, *mon étoile*." Still, Marco hands over the baby to Lynne, who brings her closer.

Something inside me quivers at the sight of that precious face swaddled in a pink blanket. I half-listen to Lynne and Ryan banter back and forth. Instead, I hazard a glance at Marco Houde—a man I know only by association with Lynne. In his dark gaze is something I recognize deep inside myself—ghosts. But as I watch, they float away once he wraps up his wife and daughter tightly against his side.

Witnessing that causes an ache to build in my chest making me recall what I need to talk to Lynne about.

I need to figure out how to fix the mistakes I've made with Kelsey because if she can't forgive the ones made accidentally, will she ever be able to forgive the ones I've caused deliberately?

With that in mind, I enter the conversation. Clearing my throat, I ask Lynne, "Tell me what a man has to do when he needs to grovel on his knees. Badly."

Marco roars with laughter when his wife sniffs the air and declares, "Well, Ben, a shower wouldn't be amiss. Or was that Danica soiling her diaper? I can't be sure."

CHAPTER TWENTY

Benedict

I GROAN WHEN THE LIMO STOPS OUTSIDE THE BOUTIQUE EASY ON ME on Royal. "There's no way there's anything your size in there."

Ryan growls. "This is my payback for meddling—more favors."

"Oh?" I ask on a yawn.

"Emily has some dresses she needed to be delivered to this store. Since Lynne and Marco were flying down on the corporate jet, my darling niece—"

"Which one?" I interrupt. Ryan's family needs its own genealogist at this point.

"Jenna. She decided Lynne could bring the dresses to New Orleans, and one of us could drop them off."

"Ryan, they do realize you're worth billions," I offer cautiously.

That's when I'm blasted with the full force of his smile. "And they don't care. The only thing that matters is we're family. Money means nothing. Love does. Running three dresses up into that store means nothing when it comes to family. You'll quickly learn nothing will stop you once you're on the path of love, my friend." With that, he slides out of the car. I close my eyes and rest my head back against the seat.

It could be five minutes or five hours later when my phone pings with the ringer I've set just to Ryan. His text is flagged as urgent. *Get in here. Stat!*

Shit! I hop out of the back and scroll through my phone to see if I missed any calls. No. I'm wondering why Ryan's message is holding such urgency. I catch a glimpse of myself in the reflection of the window and wince. No wonder Ryan was so adamant about me not driving, and Lynne wondered who smelled more. I look like I've been run over. Wearily, I hope whatever I'm about to walk into doesn't involve motor functions as I'm not sure I can stay standing for it.

Before I cross the threshold, I pause when I recognize the Amaryllis Designs logo in the shop window. Wondering if there's something wrong and Ryan needs a lawyer to help out his family, I announce my presence, "Benedict Perrault. I represent Mr. Lockwood's legal interests. And you are?"

I never expect to hear a familiar voice acidly answer back, "Funny you should show up. Tira and I were discussing the kind of guy who would take a woman's number and not call."

I blink my eyes, rapidly certain in my exhaustion I must be imagining an enraged Kelsey standing there before me. But no, she's magnificent in her fury.

"Kelsey," I breathe out. It's heavenly to say her name, even if there's an odd fuzziness on my tongue that tastes like leftover Chinese food.

CHAPTER TWENTY-ONE

Kelsey

Artfully arranged, the dresses in the window display almost appear to be a summer sky with Emily's enticing creation front and center. The effect entices a customer closer to sit beneath them for a spell. Maybe it's my author's imagination, but it reminds me of the few rare memories I have of my parents when we'd vacation down at the beach, where the ocean would bleed into the sky above, dotted with the white of boats and clouds. Wistfully, I recall those being halcyon days, feeling like I could simply reach up to pluck a dream out of the sky.

I shake myself out of my reverie before my foot touches the lowest step. At least at Easy On Me, dreams can be purchased. Cynically, I climb the stairs thinking it's better this way. I don't have to wish, hope, or cry when they don't come true. I'm in control of what happens here. Just like I should be in every aspect of my life.

The fact I don't feel like I am propels me through the door.

I begrudgingly give a heartfelt thanks to Lisa Perrault for the shop recommendation. *Emily would love to see the way her designs are displayed here.* I catch sight of the azure blue gown in the window and know I'm going to have to try it on. With my arms slightly extended, I imagine wearing the embroidered gown.

"Sugar, you look like you just found out Santa Claus is real," a honeyed voice says from behind me.

"He is," I whisper. "And it's the Tooth Fairy who bestows the secret elixir on fashion designers." Turning to meet an amused pair of chocolate-colored eyes, I smile broadly. "And the Easter Bunny delivers the goodness to store owners."

Dark hair cascades down her shoulders as she laughs. "Welcome to Easy On Me. I'm Tira."

Holding out my hand, I say sincerely, "And I'm screwed."

Hers tightens over mine as she shakes her head. "Darlin', what you're doin' is makin' my day."

"No, really," I assure her earnestly. "I'm supposed to be buying a home. I've been so good about reining in my shopping habit. But there are days when you just need a pick-me-up." Spinning around again, I blink. "But how am I supposed to choose just one dress?"

"Why don't you sit a spell? Let me get you a glass of wine, and then you can decide," Tira suggests. "White or red?"

"White." The alcohol will help reduce my inhibitions just enough so I'll be even more agreeable. Like that's going to be a problem. I rub my fingers over the delicate beadwork on the edge of a pair of shorts I have to try on.

It's becoming more dire by the moment.

"Give me just a second." Tira pats my hand before walking toward the back.

Cocking my head to the side, I ask sincerely, "Are you taking applications for part-time best friends? Because if you are, I'd like to apply." Tira's laughter reaches me from where I'm sitting.

A few moments later, she comes back with a full wineglass. Handing it to me, she gestures to a chair and sits opposite me. "Now, I've learned over the years there's not much some quality shopping won't take your mind off. So tell me what size you are and what you'd like to start with."

"An eight and the Emily Freeman in the window," I tell her dreamily.

Chuckling, Tira heads right for the embroidered gown with the illusion back that looks like Emily custom-made it for me. "Since we're going to be here for a while, why don't you tell me your name."

Out of habit more than anything, my pen name flows from my lips. "Kee. Kee Long."

I didn't expect the reaction it gets me.

Tira's eyes flare wildly. "Seriously? The writer of those wonderful books?" I nod, although Tira's "wonderful" compliment is entirely subjective. "Oh my, if my sister were here, she'd be singing your praises. I swear she and her husband could never get their son to read a darn thing until someone gave him one of your books. Now, we fight to see who can get to the bookstore the fastest."

A warmth steals through me at Tira's kind words. "Thank you so much," I say demurely.

"Drat, would it be terribly rude to ask you to sign one?" When I shake my head no, she beams. Just then, her phone rings. Frowning, she greets the person. "Oh, Ryan! You're stopping by? Your timing is impeccable. I have a . . . friend"—I nod emphatically at her word selection as Tira chuckles warmly—"trying on the last one now. No, don't you dare wait until tomorrow, or I will call Jenna myself. Yes, I know you're doing her a favor, but this is important, and trust me, it will be appreciated. All right, *bebe*. See you soon." Disconnecting, she returns her focus to me before sighing exasperatedly, "Men do not seem to appreciate the urgency of retail therapy."

I lift my glass to salute her astuteness. "Problem with your delivery driver? I generally try to bake cookies for mine or tip them extremely well. Especially when I have massive orders of books being delivered."

Tira chokes on thin air. "I'm not certain he'd be amenable to a financial reward. Now, tell me about this home you want to buy. Does it have room for all your fabulous clothes?"

"Not yet, but now I'm determined it will," I toast her.

"Atta girl. Now let's get started." Tira rubs her hands together gleefully. "Other than the Amaryllis Design, what else? I saw you admiring the shorts."

My anticipation rises as I nod. "The white ones." I point to the pair that captured my attention a few moments ago.

Tira's smile widens. "We're going to have so much fun."

And for the next while, we do.

"I think you found your casual designer, darlin'. You already knew Emily was your formal go-to," Tira drawls as she adds another hanger to my ever-growing pile.

"I mean, think about it, clothes are better than men. You can mix and match, have multiples, and they won't let you down unless you do something stupid to them like drool." I was thrilled to find Tira has a shoe selection worthy of her clothes. I whirl around in a slip dress and matching pair of four-and-a-half-inch royal blue stilettos that cradle my feet. "Tell me, after everything I shared, would you be willing to give this guy a chance?"

"Probably not. And maybe he isn't the right one, but here's the thing, Kee. You're going to want to bend to let someone in someday. Are you at a place in your life where you've forgiven enough to do that?" She busies herself fiddling with the bag.

I absorb her words like a blow. No one, Ava, Jillian, not even Val, has ever seen the part of me that hasn't quite forgiven Benedict for what he's done to me. They all recognized I was still hurting, but no one has ever spoken of my anger. Until now, until this stranger. "How did you guess?"

"That you haven't forgiven this man? Sugar, it's written all over you. And it bleeds out of your soul onto the pages of your books."

How many times had I heard those words and never appreciated them more than at this very moment? Tira continues, "Your first few books were so relatable because you had so much fury in you. Don't we all feel that about something in our past?"

"And now?" My voice trembles. This is worse than any critic; this is the opinion of someone who devoutly reads my words.

Her heartfelt words set my soul at ease. "Pilar is in transition—much as I imagine her creator is. The question is whether she'll let go of her burden and soar without shadows, or will she be pulled down into the mire?"

"I wish this were something I could figure out as easily as I do a difficult chapter." My eyes drift closed, and I click my heels together slowly. Once, twice, a third time.

"Did you just wish yourself home?" Her laughter is like a boomerang around the store.

With a quick smirk to hide my embarrassment over being caught making a wish, I shake my head. "That was a wish for the fall line to come out sooner rather than later."

Our giggles muffle the bell over the store. But nothing hides the dark whiskey voice that says, "You're lucky I love my family, Tira. We've been awake for three days straight trying to fix a deal." Both of us turn, and I see male perfection sauntering toward us, holding a handful of garment bags out to Tira. "From Jenna. She said there are three of them."

Tira claps her hands together before giving the wild-eyed man a brief hug and relieving him of his burden. "That's what I'm expecting. Kee, this is Emily Freeman's brother-in-law, Ryan. Ryan, this is Kee Long. She's an author, sugar."

"We know each other," I begin slowly as the shock of recognition hits both our faces. My eyes narrow suspiciously on the man in the rumpled suit.

"Do you? How?" Tira exclaims. "Ryan. You never mentioned you knew Kee Long."

He shrugs his shoulders. "That's because I know her socially. I never expected to run into her in the middle of a dress shop in New Orleans."

I fling my hands into the air. "Oh, for heaven's sake, Ryan. Stop acting like Caleb. You look just like him right now—like you're putting together some mystery, and you're hungry for more information."

His lips curve up. "I didn't know you knew Caleb that well, Kee."

I admit. "I've met him once or twice around the mansion when I've gone for dress fittings with Emily. Normally he asks if I want anything from Genoa."

Ryan roars with laughter. His eyes take on the same sparkle that Caleb's had when he popped his head inside Emily's studio the last time I was in Collyer and took everyone's lunch order at Cassidy's bequest. "That absolutely sounds like my brother. When were you last in town?"

"If you two don't mind entertaining yourselves for a minute, I'll be right back," Tira promises. She rushes off toward the back room with the three dresses.

Knowing I'm talking to one of the world's youngest billionaires, it doesn't seem harmful to admit, "I actually just moved from there. My cousin and her husband own the coffee shop in town."

He actually staggers back. "Matt and Ava are your cousins?"

"Well, just Ava. Our mothers are—were—sisters. They're both deceased." I'm not admitting to anything that can't be found in my press kit.

"Well, I'll be damned. Now I truly am surprised we haven't spoken more than a few words before now, Kee. I mean, catching sight of you at the Collyer Charity Ball or at my family's annual barbeque doesn't really count." Casually, Ryan leans against a pillar. Sliding his phone from his pocket, he frowns before sending a quick text. Dropping it back in his jacket, his lips curve in amusement when he sees the familiar Amaryllis Designs logo hanging by Tira's point of sale. "So I see your enjoyment of Emily's designs continues."

Before I can let him know I'm certain my love of Amaryllis Designs is an obsession that will never end, Tira comes rushing back in. She holds a copy of my most recent release in her hands. Her voice is hesitant. "Kee, I hope this isn't inappropriate, but I have to confess something."

"What's that?"

"I designed the window display based on your cover. Would you mind signing your book for me?"

After I regain my wits at the honor of something so beautiful being done because of my work, I immediately reach for the book. I murmur huskily, "Do either of you have a pen?"

Tira fist pumps the air, causing Ryan's mask of composure to drop into one of amusement before he reaches into his pocket to slide out a Mont Blanc.

I run my hand lovingly over the cover to *Forgotten*, the latest hardback in my series. The cover designer went all out with the blue tones, appealing to both boys and girls. Flipping quickly to the signature page, I think for a minute before I lower the pen to the paper.

Tira,

Life's path isn't defined by one moment, one heartache, or one love, but a series of them. No event is meant to be forgotten. Instead, weave them together to form the cloth your life will be cut from.

You have gifts that are extraordinary. Having just been exposed to them, I know they will guide you true.

They've already helped me.

Thank you for the warm welcome to the Big Easy.

XOXO,

Kee Long.

Blowing lightly on the ink, I find Tira and Ryan close together. Tira breaks the silence between us. "I'll always cherish that, Kee."

"Do you want to see it?" I offer. But Tira shakes her head.

"I'll read it later. However, I'm not opposed to getting a picture. That is if you don't mind?"

I move to stand next to her. "And feel free to tag me in it on social media."

Tira's jaw falls open. I wing up a brow. "After what you did for me all day? Please."

"What did she do?" Ryan asks curiously.

"Brighten my day, cheer me up about a guy, relieve me of the down payment of my mortgage, you know. Nothing major." We all share a laugh as Tira hands her phone to Ryan.

"Why don't you stand by Tira's display," Ryan suggests. "Then I can get the shop logo in the back."

We move over. Tira drapes her arm around my shoulders, and I wrap mine around her waist. "So, what kind of man got you down?" Ryan says as he fiddles with her phone.

"Oh, just the kind who takes her number, promises to call, and then ghosts her." Tira's outrage on my behalf feels good.

I nod even though the ache inside over Benedict's actions hasn't abated, even with my new friend's defense or the new clothes I'm adding to my collection. "Sad, but true."

"Do you think he might have had a good reason?" Ryan holds up the camera. "Smile pretty, ladies."

We both beam at him. "Thank you so much for doing this, Kee. It's made my year," Tira tells me.

I give her a quick hug. "It was nothing. Coming in here was one of the best decisions I ever made. You're a treasure."

There's a choked sound from across the room. "I don't believe those are the words I used when Jenna was asking me to bring the dresses over. I might have wanted to have strangled you at the time," Ryan mutters.

Tira sticks her tongue out at him just as the door opens and a familiar voice calls out, "Benedict Perrault. I represent Mr. Lockwood's legal interests. And you are?"

And there's Benedict, looking like he's worn the same suit for a week straight. "Jesus, Ryan. Are you making your employees sleep at the office now?" Tira teases. Her smile is wide and genuine. "And what does Ryan need legal representation for in here, darlin'?"

My eyes flit back and forth between all of them, but they narrow on Ryan, who gives a small shrug. My voice sounds like battery acid when I find it though. "Funny you should show up. Tira and I were discussing the kind of guy who would take a woman's number and not call."

His head swivels my way, and I get a good look at his face. "Oh my god, Ben! Did something happen? Is your dad okay?" Forgetting how furious and hurt I am, I hurry forward and lay my hand on his arm. He looks awful. His eyes are rimmed with red. His face is wearing a rough stubble, and I wrinkle my nose because the stench is overpowering. I hope like hell before he falls asleep he finds the energy to find quality time with a shower.

"Kelsey." He breathes out my name, and for the first time since we saw each other in the bar at the Westin, I kind of wish he didn't. I can identify the Chinese food he ate—quite possibly days ago—on his breath.

"I'm not this bad about taking care of myself when I'm in the middle of a book. What the hell happened? Did you get mugged?" Maybe that would account for the stench fouling up Tira's magnificent store.

"Told you that you smelled a little ripe in the office, Perrault," Ryan offers.

I whirl on him like a tigress with fresh meat. "You did this to him?"

"Technically, a major problem that would have left hundreds of people out of jobs did," he tells me gently. My mouth falls open. Ryan continues, "However, Ben once again figured it out in time to save the day. He's kind of the office Superman. But Clark Kent knows if he shows his face at Lockwood Industries in the next forty-eight hours, he's fired."

Ben flaps a hand in Ryan's direction in acknowledgment. I wince a little as his arm goes up and down with the gesture. I wave my hand back and forth in front of my nose. "You should really stop doing that, Ben."

Tira slaps her hand over her mouth, trying to hide her amusement.

Benedict straightens and focuses the last of his energy on me. On me! "I was going to call, Kels. I had planned to ask you to dinner, somewhere quiet so we could talk, but this deal blew up at the eleventh hour. We've been finalizing it for months. Then I was going to text, and . . . Forgive me, please," he whispers.

I reach up and place my fingers on his mouth. I can't help the race of my heart when he puckers them and kisses the tips, taking me back to the room in Savannah where those same lips scored every inch of my skin.

I may be the biggest fool, but I murmur, "For this, okay," as I let my hand trail away from his face.

Before it reaches too far, he captures my fingers against his chest. I wince as I feel the crust of the food that's landed against his blue dress shirt. "Have dinner with me tonight?"

"How about you sleep for the next twenty-four hours before you worry about dinner so you don't pass out on your plate?" I suggest instead. Besides, I need the time to get my head around the fact I'm agreeing to go out on a date with Benedict Perrault.

He presses my hand tighter. "Kels, I want to see you again. I wanted to the minute I woke up and knew you were gone." His voice is pitched low enough so only I can hear.

My heart sighs in my chest while my mind tries to tug me back behind the barriers I've lived so safely behind for so many years.

"That sounds . . ." I hesitate.

"Yes?" he urges.

Slamming the mental door on my mind for the time being, I duck my head. Studying what must be the remains of some kind of Italian and a stain of something orange-pink that I'd bet is sweet-and-sour, I reach for what my heart wants. "It sounds perfect," I admit.

"Then I'll text you when I wake up." He cups my cheek with his long fingers.

"Okay." When I lift my face up, my wariness must show through.

"Better yet—" He pulls out his phone and types in something. I hear a distant ping from my phone. "There's the address of Commander's Palace. I'll call them on the way back home for a reservation tomorrow. I'll text you the time."

"You have the phone number of the restaurant memorized?" I hear Ryan snort behind me, but I give him no mind.

"I'm there . . . a lot. I'll explain when I see you?" His voice is hesitant. Hopeful.

And it's with that I lose the rest of my reluctance.

"That sounds good." I see the relief in his eyes before the fatigue settles back in.

"Great. Ryan? Can you have the car take me home now? I'm about to fall on my face any second."

Flushing a little, I spin around to find a smirking Ryan and a smiling Tira. "Least I can do, buddy." Flashing me a smile, Ryan walks around us to the door. "A pleasure to meet you." After a heartbeat, he murmurs confusingly, "Finally."

Benedict, who's swaying on his feet, doesn't move. Finally, I murmur, "I'm just a text away if you wake up and want to talk. I'm not going anywhere."

He deflates as if my reassurance was what he needed. "Good. Okay. I'm going to go to sleep now."

"I think you need to," I tell him gently.

"Night, Kels."

I glance out the window at the picturesque New Orleans day before braving my olfactory senses and rising on my toes to brush my lips against Ben's bristly cheek. "Night, Ben."

With a flick of his hand to Tira, he staggers toward where Ryan's holding the door. Both men disappear.

Tira steps up next to me. "So? Which do you prefer? Kelsey or Kee?"

With a sigh, I turn to my new friend. "It's been so long since I've been comfortable in Kelsey's skin. There are very few people who call me that name I feel comfortable with."

"Benedict's one of them?" she says knowingly.

"No." And while she rings up my purchases, I talk a little about how I moved to New Orleans to be with Valeria, Darin, and my soon-to-be niece.

But I also reach out and touch the petal embroidered on the Amaryllis Designs bag. *At least I know what I'll be wearing to dinner tomorrow night.*

CHAPTER TWENTY-TWO

Benedict

I COLLAPSE FACE FIRST IN MY BED AFTER THE LONG SHOWER I promised everyone from Ryan, to Kelsey, to my sister—who declared I smelled, "Rank. Ben, burn those clothes ASAP."

Spread out with the droplets of water drying on my back in a prone position, I immediately fall asleep.

The industrial fan overhead chills my skin after we finished a brutal workout. It also masks the sound of the jeering laughter as we're forced to pull our swimsuits up in between our cheeks with our backs to the crowd of fellow students.

I feel a quiver ripple through my muscles as the bristles of a broom scrape across the skin of my ass. And I pray. Please, no . . .

A few yelps from my fellow teammates emerge after a loud whoosh through the air.

Then the heavy weight of his presence behind me. My head drops in defeat, knowing there's no one to save me—us—from what's happening.

I absorb my slap on the ass from the bristles of the broom before a stack of potato chips is wedged between my thighs where the suit meets my rear. A snarled, "Don't you break a single chip. If you do, you'll be eating all of them, ass muncher."

I jerk my chin up once, prepared to remain on my knees all night if necessary. So long as I don't have to experience . . .

WHOOSH.

The smack of the broom against the side of my leg causes me to clench my buttocks involuntarily. Fuck, the chips. *I quiver as I absorb another hit on the other leg without moving.*

"Dude, aren't you taking this too far?" I hear a voice ask. I didn't dare turn around to figure out who it was. The debasement might escalate far worse than it already has.

There's a scuffle behind me. It goes on for some time until an alarm stops it.

An alarm? I blink a few times before I realize the alarm that's going off is on my phone. Snatching it up, I ignore the sweat dripping down my torso as I read the reminder I set myself. "Call home. Get a reservation for Commander's Palace."

Scrolling down on my favorites, I take a moment to feel the tug of seeing Kelsey's name among the other people who can reach me no matter where I am or what time of day. Then I press the number to call my parents.

"What's up, Ben?" My father gets right to the point.

"Is there any way possible you can get me a reservation for two at Commander's for tomorrow night?"

He laughs. "Cutting it close there, buddy."

"I wouldn't ask if the lady herself wasn't special, Dad."

"Oh?" One thing I love about my father is he's curious, but he won't pry.

I give him the information he's seeking. "You might remember her. It's Kelsey Kennedy." Then I wait.

His reaction doesn't surprise me in the slightest. He's incredulous. "You found her?"

"More like we found each other. Dad, she's remarkable. Even more so than I remembered."

"Considering what an influence she's had on your life, I'd say she's worth my placing a phone call to an old friend." I let out a sigh of relief. He goes on, "And Ben?"

"Yeah, Dad?"

"Give her your truth. She deserves to know why you did what you did to her." With that, my father hangs up.

I'm still clutching the phone long after my father disconnects. Tell Kelsey the truth?

Impossible.

I can barely live with the knowledge myself.

CHAPTER TWENTY-THREE

Kelsey

THE CITY OF NEW ORLEANS HAS BEEN DESCRIBED AS PURE temptation.

For me, that feeling is amplified by the seductive aroma of magnolias and the sweet lilies wrapping around the city. As the warmth of the day passes, their scent becomes more fragrant, forcing an enormous shift in emotion. Barriers separating sinners from saints vanish in the fiery heat making everything more accessible—people as well as places. The sultry air makes the most heinous sins forgivable, so long as they're wrapped in the city's seductive scent.

The night air certainly suits my mood, I conclude on my way to Commander's Palace. With the top of my sports car down, the ends of my scarf flap in the wind as I make my way toward dinner with Benedict.

Turning left on Lasalle, I keep an eye out for the quick right I need to make onto Washington Avenue.

Spying the distinctive turquoise and white striped awning, I forgo searching for a parking spot and pull up to the valet. Unwrapping my hair, I drop my scarf into the center console before raising the roof in the event the skies open up later. As soon as the latches are secure, I nod to the patiently waiting valet who opens my door. Grabbing my clutch, I slide out. "I'm meeting someone for dinner."

"Of course." He hands me a ticket, and I give him a smile and a folded bill. He nods in appreciation before sliding behind the wheel of my car.

Taking a deep breath, I walk inside and up to the maître d' who greets me. "Good evening. Welcome to Commander's Palace. Do you have a reservation?"

"I'm meeting someone for dinner," I repeat, my voice quiet.

"Do you know if your party is here yet?"

I shake my head just as a shot of awareness jolts my system. My eyes drop down to the fingers smoothing the crease of my elbow.

Benedict's voice comes from behind me. "Hello, Elliot. A reservation was called in yesterday. I believe there should be a table for two in the Garden Room."

Turning, my heart stutters in my chest when I see how gorgeous he looks in a gray suit with a black shirt that highlights the brilliance of his extraordinary blue eyes even more. I'm completely flustered when his gaze rakes over me before murmuring, "You look beautiful, Kelsey."

"Thank you," I say automatically, even if I believe it about as much as I believe I'm about to win the Louisiana State Lottery. I'm trying to formulate a coherent sentence, but his next words stop me cold. As menus are being gathered so we can be taken to our table, he whispers against my ear, "That dress you're wearing was designed to drive every man in this place wild."

"It's the designer."

He shakes his head slowly in response, dragging his nose against the tendrils of hair that I left down. "It's the woman wearing it."

I look down to make sure we're talking about the same person I checked out in the mirror before I left Val's. The azure blue floral embroidered gown Emily Freeman designed has cap sleeves with an illusion back dipping almost to my waist. The regal lines don't require much adornment, so I opted to pair it with strappy black heels and a large black pearl ring. I figured the look was elegant enough for a place like Commander's Palace.

Before I can reply, a host quietly approaches us. "Mr. Perrault, your table is ready. If you'll follow me."

"After you, Kelsey." Ben slips his hand firmly against my lower back, guiding me forward. The warmth of his hand burns through the fine mesh, stoking fires inside me. And judging by the way his jaw firms, Benedict as well. We're frozen for one heartbeat, two before he applies the slightest bit of pressure, encouraging me to cross through the elegant restaurant.

We finally weave our way toward a side room when I come up short.

"Oh my," I breathe. "Look at that oak tree."

"It's stunning, isn't it?" Benedict murmurs.

"It's like sitting on the edge of the highest branch, perched for flight. It's the feeling of excitement without the fear of wanting to try," I whisper.

His fingers slide across my back as he pulls me against his side. "I've been here a million times, and I'll never see this view again without thinking of you." Brushing a kiss against the side of my head, he guides me to our table.

Right next to the window.

"How did you manage this at the last minute?"

A flash of humor passes across Benedict's face. "Well, I suspect the phone call I made home yesterday helped."

"What do you mean?"

"My parents are longtime friends with the owners." Lifting his water glass to his lips, he waits for my reaction.

I frown. "They didn't have to cancel someone else's reservation for us, did they? I'd feel very uncomfortable about that—as lovely as this is," I tack on hastily.

Putting his glass back down, he reaches across the table for my hand. "One of the things I've always liked about you, Kels, is you never cared about the fact I was a Perrault."

Sliding mine back from under his, I gaze out at the oak tree that's withstood so much damage and remained standing. Nothing and no one has managed to drag it down. "Why would I care about something as trivial as money when I was much more concerned about finding someone who would dare to be my friend?" As I reach for my water, my hand is stopped.

"I was your friend," he rasps. Before I can work up the fortitude to broach a conversation that's long overdue, a waiter appears to ask for our drink order.

Since I drove and hope Benedict and I talk, I'll allow myself one drink I can nurse for most of the night. I tip my head toward the waiter and request, "A French 75, please."

"Would you like to finish that with gin or brandy, ma'am?"

"Brandy, please."

"And for you, sir?"

"An old-fashioned. Scotch," he adds before the waiter can ask.

"I'll have those right out." He disappears as quietly as he appeared, leaving us caught in the space between harsh memories and magical views. I decide to span the time between us by explaining.

"Everything I told you the other night was the truth."

"Except your name," Benedict interjects. I tip my head in acknowledgment.

"Except my name." Tracing my finger up and down the cold water goblet, I admit, "With or without my journal being plastered all over the walls, it likely wasn't hard for you to realize I'd started to . . . care . . . about you."

His face softens. "Those kinds of feelings are difficult to hide. Even as young as we were back then."

I lift my glass to my lips, trying to figure out what to say next when our drinks are delivered, giving me a much-needed reprieve. "Thank you," I murmur as the glass is set down in front of me.

"Are you ready to order?" the waiter asks as he places Benedict's glass in front of him. I'm about to say no to buy myself a few more minutes when Benedict requests, "How about giving us a few moments with our drinks?"

"Certainly, Mr. Perrault. I'll check back with you in a while." He disappears. I touch the long stem of the fluted glass lightly before asking, "What shall we toast to?"

Benedict lifts his glass. "To reconciliation? I think we've been through enough rough patches to get here."

I still, my hand falling away. "Maybe it isn't supposed to happen. Not all stories are supposed to end well. I know for sure you were forced to read *Gone With the Wind*." His grin disarms me.

"True, but can you think of something better?" His eyes are steady over his still-uplifted glass.

Not without anticipation and fear, something I experience at the start of every book, I lift my glass and touch it to his. "To reconciliation," I repeat. Holding each other's gaze, we each take a sip before lowering our glasses.

"So, it wasn't a lie, and it wasn't payback." He raises a brow in question.

I promptly shake my head. "No, it wasn't either of those things."

"Then what was our night in Savannah supposed to be?"

I lift my glass and take another sip for courage. Staring down into its pale-yellow depth, I admit, "Maybe it was a gift to the teenage girl who still lives in a small corner inside of me. I ended her story that night. I gave her the fairytale she never had in high school to heal the pain she still harbored inside." The swirl of the bubbles from the sparkling wine captivates my attention.

"Wouldn't that gift have been more meaningful if you admitted who you were to me?"

I shake my head. "I was afraid to take a chance. What if you weren't the Benedict I'd remembered from the hours of tutoring? What if you turned out to be the same man who . . ." . . ."

"What if I turned out to be the same man who would hurt you the same way I did on our graduation day?" he concludes grimly.

"Yes." Lifting my head, I meet his stricken expression. "I fell for a boy and was shattered in the end. What if the man did worse? I could get a feel for who you were as my alter ego. Suss you out, as it were."

"Jesus." He takes a swallow of his drink. I rush to continue.

"There's no going back to change the past—either what happened back in high school or recently."

"And in the meantime, we shared something so explosive, we might have left scorch marks on the sheets in Savannah," his honeyed voice concludes.

I blush. "Well, there is that."

"Yes, Kelsey, there is." We each take a sip of our drinks without losing the other's gaze. After he lowers his glass, he asks, "The question is, what are we going to do about it?"

"About what?"

"About all of it. Do we forget our past and move on?"

"I . . . I don't know."

He leans forward and reaches for my hand again. This time, I let him keep a hold of it. "I don't want you to be just a regret from my past."

"Then, what do you want me to be?" I wonder aloud.

He shakes his head. "I'm still trying to figure that out."

"Along with dinner?" I joke lightly, trying to bring us around to a lighter topic.

A smile breaks across his handsome face. "Getting hungry?"

"Yes. That and my best friend bet me I wouldn't try turtle soup." His laugh is a more mature version of the one I've dreamed of since I was a teenager—low and husky.

"If you're going to have it anywhere, this is the best place to try it. They're renowned for it here." Lifting his arm, he calls the waiter over. When he's at our side, Ben says, "I think the lady is ready to order her appetizer."

"Turtle soup, please," I say without hesitation.

"Gumbo, for me. Thank you." After the waiter leaves, he asks, "Ryan lambasted me pretty hard in the car after we left?"

"For what?"

"Apparently you and my boss know one another?" Benedict wings a brow upward with unasked questions.

I hedge. "I wouldn't say we *know* each other. We have a number of mutual acquaintances. It was a surprise to see him act as delivery boy."

When I explain about the shock of recognition and ferreting out my loose connection to Ryan's family, it leads Benedict to ask why Tira and I were standing in the front window. After I bashfully explain about the book I signed, Ben lifts my fingers to his lips. Brushing them back and forth over his full lower lip, he smiles. "And there's the girl I know shining through the woman sitting in front of me. Nothing but sweet grace."

I blush and duck my head, but the compliment does more for my soul than any other I've been given in the last fifteen years as my body's morphed from grotesquely obese to fit. And most importantly, because it came from Benedict's heart.

It turns out turtle soup is divine. So is every dish at Commander's Palace. But it has nothing on the charming man sitting across the table from me.

Benedict is a perfect date, regaling me with stories of Harvard law school, how he ended up working for Lockwood Industries after working for one of the top law firms in the nation, his friendship with his best friend, Cade, that spans back to college, and what an enjoyable pain it can be to have his sister living with him. His comment of "She wants to do so much more than being a teacher. How could I not help her?" makes me realize that the Benedict I crushed on, my Ben, is still in there.

A little voice inside me whispers, *Maybe there was a good reason for what he did.* It will give me something to think about, that's for sure.

In response, I tell him about living in Southern California, Val, and moving to Connecticut to be closer to my cousin. I give him a rundown of the characters of the random people I've seen strolling the streets of Collyer—

"Beckett Miller, Ben! I mean, one day, he's just coming out of the grocery store with one arm around his wife and the other holding a bag of groceries."

Benedict's amused at my exuberance. "Ahh, now it all starts to come together. Collyer, Connecticut apparently is the metaphysical center of the universe."

I choke on a sip of water. "What makes you say that?"

"Everyone has been there, has a connection there, or has lived there." At my quizzical look, he asks me, "I'm certain you've heard of Hudson Investigations?"

"Certainly, since Ryan's brother Caleb co-owns the company and he's married to Cassidy Freeman-Lockwood."

Benedict's face gets serious. "I feel I need to be upfront with you, Kelsey."

I frown. "All right?"

"I had you investigated by Hudson Investigations."

Outrage surges through my system. I begin to slide my chair back when Benedict lays his hand on mine. "It was years ago. I was trying to find you. I wanted to find you . . . no, needed to."

Confusion fans the emotions brewing inside me even higher. So there can be no misconception, I ask, "You were trying to find *me*?"

"Yes."

"But, why?"

His fingers tangle with mine before I'm pinned to my seat with the intensity of his gaze. "I knew we were always meant to reunite."

I inhale so sharply, my dress shifts causing my napkin to fall from my lap. His lips form a crooked line. "I'm going to need you to avoid breathing like that."

"What?"

He tips his chin down before murmuring, "I'm already in hell imagining what you have on under that dress. Don't make it worse, Kels."

My fingers spasm around his. We're trapped with so many undercurrents, I'm not certain which one to ride out.

Just as I'm about to speak, we're interrupted by the waiter handing me a clean napkin. It breaks the bubble of tension around us. "Maybe we should eat," I suggest.

"Good idea." But the intensity still hovers between us. And I can't forget what he said.

Benedict tried to find me.

Fast on its heels is the question I still don't know the answer to: *What would have happened if he did?*

Is this what Ava, Jillian, and Val all meant when they said it was time for me to chase my happiness? Would I have reached out to him or pushed him away?

Uncertain of the answer, even now, I guide us back to safer topics. We begin debating all the divergent paths our lives have taken us on and what we've held steadfast to. I'm telling him about the best pizza in the world in a tiny town called Ridgefield. "I'm telling you, Ben. It's the best pizza on the planet. It was one of the first places Ava took me to when I moved there."

"Sounds like it's worth braving a trip into Yankee territory," he drawls. I pause with my fork halfway to my mouth.

"Do you mean the world north of the Mason-Dixon line or the baseball team?"

"Both."

My fork clatters to my plate as I glare at him. "Tread carefully, buddy. I lived there for close to six years."

"And you lived in the South for eighteen. More if you count your time now. Where's your allegiance to the Braves, Kels? I lived in Red Sox territory and managed mine," he counters.

"Dead," I retort. "I'd root for the Dodgers first if that tells you anything."

"It tells me you need to go to a ball game."

"As long as you don't mind my wearing pinstripes, that's fine."

He shakes his head in mock tragedy. “And you had such potential as the perfect woman until just now. What happened to you?”

“First, no one is perfect. Second, I saw the world and discovered it’s a place filled with a beautiful reality where the best people aren’t judged by anything but by what’s in their hearts. Third, I learned there are better things in life than following the crowd.” I slide a bite of my tartare between my lips as I watch his part in shock. But I plow on. “I’m not who I was yesterday or who I was the day before. Wouldn’t that be boring?”

The smile that crosses his face causes my stomach to clench and my nipples to tingle inside my lace-edged bra. “Yes, yes, it would be.” When I don’t respond, don’t move, he encourages me, “Finish eating. The desserts here are fabulous.”

“I’m not sure I can manage one,” I admit ruefully.

“Then we’ll just sit here with coffee, and I’ll keep discovering more things about you that fascinate me.”

Somehow, I manage to eat another few bites, but I don’t know how. Not when my heart and my stomach have flipped spots.

CHAPTER TWENTY-FOUR

Benedict

I escort Kelsey through Commander's Palace so we can retrieve our cars, but I don't want to. Every step we take together toward the entrance means our night's ending. I want to pull her back into the alcove we were nestled in for hours and let the atmosphere continue to keep alive the hope there's more than just forgiveness to be found with her.

Much more.

As we step outside, a mournful sax wails down the street. Kelsey shivers. My hand slides up her back to cup her shoulder. "What is it?"

"The soul of this city just hits me here." She presses her hand into her stomach. "Whether it's through tragedy or beauty, they come together as one. It's a special kind of bond that I've never witnessed before."

Even as I tighten my arm around her to tuck her against my side, my breathing starts to quicken. I need to feel her lips against mine again.

We haven't been just us without hiding anything since the last time we were in Mrs. Wiley's classroom alone. Not even when our bodies were entwined so intimately with the hotel sheets have I felt this connection. I need to taste her as we learn each other for who we are with our secrets unraveling a little at a time. I need to see the gray eyes I knew then in the woman I'm holding now. I didn't lie to Kelsey when I told her I thought she was amazing and beautiful over fifteen years ago. I need her to believe that. And there were reasons for the pain we suffered. Because, yes, damn it, I was hurt too. *But can you ever tell her the reasons why?* I think jadedly.

The primal urge clawing at my insides, the need to lay claim to her lips here in my city—our city—where we're just us with no bad memories between us.

Yet.

Just as she's handed the valet her ticket, I drag her around the corner of the building. Sputtering, she asks, "What the hell, Ben?"

"This." My head lowers. I capture her lips with mine as I press her body back against the turquoise clapboard.

I was going to give her a gentle kiss at her car. I intended to take us back in time to the kiss I almost gave her as I hugged the breath out of her in the classroom and murmured, "You are so incredibly amazing and beautiful. And I'm going to miss you so damn much." I'd just put her down after spinning her around in jubilant glee, and for a heartbeat, a second, an eternity, a feminine awareness lit her face. In her eyes, there was a knowledge I was feeling something more than gratitude. And if Mrs. Wiley hadn't flung open the door, I know it would have been the first time our lips met.

A sweet kiss for a sweet girl.

The kiss I'm giving her now isn't that. It's reverent but wholly sexual. I brush my lips across hers once, twice, willing them to part. On a gasp they do, and my tongue accepts the invitation immediately. I taste the creamy coffee she had in place of dessert on her lips. Aligning our bodies so our hearts touch, I cage her head between my arms as I deepen the kiss further, ravaging her mouth as I did the night of the reunion as I lay atop her glorious body. Her arms wrap around my neck, pulling me closer. A moan escapes her lips, hidden to all but me by the sax playing nearby. Need swirls up between us, merging with the heat and hunger in the warm summer air. It prompts me to want to drive the kiss higher, even as it makes me want to treasure her.

Tearing my mouth away, I trail kisses behind her ear and whisper, "Kelsey." I'm burning up for her again.

In contrast, she freezes. Pressing a hand against my chest, she pushes me back slightly. "I know where we took things in Savannah, but I'm not ready to go there again."

"This isn't going away between us," I point out, breathless.

"No, but it doesn't mean I want to rush this either."

"We also have a hell of a history," I say when there's nothing more that I'd like to do than hitch her skirt over her hip and feel the smooth length of her thigh wrapped around my waist. Again.

And after the words are out of my mouth, I could slap myself for saying them. "Yes, we still have that between us, don't we? I answered a lot of questions tonight, counselor, but you didn't. How is that? Why is that?"

Shit. Immediately I try to regroup. "Kelsey, that wasn't what I planned between us." I honestly wanted to discuss with her our past in a controlled setting.

Controlled, something our pasts weren't. Not for either of us. She just doesn't know it.

"What did you plan, Benedict?" When I can't get the words out fast enough, she supplements her own answer, "Of course. Picking up where we left off in Savannah."

I want to yell at her incorrect assumptions, but I'm still trying to put the right words together to make her stay. She backs away, edging closer to the corner and escaping. "Good night, Benedict. Thank you for a lovely evening."

Damn, how do women move so fast in heels that high?

Unfreezing, I realize everything that needs to be said. I make it around the corner to spy her hugging her arms tightly before sliding into a BMW waiting at the curb.

Pulling out my phone, I immediately begin to text her, but I wait to send it. I don't want to upset her while she's driving. I know I won't forget to send this one.

Instead, I hand my ticket to the valet and wait for my vehicle to be pulled around. About fifteen minutes later, waiting for my garage door to open, I finally hit Send.

The first time I thought about kissing you, you were wearing a pair of black leggings and a purple tunic. I'll never apologize for that kiss. It should have happened fifteen years ago. But even if I won't apologize for that, you should know I tried to do it back then—apologize, that is.

I lower the garage door and walk out the side entrance before making my way to the back of the house. Lisa looks up from where she's studying on the couch. "Hey! How was your date with Kelsey?"

My phone chooses that moment to ping. "Give me a second, and I'll let you know." I read the message.

When was that? she writes back.

The day after graduation, but you were already gone. Damn it, this shouldn't be over text.

There's a long pause before she says, *I agree. I thought we were going to do that tonight.*

We were. But then I got lost in the moment, I write back.

That doesn't bode well, Ben.

Leaning against the counter, I silently agree. A large part of me knows I should just meet her and let her go. I'm no good for whatever beauty her future holds. I'm more tainted by my past than she could be by hers. Kelsey's had the ability to transform herself into someone different, but how do you transform something so ugly, you'd do anything . . .

An incoming text pulls me from traveling down a bleak road. When I read it, I'm floored. And the dark part of me that's trying to pull me away loses its grip when I'm lassoed in by her words.

I'm struggling with this, Ben. There's a part of me that wants to walk away because I can't, won't, be hurt like that again. Then there's the part of me that can't because it's you.

I'm clutching the screen so tight I'm afraid it might crack. Again, Kelsey's words undo me. I read them over and over until they're memorized.

Lisa gets frustrated waiting for my answer. She shoves herself off the couch and gets to her feet. Standing in front of me, she waves her arms. "Hey, Ben? You in there?"

Quickly, without answering Lisa, I type back, *Please, let me see you tomorrow. Let me give you the words you deserve in person.* I'm desperately praying she says yes because I owe her a long-overdue apology and a reassurance that whatever *this* is, it isn't because of what happened before. It's because we're here, we're us. And my heart's pounding just as hard as I hope hers is.

After trading a few texts back and forth, we decide to meet at Audubon Park. I get confirmation we'll meet in the early afternoon. Then I receive a text that causes a broad smile to break out across my face. I slip my phone into my pocket before I give my full attention to my sister.

Lisa's impatiently waiting for me to finish. "Aren't you supposed to make plans for your next date when you're, say, on it?"

"Not when you almost screw it up."

"Oh, Ben." She lays a hand on my arm sympathetically, right before she punches me. "Don't screw up."

"I can't seem to not manage it around her," I admit.

Lisa gapes at me before a wonky smile that used to cross her face before she would tattle on me to our mother appears. My balls draw up in fear. "What?" I demand.

"Nothing," she demurs.

"Lisa," I say warningly.

"Just that watching you go down for the count is going to be an extra form of entertainment I didn't realize I'd get when I moved here." She turns and laughs over her shoulder as she returns to the couch. Picking up the textbook she was reading, she tunes me out.

Shaking my head, I make my way down the hall and head upstairs to my suite of rooms. Stripping out of my clothes, I crawl between the sheets thinking of the last thing Kelsey sent me over text.

I'll see you tomorrow.

Maybe our path in life isn't predetermined by the things that happened to us or even by a single action. Perhaps it's determined by our willingness to humble ourselves to correct the wrongs.

If so, maybe I have a chance at not only redemption but happiness.

Finally.

CHAPTER TWENTY-FIVE

Kelsey

I DON'T KNOW WHAT THE HELL I'M DOING. WHAT POSSESSED ME TO agree to go out with Benedict again? What is it he expects from me? It's got to be something. After all, something that burned that hot couldn't lead to something more.

Could it?

Agreeing to meet him at Gumbel Fountain in Audubon Park seemed like a good idea last night, but in the light of day, while yanking out everything in my dresser and closet, trying to find something to wear that doesn't make me resemble an exhibit at the zoo, I'm not so sure.

"Maybe I should text him and cancel," I grumble aloud as I toss another pair of shorts on the bed.

"I'll hide your phone if you even reach for it. You are going to go long enough to get your apology, Kelsey, so help me God," Val warns me from the now open doorway.

Startled, I spin around. She's rubbing her hand over Lucy, who seems to be getting bigger inside her mama's belly each day. "And stop worrying about what you're going to wear. Who cares?"

"I do since I'm judged every time I walk out the door," I return.

"The only person doing that to you anymore is you," she retorts.

Startled, I drop the sixth pair of shorts I'd planned on trying on.

"Hold on to everything you've managed to accomplish, Kels, and stop berating yourself for the fact you're not perfect. Hell, am I?"

"You always have been," I tell her sincerely. Because in my eyes, Val is everything: beautiful, loving, and smart.

"That's because you love me. Don't you see? If someone loves you, they forget about your imperfections and focus on all the beauty that comes from within."

Walking over to my bed, I sit on top of all the discarded clothes and pull my knees into my chest. "What am I doing, Val?"

"Other than sitting on half your closet?"

"Cute. I'm not certain I can handle this—him," I admit. I'd shared what happened on our date plus the texts with Val this morning.

"Darlin', who says you're the one who has to? It seems to me like he's the one who needs to speak up and say what's on his mind."

"Have you ever known a man to do that?" I demand.

"Just Dare when he . . ."

"Stop talking. Right now."

Val laughs when I flop back groaning. Sobering, she asks, "Do you think there's something worth exploring?"

"Maybe, but how do I not resent it's happening now because of the way I look? I'm proud of who I've become, but sometimes I want to be loved because of being attractive inside." I voice my frustration. My eyes finding hers, I smile ruefully. "You know, the same person I've always been."

"Get it out in the open, and you let him explain like the man he's supposed to be. And as for your struggle about not being seen as attractive on the inside, let me remind you, you were asked out plenty before you ever had the surgery."

I snort derisively.

Val hauls off and punches me in the arm. "Don't give me that crap. I'm not talking about at school but after. That cute PA at the surgeon's office asked you out constantly. What was his name again?"

I dismiss her words with a wave of my hand. "Josh? He was nice. I'm sure it was just as friends."

"Right," she drawls sarcastically. "Friends. That's why he looked like he was sucker punched when you ran into him with an actual date."

I flush before averting my eyes. "This is the problem with having a best friend. They know too much."

She smiles before her face gets serious. "I need you to make me a promise."

"Okay." And I agree because there isn't anything I wouldn't do for her.

"Hold on to all you are and try to forget the negativity that's been thrown at you. Most of the time, people have their own issues they're taking out on someone they perceive is weaker than they are." Shifting to the end of the bed, she looks at the mess I've made of my summer casual wear. "Now, if it were up to me, I'd wear your blue shorts with the berry camisole and espadrilles."

I shift my hips to pull out most of what Val suggested. "You think?"

"Bring a shirt in case you go inside," she suggests. Remembering my blue and berry cotton striped button-down hanging in the closet, I realize it's perfect. Casual yet cool. Making her way to the door, she turns. "Oh, Kels?"

"Yeah, babe?"

"One more thing?"

"Uh-huh." I'm already folding my clothes to put the explosion of my wardrobe away.

"You're an adult now. You're not forced to stay anywhere. If you're unhappy, then walk away. That's allowed too." With that sage advice, Val leaves my room.

Tears burn my eyes when I realize I've never really done this. I'm thirty-three years old and never really dated because of the locks I placed on the cages I guarded my heart with years ago.

In one of our heart-to-hearts back at the Coffee Shop in Collyer, Matt said eventually I'd find someone who'd be worth taking more than a superficial chance on. "Don't feel you need to conform to being anything, Kelsey. Take life, love, and relationships at your own pace. Just be you."

"And what if that means being alone?"

Matt shrugged. "Look at how long it took me to find the other part of my soul. I'd say it's worth the wait of not settling." His all-knowing gaze met mine as I lifted a heavy white mug filled with coffee Ava had just topped off. "Don't settle for anything. You've had to give up on your dreams for far too long." With those words, he shoved out of my booth and headed back into the kitchen.

Pulling myself from my memories, I head toward the bathroom to get ready, wondering how I'm going to push the past far enough away to live in today and enjoy the beautiful day outside with a man I'm intensely attracted to despite past concerns and present wariness.

"How are your grandparents?" Benedict asks me in between popping grapes in his mouth.

Even though it's not what we're here to talk about, I'll give him this as an icebreaker. I assure him, "They're wonderful. Loving retirement in Florida."

"Where's home for them now?"

"A little town just north of St. Augustine. There's a fifty-five-and-over community they live in." Thoughtfully, I reconsider my words before adding, "It's not a retirement community as much as it's a perpetual cruise ship. The activities program printed is almost as thick as one of my books."

Benedict chuckles. "So, things like bridge, canasta?"

I rear back, horrified. "Hell no. Pop-pop would go insane. He's already thrown out his back twice with the competition-level paddleball and bowling league. Nana swears that if he pulls this crap with ping-pong, she going to sign him up for quilting."

"And that's a problem because . . ."

"Because he is a retired tailor—it's a form of torture for him to see some of the messes that happen. He comes back to their home ranting about how he could teach the class better," I confide. "It's Nana's perfect revenge."

By this point, Benedict's dropped the grapes to the blanket because he's laughing so hard. "Has she done this often?"

"Twice that I know of. The first was after he didn't listen to doctor's orders and went back to paddleball too soon. The second was after . . ." I clamp my lips together.

"After?" Benedict rolls to the side and raises his brow in question.

"Well . . ." I hesitate. "Ava and I gave them a present for their fiftieth anniversary. He threw a right fit over it, refusing to accept it, yelling and everything. Nana told him to get over it. Since he didn't by the time we left, we each received a beautiful quilt as a thank you a few weeks later."

"What was the gift?"

I shift uncomfortably. "It wasn't that big of a deal. I mean, Ava helped." I'm avoiding answering.

"Kelsey, did you get them a trip? A car?" At the negative shake of my head, he smirks. "A house?"

I studiously avoid his gaze as I reach for the bottle of water and take a drink.

"Wait." He sits up. "You're not kidding. You bought them a house?"

"No, what we did was pay off their mortgage. Pop-pop didn't take kindly to it," I reply defensively.

"I can imagine."

I turn on him like I've just been transported back to Nana's kitchen three years ago. "And why the hell shouldn't I? I was clinging to life by my fingernails when I lived with them. They're what kept me on this side of sane. I—we—paid off their mortgage. So what? I already owned my own home," I argue hotly. Benedict opens his mouth to speak, but I don't let him. "Why shouldn't they get a chance to live a life full of riches? Should I hoard it for myself, maybe buy some more shoes with it?"

"I was just going to say . . ."

"They taught me everything about the kind of person I should be and the love I deserve."

"Then you should have bought them the house and a car." When my head snaps around, his blue eyes are burning into mine. The hottest part of the flame is searing me as he continues to look at me without saying anything, but when he does, my heart backs up into my throat. "It's hard for men to admit we're not always doing the right thing, that accepting help is okay. There's something inside of us—either we're taught to believe or it's genetic. I don't know—that makes us feel responsible for the well-being of those we love. Sometimes, it takes that person to point out the error of our ways before we can let someone else in. And unfortunately, it's often too late to make amends."

My lips part because while I know what he's saying is true about what happened with Pop-pop, I know he's asking me more. The question is whether the forgiveness he's seeking will be as generously offered as I did for my family.

And I just don't know. Not yet.

"I think that depends on the transgression," I whisper, lost in the swirling depths of hope and torment before he ducks his head so I can no longer see his face.

"So, quilts work?" he asks in an attempt to distract me.

"I think it was more the hug that came with it since Pop-pop brought them to Connecticut himself."

Ben slips on a pair of sunglasses. "Good to know. Kelsey, I'd like to ta—"

Alarms clang in my head. He's about to bring up the past. My breathing becomes shallow. *No, I can't do it. I can't go there. It doesn't feel right.* Taking Val's advice and shifting away from the conversation we've not yet had, I rudely interrupt, "What about your family? I know your sister is here."

Benedict's smile is bittersweet. "Yes, Lisa's here. She was teaching in Georgia, not too far from our family. She had a full life—great job, engaged to be married, planning her wedding, when she found out her college sweetheart was cheating on her."

"Ouch." I wince in empathy. Poor Lisa. But in my mind's eye, I think of the beautiful woman I ran into at Café Du Monde. "She looks like she's happy here though."

"Yeah, she is. When it first happened, it broke her up into a million pieces. Mom and Dad offered for her to go home to Skidaway, but she's almost twenty-nine. She couldn't face the idea of that. I offered her a new start here. That was a few years ago."

"Is she working?" I vaguely remember from that embarrassing interlude something about classes, but I can't recall clearly.

"She was, but she stopped at the end of the last school year. Now, she's getting her master's in psychology. She's a certified teacher but wants to become a guidance counselor. She does some volunteer work as part of her course of study." He lets out a short bark of a laugh. "I wonder what Mom and Dad are going to think when they realize Lisa plans to stay down here and not move back to Georgia when she's through with school."

I gnaw on my lower lip. "Speaking from experience, I think they'll be shocked and hurt, but do everything in the world to cover it up."

"Is that what happened with your grandparents?" I nod tentatively. Benedict reaches over and rubs his hand over the top of mine in comfort? Empathy? Just because he wanted to touch me? I don't know. "When?"

"When what?" I ask blankly because with the way his thumb is moving back and forth slowly over the top of my wrist, I'm feeling brain cells leak from my head and water the earth beneath us. *It's going to be brilliant grass,* I think wildly when he squeezes my hand before letting it go.

"When did you tell them you weren't coming back home? To Savannah, I mean," Benedict clarifies.

I twist my head to avoid looking at him. I focus on a couple of Frisbee players, then a girl flying a kite with her father behind her. I shake my head, not wanting to answer.

"Kels?" There's concern laced with worry in his voice. I'm not going to be able to put off answering him. But for some reason, I don't want to because what I'm about to say is going to hurt us both, taking us from the idyllic peace we've enjoyed up until now into something much darker.

Our past.

He reaches over to touch my arm, but I jerk it away. Taking a deep breath, I blurt it out. "I told them seconds after I hugged them goodbye before I pulled out of the driveway. It was the day after our high school graduation. I told them I was never coming back to Savannah—to the city that had caused me so much pain. And until the reunion a few weeks ago, it was a vow I kept. I'd never once been back."

CHAPTER TWENTY-SIX

Kelsey

His sharply indrawn breath stills every movement in Audubon Park. I feel on display—just like I did that day at graduation. With all eyes on me. The Frisbee players seem to have stopped; the little girl with the kite is avidly watching.

And I know Benedict's focus is solely on me. I can feel it even if I'm not returning the look in kind. Then I hear laughter, lots of laughter. And flashes of memories make me shake.

Oh my god! She's running. I'm surprised the stage isn't collapsing.

Who knew a monster could run that fast?

It's called ambling by a beast, you moron.

Jesus, do you see the way that fat's jiggling? I wonder if she ends up with bruises.

Flashes of the comments flung at me along with the jeering laughter as I ran off stage at our high school graduation race through my head. It's too much. I push myself to my feet. "I thought I could . . . with you. I'd give just about anything to be able to . . . Fuck!"

I don't make it a step before his hand wraps around my ankle. The next thing I know, I'm flailing backward helplessly, windmilling my arms. Shit, this is going to hurt. Tears prick my eyes as I think about how embarrassed I'm going to be. So be it. It's not like I've never been humiliated in front of this man before.

Instead, I find myself caught by a strong pair of arms. "Where were you going?" Benedict's voice is guttural.

I twist and turn in his arms. "Away. I can't hurt you, but I can't . . . I'm not ready . . ."

"Then tell me that, damn it. We'll back off this conversation until you are—we are. But don't run away from me. Not when I don't know if it will be another fifteen years before I can find you again to say I'm sorry." His voice sounds broken. "And I am, Kelsey. So, so sorry." Benedict lays me down on the blanket, and I hazard a look up at him. Fear, determination, and something I can't quite name chase each other across his face. He aligns his long, lean body against mine. My heartbeat picks up in anticipation.

"In all my life, it's only been you," the words escape my lips before I can stop them.

"What do you mean?" His brow lowers in confusion.

In for a penny. . . "Only you have been able to take me from dreaming with the clouds to flat on my back in the span of a heartbeat. I'm not sure I care to understand why."

My hands grip his shoulders as he angles up sharply over me, intent in his every movement. "What are you doing?" I whisper.

"This," he murmurs. His head lowers down, his lips fitting to mine. His broad shoulders block out the sun more effectively than the trees above us. I let out a gasp before wrapping my arms around his neck and pulling him closer.

Can salvation and forgiveness be exchanged in a kiss? Does a perfect day wipe out the pain etched in my memory of a horrific one? No, but maybe it demonstrates life isn't always going to disappoint me. I've been so on guard, protecting myself from the past I suffered, the scars in my mind and heart, I'm scared to allow myself the reward being offered to me.

As Benedict's lips whisper over my face and down the side of my neck, I rake my nails through his thick hair. "Never been like this," I gasp. My limited experience before Benedict wasn't altogether unsatisfying, but it never made my head spin. A kiss never made me forget the world turning around me at a million miles an hour and coming to a sudden halt. It never had the power to sweep my legs out from under me when I was already weightless.

It never stopped the ache I live with in my head and my heart.

"You make me need, Kels," his voice rasps in my ear, sending shivers down my spine. "You make me wish."

"For what?" My lips trace the shell of his ear. I let out a small gasp at his next words.

Brushing my hair away from my face, he mutters more to himself, "For a moment in time where I could make you forget the pain I caused you. To not be terrified to show you the man I really am."

He rolls until I'm lying on top of him. Even as I brace my elbows on either side of his head, he wraps his arms around my back, holding me in place. "I would have you lie on me like this forever if I could," he says tenderly.

A cloud of doubt passes through my mind. "I wouldn't have been able to years ago." I start to push up and away, but his arms tighten.

"I want you to hear me. I went to that reunion looking for you." At my dubious look, he tightens his arms and continues. "I spent the entire plane ride preparing myself for how I was going to handle meeting your husband, hearing about your kids." At my shocked gasp, he groans. "Yeah. So, don't for a minute doubt I didn't think of you as a desirable, sexual woman before I found out who you were. I guess I'm just damned lucky some man hasn't been able to win your heart. Or have they generally been idiots who can't see past their noses?" He uses his to brush against mine, setting off sparks between us.

My fingers trace his brows above his sunglasses. Even as I'm absentmindedly stroking him, my mind wonders if I'm not stronger for the agony of what I lived through. Otherwise, would I appreciate the simple perfection of a moment like this as something to be cherished? "I refuse to comment either way," I declare resolutely.

Benedict's shoulders arch off the ground, he laughs so hard. "I think that is your answer."

"Maybe. At least that's been my experience."

He jackknifes us both up into a sitting position. "You haven't had good relationships?" The note of concern starts picking away at the lock on the next door of my heart.

Damn him.

I decide to lay the reality of what high school did to my social expectations on the table. It's past time.

"Relationships imply I gave people a chance, Ben," I say softly. "I've been reminded recently by the people closest to me that I wasn't exactly open to that."

"Why?" The question is torn from him. It scrapes the walls of my heart to listen to the brittle sound of his voice. "How could no one see the remarkable beauty you are?"

Unable to believe the words coming out of his mouth, I reach over and pluck his sunglasses away. His blue eyes hold as many demons, if not possibly more than mine. They're also pulling me under with the same unnamed emotion my heart began to fall for years ago. Shaking my head, I pull myself back from the brink before I know everything. I remind myself there's no happily ever after in words unspoken.

Instead, I press my hands against his chest and tell him bluntly, "I am the collective of everything said or done to me. Like everyone else who's ever contemplated a relationship, there's been miscommunication and misunderstandings. I wouldn't blame either party." Though I didn't try that hard out of fear of rejection. Lamely, I add, "Things just didn't work out."

"At the end of it all, I want the simplicity of a man who will be willing to sit on our front porch holding my hand," Ben quotes me to me softly.

I rear back as if I've been struck. "You remember that?" I wrote those words in an essay about my vision of love during our creative writing class. Benedict wrote a short story inspired by his parents, he told me. Fear courses through me. As he's trying to prove to me he wasn't joking, that back then, he did like me, care for me, and maybe found me beautiful, he still slid a knife into my heart.

Moving his fingers behind my ears, he tugs my glasses off. Now, neither of us can hide. And neither of us is capable of escaping the penetrating stare of the other. "I remember everything. And I know that what you just told me was to protect yourself or me."

"What makes you think you know me so well?" I demand, struggling to put some distance between us, but his words still me.

"Because I can never get close enough to make it stick. My mind replays every mistake I made with you."

I initially try to swallow the bitter words that maybe neither of us would be so broken, so unable to be with someone if it hadn't been for the way he did me dirty because that's not the truth—well, not the whole truth. Then I decide to hell with protecting Benedict's feelings when he never had a care for mine.

Yanking myself out of his arms, my voice is trembling when I bite out, "Is that what this is? Do you figure if you can have a 'normal' relationship with me, you'll be able to move on with your life? Because if that's the case, I'll save you the hassle. Go forth, do good things, and don't be an asshole. It will be great for whoever is worthy enough to end up in your perfect world."

Benedict shoves to his knees and squares off against me. "Is that what you think this is?" he demands.

"What else could it be? No one wanted to be seen with me back then. Now? I guess it's okay based on what I look like. I don't know what kind of game you're playing." Wearily, I run my hand through my hair.

"And what about you?" Benedict's words slap at me. "What did you come to that reunion for if not . . ."

"To shove it down their goddamned throats!" I yell as I surge to my feet. "I had every damn right to shove it down every one of your throats that I wasn't some broken, defeated, ugly—"

"And all you've managed to do was show me you weren't ugly," Benedict interrupts coolly.

Staggered, I step back as if he slapped me. The wedge of my shoe sinks into the soft grass. I feel the tickle of it around my ankles as I begin to back away.

"Jesus, Kels, I didn't mean . . ." He scrubs his hand up and down his face.

"I think, Benedict, the problem is you very much did mean it. Just like you meant what you said at graduation," I whisper tragically before I turn and walk briskly toward the park entrance.

I ignore his repeated attempts to get me to stop by calling my name.

After all, when you're barely hanging on, you can't stop to answer questions.

CHAPTER TWENTY-SEVEN

Benedict

After I get back from my abysmal second chance with Kelsey, I lock myself in my study. There I study a piece of glass I had etched with words that have been my only lifeline to Kelsey Kennedy for far too long.

"The worst thing that's happening to you is the best thing that will ever happen to someone else. All you can do is move past it. After all, if life were meant to be easy, I'd have already won the game." I read the words aloud to the empty room. "You were the best thing that happened to me, Kels. I keep trying to make amends for what I did. I don't know how."

Yes, you do. Tell her the truth, a little voice inside me whispers.

I shudder inside, immediately rejecting the idea of Kelsey knowing the true crimes perpetrated at Forsyth weren't those witnessed by the average student body member.

They were saved for the elite.

CHAPTER TWENTY-EIGHT

Kelsey

I SPEND THE NEXT WEEK LOCKED AWAY IN A PASSIONATE RELATIONSHIP with my computer.

Seconds after I burst into her house with tears leaking out from behind my sunglasses, Val's "What the hell?" did little to soothe my ragged emotions. Nor did her "Do I have to kill him?"

"I'm never going to escape what I was," I sobbed briefly before rushing away to find the one place I could seek solace and resolve all my problems.

My writing.

I threw myself back into the story I thought I had plenty of time to complete before receiving a call that put an enormous burden on my exhausted shoulders. But it was one I gladly accepted by the time I hung up the phone.

My publisher contacted me to ask if it would be possible to move up the due date of my manuscript by over a month since another author I'm friendly with had been in a life-threatening automobile accident. I assured them it would be no problem before asking what kind of help the family needed.

As for the book, Pilar's struggles were almost resolved and she would emerge stronger but still not overall triumphant. In this installment of the Pilar Martell series, Pilar decides to try out for the swim team only to be told that she'll be kicked off if she's more than five pounds overweight. She's secretively and dangerously running laps around the cul-de-sac where she lives with trash bags strapped to her chest by duct tape, hoping to drop weight before weigh in.

Throughout the book—and with Val's expertise as a dietitian—I demonstrate the effects of malnutrition and dehydration. Pilar passes out in the water, almost drowning, during tryouts.

When questioned, she tries to deny it until the doctor talks to her privately. "I went through the same situation, Pilar. I feel your agony. But true happiness is found in what you accomplish for yourself, not because someone else decrees you don't fit a perfect mold." Dr. Reilly lays her hand across Pilar's compassionately. Pilar yanks her hand back.

"Do you? Then why haven't you stepped in when they've touched me? Shoved me? I'd have rather drowned than let this go on."

Suddenly Pilar feels another presence in the room. And there he is.

After typing the word "mold," the growling in my stomach makes me wonder if there are any Jell-O cups in the house. Stretching, I shove away from my desk and open the door to something even better.

The sound of a blender.

"Aren't you both supposed to be working today?" I tease Val and Darin.

"She lives," he cries. I smile in rueful acknowledgment over the fact I may have been here, but I haven't exactly been present since my aborted picnic in the park.

"And for the record, you've been in the cave a week." Val's voice holds more than a touch of amusement. "I hope whatever torment wave you were riding was productive."

"It'd better be." I quickly tell them about the call I got from my publisher.

"Oh, how horrible!"

"So, that deadline I wasn't under? I have four days to turn in the book for editing," I say grimly before taking a sip of a power smoothie Darin slides in front of me.

"Well, I have the perfect way to celebrate when you're done," Val announces.

"What's that?" I take another slurp of berry deliciousness that I know has all kinds of good things blended together.

"How do you feel about coming down to talk to the kids at Morgan's about your experience?" Val names the woman who runs the center she volunteers at. Most of the boys and girls there have suffered through some emotional devastation, whether that be the trauma of homelessness, drug-addicted parents, physical abuse, or even school bullying. "It might help them to know there's a path other than gangs, drugs . . ."

"Sex," Darin pipes in.

Val nods. "That too. I found out today one of our juniors, Melissa, is pregnant for the second time. We'll do all we can, but . . ." Her voice trails off, telling its own tale.

"There's only so many lives you can touch," I murmur, heartbroken.

"Exactly."

I tap my fingers against the counter. "Let me call Jim with an update on the manuscript and see if he can get some of my published books shipped down here to give away. But how about I come in at the end of the week to talk with Morgan? Get the lay of the land? See if there's a place for me there. That gives me plenty of time to finish, and then I can figure out what I want to say." And how I want to say it.

Val jumps out of her chair and runs toward me, her stomach bouncing like one of the balls Darin used to dribble on the court. "Jesus, hold on to my niece if you're going to move like that!" I joke right before she slams into me.

"You won't regret this," she promises me.

"I've never regretted anything with you," I murmur. Giving her one more tight squeeze, I pick up my drink. "It's time for me to make a quick call and head back to work."

"I'm dragging you out for dinner," Darin warns. "You're wasting away."

I blink a few times. "The thought of that is utterly incomprehensible but sweet of you to say, nonetheless." With a quick wave, I head back to my room to immerse myself again in a world I understand with every fiber of my being, a world where the girl doesn't end up with the boy or a perfect ending but the ending that fits the reality she lives in.

Five days later, Val and I are standing in the basketball courtyard behind the building that holds Le Cadeau, Morgan Evans's youth awareness program. The program built on the premise that each child is a gift is a nonprofit in an area of the city that needs its youth to have strength in themselves to avoid the overly abundant temptations awaiting them. Wide-eyed, I turn to Val and whisper, "I'm surprised Dare hasn't tanned your hide for coming down here while you're pregnant."

"What makes you think he hasn't? Or that I haven't enjoyed it?" Unable to stifle the laughter, we draw the notice of several of the older teens who are sitting on the nearby bleachers.

"Hey, Ms. Val!" one calls out. "How're you feelin'?"

"Big, Lena," Val calls back. "Want to do me a favor and round everyone who's here inside?"

"Can do," says the pretty blonde, who I notice with some shock is the second pregnant girl I've seen since I walked in the door. She pushes up off the bench and trudges away.

"Should I . . ." But Val stops me.

"These kids may be broken, but they have their pride. You'll learn that fast. Come on." She slings an arm around my shoulders. "Let's get you inside and set up."

But before we can move anywhere, a familiar face steps in front of us. "Kelsey? What are you doing here?" Lisa Perrault's bright smile beams at me.

I falter. I haven't responded to Benedict since his highly insulting comment at Audubon Park. I was too busy channeling my hurt and frustration into finishing my book. Now, knowing I have unfinished business left to deal with, here's his sister. What the hell am I supposed to say? "Um, hey, Lisa. I didn't know you volunteered here."

"I just started last week. I'm on a rotation through the program I'm working with at school. Every six months, they have me working at a new location in the inner city," Lisa announces proudly.

"Oh, that explains how you and Val didn't recognize one another?" Val didn't have a clue who this woman was when we saw her at Café Du Monde.

"Val?" I nod even as Lisa shakes her head. "I've heard about her from Morgan but haven't met her."

Val comes up behind me and shoves me inelegantly in the side. I barely hold back snarling at her before dryly introducing the two women. "Now do you remember my best friend, Val Macondo?"

Val steps around me and smiles. "Hey, Lisa, right? Morgan mentioned a 'Lisa' was volunteering here now. I didn't realize it was you. I've been off the last few days, or we'd have met officially sooner." The two women shake hands.

Lisa grins. "Have you been chaining her to her bed again? I know of someone desperate to reach her who's becoming more and more of a pain in the ass to live with by the minute."

Before Val can defend me, I speak up for myself. "I was under a tight deadline." *And I didn't feel like having your brother try to backpedal his comment about me still being broken*, but I rein that in. "One of the authors who publishes with the same press I do was in a terrible accident." At Lisa's horrified gasp, I nod.

"Oh, how horrible. Will they be all right?" Her concern is genuine.

"Eventually. But the worst thing he can do is look at a computer. Now he has time to recover from his concussion."

"And since you have a large number of overlapping readers, no one is going to be too disappointed." Val connects the dots for me.

"Exactly."

"So, is that why . . ." But Lisa doesn't get a chance to ask what I suspect she's going to because Morgan joins us.

"Kee?" Morgan is a tall, lovely redhead with a scar that runs from behind her right ear down her neck. Val told me she got it in college after she was brutally attacked coming home from a frat party. Instead of hiding, she returned to the city intent to help others realize they can survive no matter what life throws at them.

She's exactly the kind of person I want to know better.

"The kids are inside waiting for you. But before I forget, I need the address of your publicist." Morgan's face is awash in shock. "They sent so many books—and not just yours. There are books for all the children, regardless of age or gender."

I grin. Jim came through in a big way. "I'll be sure to leave it with you."

We all begin to make our way inside when Morgan lays her hand on my arm to stay me. "I just want to be sure that volunteering won't interfere with your writing schedule."

I stop in front of a set of clear glass doors. Turning toward the remarkable woman, I ask, "Have you ever felt like it'd be easier if you ran away? If you disappeared? If your life was over because the dejection you feel when you're alone is more rewarding than the time you spend with someone else?"

Morgan acknowledges my questions with a bob of her head.

"Then you understand I'll find time to ensure history doesn't repeat itself." With that, I push open the doors to the curious but wary faces.

I stand to the side while Morgan introduces me. "We have a new volunteer on staff. She's going to be working with Val closely and taking over Val's hours once she has the baby. I want to introduce you all to Ms. Kee. You all know the rules: treat her with respect unless she shows any disrespect. Then you come directly to me." All the kids in the room, from the oldest to the youngest, nod. The atmosphere relaxes when they realize I'm no threat. Teasing that ensues from a long-built trust commences.

"Ms. Val, you know you're not going to be able to stay away," one of the older boys sasses from the back.

Val laughs but admits, "Probably not. But see, Kee's my best friend. I figure if anyone's got a chance of keeping y'all in line, it's her."

"Kee? Thwat's a pwetty name," a girl with perfect pom-poms in her hair lisps through her missing teeth. I give her a beaming smile.

"Thank you. I chose it for myself," I reply.

That sets off a massive rumble around the room. "Cool! I want to be known as Dr. Ponch from now on. You know, like the lake," a boy calls out.

"Don't you mean Dr. Paunch? You know, like his stomach?" There are snickers around the room as a different boy in the back is pointed at. The first boy cackles.

I don't even crack a smile. "There's something you should know about me. I'll be your best friend or your worst enemy. But the one thing that will slide you right from one side to the other is cruelty. People used to try to break me every single day of my life. Sadness was my constant companion. So, you want to hang with me? Drop the attitude toward each other." I look over at Morgan, who's nodding.

"I deliberately didn't tell you about Kee because she will do that herself tomorrow. But you should know she's Kee Long, author of the Pilar Martell series." All the older kids in the room gasp. The younger ones twist around in confusion. Morgan explains, "These books are written from her soul, and now, there are several sets of them here because she gave them to us as a gift. Ms. Val asked—and Ms. Kee agreed—that tomorrow, she will talk about the inspiration behind that series. It's something she's never done before."

I break in, "But it's about understanding and respect. If you don't think that's cool, then maybe this isn't the place you want to be."

There's a lot of "I'll be here" and "Dude, you better not take my spot," but for the boy who was taunted earlier, it's like I'm standing in front of a mirror looking at myself fifteen years ago. But there's something twisted. The look in his eyes when he dares to make contact with mine hurts me. I don't know how to handle him without talking to Morgan. So, for now, all I do is take a deep breath and smile. "I hope you'll all be back."

When I turn, Lisa's standing right behind me. "You have no idea the strength you're about to give these kids."

Turning around, I glance back at the boy who was mocked earlier. He's off to the side where my books are stacked, touching the cover of one with a reverence I think I have when I see each one for the first time. "I think I understand better than you think."

Val and Morgan join us before we're swarmed by kids. But out of the corner of my eye, I keep trying to make eye contact with the boy to let him know he's not alone.

None of us are, even if we have doubts.

CHAPTER TWENTY-NINE

Benedict

Almost two weeks, at least twenty texts, and I'm no closer to reaching Kelsey than I was when she ran out of Audubon Park.

I fucked up.

After I let myself out of my study, Lisa was eager to ask me how my latest date went. I just shook my head. Less than an hour later, I sent my first text.

I'm sorry. Please talk to me.

What I lost sight of when my temper snapped over her absolute disbelief in herself was Kelsey still has a right to be angry with me. She doesn't know the truth. She doesn't know what could have happened to Lisa. She doesn't know what happened to me. She has no idea of the insults she keeps piling on me when she lumps me in with those pieces of shit from high school. I thought I was ready to face her in Savannah with a heartfelt but simple apology, but I factored none of her feelings in.

I was so wrong.

I can say "I'm sorry" a million times, but I've done a shit job at proving I don't mean to harm her again. And Kelsey's far from an idiot. She's protecting herself from me, from her past, and all the pain associated with it. Instead of patience while I figured out how to explain something I never thought I'd have the chance to, I erupted like I was the injured party.

In the meantime, I keep trying to reach her. I've had no success, and I'm completely miserable.

I can't let go, I think frantically as I begin to text her again. *Kels, I'm so sorry. I was wrong. Can we meet . . . ?*

I'm interrupted by Lisa walking into the kitchen, laughing. *I don't even remember what laughter feels like,* I think sourly. I keep typing, and then I erase the text I started to send.

I need to be open, apologize for something I didn't mean to say. Again. But how? How do I even begin to explain my asshole remark when I'm already on probation for the soul-shattering insult I hurled at her years ago?

I'm doing my best to ignore Lisa as she chatters away about the kids at her new volunteer center—not because I don't care, but because she's been talking about them nonstop. From what she's described, it's a great organization that focuses on destructive home life, bullying, and abusiveness in the school. Then I hear her side of the conversation.

"Nice job!" Lisa pauses. "That's incredible. And we're so thankful for everything with your publicist."

My ears pick up at that. *Publicist*? I close out the text app so I don't send Kelsey a bunch of gibberish. Instead, I open a Notes page and begin typing the idea for a new text while I blatantly eavesdrop.

"Right. Talk about a happy coincidence to see you at the youth center today." Lisa pauses before exclaiming, "I know, small world! No, that's crazy that Val and I only met for the first time. I don't know how much we'll work together. Morgan said she likes to spread us out. She called all-hands-on-deck because you were coming in." There's a pause where Lisa listens before a huge smile breaks out across her face. She turns partially away from me before gushing, "Thanks, Kelsey." *My Kelsey*? I straighten up, my phone clattering to the counter. Lisa continues blithely on as if she hasn't just earned an interrogation when her call ends, the likes of which I haven't given her since I was home from college break and realized she was dating.

"That means a lot. I mean that from the bottom of my heart. It's been my dream to work with kids who need extra emotional support. And the volunteer work I'm starting for Le Cadeau? It's my dream come true." Another pause. "Well, let's just say after you and Val left, the kids couldn't stop talking about the donation of your books." Another pause. "No, he spent his time reading and didn't interact with the others. I agree. So many of those kids are affected by those very issues. Have you given more thought to what you're going to . . . really?" Lisa starts jumping up and down like a kangaroo in the kitchen.

I'm more than a little scared, to be honest, even if I plan on attacking this particular doe as soon as she hangs up the phone.

"Okay. Fantastic. So, tomorrow around four? Wonderful! We'll see you and Val then! Bye, Kels!" Lisa hangs up the phone with a war whoop that I haven't heard since her days on the soccer field. Then she turns and stumbles.

"Uh-oh."

"Not exactly how I would have phrased it. You do realize I—"

"Was a complete ass? Yep," Lisa chirps.

I glare at Lisa like she's an opponent in the Lockwood boardroom.

"Val was arguing with Kelsey in the background that she should respond by telling you to 'go to hell' after one of your texts came in. Kelsey was conflicted," Lisa confides. "Whatever you did must have been monumental, brother."

"I said she was still broken," I admit morosely.

I should have been expecting the punch, but I wasn't. That's likely why Lisa managed to knock me off the stool and onto my ass. "Hey," I protest.

"You deserve to be called an asshole, Ben!" she shouts. "What the hell were you thinking?"

"I wasn't!" I yell back. "I couldn't stand her lumping me in with the people we graduated with!"

Silence descends on the kitchen. "Are you ever going to tell me the extent of what they did to you? Are you going to continue to carry the burden? The things you've held inside?" Lisa comes around the side of the counter and wraps her arms around me from behind. Her chin rests against my shoulder.

I stiffen. "What makes you think there are things I'm holding back?"

"What makes you think I'm an idiot?" she counters.

"Lisa," I begin jaggedly.

Her hand slides over mine from behind as her head rests on my shoulder. I don't stiffen until her thumb runs over the scar on my right hand. "It kept happening after you left."

Nausea churns in my stomach. I struggle to get away. Crawling in front of me, she grips my forearms to hold me in place. "Do you think they didn't tell me that's why I was spared, Benedict?"

I glance around the kitchen, searching for anything—a cobweb, a crumb—anything but the agony in my sister's eyes. "It's my burden."

"It's my salvation," she counters.

My eyes whip to hers. I find nothing but pools of love reflected back at me. "How could you believe I'd love you less if I knew?"

"Because Kelsey was a part of it." Just saying the words aloud relieves the weight sitting on my chest. My body sags into Lisa's.

"I guessed that."

"What?"

"You were on a mission, Ben. You hated Forsyth. Yet, you went back to every reunion? Either something—or someone—had a hold on you."

"You're too smart for your own good," I mumble.

"And you need help. You're the one who can't handle the past—not Kelsey. You can't keep sabotaging her happiness." Lisa lets me go, pushes to her feet, and turns to walk away.

"Lisa?" She stops. "I live with it just fine."

"You don't live with anything if you lash out at the people who will make you look back. Do you feel that way about me?" With that, she turns and leaves the kitchen. Her words hover in the air.

Shoving to my feet, I pick up the coffee in front of me to take a sip, but my stomach rebels at the idea of swallowing anything. I slam the mug down, and the force causes the handle to break off in my hand, leaving a small trickle of blood from the shard of chipped ceramic.

Aw, look at how well he's taking it.

What a good newbie. Don't hurt him too much. He still has to race this week.

Rough male laughter rasps at my ear, "You heard, Cap. So, no more of this." Another sharp movement that seems to bleed into another.

As they release my body from the hold, I refuse to let them have the satisfaction of hearing me cry out, so I bite down on my hand.

And only I notice the small trickle of blood . . .

Snapping out of the memory, I realize I need to talk to Cade. If there's one person who truly understands, it's him. And before I can beg my sister to get me entry into Le Cadeau, I need to have an excuse for why I snapped.

Because I can never admit what happened. Not to anyone who didn't endure something similar.

CHAPTER THIRTY

Benedict

A FEW HOURS LATER, CADE AND I SIT IN A CORNER BOOTH IN A SEEDY dive in the Quarter. I just got finished explaining everything that's happened since the night of the reunion. He's been remarkably silent, which, for my overly opinionated best friend, is a damn miracle. "I don't know what to do. How do I fix this?" I ask morosely.

"You're not going to like my answer."

"What?"

"You have to tell her."

I immediately shake my head. "No way. No how." It took everything left in the withering part of that long-ago defeated child to explain to my father and the president of the school why I did what I did. There's no way I can tell Kelsey what I never want to remember but can't seem to forget.

"And to find out tonight it was for naught? That Lisa still suffered some sort of hazing after I left Forsyth?" I shudder.

He holds up a placating hand. "I'm not saying tell Kelsey all of it. Hell, I'm not sure I could ever share that with a life partner. What we each lived through . . ." He shakes his head. "No one should have that in their head."

Since I agree, I don't bother responding. I tag my drink and lift it to my lips, waiting for him to continue.

"But Kelsey may not be able to separate what happened on your graduation day from the man you are long term without understanding. You were her friend, Ben, then, suddenly, you weren't."

"I was her friend a hell of a lot longer than—"

"It doesn't matter," Cade interrupts ruthlessly. "If you went by that logic, then you'd still be friends with—"

I cut him off. "I get your point." There's no way of that ever being the case. Ever. "So, I killed it all, every chance we had between us of ever being friends?" *Of more?*

"That's not what I said."

"That's what you implied," I snap back before taking a drink.

"Jesus, Ben. When did you lose your ability to think?" Cade drawls sarcastically. "Would a woman who's been so hurt by a man ever give him a shot if some part of her didn't care?"

My eyes widen a fraction as Cade sighs. "You're an idiot. From the moment you realized who she was, you should have straight up apologized. You have to get her beyond thinking you're the reason her life was such shit. From what you've told me, you were her safe harbor."

"All except one time," I say grimly.

He agrees. "Except that one time."

There's silence between us. "If I were her, I'd be holding back too—waiting to see if you've changed." I start to squawk, and Cade holds up his hand. "Man, I know you weren't like that, but think about it from *her* point of view. She thinks you flipped on her. She doesn't understand *why*." His emphasis on the last word finally penetrates.

"You mean I explain why I hurt her without . . ."

He finishes my thought. "Going into the details about everything that happened to you? Yeah." Grunting, he grabs his drink and tosses it back. "Though if this goes the distance, I suspect you'll end up telling her everything."

I shake my head emphatically, not at the idea of Kelsey and me, but at the thought of baring my soul that way. Cade gives me a half-amused, half-sardonic grin.

"We'll see. Now, what's your plan?"

"Talk to Lisa. Convince her to help me get in the same room as Kelsey."

Standing, Cade tosses a wad of cash on the table. "Then let's go find your sister."

When we get back to my house, Lisa's car is gone. "Come on in and hang out for a while. You can catch me up on what's been going on with you."

He shrugs. "Not much."

I walk over to the fridge and pull out a couple of beers. After I hand one over, we make our way into the living room. "You still with . . ." But I'm stuck on the name. Cade flies through women like they're diapers on a newborn baby.

Before I can even try to think of the name, Lisa's voice floats out from the kitchen. "Don't strain yourself, Ben. You work your brain hard enough at the office." Cade's eyes flare at the sound of Lisa's voice, but he doesn't reply to the blatant smackdown. Instead, he calmly lifts the bottle to his lips and sucks back some of the dark ale.

Lisa pokes her head in briefly. Our eyes connect—hers offering an apology for our earlier disagreement, mine hopefully conveying it isn't required. But when her gaze shifts to Cade, the look she gives him would fry an egg. She sniffs as if she's smelled something rotting in the kitchen.

Cade's words from the pub crawl insidiously through my brain. No one should have the kind of pain we've both lived through swirling in their memories. But how long have I been locked in my own head that I haven't been able to see what's staring me right in the face? The way Cade and Lisa circle each other with one holding a chair and the other a whip, it's so obvious she's keeping him at a distance to avoid being hurt.

Just like Kelsey's doing to me.

After tonight's conversation, I feel like an idiot for not noticing what's been in front of me for years. Like me, Cade's been so wary around someone he cares for—my sister—because it's a lot harder to expose your ghosts to someone who matters.

With the same exact reason as the one that keeps me screwing up my chances with Kelsey time and time again—complete and utter terror of their opinion. But now, I know what Lisa feels. I have an inside track that could help two people I love find their way to happiness.

Even if I can't be reunited with my own.

"Hey, Lisa," I call out. Footsteps pause in the hall. "Come here for a moment."

"What the hell are you doing?" Cade hisses as my sister makes her way back into the room.

"The same thing you both have done for me," I mutter to him as I stand and pick up my beer.

Walking to where Lisa braces herself in the entrance of the family room, I pass a hand over her dark hair before tipping her face up to meet mine. Softly, I tell her, "Maybe you both should just work things out. I'll be in my study trying to figure out a way to get Kelsey to talk to me."

It takes a moment for my words to penetrate. When it does, her small frame goes rigid. Her eyes immediately leap in Cade's direction. Cade's head is dropped beneath slumped shoulders. It's a defeated posture I know well as I've recently sat for hours in precisely the same position, wondering if the darkness that's surrounding me will ever lift.

Brushing a kiss on the top of my sister's head, I walk down the hall.

Along the way, I hear my name. Without turning, I call back to her, "I wouldn't leave Cade alone, Lisa. He might leave."

"You realize you just gave me the okay to go after your best friend?" She sounds like she's questioning my sanity.

I turn around and lean against the wall. Crossing my arms and my ankles, I give my sister a one-sided smile. "I can think of no one else in the world who I'd trust your heart with. And I can think of no one else who can find his." Pushing off the wall, I walk back in her direction. Out of the corner of my eye, I catch Cade in the doorway behind her, staring at us like we're insane. "He's the best man I know, and you're . . . you. I'm just sorry I had my head up my ass so long I didn't see it before now." Sincerity rings through my voice.

Indecision flickers across her face before she blurts out, "Stop texting Kelsey tonight. Promise me."

My brows lower into a *V*. "But, Lisa, I . . ."

Placing her hand on my biceps, she squeezes it. "I'll bring you to the center tomorrow. You need to hear what she has to say, Ben. You need to hear what it was like from her perspective and compare it to your own. Maybe then you can find the words to make things right."

"When did you become so wise?" I ask her.

Her head turns, and she locks gazes with Cade. "Right around the same time I realized that a broken engagement was the best thing that ever happened to me."

Cade lets out a quiet, "Damn."

I smile. "You said it yourself, buddy. If this goes the distance . . ."

"Fuck you, Perrault."

Lisa, quick as a whip, advises him helpfully, "Wrong Perrault to make that offer to."

Cade groans, but it's filled with laughter and something I haven't heard from him in years.

Hope.

"Good night, kids. Keep the noise down," I call out as I make my way toward my bedroom instead of my study because I don't need to stare at Kelsey's words. I need to be rested to face them.

"Night, Ben," Lisa calls back.

"Night, buddy."

With a grin, I enter my suite, wondering if Cade's going to be here tomorrow when Lisa and I leave for the center. For both their sakes, I hope so. It'd be nice if the hands on the clock of love stopped standing still for one member of this family.

CHAPTER THIRTY-ONE

Benedict

"What the hell was that about, Benedict? How could you do that to that poor girl? She saved you!" my father shouts at me, disgust in every line of his body.

"Dad." Just his name. Tears are falling fast and furious down my face. My heart is shredded because I saw what I did to Kelsey. My sweet Kelsey. My light.

"Listen to me. We will be returning to Forsyth today. Right. Now. You will make your apologies."

I shake my head frantically. "Not that." Please God, don't make me go back to hell when I've just escaped it.

He seems to grow in size as he storms at me. "You will do as you're told."

As he reaches out to grab—what, I don't know—I let out a shriek of primal fear. My hand flies into my mouth as I back away from him. That stops him in place. The blood drains from his face. "Ben? Son?"

"Don't make me. Please stop. Don't make me," I mutter around the skin I'm chewing on my right hand.

Harsh breathing is the only sound in the room for long minutes. Then a quiet, "Benedict, son?"

Son? I blink and find my dad reaching out for me—hand outstretched beseechingly. We're both on the floor of his study, and I'm curled in a corner.

"No, no, no," I moan. This can't be happening.

"Son, I need you to tell me that you know who I am," my dad says.

"Dad."

"That's right, Ben." His voice is overcome with emotion. "It's Dad. And I'll do everything I can to protect you."

Lips trembling, I say, "They said . . . they said . . ."

"What did they say, son?"

"Lisa." I just say her name.

That's when my father decides explanations can wait. He crawls on his knees until he can wrap me up in his arms and rock me back and forth.

I didn't mean to snuff out my light. I just had to keep someone else's burning.

CHAPTER THIRTY-TWO

Kelsey

"Words have the power to come back and haunt a person long after you've forgotten about saying them. Think about your favorite song. What kind of emotion does it make you feel?"

"Happy," one of the center kids calls out.

"Ready to dance," another yells.

"You're always ready to do that," one hollers. The room laughs.

"My favorite songs are the ones my nana sings. They're kinda soft and they're pretty," a little girl pipes up. The room goes quiet at her words.

"Some of the best songs are like that," I assure her. Her brown eyes brighten as I get close enough while I walk around the room to lay a hand gently on her shoulder. "But what if a song made you sad? Would you want to replay it over and over in your head? Unable to not hear the words?"

The chorus of "no" is overwhelming. "Then end the cycle right now. Because the words you say to each other matter. I can hear what was said to me when I was your age in my head just as clearly as if one of you said the words to me today."

My words ring out clear across the room. "I was humiliated. I tried to stay under the radar. I was physically assaulted. And guess what? Right now, even overhearing one harsh comment, I, too, can be transported back to my nightmare called high school. Is that what you want to be known as? Mean? A bully?"

I make my way back up to the table in the front of the room stacked with my books. Last night, Morgan pleaded for me to do an impromptu signing for these kids. "This is a unique way to drive your message home, Kee." I was concerned it would come off as pretentious, but Val was all for it. "It gives them motivation, Kelsey. Let them see what else is an option instead of the lives they're falling into."

I pick up the first of Pilar's stories. "You asked me how I started writing the Pilar Martell series. I had to purge what was still wounding me, what still had the power to control me. I wanted to make it so the people who hurt me didn't have the power to when I ran into them again, and I was sure I would."

Taking a deep breath, I meet Val's eyes. She nods, even as she swipes her fingers under her lashes. "You become who and what you are not only because of the things that happen around you, but because of things done to you. Learn from what's happened to me and become a better person, a better friend, a better human. Be the voice for people who can't." I stop talking to take the pulse of the room.

And that's when I spot Benedict leaning against the wall with an expression of awe mixed with pain.

Who the hell agreed to let him in here? I think furiously. But I know it must have been Lisa trying to mend the breach between us I still wasn't sure how to handle.

Because like I just told these kids, words hurt. And when they're said by the man who managed to lay inroads to your heart, they leave you with no obligation to be kind, no duty to be polite, and no responsibility to care for anyone's emotions but your own.

Pretending as if Benedict is nothing more than one of the motivational posters tacked up around the room, I return my attention to the reason I'm even standing in the room baring my soul to begin with—the kids of Le Cadeau. Some of them are smiling, some have expressions of mild distress on their face, but one—the boy from yesterday—looks like I simultaneously shot him even as I pumped his heart full of life-saving blood. It's hurt and pain, war and peace. It's like looking into a mirror.

Catching Val's gaze, I flick my eyes over to the boy. She gives an almost imperceptible nod, understanding my concerns. "Okay, everyone!" I clap my hands together. "Normally there are people who help me with this, but what I need you all to do is to line up . . ."

The sudden scraping of chairs overpowers my voice until Morgan lets out a sharp whistle. "Keep calm until Kee's done talking."

"Right, as I was saying. If you all line up, I'll be happy to sign the books I have here." I gesture behind me. "Ms. Morgan's going to take pictures to hang up around the center. With her approval, I was hoping we could name it after the title for the next book I plan on writing for Pilar. I just finished *Humility* and sent that one off to the publisher last week. My next one, I plan on calling *Strength*. That is if you all approve?" The murmur of excitement causes the same emotion to swell up inside me as well.

There's not going to be another chance for someone to take away my self-worth. The last chance for that happened at Audubon Park. I don't have to justify my emotional reaction to the bullying I endured. I won't apologize if Benedict can't understand my emotions or won't own up to the part he played. I know the hell I lived every single day, and if I can help one child be a better person because of it, I'm going to.

I don't owe anyone an explanation.

Moving around to the back of the table, I pick up the first book, open it to the title page, and look up into the smiling face of the anxious girl in front of me. "Hi, sweetheart. What's your name?"

"Mara," says the adorable girl with a missing front tooth.

"Can you spell that for me?" After she does, I carefully pen her name in the book in print so she can read it. "How old are you, Mara?"

"I'm six."

"So, this book may be old for you now. I want to make sure you have an adult's permission before you read it," I caution.

She nods. "Nana reads your books. She said I could get one, but I'm not allowed to read beyond the dead . . . deadi . . . what's that word?"

My heart melts. "Dedication. Do you know what that means?"

She shakes her head.

"When authors write a book, they often give a special thank you to the person who supported them while they wrote it. Did your Nana tell you who this one's dedicated to?" At the shake of Mara's head, I tip mine over to my best friend. "To two people. One is Ms. Val. She's my bestest friend in the whole world."

Mara's eyes get round. "Would she sign it too?"

I laugh and hand Mara a spare pen. "I bet she will if you ask her."

"Not until we get your picture," Morgan interrupts. "Mara, why don't you go behind the table with Ms. Kee."

Mara comes behind the table and wraps her thin arms around me. "Ms. Kee, can I ask a question?"

"Of course."

"Kee's not your real name, right?"

I swallow a lump in my throat as I recall how I chose the name Kee Long. "No, sweetheart. It isn't."

"Why not? If you wrote this book, why's your real name not on it?" Ah, the beautiful simplicity of childhood before reality spoils it.

"Because, sweetheart, sometimes people can be not so nice, so you have to come up with a special name to protect yourself," I try to explain simply.

The little boy next in line says boldly, "I like it. It reminds me of the name King Kong." He lets out a roar to the delight of the other kids, who laugh.

My eyes drift to Benedict, who is still. He's as pale as the white wall supporting him. "Yes, I guess it does kind of remind you of King Kong." Turning my attention back to Morgan and Mara, I say, "Now smile and say 'strength'!"

We both do before she scrambles off. Soon, I'm onto the next boy, the one who thought my pen name was cool.

Damn right it is.

An hour later, the last child approaches. It's the boy I saw in the audience earlier. I don't hesitate before standing and walking around the table. I hold out my hand. "I'm Kee. I noticed you in the audience."

He mumbles something. I bend down, not letting go of his hand. "Darlin', I'm sorry. If it's just me because it's been so loud in here, I'll apologize. But I didn't catch your name."

Lifting his head, I see he has one blue eye and one brown, and the brown appears to have either a faint birthmark surrounding it or a bruise. More clearly, though still softly, he says, "I'm Max."

"It's nice to meet you, Max," I say sincerely.

He shrugs as if indifferent, but I see a light flush cover his neck. A neck with small skin tags on it, I notice. "Tell me, Max, what do you like to do?" I ask casually while reaching for the last of every book.

He greedily takes in the stack I'm accumulating in front of me. "I love to read. Like, a lot."

"What grade are you in?"

"I'll . . . I'll . . ."

"Take your time," I say softly.

He rushes out. "I'll be going into ninth grade in the fall, ma'am."

"Kee," I correct him. "Or Ms. Kee. I'm going to be around the center quite a bit."

"But no one wants to be around me 'cause I'm too ugly," he blurts out. "Even my momma swears I have a face that would break a mirror." And a tear I'm sure he'd rather die than surrender slides out of one of his unusual eyes.

And when that happens, my heart shatters into a million pieces. How did I think I could be healed by writing a bunch of words when there are children who need to see there are people who will stand behind the things they say?

"Max, why don't you join me over here?" I cajole softly.

Slowly, the teen shuffles around the table, his whole body strung tight in anticipation of another rejection. In his hands, there's a dog-eared copy of *Betrayal*—the first book I ever wrote. "What was your favorite part of the story?" I ask him, nodding at the book in his hand.

"The first time Pilar stands up for herself," he answers without hesitation. Then, in a moment I know I'll never forget, he begins to quote me to me, "I hope the time I spend enduring this is guiding me toward something. Otherwise—"

I join in, "What's the point of the struggle? The suffering? Is there a life beyond this pain?" Without thinking, I reach out to grip Max's free hand.

He shudders as if touch is a foreign concept to him.

"There is." Tears clog my voice as I speak to the young teen who's hurting in ways I know intimately. "I found the way to the other side."

"Can you show me the way to get there?"

I shake my head. "But I can talk with you about the tools I learned to get me through."

"You'd do that for me?" he asks in disbelief.

"Absolutely," I say firmly. "I wish I had a place like Le Cadeau to come to when I was your age. Who knows if it would have made a difference?" I squeeze his hand, then begin to loosen my grip. But suddenly his tightens with such a strength, my eyes fly up to his.

"Do you know what Le Cadeau means?"

I nod. "The gift. All of you are, you know. Not just to Ms. Morgan or Ms. Val, but to people you haven't met yet."

"I'm not sure if I believe that," he says starkly. He tugs his hand away and pushes his straggly hair away from his face.

"You will when you're ready to." I let that sink in for a moment before I reach for the pen. "Do you want me to sign your book, Max?"

He nods and hands it over. I touch the worn cover reverently, knowing this is a beloved treasure while I think of the right things to say to a boy who needs to feel worthy and to give him the strength to go on to his tomorrows where there might not be people to help cushion the pain of his struggles and celebrate his triumphs. With gentle care, I flip to the title page.

And I write.

This isn't a quick note. I take my time writing a message to a boy whose soul touched mine in a place where in a perfect world no one should ever meet—on the hunting ground for bullies. I know we're strangers, but we're not when it comes to the hurts of our hearts. When I'm done, my not-so-perfect penmanship has covered the front and back of two pages. I blow lightly on them before I turn to hand him his precious treasure. Then I turn to the stack in front of me and begin writing. When I'm done, each book in the series has a quick message of encouragement.

There's an awestruck look on his face. I bite my lip to hold the tears at bay. "Let go of the words they throw at you. Don't keep them inside. Don't let them eat at your soul, and you'll be just fine, Max." Sliding the books in his direction, I stand and wait for his reaction.

His lips tremble before he picks up the books, turns, and walks away. He gets halfway across the room before he stops. "Ms. Kee?"

"Yes?"

"How long did it take before the words they said to you didn't matter?"

They'll always matter. I don't say that aloud. Instead, I say, "They started to matter less when I began to write." I nod to the books in his hands.

He offers me a fleeting smile, but a smile, nonetheless, before exiting the room. Dropping the pen I'm still holding, I sag against the table and rub a hand over my heart. "Jesus. I feel like I just relived my nightmares. Only I'm awake."

"I now have a better understanding of what your life was like during high school. Is that what you felt like?" My head snaps up to see Benedict in the doorway. His expression is somber. Intuitively, I know he must have overheard my conversation with Max.

Part of me feels like a private moment was violated, but another part of me wants him to understand how deep my scars run. "Yes."

He slowly approaches until he's a few feet away. I can't read the expression on his face. "Then, to be honest, I'd have wanted much more than you to shove your success down our damn throats. I'd have wanted you to slice them instead."

He closes the distance between us before reaching for my hand while I try to pick up my jaw from the floor as I process what he said.

CHAPTER THIRTY-THREE

Kelsey

"Let me apologize," he rasps.

I try to turn from him, but he won't let me. I tug my hand away and wrap my arms around myself protectively. My eyes close instead as a barrier of protection as conflicting emotions play tug-of-war with my heart. "This seems like a conversation we've had before. It didn't turn out very well." Glancing at him beneath my lashes, my lips twist cruelly. "After all, I'm still dam—"

"Don't," he begs, interrupting. "Please. I'm so sorry for what I did—then and now. There are reasons, and you deserve to know what they are."

I hold firm as he steps closer, my arms still wrapped around my body to ward off the blows I'm sure are to come. As Benedict speaks, I brace myself.

"I have wronged you in so many ways. It's laughable to ask you to give me another chance. But I am. I need to be able to explain. You deserve to understand why."

"What you don't know is I'm tired of fighting you, of fighting myself. I'm so tired of being wounded over and over when I try to live normally. It's just easier to live behind my barricade. But you? For some reason, my defenses are weaker when it comes to you," I admit. Ignoring the flare of his eyes, I go on. "I can't see the point of subjecting myself to the same repetitive cycle of being damaged again by a hurt I didn't invite or earn. Is it always going to be like this, Ben?"

He's already shaking his head before I'm through speaking.

"It won't. I promise."

I study him silently, searching for some indicator this isn't another opportunity for him to knock me off my feet again. Instead, I find the same signs of restless nights I've been suffering that I, at least, was able to cover up with makeup: dark circles under his eyes, a paleness to his skin, a tightness around his mouth. Combined with the attempts he's made to reach me in the last two weeks, I weaken.

And besides, he's right. I deserve to know why, so I can put my past behind me where it belongs. And that may include him.

"One chance. And we'll talk about the past and why you hurt me, or you can walk out that door right now."

I barely complete my sentence before Benedict has stepped into my space. His fingers are dragging down my face. "The way I feel about you has kept me up more than my fair share of nights. And not just in the last few weeks," he starts.

But I remain firm despite the part of me that wants to capitulate to the young girl begging me to throw myself in his arms. "This is your last chance," I warn him. "I explained why I hid in Savannah. You'll talk to me about what ruined what I thought was our friendship, or I'm walking away for good. I don't need to restart what I managed to leave behind." I wrench myself away and move back to the window overlooking the courtyard.

"And what was that? What did you leave behind, Kelsey?"

"So much pain. It's a wonder I couldn't fly when the burden was lifted." I speak softly but fill the words with so much emotion.

I feel him come up behind me. He cautions me, "I can't promise we won't feel pain, even if we fight."

Spinning around, I agree, "There's fighting, and there's being cruel. What you said . . ."

"Was my inability to deal with what happened back then. Once we talk it out, I hope you'll understand." His voice is sad in a way I've only heard when discussing the past.

I cock my head to the side, trying to read him. He shakes his head. "It isn't for here."

"Okay? Then when?" I demand.

Pushing a strand of hair back, he says, "Start again with me. Get to know me now. Then when you feel like maybe you trust the man I am, and I know the woman you've become, we'll lay it all out."

I give it careful thought before nodding. A relieved expression crosses his handsome face. I ask cautiously, "What does this mean, getting to know each other?"

"I don't want to ruin my chances at having you forgive me—and I hope like hell you'll let me make plans soon—but I actually have to go back to work before Ryan fires me." His eyes search mine with concern that I'll be upset we're not racing out the door into the sunset on a white steed. The reality is, I can use the time to get my head on straight.

I decide to lighten the mood. "I know your boss and his family. Somehow, I get the feeling he's got this romantic streak in him."

"For his husband, maybe. Normally, he's just barking orders at the rest of us." Benedict's humor washes over me even as I begin gathering my belongings. He comes to stand next to me. "At first, he courted me. Tantalized me with seductive words like hundred hour work weeks and international cases."

I slap my hand over my mouth to hold back the chortle that wants to escape. Ben lets out a long-suffering sigh. "Now, we only spend time at the office. It's like I'm his dirty little secret."

"I'd have to argue that, Counselor. I do believe he took you to a boutique—in a hired car, no less. And you weren't even looking your best at the time. It was so romantic. All you needed were roses, and you would have been a whole new take on *Pretty Woman*." I burst into laughter at the dumbfounded look on his face.

I'm too busy trying to regain my composure to realize Benedict's tugged me into his arms. By the time I do, I gasp. "Just for that, I'm never going to bring you roses," he teases.

"That's okay. I prefer daisies," I say automatically.

"Pink ones, if I remember correctly," he murmurs, alluding to the fact he's already seen me naked. *Damn.*

"No. No bringing up that night," I warn him, forcing myself to slide out of the warmth of his embrace. "Go, do whatever it is Ryan makes you do at work." I point to the door.

The corner of one side of his mouth lifts before he backs away. I let out a breath I didn't even realize I'd been partially holding when he turns away. What scares me is when he says, "Isn't it difficult protecting such a soft heart?"

I square my shoulders. "I'm strong enough." I refuse to admit he's right.

He nods. "I don't doubt it. I was just thinking after all this time, maybe you might want some help."

"If I find someone worthy of it, I'd hope they'd hand me theirs, and they'd have mine. So, I'd still be carrying the burden of a heart, just not my own."

What crosses over his face makes me glad we're going to have this time getting to know each other. Because at that moment, I see pain, hatred, and anger mixed with love, passion, and hope.

What happened to you, Ben? I want to shout. But I hold it back. Instead, I ask, "So, I suppose I should answer one of your many texts?"

He whips out his phone. His fingers fly before I hear a ping from the depths of my purse. "Answer that one. I'll talk to you later. I'm heading back to work." With a wink, he leaves me standing in the common room of Le Cadeau, wondering if I'm a fool for jumping on the spinning wheel again. Reaching into my bag, I pull out my phone.

There's a text waiting from Ben. Unlocking my phone, I open it.

Meet me at Café Du Monde tomorrow morning at 7:30. I'll buy the beignets.

Part of me wonders if I am a fool because I respond, *You'll buy the iced coffee too.*

Within seconds I get a single word back: *Deal.*

For just a second, I'm taken back to when Ben would ask if there was anything he could bring me when I'd be tutoring him. "A soda? A coffee? A bottle of water? We talked for over an hour, Kelsey. You have to be thirsty," he protested.

"I don't need you to buy things for me, Ben," I told him.

"Then consider this something I want to do. Friends do nice things for one another. Now tell me what you want to drink?"

I told him water because I figured this way no one would realize the drink would be for me if he were seen with it.

What happened between the boy who wanted to nurture me that I fell for and . . . I don't even let myself think of it, knowing I'll back out of coffee if I do. And for whatever it's worth, Ben's right. I need to trust him enough now to talk honestly about my questions about the past.

And to believe his answers when he gives them to me.

Eventually.

When the time is right.

Because I want to get to know the man a little more before I determine if I'm going to hold him accountable for the acts of the boy.

CHAPTER THIRTY-FOUR

Benedict

A WEEK LATER, I'M FEELING A RUSH FLOW THROUGH MY VEINS. IT'S different from the one I feel when I'm with Kelsey; it's just as powerful but in a completely different way. "If you'll initial here, here, and sign here, Mr. Larruscain," I ask politely, while inside, I'm running around the boardroom table with my hands raised above my head in sheer ecstasy. The hawklike features of the chairman and CEO of the company we've been brokering the deal with over the last several years break into a smile before he picks up the pen next to him. Murmuring in Spanish, he scratches his initials where I had my paralegal flag and scrawls his name with a flourish.

It's done.

I wait for the small stack of final contracts to be passed to me and lay them facedown in the folder marked TO BE FILED. Standing, I hold out a hand. "Congratulations, sir. This is an exciting time for you."

"Yes. It will leave me much more time for family." He clasps my hand, laying a wrinkled but still firm one on top of it. This is a man who stood at the helm of a superior company for over forty years. He made the best decision for the company's immediate future while setting it up for long-term success. I accept his unspoken thanks for the work I did to help this deal to close.

I turn and shake Ryan's hand. "Congratulations to you as well. I see extraordinary things for the future."

"An excellent job, Ben," he compliments before he goes off to talk to the members of the Larruscain team.

I shake my head. "It was a team effort, as always. It always is." Carol's moved next to us after offering her congratulations to the senior Larruscain.

"And that's why Ryan insisted we invite the entire team to a party to celebrate tonight," Lynne—who was present to oversee the monetary transactions as third-party broker—slips in smoothly.

"I'll be sure to pass that along," I assure her.

Ryan, having just finished talking with the members of the Larruscain team, joins us. "Did we reserve the entire courtyard at Brennan's?"

Carol nods. Ryan says, "Excellent. I invited Bastien and his team to join us as well."

"Of course. I had planned to invite them when you finished speaking with them."

Then Ryan turns an innocent smile at me. "You should invite Kelsey, Ben. I'm sure she'd love to get to know your coworkers."

"You're an ass," I retort immediately. It's not that I don't want Kelsey by my side, but the party tonight might be taking a step she's not ready for. Even though we've had breakfast or lunch every day since we were at the center last week, we're slowly getting to know one another. We've caught up on big things and little things that have had no importance. I talked to her about how I met Cade in college, starting a friendship that led to a possible relationship between him and my sister. I had her howling when she found out I not only short-sheeted his bed in college, I replaced his can of shaving cream with spray hair dye right before a formal ring ceremony.

"How did he retaliate?" she asked as if there was no question. Which there wasn't.

"Let's just say my head was never quite so smooth for our next swim meet," I admit with a laugh.

Kelsey laughed as she sipped her iced coffee.

As for me, I've learned Kelsey still has a passion for Hemingway, and she loves modern poets. "They have a perspective on humanity that is unparalleled and isn't biased by anything." She also has "an unhealthy obsession for clothes, Ben. Really. I could live in sweats, but I *need* to shop like some people need food. Or water." Frowning thoughtfully, she tacked on, "Maybe air."

"No wonder why you and the shop owner at Easy On Me hit it off." I grinned, taking a drink of my club soda.

She scooped up a small bite of food before shrugging. But there was a light in her eye I hadn't seen since we used to argue about the merits of whether there was such a thing as too many adjectives to describe a noun in a sentence.

It was just dumb luck Ryan and Jared showed up while we were enjoying jambalaya during lunch yesterday. Kelsey happened to be shoving her bowl under my chin to catch my lunch from landing on my shirt. "You tend to wear too much food, Counselor," she teased me right before her beautiful gray eyes got enormous in her face. "Um, hello," she said, her voice uncertain.

And there was Ryan. Jared, I didn't mind so much. Shoving us over, they ordered a couple of bowls of jambalaya for themselves. I kept giving Ryan killer looks for crashing my date. Unfortunately, I couldn't do the same to Jared, who got along with Kelsey like they were long-lost best friends.

"Hold on—" Lynne lifts her hand. "Ben's dating someone, and you didn't say anything?" She immediately punches her former boss in the shoulder. I feel infinitesimally better until Carol snaps, "Can the two of you behave? We're in the middle of a business meeting."

Chastised, we all look at her, abashed. "You really should invite her, Ben. She'll enjoy seeing Jared again," Ryan encourages.

Suddenly, I'm the one who's rubbing my arm. I glare at Carol. "What was that for?"

"That's for Jared—who doesn't even live here!—getting to meet someone you're dating and I haven't."

"Tira's met her too," Ryan adds helpfully.

Carol bares her teeth, and suddenly, I'm terrified the marketing department is going to revolt.

I shoot Ryan a fulminating look. "Listen, I'll call her. I'm not putting any pressure on her though."

He nods. "Fair enough. I think you're going to be pleasantly surprised."

I'd love it if I were. Giving my bosses a quick grin, I grab the files so I can head back to my office. "It was a good day."

"No, it was an excellent one," Ryan corrects. He rubs his hands together. "Now, go find out about your woman, and let's celebrate."

I only wish I could call Kelsey my woman, I think glumly. As I make my way back to my office, I stop by my senior paralegal's desk and hand him the files. "Great job. There's going to be an invitation from the bosses . . ."

"It's already in our inbox." Vince grins. "I, for one, am not above drinking martinis on the company dime."

I laugh. "Why does this not surprise me?" I slap him on the shoulder. "Thanks for all your hard work."

"My pleasure, boss. Let me get these filed, then do you mind . . ."

I shake my head, laughing. "Go. Head on over to the party as soon as those are scanned, emailed, and filed."

Vince scrambles to organize the piles of documents. I know before I step foot out of the office, all the principals will have an electronic copy of the contract in their inbox. It's what makes him utterly invaluable to Lockwood Industries and me.

Entering the sanctity of my office, I pull my cell out of my jacket pocket. Flicking the switch on the side to turn it off Silent, I unlock it to see a text from Kelsey.

Darin and Val are going out for a date night tonight. I know today's been a long one for you? Want me to cook dinner?

My heart is pounding in my chest. Earlier in the week, Kelsey told me all about her plans to buy a home. Laughingly while enjoying a mouthful of shrimp, she explained, "I love the time I get to spend with Val and Darin until the baby's born, but soon, they're going to need the space I'm taking up."

Taking a sip of my drink, I asked, "It's not crazy with three adults living there?"

"Nope. Val and I lived together our senior year off campus. With the amount of time Darin spent there, it was like having a third roommate." She snickered. "There were ballplayers in and out of our place constantly. I distinctly remember telling Darin that I wasn't feeding a basketball team." Her head cocked to the side. "What's that look on your face?"

I tried for a look of innocence. "What look?"

"That look that is a cross of remorse and annoyance."

I reached across the table for her hand. "Likely my regret that I didn't get to spend that time with you. And irrational jealousy that some no-name ballplayer's been lucky enough to have you cook for him, and I haven't," I teased.

Kelsey opened and closed her mouth. My eyes narrowed. "What?"

"Well, one of them wasn't quite so no-name," she hedged. Naming a former NBA star-turned-coach among the guys who are tight with Darin, she shrugs at my amazement. "Basketball was a big thing at Pepperdine," she reminded me before tacking on, "You should have seen us line up to get student tickets. We'd camp out overnight during playoffs. Some people would even bring the couch down from their dorm room!"

Leaning forward, our hands still clasped, I brushed her fingers with my lips. "I love you had that," I admitted.

Her brows lowered in question. I clarified my response. "The whole college experience."

"If it weren't for Val and Darin, I honestly don't think I would have," she admitted. "I was too withdrawn. It took a long time for me to build up my confidence."

"Well, just so you know, you can always cook for me anytime. I'm definitely not as high maintenance as any of those college guys," I teased her gently.

She laughed before shoving my hand away.

Now, staring down at my phone, even with the thrill of success still racing through me, I wish I didn't have to attend the party at Brennan's. There's nothing more I'd like to do than spend the night enjoying a quiet evening with Kelsey. Ryan's words ring in my head. Before I know it, I'm typing, *How about joining me for a last-minute work event?*

Tossing my phone on my desk, I lay my stack of files down. A few moments later, it pings with an incoming text. *Can you be a little more specific? Is this the kind of event where I need to find a black-tie dress in under an hour and kill you later?*

I burst out laughing. I should have known to have been more specific to a writer, especially one with a clothing obsession. *You have an incredible imagination.*

Within seconds I get her reply. *And the ability to do mean things to you in print. Remember that, Ben.*

With a grin, I type, *We just closed the big deal we've been working on. The company is paying for everyone involved to go to a place near the office called Brennan's. We'll all be in work attire.*

Congratulations! Is this the Chinese/Italian food on your suit deal?

I snort out loud at her response. *I'm never going to live that down. Yes. It's finally done.*

Let me know when and where to meet you.

I'm about to type when another text comes in. *And Ben, I'm so thrilled for you. I know you worked hard for this.*

The warmth of her words steals through my body and my soul.

The way they always have.

Quickly, I look up and then paste in the address to Brennan's in our chat before I begin to tie up a few loose ends so I can celebrate this incredible success for all of Lockwood Industries.

A few hours later, I'm standing with a glass of bourbon in my hand when a vision glides into the courtyard. Amid a sea of black, dark blue, and dark gray suits, the silvery gray of her sleeveless dress stands out like a beacon. My breath catches as her hair gleams like luxurious mink under the lights strung overhead as her head swivels from right to left. Then all the breath leaves my body when our eyes meet. I almost fumble my drink when she slowly smiles at me as she continues to weave her way through the bodies to make her way to where I'm standing.

"Hey," Kelsey says breathlessly. Reaching up, she brushes a kiss on the underside of my jaw. "Sorry I'm late. It was impossible to find parking."

My arm slips around her waist as naturally as breathing. "I'm just glad you were able to make it." I curl her close for a one-arm hug.

"If this party is anything to go by, it seems my earlier congratulations were fairly lukewarm," she teases. "Either that, or is Brennan's code for the employee cafeteria?"

I let loose a laugh that has several people turning their heads. "With the amount of time we spend eating here, we should negotiate an employee discount," I tease in return. "You look . . . beautiful isn't the right word, Kelsey. Luminescent, perhaps?"

Her head ducks shyly as a stain of color brightens her cheeks. "I . . . thank you. I hoped this would be okay. I looked online to see what people normally wear here. It wasn't much help." She frowns, making her so adorable. I want to kiss her, claim her, in front of everyone here so they know she's mine. But I can't. I don't have that right. Not yet, anyway.

The hand still holding my drink comes up next to her face. I run my thumb along her jaw. Her eyes flare in response. The heat between us has been simmering. Each time we've left each other, my lips have met hers in some way: a sweet brush, a quick press, or a delicious taste that leaves me aching for more. I want nothing more than to sink inside her luscious body again, but I owe her everything before that. Well, as much of it as I'm able to surrender.

So, after the barest of caresses, I've walked away with nothing but Kelsey on my mind, every moment, every second.

Leaning down, I brush her nose with mine. A puff of air escapes her lips. "Have dinner with me tomorrow night at my place? I was going to ask you to dinner tonight before the party came up—somewhere quiet so we can talk. And then I got your text."

The black of her pupils eclipses the gray of her eyes as they dilate. We're suspended in our own world, lost in this moment, in each other. Centuries of time could be racing by us, and I don't think either of us would notice. She steps closer, her curves fitting all my hollows. Her whispered "Yes" sets me aflame.

I barely restrain myself from bending her back over my arm to show her what she does to me. Instead, I step back. Loosening the band I have around her waist, I hold my arm out for her to slip hers through. "Come on," I grate out.

At her quizzical gaze, I lean in slightly. "It's either introduce you to a few of my colleagues or do something completely inappropriate."

"Well, we can't have that, can we?" Her voice is rich with laughter.

"For now, Kels. For now," I growl softly as we approach one of the lawyers on my team and his partner, who works in marketing.

The wicked smile she sends me tells me she wholeheartedly agrees.

CHAPTER THIRTY-FIVE

Kelsey

THE NEXT NIGHT, I PULL UP TO THE ADDRESS BENEDICT TEXTED ME. I'm remarked at how close of a drive it is to Val's. "I didn't know he lived in the same general area of town."

Darin advised me, "The homes on his side of the park are stunning but have such low turnover. If you found one over there, I'd tell you to snatch it up—even a fixer-upper."

Parking my car in the circular drive, I briefly sit to admire it before sliding out. The decor screams New Orleans to me with the herringbone-patterned brick driveway, the immaculately painted wood railing on two levels accenting the Confederate blue paint. I'm a little surprised I don't see a historical plaque as I approach a front door that's, oh wow, lit by gas lamps.

Someone went through a hell of a job restoring this place the right way, I think admiringly.

Before I ring the discreet brass bell, I do a quick check of my outfit. Even though Benedict said casual, I decided on the royal blue slip dress and matching blue heels I bought the day I went to Easy On Me. With a silver bracelet my grandparents gave to me gleaming in the twilight, I'm about to announce my arrival when the door flies open in front of me.

I take a step or two backward when Lisa bounds out. "Hey, Kelsey! Good to see you again. You look beautiful. I'm just on my way out. I'm meeting up with someone." She leans in and gives me a quick hug, which I automatically return. Her brows wiggle, which causes me to burst into laughter, relaxing me when I didn't know I needed it. "If you go straight back, Ben's in the kitchen. Ignore the mess." Blasting me with a friendly smile, she scurries past me toward the cute Mini Cooper parked on the curb.

My head is reeling. I take a deep breath to steady myself. The intimacy of the evening hits me. Benedict cooking dinner for me at his home? Never in the juvenile fantasies I had about this man did I ever contemplate something like this being so incredibly sexy. Then I remember his words. *I had planned to ask you to dinner—somewhere quiet so we could talk . . .*

My stomach roils, anxious. I hope the small pouch can tolerate consuming some of what he's going through the trouble of cooking. Crossing over the threshold, I close the door just as Ben comes forward dressed in a button-down and dress slacks. He looks as if he just stepped off a live cooking show, not as if he's been the one to slave over a hot stove. But damn. I just inhaled a good whiff of his cologne. I swear that's what makes me babble, "Something smells delicious."

His smile ratchets the pounding of my heart up a notch. "I thought I heard Lisa talking with someone." He leans against the door jamb, intuitively giving me space to absorb the fact we're alone in his home. It's our first time together in a nonpublic place since our night together in Savannah.

Breathe before you pass out, Kelsey, I scold myself. I exhale entirely before informing him. "I was just about to ring the bell, but she told me to come in. She's like a whirlwind. Does she always have that much energy? I don't recall being much older than her, but I'm pretty sure I feel . . ." I pause to find Benedict smiling at me.

"Ancient? That's the way she makes me feel most of the time. My little sister has enough energy for four people. It's a good thing she volunteers at the center. I think the kids are the only thing that can tire her out." Pushing away from the frame, he walks toward me, his hand extended. "You offered to cook dinner last night. Do you enjoy it?"

"I do. I've never had any complaints." I can't help the way my heart skips a beat as he closes the distance between us.

"Come on. I'll give you a quick tour, and then you can tell me if there's anything you don't want in your pasta." His hand touches mine before he gives it a quick squeeze.

"Wow, a classy joint. I can custom order off the menu."

Winking at me and giving my hand a quick tug, Benedict says, "You have no idea. Now, let me tell you about the house. Although it looks historical, it's a fairly new build from 2004. The owners lived through Katrina and subsequent storms. They decided they were done with New Orleans. Despite the number of years since then, I still got it for a steal."

"Was the house damaged?" Hurricane Katrina is the most destructive storm to strike Louisiana. It wouldn't surprise me if I were given a litany of items that needed to be repaired. I'm shocked when Ben shakes his head.

"Not a single thing. The owners decided they didn't want to live with the uncertainty anymore, so they moved back north." His voice takes on a note of empathy. "Despite my realtor telling me I could have likely negotiated more, I couldn't do it. This was my dream home, Kels. They were a lovely retired couple who had just put the finishing touches on it when Katrina hit."

"Where do they live now?" I ask casually as I run my hand over the back of the warm brown leather sofa that dominates the room.

"North Carolina," he answers immediately. I begin to smile, but his next words wipe that right off my face, leaving me free-falling from a multitude of feelings. "There was someone from Forsyth who was a few years younger than we were—Chad Zhang. He's a realtor up there. I touched base with him through my family to explain the circumstances. He and the other realtor reduced their commissions to get them in a home."

I remember Chad Zhang. While not as overt in his distaste for me as others were, he still didn't try to curtail the bullying that drove me to the brink of all reasonable sanity levels time and time again. Pulling slightly back, I dig my shoes into the plush area rug. "What are we doing?" I whisper suddenly, interrupting Benedict's explanation that the porch wraps around the front and both sides of the house.

He stops and turns to face me. "What do you mean?" Confusion is written all over his handsome face. It hurts, physically hurts, to look at it. I duck my head so my hair falls to cover my face. Warring emotions of fear and pain come crashing into me.

"This was why I left that morning in Savannah, why I keep running away. I don't want to live in the past. I don't want to make promises. I don't want regrets. I don't want to feel things I've learned to lock away and subdue. I want to feel confident and successful—the things I could never feel while being tormented every day in high school."

Even by this man.

My voice quivers. "I thought I could do this, but I can't. I have to go." His expression is shocked, allowing me the chance to rip my hand away. I start to walk purposefully back to the door when a strong arm wraps around me from behind.

"Will you come with me to one room long enough for me to give you the apology I owe you and to explain? Then I won't stop you from leaving—if that's what you want." Benedict's words are a breath whispering across my head.

I want to shake my head in denial. I want to refuse him, but flashes of the time I've spent with this Benedict Perrault cause me to pause. Stepping away, I turn around and say, "I reserve the right to walk away, Ben."

"And all I can do is pray to God you don't. Please, give me a chance to show you the heart of my home. It might help . . . maybe you'll understand." Benedict steps forward and reaches for my hand again. Bypassing the dining room, set for an intimate dinner for two, we pass through a set of double French doors into a study lined with bookcases. Dropping my fingers, he invites, "Feel free to look around."

I take him up on it. Because this, this is the room that feels like the Benedict I've had the chance to get to know: smart, sharp, intense. Masculine. Dark wood plays off bright light streaming in the windows. There seem to be hundreds of books interspersed with family photos. I pick up a silver-framed photo of him and Lisa taken on the beach. It doesn't look too old. "When was this taken?" I turn and face the picture toward him.

He smiles. "We went to Tybee Island with Mom and Dad for their anniversary a few years ago." A soft protective look drops over his face whenever he speaks of his sister.

I can't help but react to it. My fear begins to ebb away. "You two are close."

"We are. I'd do *anything* for her, Kels." There's something profound in that statement, but I don't touch it right now. Turning, I place down the frame and continue my turn around the room until I stop dead.

"The worst thing that's happening to you is the best thing that will ever happen to someone else. All you can do is move past it. After all, if life were meant to be easy, I'd have already won the game." I read aloud my own words. Words etched on a small piece of glass sitting in Benedict's study.

Words I used in my first book, *Betrayal*.

"I thought you didn't know who I was?" I turn to him accusingly, my lips trembling.

"What do you mean?" Ben's long stride brings him to me. He runs a finger down my cheek.

"I used these exact words in my first book."

"And you also gave them to me the first time you helped tutor me. Did you think I'd forgotten?" His deep voice holds a note of poignancy I'm not sure I can handle.

"No, there's no way you'd remember that," I whisper helplessly. I was sure he'd forgotten about all the times we spent talking, all the moments after he'd be done with practice, and he'd come to me smelling like chlorine with his hair slicked back. After I'd finished helping him with writing, Benedict—my Ben—would open up to me.

At first, I thought it was some trick, but he never asked me anything about myself. Eventually, we'd talked about everything and nothing, our hopes and our dreams.

Our mutual desire to graduate. To leave Forsyth. To see the world and what it had to offer.

We shared secrets. We'd become friends.

Reaching the delicate glass, I hold it in my hands as flashes of moments cross my mind. Including remembering sitting alone on a Saturday night, imagining what it would be like if I were an average teenager, not an obese one who had lost all semblance of her self-esteem due to the systematic hell she was put through for so many school days.

"I didn't forget a thing. I cherished the time we spent together. And I sacrificed more than you know when I hurt you that day." The look on his face is terrible, as if he's reliving every horrible moment of graduation day along with me.

"Did you?" I whisper. My hands are shaking horribly, but I can't seem to move. All I can do is stare at the words I wrote when I was living in hell. "Did I really mean so much to you back then? How could that be when for all those years, my memories included you shattering what was left of my heart?"

My hands are slick as the sweltering heat of the Georgia summers. Tears blur my eyes. I hear a crash as the fragile glass slips from my hands unintentionally, but it shocks me nonetheless. "Oh my god. I'm so sorry. I didn't mean . . ." It's shattered—just like he broke my heart into bits on graduation day. I run for the open door.

I don't make more than a step.

His strong arms wrap around me, holding me. His voice is broken in my ear when he grates out, "They threatened Lisa. It's the only reason I hurt you. I went to tell you the next day, but you were gone."

I struggle against him, wrenching out of his arms. Moving away from him, I back up against his desk until I can't move any further. Despite my regret over physically damaging something in his home, I lash out, "What the hell could they possibly have threatened her with that would be so damn awful you would do that to me?"

The sun from the square transom windows over the built-in bookcases pours down on him, beaming in warmth where I feel none. Benedict slowly approaches me until his body fits itself against mine. His head drops down until his mouth is against my ear.

"I hurt you that day because they promised me they would take turns raping my baby sister as part of her soccer hazing when she played varsity for Forsyth if I didn't. That's what I traded your heart for, Kelsey." His breath is jagged against my ear. "And you know what? I'm not sorry. I'd make the same decision again tomorrow and the next day. I'll spend the rest of my life apologizing if I have to, but I had a choice, and I made it." His lips brush my cheek, gentle in its apology for hurting me and unabashedly proud.

I yank my head back in shock. Benedict tentatively lifts a hand to my face, and I lean into it. Now I understand. And he's right. He did the only thing he could because I know the people who walked through those halls. There's no doubt in my mind they would have done it without blinking an eye. After all, look at what they did to me? "Dear God in heaven. What kind of monsters lived inside the walls of that school?"

But then, I already know that answer. "I was so self-absorbed, I believed they were only hurting me. Was I any better than they were?"

He pulls me flush against him. "You became my moral compass, my light. Never say that."

My hands slide up around his neck. I lean into his chest and let out the first sob.

For his sister.

For him.

And for me.

CHAPTER THIRTY-SIX

Benedict

SOMEHOW I'M GOING TO HAVE TO BE ABLE TO ANSWER QUESTIONS I'VE struggled with having the answers to for years.

When Kelsey pulls back, I brush the damp hair away from her face. She stumbles with the first one while I mentally brace. "They didn't . . . she's . . . Lisa?"

Something inside me relaxes marginally. I reassure her, "Never experienced the sort of physical pain that left the scars of the emotional agony you endured."

She blows out a loud sigh of relief.

I knew bringing her into my sanctuary, with her possibly being dragged back to Forsyth by seeing her own words was a chance—a big one. But when she was ready to bail because of the mere mention of someone's name from school, I took it to get us both out of the past to the here and now, where we need to be with each other.

Never in the past, not if I can avoid it. And it appears she wants to as well. Something inside me eases with that knowledge.

"I need to apologize." Her voice is low and sad.

I cup her chin and tilt her face up. The light highlights the dusky rose of her cheeks and softens the hollows. "For what?"

Her head still clasped within my fingers, I can feel as she nods at the shards of broken glass behind my shoulder. "For breaking something you treasure in your home, though that was an accident. For not telling you who I was that night. For being selfish about my pain. Losing my temper. Is there more?"

For thinking I was one of them. But as quickly as the thought comes into my head, I shove it aside. As a lawyer, I've been trained to evaluate the evidence presented to me. Even though my heart wants to scream aloud asking how she could think that about me, I can't. Not unless I'm willing to tell her the whole story. As it is, even with the explanation I just gave her, it's going to take time to fully earn my place back into her heart. I'd destroyed what was between us cruelly, deliberately.

Intentionally.

I've been living life, but I've been numb waiting for the chance to accept the punishment and consequences for my actions. That is, after the reality of pain left me with a void so great I had nothing else to fill it with. "When I had the glass made, it was because the hurt was better than the emptiness. Feeling the never-ending reminder was better than the void. And above all, it gave me hope that maybe I could change things."

Kelsey swallows convulsively but doesn't interrupt. "I had it made because it reminded me of you and all the reasons why we weren't so different back then. It's going to take time for you to forget hurting you was intentional, Kelsey, though I didn't have cruel intentions. Even though I can't vouch for a single other person, I had reasons. I hope you can get past the pain to understand that I . . . cared for you," I conclude.

A veil of disquiet settles over her face. "Are you going to hurt me the way you did?"

"Kels, if I hurt you again, it will never be the same way I did back then," I tell her honestly.

And for that, I receive a small laugh and a light punch in the gut. "How about you point me in the direction of a broom to sweep this up and we . . ."

I stiffen at her mention of a broom. "How about I not?"

She frowns at my reaction. I brush a kiss against her forehead to distract her. "How about I set you up with a glass of wine in the kitchen? I'll come back, clean this up, and then you can watch while I cook."

Even as I'm talking, I'm pulling her from the room. She digs in her heels at the entryway to stop our movement forward. "Ben? I want you to know I'm truly sorry." She waves her hand back toward the mess. "I'm sorry for not being able to turn back the clock and listen. Maybe if I hadn't run, things would have been different. Not just between us, but for us." She squeezes my hand before she steps past me down the hall.

Once she's out of hearing range, I whisper to the empty air, "And I'm sorry for not being strong enough to save us all."

CHAPTER THIRTY-SEVEN

Benedict

"That was delicious," Kelsey compliments me on the spicy grilled shrimp I paired with pasta salad. After vacuuming up the glass, I gave her a few options for dinner. She was unable to make a decision, haunted emotions written all over her face. I decided what to make and just started cooking while keeping a sharp eye on the woman sitting at the counter in front of me.

She gently wipes her lips with her napkin before setting it on the side of her plate. "I'm stuffed."

I frown when I realize how little she's eaten. Maybe four of the six jumbo shrimp I slid on her plate are gone and about half of the salad. Meanwhile, I must have devoured three times what she did on my first go-around. Maybe she's still upset until it strikes me, she didn't consume much at Commander's Palace, nor anywhere else we've eaten when we've been together. I question, "Did you eat before you came?"

She frowns. "Of course not. Why?"

"Because you barely ate. Was it too spicy?"

"Not at all! If you want spicy, you should try this small Mexican place down by the border Val and I used to go to all the time when we were at school." Her laughter emerges much freer. However, she still doesn't pick up her fork.

"Then did you not enjoy it?" I'm confused. I mean, I've dated women who don't eat a lot when they're out with men, but this is smaller than a child's portion.

Kelsey freezes. "I enjoyed it." Her voice is barely audible. She ducks her head.

Reaching over, I tuck a lock of hair behind her ear. A warm blush staining her cheeks. She's fidgeting with her napkin, twirling it back and forth between her fingers. "Hey? What is it?"

"I . . . It's just . . ." Squaring her shoulders, she sits back. "I refuse to be ashamed of my decisions."

I sit back and pick up my glass of wine. "Of course not. What decision?"

"How I changed—how my life changed."

Confused, I shake my head a little. "Why would you be? You've worked so hard to attain . . ."

"I had gastric bypass surgery," she blurts out.

My jaw unhinges. "What?" I've heard of the medical procedure certainly, and many famous stars have had it done, but most were ridiculed for putting the weight back on so quickly.

"Most people sneer when they hear that. They think I took the easy way out and didn't try hard enough to lose weight. But I did." She leans forward to impress upon me how earnest she is. Her gray eyes turn stormy. "For years, Val and I worked out almost daily. She helped me monitor what I ate. And I worked with doctors long before I finally went to a surgeon for assistance."

I understand the words she's saying, but I can't quite put it all together. "You mean . . ."

"I had a doctor remove part of my stomach and intestines to help me lose weight, yes." Her voice is devoid of emotion. Rote, as if she's had this conversation many times. I expect she has, but there's something else there. My eyes narrow on her carefully.

She's anxious—no, fucking terrified—of being judged. Again.

I put my glass down. My fingers trail along the stem. "I admire the decisions you've made." Her expression clearly shows her disbelief, making me want to stand up and fight her more recent battles for her. How much heartache can a single person endure in one lifetime? "Jesus, Kelsey, deciding to have this surgery couldn't have been easy."

Still not meeting my gaze, she runs her finger over the lip of her glass. "It wasn't. But I was so tired of not being enough. Of working so hard for what? A sympathetic smile when I'd arrive at another party alone. A pity date where a friend would take me to a major dance. You see, high school was a nightmare I would never wish on my worst enemy, but college was a metamorphosis. I went in ugly, wrapped myself in a cocoon, and after it was over, emerged entirely different."

"So, college wasn't better for you?" My heart aches, but that pain lessens when her smile spreads across her face.

"Oh, it was completely different. Trust me when I say, from the first day there, college gave me the will to survive what Forsyth stripped from me."

My pride and shame go to war with each other. For the moment, pride wins out. I say honestly, "You are utterly incredible."

A flush stains her cheeks. "I wouldn't go as far as to say that."

"What are the statistics for people regaining weight after a surgery like yours?" I challenge her. I'm unsurprised when she begins rattling them off. "So, what you're telling me is you had this procedure over ten years ago, beat the curve of the amount of weight you were anticipated to lose, and kept it off longer? That's not the luck of the draw, Kelsey. That's strength of character—something, I might add, you've always had." I finish off my wine and push to my feet.

Reaching down, I hold out my hand. "After everything, will you trust me?"

She's staring straight forward, her dinner napkin clenched in her hands. She's lost in a world I have no way of reaching her in, so I bring her back to this one by gently reaching over and brushing her hair behind her ear. Startled, she smiles. "I'm sorry, did you say something?"

"Do you trust me?" I repeat.

Something inside me heals when she doesn't hesitate. "Knowing what I know now? Unequivocally."

"Come with me." I cup the side of her jaw as I draw her to her feet. She drops the napkin in the vicinity of the table. It flutters to the floor in a heap of cream-colored linen. Taking her hand, I guide her to the back door. Flicking a switch, I turn and face her before asking, "I want to show you something. Will you let me?"

Clasping her delicate hand in my larger one, I open the back door. The hours I spent at Lisa's direction hanging the thousands of lights in the trees become worth it when Kelsey gasps with pleasure. "Ben . . ." She breaks away and steps down the few stairs on her own. Moving across the stone patio that connects our garage to the main house, she spins around, arms and hair flying wide. Her face is radiant when she faces me again. For this moment, everything is the way it was fifteen years ago. We've finally reunited the souls we have been searching for.

Freely

It's more than I ever hoped and dreamed for, but before I can cross to her, I need to say what's been on my soul.

"You're beautiful," I rasp. I jump past the last steps and am in front of her before she can protest. "You are. It has nothing to do with this"—I drag my fingers down her face until they rest upon her heart—"and everything to do with what's here."

The strung lights enhance the ones twinkling down at us overhead. Pulling her closer, I tip her chin up. "Can you see that star right there?"

She names it easily. "The North Star."

"You've been mine, Kelsey. My guiding compass even when you weren't in my life." Her shock is evident. I stumble on. "I read a poem once that said the North was supposed to represent wisdom. Even . . . even when you weren't in my life, you were in my heart. My touchstone. Who knows? We kept orbiting each other—Harvard, Collyer. Yet, nothing until now. I just don't know why life kept me waiting for you. We were so close."

"What does the poem say happens in the South?"

I swallow convulsively. "A person is supposed to find the wisdom of their heart."

What happens next should have dropped me to my knees. The fingers at my jaw urge me to look down. She hums, "Maybe it's time to go south."

And in my arms is everything. The few dreams I've been blessed with can't compare to her upturned face radiating forgiveness and more. My forehead crashes down to hers. A harsh sob is ripped from my chest. I'm unsuccessful in suppressing it. But as overcome as I am, I'm not so blinded by my own tears that I can't see the ones dribbling from her eyes.

"Maybe if I'd found a way to explain back at school, hired a different investigator years ago . . ." I begin. But Kelsey lays a finger across my lips, staying my words.

"Who knows if we'd be standing here right now. I didn't break away just because of you. I needed to find out who I could be on my own." She reaches up to brush her own tears away, but I beat her to it. Slowly, back and forth, my thumbs wipe away every tear of precious reconciliation I know deep down I don't deserve. Each one is like a moment with her—a gift I'll never take for granted. Soon, my lips begin to trail across the wet tracks left across her face.

"I've prayed for the chance to make up for the past," I choke out. I hear a clap of thunder and lift my head to the sky, afraid we're going to get poured on in a summer storm as my punishment to counterbalance the abundance of joy coursing through me.

When I bring my eyes back to Kelsey's, I realize the storm brewing isn't in the air and isn't a fragment of the one raging inside my soul. It's because the woman I'm holding in my arms has already risen from her demons stronger than she was before.

So how weak does that make me?

Desperately, I shove the thought aside as I thread my fingers through her hair. Tipping her chin up, I seek permission to bridge the space of air between her lips and mine under the sultry night sky. Because once my lips touch hers, there's no going back.

Not now. And maybe not ever.

Kelsey's hands slowly slide around my neck, tugging my face as close to hers as possible without our lips touching. "Kiss me, Ben. Do it under the stars where a million wishes can be made. Kiss me knowing whose lips you're taking. Do it knowing I'm the same girl I was at seventeen, the woman you took in Savannah, and that I'm going to make mistakes. I've changed, but I'm . . ."

Before she can continue, my lips have crashed down on hers, swallowing her taste. Because I already know who she is.

Mine.

CHAPTER THIRTY-EIGHT

Kelsey

Stumbling inside, we're so close to one another that I can feel Benedict's breath brush the wisps of my hair off my forehead. This isn't the wild pleasure we'd surrendered to the night of our reunion in Savannah. I suspect a single kiss is going to make me weep. The touch of his hands is going to be more potent than anything I could ever dream of because he knows it's me he's touching.

This is real. We're real.

I still can't forget the pleasure his body brought to mine. I'm shivering, aching for the pleasure I'm already anticipating. But it would be different if it wasn't him. A sigh of pleasure escapes my lips as his fingers trail over the silk of my dress, pulling my hips tighter against his.

The first time he touched me, I didn't appreciate why his heart synchronized so perfectly with mine. Or what it meant when his fingers left goose bumps in their wake. I didn't understand that our bond goes beyond our minds and our hearts; it's woven into our souls. Somehow, this man became more than a fantasy. He became my reality. He's my every wish, my biggest regret, and my deepest fears, all wrapped up in one devastating package.

Tentatively, I reach up and cup his jaw. He ducks his chin and places a lingering kiss on the center of my palm. "Are you nervous?" The tenderness and seductive rumble of his voice wraps around me like sexy velvet.

I curl my body closer and nod. "But I'm not certain why. It's not the first time."

"Isn't it?" Bending down, Benedict catches me behind the back of my knees, shoving my dress well above my thighs.

With a yelp, I instinctively wrap my legs around him. "A little warning next time." I whack him on the shoulder.

He grins and just that easily, I'm transported back to the moment when his bright blue eyes were shining down at me the day he found out he got into college. That same expression is causing feelings to well up inside of me. It's not because of how he's touching me now, but because of how he already did years ago. I begin to tremble from head to toe.

"Kels? What is it?" Benedict backs me into the nearest wall, bracing me with his lower body so his hands can frame my face.

"I . . . You really did have feelings for me back then," I whisper, finally believing. I want to laugh and cry.

What I feel, finally, is what everyone has wanted me to feel.

Happiness.

Joy.

Benedict unwraps my legs from his waist before he pushes me flush against the wall. Rocking his hips against mine, he confesses, "I think what I felt was a man's feelings in a young boy's body. I was, am, intrigued by you. I was, am, protective of you. I was, am, aroused by you." Twirling a lock of hair in between his fingers, his mind goes exactly to where mine was—to the moment he told me he got into Harvard. "You'll never know just how close you came to being kissed that day."

My breath catches in my throat. "I thought . . . maybe . . . but then . . ."

"Let me show you what was really on my mind." Pulling back, Ben leans down to straighten my skirt.

I giggle. He shoots me a quizzical glance. I flick my hand toward my skirt. "This isn't what I was expecting."

"Oh? What did you have in mind?"

"Something along the lines of Savannah," I toss out.

Heat flares in his eyes. His cheeks turn ruddy.

Before he can speak, I draw a finger down the front of his shirt and remind him, "Where we could barely get the hotel room door open before we were leaving a trail of clothes from one end of the room to the other."

"Hmm, that has possibilities." Straightening to his full height, he bends to wrap his arms around the tops of my thighs. "So does this."

Before I can question what he means, Benedict lifts me and begins twirling me in the wide hallway. He yells, "I did it, Kelsey! I got in!"

Tears prick in the back of my eyes. "Congratulations, Ben." Unconsciously, I say the same words I did all those years ago. My hand lifts from his shoulder to cup his cheeks.

Just like I did before.

He lets me slide down the front of his body before his thumb sweeps away the remains of my tears. "I couldn't have done it without you. None of it. I couldn't have made it into school, and I'm so damn sorry." Then the rhetoric changes and my heart loses the last barrier it's been holding—both the girl of the past and the woman I am now. "I'm sorry I'll have to use you to save my sister. That you'll leave me before I can explain. I want to tell you the truth because you're behind all the good in my life. There's no light at Forsyth except for you. And I will deliberately put yours out."

Pressing closer to him, I whisper, "I understand." Because now I do.

His forehead leans down and rests against my crown. It's so similar to what happened that afternoon and yet so different. This time, I recognize not only my heart pounding but Benedict's as well. When I pull back to see the truth in his eyes—exactly the way I did in Mrs. Wiley's classroom—I understand what his narrowed eyes and harsh breathing mean.

I didn't then. How could I when I never believed in myself?

My heart is knocked out of my chest when I understand the man I've longed for in the depths of my heart for so long wanted to kiss me then. As much as he wants to now.

"Kelsey . . ." My name is barely a whisper—just like it before—only this time, there's no door creaking open, causing us to jump apart. This time, when Benedict's head lowers, his lips tentatively touch mine. He pulls back just far enough so he can murmur, "That's the kiss I would have given you then, sweetheart."

"And now?" His lips curve. With our faces being so close, I can feel them. My heartbeat goes into overdrive because he doesn't bother to say anything.

He shows me.

His lips press back down onto mine and they sweep across once. Twice. I dart my tongue out, which has the inadvertent effect of touching his as well. We both groan aloud. His head dips again, and gripping the back of my neck, he lifts me into his kiss.

He possesses my mouth, much like he owns the deepest, darkest parts of my heart. My lips part and his tongue slides inside, taking control of my mouth with each smooth glide back and forth. My tongue thrusts against his, staking my own claim.

Long moments later, when we part, we're both gasping for air. The way he's cradling me against him allows me to feel the rapid staccato of his heartbeat. His next words are ripped from him. "Stay. Stay all night. Don't let me wake up without you again."

I may be emotionally stripping myself more than I'll be physically naked later by uttering one simple word, but I do it anyway. "Yes."

The next thing I know, I'm airborne as Benedict swings me up around my thighs and starts making his way down the hall, his laugh more carefree than I've heard in the weeks since we've reconnected. There's unbridled joy on his face I want to memorize because it's captivating.

But before I get the chance, we're crossing the threshold of double doors that he shuts behind him with a sharp kick.

CHAPTER THIRTY-NINE

Kelsey

Benedict kisses me senseless for the longest time after he lays me down on top of his bedspread. I get lost in the way his lips and tongue drive me to madness before a whimper escapes my throat.

Finally, he tears his mouth away, but only to subject me to more pleasure as he drags his teeth down the sensitive column of my neck. Over and over, lips, tongue, teeth tantalize me until soft moans roll one after another from my lips. He can't help but hear them because I can feel him smile against my neck. But I get no reprieve before he resumes his seductive torture.

This merging of our bodies is my final step out of the past for us both. There will be no more looking back, no more barriers between us after this. We were the Kelsey and Benedict of then, and we've morphed into the people we are now. And if I'm blessed, we'll become the us we were meant to be.

Rolling him to his back, I straddle him and whip my dress off over my head, leaving myself clad in nothing but a matching set of barely-there lace bra and panties. He pauses in the act of destroying my body to shoot me a heated look from where he's lying between my thighs. Sliding his fingers back and forth beneath the hem of the lace, he orders, "Unless you want these to have the same fate as the last pair I took off, I suggest you lose them. Now."

Leaning down, I press a kiss on his lips before teasing him, "Not until you lose some clothes too, Ben. This isn't a one-way strip show."

I fall back as he lurches from the bed ripping his shirt off with one hand without unbuttoning it. I'm paralyzed as he reveals an upper body every woman dreams of—strong shoulders, muscular arms, and a stomach a god would weep to have. It leads down to tapered hips his dress slacks cling to only with the assistance of a leather belt. Dimly, I hear the jingle of his belt loosening, but I'm in a dream state. I could live off the sight of his body alone. Out loud, I throw out a little sass as I relax into the pillows behind me. "I feel like I need music for this."

Benedict pauses in the act of shucking his pants. He amusedly threatens, "You know what I'm going to do with that smart mouth of yours?"

"No, what?" I slide my fingers through my hair before letting them rest on my shoulder. After fiddling a bit, the strap of my bra falls off my shoulder nonchalantly. When the only sound he makes is an audible inhale, I feel empowered. Before I can move, my mouth becomes otherwise occupied as Benedict's crashes down on it, almost daring me to defy the urgency in his kiss.

Happily, I realize when he joins me back in bed, it is without a single stitch of clothing on to impede my hands. He braces himself above my body and is just about to lower his weight against me when I press a hand against his chest, just over his heart.

"Your body is a work of art, but the place I'm touching is magnificent." I feel a large thump against my hand as his heart imprints itself against my soul. And I want to do the same for him.

My hands smooth down to his stomach. My reward is when his muscles quiver beneath my touch across the expanse of his skin. I can't keep my hands still, roaming them from his washboard abs to his broad chest. My fingers target his hard nipples. I already know from our previous night together they are super sensitive to being rolled, licked, and sucked. Pulling my hand back, I wet both my thumb and forefingers before reaching over and twisting them. Hard.

He groans, his head dropping in sweet agony. "Jesus Christ," he rasps.

"Let me touch you. Feel you." My body is aching for his touch, but that can wait. I need to give this man pleasure.

If I have my way, I'll give him everything.

Seeming to understand without words, Benedict capitulates to the hunger that must burn in my eyes. His fingers, hovering near my shoulders, slide beneath me to make quick work of the snaps at my back. My arms lift so he can pull my bra away from my sensitive breasts. Then I gasp as the air gives them sweet relief and taunts them.

He stares down at them in wonder. "I never thought I'd get to hold you like this again. I want to spend all night cherishing you, Kelsey," he says, right before he lowers his head and licks one tight bud and then the other back and forth before sucking one nipple firmly into his mouth.

I arch off the bed, crying out. Every time his tongue lashes at me, it makes me wetter. Now, the sensation is like a constant pull against my aching clit.

Wrapping my legs around him, I arch my lower body into him.

Benedict pushes back against me with his hard cock as he switches breasts, treating my other nipple to the same treatment even as he reaches over and pinches the one he just abandoned.

My head rolls back and forth on his pillow. "Have to touch you," I groan. It's a need. My nails scrape at his flesh until suddenly I'm whirling through the air, carefully being flipped over.

Benedict has a devilish cast to his face as I'm once again astride him. "This way, we both can play," he says, breath rasping.

Lowering myself down to him, I grip his jaw to hold it in place for a thorough kiss when I feel his hands slide down the back of my panties before he growls, "But, sweetheart, it's time to lose these." He slides his hands over my hips, dragging the lace over them, likely stretching them beyond repair.

Like I give a shit.

When they catch between us, I lift, giving him the room to slide them further down my thighs before I then twist from one side to the other to push them down my legs and kick them off the bed. Elongating on top of him, he strokes his hands from the backs of my thighs to my shoulders before simply holding me close in a sweet hug where he breathes me in.

"God, I missed you when I woke up and you were gone."

My hair brushes against his jaw as I duck my head when I confess, "I almost stayed."

"You're kidding." Shock and an emotion I can't identify fill his voice.

"I had a moment before I walked out the door where I almost said the hell with it and crawled back into bed. I knew if I did, I would have told you everything. And . . ." I finally admit the truth to myself as well as him. "I was petrified of your reaction. After all, I was just me."

He rears back as much as he can before rolling us again until he's back on top. I'm wrapped tightly in his arms. He's holding me to him as he devours my lips, showing me what my revelation means to him.

"And you're all I want."

Losing the last fragile illusion of control, Benedict kneels in front of me. Wrapping my legs around his hips, leaving my core completely exposed to his exploring hands, he strokes the bare lips of my drenched pussy with a teasing, delicate touch. "Oh my god. Don't stop," I manage to get out as his fingers dance along my clit before they work their way inside of me slowly.

I can barely get in enough air to breathe.

His rough laugh tells me I'm not the only one affected. He thrusts his hips into my wandering hand as I blindly reach out and grab his cock.

His guttural groans draw even more slickness from my body. It's almost as much of a turn-on as what his destructive touch is doing. I stroke up and down over the hard length when he groans, "You're magnificent." My fingers graze over the head and swipe over the bead of fluid leaking from the tip. Catching his eye, I lift my fingers to my lip and taste him. It's not quite the way I want to, but I can't slip my mouth around him from this angle.

Later. Definitely.

The feral sound that emanates from his throat causes me to shiver, but I end up whimpering when he removes his fingers from my drenched core to unwrap my legs from the viselike grip they have around his hips. I begin to protest until he slides down the bed. He braces himself as he spends an inordinate time kissing the flowers on my stomach along the way, causing hot tears to burn behind my eyes.

All thoughts fly out of my head as he situates himself between my spread thighs. He parts my folds, exposing my bud to the air. I swear it throbs even more before he lowers his head and lays waste to me by flicking his tongue back and forth over it.

"Ben, yes! There. More, please." My hips arch of their own volition into his mouth as he claims me. My fingers fly into his hair to hold him against me. He kisses the sensitive nub and licks it before opening his mouth and sucking the bud fully inside, just like he did my nipple.

I scream my pleasure out. "Ahh!"

With no mercy, I'm scoring his shoulders with my nails and gasping his name over and over. My legs fall open wider. That just spurs him on. First one finger, then two slip into my pussy. I can hear my wetness slicking his fingers as he continues to drive me up and over the edge of madness until my inner muscles clamp down tightly against his fingers, squeezing hard once.

Twice.

I arch before spasming rapidly.

My body sinks back against the mattress, spent.

Benedict licks my folds gently to soothe me as I come down from the high. Soon though, I want more.

"Please," I beg. He looks up from between my legs, and I swear there's nothing that's affected me more than seeing the sheer joy on his face. "Take me."

"With pleasure." He prowls up between my legs, levering himself above me. Reaching into the drawer, he pulls out protection. I bite my lip in anticipation as he quickly sheaths himself. He nudges the head of his cock against my pussy. "Look at me, Kels."

My eyes fly up to his as his forehead lowers to mine. He pushes inside me, slow and easy. I moan in pleasure even as my core takes a moment to adjust to the width of his cock. "It feels so good to be inside you again."

Tears I thought had fled after I had such an intense release burn again at the back of my eyes at his words. He means it. My mouth opens in wonder. Me. Kelsey. I lift my hips and wrap my arms around his neck as pleasure floods every inch of my skin, my heart, and my soul. His hips pull back before he thrusts again, plunging deep. His forceful strokes take my breath away and give me life all in the same instant.

My hands slide into his hair as he arches his cock into me again. "You're so tight." Benedict leans down and nips my shoulder, my neck before he captures my lips in a searing kiss that mimics what our bodies are doing below, filling our souls with memories that will last so much longer than this night.

My cries mingle with his groans as our bodies come closer to the edge. There's a sweetness to the intensity that wasn't there that night in Savannah. Wrapping my legs tighter around him, I hold him as close as I can with all the jagged pieces of what I have inside of me.

This time when Benedict's final thrust throws me over the edge, all I can think is, *Is it going to be like this every time Ben touches me?* Because if it is, I may die of ecstasy.

It's my last coherent thought before he rolls me into him, and I drift off against his shoulder.

CHAPTER FORTY

Kelsey

"Tell me about this." Ben traces his fingers lightly across the daisies on my lower stomach, and I tense. "It means something more than just being your grandmother's favorite flower."

"It's not an easy story," I warn him. Because it won't be for either of us. It's going to bring up the heartbreak and heartache we're trying to move past.

His fingers stop tracing the delicate petals covering the worst of the scar over my left hip where my incision didn't heal correctly. "Is it going to take us back?" he asks quietly.

My head moves up and down against the pillows slowly. But before he can speak, I lay my hand on top of his. "We can't pretend the past didn't happen, though look at how well that turned out."

A gorgeous smile curves his lips before he kisses me. "Well, it certainly ended up well," he teases.

I can't help but laugh because he's right. Not once, but twice, we've ended up in bed over my need to forget the past never happened. Only this time, look at what I gained by not running away. Come what may, there's no ignoring the past; there's only fighting the right battles to secure my future. Whatever they may end up being.

"I had the surgery a little more than ten years ago," I begin.

Benedict's face sobers. "I've heard about how serious of a procedure it is." His hand presses hard against my lower abdominal wall. I feel the warmth around the areas where the scar tissue hasn't deadened the area. In the rest, I feel nothing.

I thought my heart was like that too until tonight.

I nod because it was. "You need to appreciate I chose to have the surgery, though it was deemed medically necessary by my insurance."

He swallows hard. "Are you . . . can you still have children?"

Tilting my head to the side, I ask, "Would it matter to you if I couldn't?"

He presses a soft kiss to my forehead before telling me truthfully, "Only if it hurt you. I don't want anything to hurt you anymore."

And while I lost my protective armor against being hurt, I start to feel the ground shift beneath my feet. *Is this what falling in love feels like?* "Oh, Ben." I lift my arms around him and pull him close so the full weight of his body is on mine.

We lie together like this for a few moments before he rolls to the side. Cupping my face, he brushes his thumb over my cheek back and forth. "If it wasn't that, what was it?"

Taking in a deep breath, I summon the courage of all the saints I've ever prayed for mercy on. My voice quivers, "When I had the weight loss surgery . . ."

I don't know why I'm afraid of his response. Maybe because I'm finally beginning to realize Ben cared about me before when I wasn't fit. He cared about what was under his hands that he's currently cupping.

My heart.

"I was so close to . . ." My voice trails away. Tears well and begin to overflow and trail down the sides of my face.

"Close to?"

"Giving up. I hated my body and the distorted image I had about myself more than I loved anything about my life. I was—no, I am obsessive about what I eat, working out, and making sure I don't put on weight. I'm not dysmorphic, but I have huge levels of anxiety over my appearance—more importantly, how others perceive me." Biting my lip, I wait for him to turn away in disgust.

Instead, I'm thrown off by what happens next.

Benedict shoves the sheets off our cooling bodies and starts to slide away. "Ben?" I ask uncertainly.

"Shh," he whispers. Brushing a kiss over my lips, he says, "Let me tell you what I see when I touch you."

Trembling, I lie beside him while his fingers glide through my hair. "It's like silk. It glides over your body as you move." I can almost feel each strand as he sifts his fingers through. "When I play with it in the light, it catches fire—much like the woman inside."

His fingers glide over my brows and around my eyes. "And here? Smoke and serenity. Your eyes are like an antique mirror, priceless in any setting."

His thumb dips down over my lips. I take a small nip, I can't help myself. His answering grin tells me how much he likes it—me. "Daring, playful, and yet ridiculously modest. The things that come out of this mouth are a constant temptation. But there are two places I'm fixated on."

I expect his hands to slide to my breasts or maybe between my legs, to feel the dampness gathering there over the intensity of feeling he's generating in me.

I'm partially right.

His hand slides between my breasts to land over my heart. The other braces above my head so he can leverage himself partially over me to lay his lips on my forehead. "It's what's in this incredible mind that captured my attention from the moment we first met years ago." Sliding down, he trails soft kisses down the centerline of my body until he replaces his warm hand with soft lips over a heart that's going wild. "And it's what's in here that's making me understand why my own beats in time with yours."

My whispered moan of his name is broken as he lays his head on my chest and breathes in the mingled sweat of our previous lovemaking. I'm already a mess of tears when he speaks again a few moments later. "So, to answer the question you didn't quite ask, no. I don't judge you for doing whatever you felt you needed to survive. I'm just grateful as fuck you came out of it healthy and with no long-term medical issues." To add a nonverbal exclamation to his statement, Benedict drops his head to the cluster of gerbera daisies covering the worst of my scar and kisses them soundly before sliding back up to take my shaking body in his arms.

"You're going to make it very hard not to fall in love with you," I tell him long moments later.

"God, I hope so" is his only response before he reaches over to turn out the lights. He pulls me close, and I lay my head on his chest.

Closing my eyes, in his arms, I finally feel like maybe I found the place where I was meant to be reunited with my happiness since I left Savannah all those years ago.

Benedict's arms.

CHAPTER FORTY-ONE

Benedict

THE SILKY SMOOTHNESS OF HER SKIN UNDER MY FINGERS IS LIKE A drug I can't get enough of.

Kelsey is asleep after we made love again, her heart-shaped ass nestled back against the cradle of my hips. And time and time again, my fingers run up and down the outside of her leg. Under my hands is the physical manifestation of the core of strength inside this incredible woman.

She stirs lightly in her sleep. I slide my hand from her thigh to her hip and squeeze gently, my fingers resting over the daisies she tattooed over the physical scars she endured in an attempt to help her facilitate removing the mental ones. My heart beats an erratic rhythm when she reaches back and pulls my hand forward to cup it against the most precious of places.

Her heart.

Dropping my head forward, I take a hit of her—a smell that's uniquely Kelsey mixed with the earthy scent of our lovemaking. I can hardly believe the way our bodies responded to one another. There was no holding back. Not an inch of her soft skin wasn't touched or tasted throughout the night.

I should be exhausted, so why can't I sleep?

Something dark stirs up, causing my stomach to churn, but I violently shove it aside. *Not now. Not ever again.*

Refusing to think about my past, I focus on a possible future with a woman —this woman. My physical anguish begins to subside. And I feel triumphant.

Maybe I am strong enough. Then again, having your soul branded by a woman can help beat back the worst demons, I muse.

Nuzzling her soft hair, I take another whiff of the scent I know even now, even though it's still new, could carry me through the everyday burdens.

Fresh regret washes through me when I think of the time wasted. How different would our lives be right now?

Before I can travel down that path too far, a delicate hand reaches behind me and squeezes my ass. "I didn't mean to wake you," I murmur, though I take advantage to lay a string of kisses down Kelsey's neck.

"I could hear you thinking. It was like a little buzz behind me."

I smother my laughter and take on an affronted tone. "There's nothing little about me."

"Mmm," she agrees.

I can't wait any longer to see her face lit by the promise of the morning sunlight. Shifting Kelsey to her back, I stretch out on top of her. "Good morning." I brush stray hair away from her face.

"I've been waiting for you to wake up," she admits as she smiles up at me.

"I've been waiting for you my entire life," I tell her honestly.

At my words, her eyes liquefy into the New Orleans sky just before an afternoon summer shower. They turn dark and stormy before a trace amount of moisture trickles out. "Ben?" My name comes out as both a question and a prayer from her sweet lips.

I drop my head and answer the best way I know how.

Soon, we're awash in the early morning golden sunlight, a tangle of arms and limbs as I again experience something I've never felt before.

It might just be love.

CHAPTER FORTY-TWO

Benedict

"What are your plans for today?" Kelsey asks me as we're eating some eggs I threw together. When she sets aside her portion after eating about half, I take a mental note for the next time I cook.

Next time. I relish the idea of a lifetime of next times. Lifting a mug of coffee to my lips to cover my smile, I know I don't get away with the fact I was staring when her eyes widen at me.

"What? Do I have food somewhere on my face? My teeth?" She makes a face that resembles a braying donkey. I shake my head in silent laughter. After a moment, she glances down at her plate anxiously. "If it wasn't that, then was it . . ."

"It was the thought I had that maybe I'll get your portions right eventually. And that led me to think we'd have an eventually."

Her lips form a perfect O. The way her hair flutters so close to her face, I can tell a breath of air passed through them, and I want to feel it on my own.

Stepping closer, I tangle my fingers in the loose strands that fell from the top knot on her head. Tugging gently, I tip her face up to mine to receive the gentle kiss I lay on her lips. If I believed in shapeshifters, in voodoo, in magic, I'd say she cast a spell on me from the moment I carried her to my room last night. The problem is we both know what happens in the dark, and it doesn't always lead us to places where the worst thing that happens is losing ourselves in each other.

Even if only one of us is talking about it.

"The feelings I have for you . . ." I pause, trying to find the right words.

"Yes?" Her voice is as weak as a newborn and as strong as a phoenix. She's triumphed where others would have caved. Instead of cracking inside, Kelsey tapped the energy at the core of her heartache and fought her way out.

How could I not love her?

Kelsey's the point on the circle where the beginning and end of the same line intersect. She represents all my mistakes, but she's also everything I've ever dreamed of. "I'll never be able to escape what you make me feel," I tell her honestly.

Sliding her arms up and around my neck, she asks, "Are you looking to?"

"Knowing I have this chance with you is making me crazy with fear, but it's because it's making me forget everything but one."

"What's that?"

I breathe into her mouth, "You," before I capture her lips in a kiss so much more potent than the ones we shared before. Our eyes are open as we let our mouths whisper secrets our minds aren't ready to speak yet.

But oh, the beauty of them.

Sliding an arm around her waist, I pull her closer to deepen the embrace. I'm just about to boost her on the kitchen counter when I hear a key in the lock.

Ah, crap.

Lisa's texting on her phone when she strolls in. At my enraged growl, she hazards a glance up. "Well, this is a first, and we've lived together for years."

"I sure could have done without it. I thought you would be out all night."

"Um, hate to break it to you, big brother, but I was." The dreamy smile on her face thrills me, and I want to punch my best friend in the face, all at the same time. "It's after nine. I've got class in a few hours. I'm not sure what you have planned for today. Morning, Kelsey." Lisa waves as she passes through the kitchen toward the stairs that lead to where her room is.

I go to pull Kelsey back in my arms, but she slaps a hand against my chest. "Ben, didn't you hear your sister?" she demands.

"I get that she's a cockblocking . . ." Then both Lisa and Kelsey's words penetrate. "Holy shit, baby! It's nine? I'm an hour late for work." I dash off to the bedroom, expecting Kelsey to race behind me.

The only thing that follows me is her laughter. "Why don't you get ready, and I'll clean up in here? I can shower when I get home. Remember? I don't have set hours," she calls out.

There's a definite smirk in her voice I'm going to have to spank her luscious ass for later. But as I'm running through a thoroughly destroyed master suite, I can't prevent the wicked smile that crosses my face. I might be facing a wrath of epic proportions at the office, but I can't say it wasn't worth it.

Every second of it was.

Still, I set a world record for showering and dressing, leaving Kelsey, at her insistence, to finish straightening up. As I race out the door, I'm man enough to admit my balls draw up in fear at the idea of my woman and my sister being in the same house alone for any length of time. God only knows what kind of war stories they're about to swap.

Pulling into my parking spot at Lockwood Industries, I scurry into the executive elevator, my head buried in my phone, trying to catch up with everything that's happened this morning.

Stepping out, I rapidly make my way to my office. Vince calls out, "Ben, wait a sec!" But I blow past him.

And immediately wish I hadn't.

Because an extremely pissed off Ryan Lockwood is sitting behind my desk.

"Want to tell me what was so important that you missed the briefing you scheduled with me and Carol for the government proposal?"

Shit. I'm completely screwed.

Quietly, I close the door to accept the royal ass-chewing I rightfully deserve.

CHAPTER FORTY-THREE

Kelsey

. .

"Spill it." Lisa bounds down the stairs the second Ben's car screeches out of the driveway. Mentally saying a quick prayer he makes it to work in one piece, I go back to scrubbing the pan he cooked in.

"I'm certain you don't want the details, sugar," I drawl.

The devilment that dances in Lisa's eyes, so much like Benedict's, doesn't reassure me any. "About the fun, spanky times with my brother? No. Not in the least. What left you standing in the kitchen looking a million miles away and so at home it's as if you've lived here forever? Yes."

Startled by her observation, I rinse my hands and dry them before turning and facing her fully. "What happened between Ben and me last night is private." I'm not even sure I could share what happened with Val. I frown as I consider that. There's nothing I've never not been able to tell my best friend. But this? It's too intimate.

Instead, I tell Lisa the truth and hope it will satisfy her curiosity and her need to protect her brother. "I didn't use to dream about tomorrows until I tangled with Benedict. Every time it's happened."

Lisa's face transforms from teasing to buoyant. "There's no going back?"

"Not for me. I guess together we'll see where this leads."

Lisa comes closer and wraps her arm around my shoulder. "You've never had anything like this? No partner or significant other to rely on?"

I shake my head.

"No other lover stood in front of you to protect you?"

I laugh, and the sound comes out hollow. "Lisa, I can count on one hand the number of people who've ever stood up to protect me." Pulling away, I turn and look over the beautifully manicured backyard. Absentmindedly, I note Benedict was in such a hurry, he left the garage open. "Some days, I still look in the mirror, and all I see is the reflection of the woman who was so obese, no one wanted to be her friend," I whisper from a place that's still so dark, I'm not sure that light is ever going to touch it.

"Ben did." The strength of conviction behind Lisa's words plus the explanation from him goes a long way to guide me out of the blackness I was beginning to sink under. Now understanding that to be true, I merely signal my acceptance.

Silence blankets the two of us as I think about sacrifice and redemption. *What exactly would I have done differently with my life if Ben hadn't done what he did? Not a damn thing*, I realize. I still would have left Savannah behind. I would have gone to Pepperdine and met Val. I would be writing. I can't name one thing I would have changed.

Except maybe never returning to face the past before now, I admit truthfully.

And finally, I start to shed the first layer of the burden weighing me down much more than pounds on the scale ever did. If I keep looking back, I'm going to miss what's ahead of me. I can hold on to my heartache, or I can trust him to hold my heart.

Empowered with that knowledge, I decide to make a concerted effort to stop thinking less of myself. Remembering Darin's comment a few weeks back, I don't choose to open my heart to Benedict because I've already done that. Instead, I promise not to talk myself out of it, not to turn away from it when the need to escape inevitably comes.

Resolute, I step back from Lisa. "I need to get going myself."

Her face falls in disappointment. I quickly tack on, "I don't think I can surprise Ben at work later looking like this?" Lifting my arms, I indicate the T-shirt and basketball shorts I stole from his closet earlier after setting his room to rights. They swim on me, but at least they provide some cover. I have no problem with going home like this, but I want to be the best me I can be when I show Ben I'm not running.

Lisa gives me a critical once-over. "Yeah. That's not exactly the dress code I've seen when I visit the office."

I snicker as I head toward his room to retrieve my clothes. "I just bet."

"Hey, Kelsey?" I stop in my tracks. Turning, I face the person Benedict would do anything for.

Anything. Even break my heart.

"Yes?" I ask cautiously.

"Be everything he's been waiting for. I think he's been holding out a long time for you," she says softly. With that, Lisa leaves the kitchen, and I enter Benedict's room to lose myself in a night's worth of memories before grabbing my clothes and slipping out the back door.

CHAPTER FORTY-FOUR

Kelsey

Hours later, I've changed into a pair of black wide-leg pants and a matching jacket in light crepe wool I picked up at Easy On Me. The jacket is a scandalous red so bright, Dorothy would have said screw the shoes, let me wish on this to get home to Kansas from Oz. Striding into the lobby of Lockwood Industries, I walk up to the reception desk and ask confidently, "Benedict Perrault, please."

A lovely young woman picks up the phone and dials a number. "Vince? Yes. I have someone in the lobby asking for Mr. Perrault. One moment." Pressing a button, she asks, "May I have your name, please?"

Just as I'm about to give it to her, a hand slides under my arm. A familiar voice says, "I'll escort Ms. Kennedy to Ben's office." Startled, I jerk my arm that's clasped in Ryan Lockwood's. The look on his face isn't entirely friendly, despite our last meeting. My heart clutches in my chest. *Maybe this wasn't the best idea.*

As I'm contemplating bailing, Ryan gives instructions to the efficient young woman, who is typing furiously on a computer for a visitor badge to be issued. When the lanyard is slid across the counter, Ryan gestures to it.

I quickly slip it over my head.

"Follow me, Kelsey. Thank you, Ms. Mitchell."

"Certainly, Mr. Lockwood," she says faintly. I'm not entirely certain if it's Ryan's impressive looks or the fact the chairman of the board just escorted someone into the building that holds her in shock. It might be a bit of both.

As we make our way over to a bank of elevators, Ryan tells me a little about the history of Lockwood Industries. I'm impressed not only with the history of his family's empire but with the obvious familial love that radiates from him as he speaks about the business, his brother. I wonder if he realizes it?

"Realizes what?" When Ryan asks me that as he holds the elevator for me, I blush when I realize I spoke aloud, but I soldier on.

"If you realize the pride you speak about the work your family does with the company is only outweighed by the love you have for them." At Ryan's startled expression, I shrug. "When you mentioned the work your brother chose over working for the corporation, your pride was impossible for you to contain." Thinking I've overstepped my bounds, I lean against one side of the elevator. Waiting. After all, Ryan Lockwood isn't the kind of man to allow for an armchair character analysis without having something to say about it.

It doesn't take long.

"I'm impressed, Ms. Kennedy. Most people don't pick up on that," his whiskey-smooth voice begins. "But if you're so intuitive, why wouldn't you understand how important Benedict's job is to him?"

Benedict, not Ben.

The elevator continues to climb as I face off against Ryan. "What makes you think I don't?" I declare fiercely.

"Oh, the small matter of a missed business meeting that was fairly critical this morning. While the part of me that's been his friend for years is pleased to see things working out for both of you, his life is different from yours. He doesn't get to float into the office when the mood strikes him."

My face flushes hotly as fury infiltrates every cell of my body. "You mean to tell me that you're perfect?" Before he can respond, I raise a hand to ward off his response. "I sincerely doubt it."

"There are those who would disagree, I'm sure." His voice is calm, controlled.

Two things I'm not.

"Mr. Lockwood, let's get a few things clear," I hiss. His dark eyebrows wing upward. "My relationship with Ben is none of your damn business."

"Except when it impacts mine," he chides me.

And that's when I blow my stack. "And second, if it were that urgent, you would have called. You would have tried his cell or come to his house to make certain he was all right, not sit on a holier-than-thou throne of righteousness! He was appalled when he realized the time. Do you not remember what falling in love is like?" *Coldhearted bastard,* I think bitterly. Poor Ben. He's had to deal with his friend acting like a miserable prick because he was late, likely the only time he ever has.

Spinning, I realize the elevator doors are open. Ben's leaning against the jamb with a massive grin on his face. "Damn, Ryan. What the hell did you say to her?"

"I think somewhere between hello and trying to pull the same crap I did to you, I found out your woman is as protective of you as you are of her." Ryan's amused smile makes me want to coldcock him. In fact, even as my fist tightens, my arm begins to pull back.

Laughing, Ben yanks me out of the elevator. I'm stiff as a board when I crash into his arms. Woodenly, I question, "So, I take it there were no long-term effects for you being late this morning?"

"Oh, there were. Ryan ridiculed me for a good twenty minutes," Ben assures me. He leans down to kiss me, but I pull back. His eyes narrow. "Ryan? Seriously? What did you say?"

Stepping off the elevator, Ryan breezes by. When he passes, he loftily announces, "Practically nothing. She went on the attack."

Why that makes Ben's lips curve, I have no idea. But I won't forget the way it feels to have him kiss me in the lobby of the executive floor with that smile being the first thing I feel against my lips since he left this morning.

I doubt I'll ever forget my first unannounced drop-in to Lockwood Industries.

Ever.

"Vince, this is Kelsey Kennedy. If she calls for any reason, put her through immediately." I shake hands with a darkly handsome man who Benedict introduced as being his "right and left hand. I couldn't do a damn thing without him."

Although I'm thankful Benedict has that kind of assistance in what appears to be an enormously stressful job, it just leaves me even more confused. If this was such a big meeting, wouldn't someone have called him within minutes of his late arrival? But I don't voice my opinion. I hold out my hand to the grinning man. "A pleasure to meet you."

"I briefly saw you across the courtyard at the Larruscain celebration the other night," Vince says. "I was trying to make my way over to be introduced then, but I guess you bailed?" He directs his question to Benedict.

"Get back to work," Benedict tells him, laughing.

"I'll have the mods ready for your review in about an hour."

Clasping my hand, he pulls me toward his office. "Then ring me when they're ready."

"Will do, Ben. Nice to meet you, Ms. Kennedy," Vince says courteously.

Just before the door slams behind me, I call over my shoulder, "Kelsey." Once we're out of the sight of prying eyes, I turn on Benedict. "What the hell has gone on today? I come by to see you—something I might add you said I could do at any time, and your boss accosts me."

His brows lower at that. Before he can get a word out, I forge on. "Then I find everyone on your team is part of some joke that I'm the butt of." My voice breaks at the end, and I realize where this comes from.

Hurt, not anger.

Damn it.

Regret crosses Benedict's face, taking my temper down a few notches. "Will you let me explain?" he asks quietly. He slides his hand up my arm to my elbow to guide me to a sitting area in his large office. Now that I've run out of steam, my eyes widen as I take in the view of the shipyard. "Wow," I whisper.

"Explanations first, tour second." Benedict tugs me down so I'm sitting sideways on his lap. "Ryan was waiting in my office this morning to give me crap about a meeting I missed."

"Oh my god, Ben. And I gave him hell in the elevator." Guilt surges through me.

"You did?" His smile is sinful and causes my heart to quicken. "Good. He deserved it because the meeting was a ruse."

"Wait. What? Why would he do that?"

"Because when Lisa went out with Cade last night, they ran into Ryan and Jared." Ben leans back, and I slide naturally against his chest. "As I'm certain you're well aware with your family connections, parts of the Lockwood family—and in my personal opinion, Ryan in particular—are a bunch of gossipy—"

"If you end that sentence with women, I'm leaving right now," I warn him.

"I was going to say busybodies. Is that better?" He's amused.

I shrug. "Acceptable. Continue."

"So, Ryan told Vince to let him know when I was coming up. He made it to my office minutes before I did to give me a hard time. The reality is, he just wanted to see how last night went." Blowing out a breath, he admits, "I told you, Ryan's heard me mention your name for a long time."

"Should I go apologize?" I ask quietly, thinking about how I told off his boss and friend.

"If Ryan were pissed, he wouldn't have been smiling when he got off that elevator, love."

"Oh." Then I get frustrated all over again. "I was pissed on your behalf, Ben. I told him—"

"Tell me later," Ben whispers. Soon sparkling blue eyes are all I can see as he becomes everything in my vision.

Who am I kidding—he's just become my everything.

CHAPTER FORTY-FIVE

Benedict

Later that night, I spit the Chinese we ordered into my napkin. I'm laughing so hard at Kelsey's play-by-play of what happened in the elevator with Ryan. "I wish I could have seen that." I'm howling. "You completely desecrated him."

"It wasn't like he didn't get a few punches of his own in there," she mutters.

Reaching over, I grab my phone. Scrolling through the contacts, I find Ryan's number. I press Send and put the call on speaker. "What do you want? Haven't I taken enough abuse on your behalf today?" Ryan answers, grumbling. I hear Jared in the background laughing at him.

I don't say a word. I just join in.

"Fuck you, Perrault. And remember, that meeting is actually tomorrow morning. Be on time," he warns before hanging up the phone.

I'm still laughing when I toss mine onto the table.

Kelsey's frowning down into her steamed vegetables. "Men are really just little boys with bigger penises, aren't they?"

Lisa, who Kelsey asked to stay and join us for dinner, has been trying to hold in her laughter. She finally can't contain it, and her own flows out. "If I'd known this would have happened . . ."

"Yes? What would you have done?" Kelsey uses her chopsticks to stick a bite of chicken in her mouth. She chews carefully, something I notice she does with every taste, then swallows.

"I'd have talked you up more. You're about to become a legend, Kelsey," Lisa declares.

Meanwhile, Kelsey puts down her Chinese carton and buries her face in her hands. "It was mortifying."

"It was quite simply the bravest thing anyone's ever done for me," I tell her softly.

Her head flies up. "Really?" The same power that's arced between us that lay dormant for fifteen years flutters in the air. The ions are almost tangible.

Lisa stands. "And this is where I bow out." Scooping up her carton, she stabs her chopsticks inside before tossing the box onto the counter. "You'll set the alarm?"

I nod, not dragging my eyes from Kelsey's face. "Good night, Lisa."

"Night, Ben. Night, Kelsey."

"Night, Lisa. I'll see you later in the morning," Kelsey says in her soft voice.

The lights in the hallway go out as Lisa turns them off one by one. Kelsey's beautiful eyes are only left illuminated by overhead pendants in the kitchen, where we're both still seated staring at one another. Putting my carton of Mongolian beef down, I stand and walk around the island. Kelsey follows my every movement, yet her breath still catches when I trap her between my arms. "I missed you today." I lean down to nuzzle behind her ear, and she lets out a long, slow moan.

Suddenly a voice yells from the hallway. "We had an agreement, big brother! No sex in common areas of the house!"

"But it's my damn house," I mutter like an adolescent boy.

Kelsey giggles before pushing me back slightly. "That reminds me. I have something for you. I need to run out to my car."

My eyes narrow as she ducks under my arms and heads toward the back door. When she followed me home earlier, I directed her to pull around back next to the garage. That's right before I gave her the extra remote to open the back gate. I want to know that Kelsey is as protected as Lisa—no, I need that.

"Want any help?" I question as I start to follow her.

"Nope. Wait for me right where you are!" The back door slams behind her.

From the back window, I see Kelsey reach into the trunk of her BMW, lifting an awkward box from the back while she has an enormous bag swung over her shoulder. She steps back under the weight of both.

I fly out the back door and catch her hips to balance her. "Don't argue. Hand it over."

Glaring at me, she says, "You suck at surprises."

I fall back a step. "This is for me?" At her sharp nod, I right myself before removing the massive rectangular wrapped package from her arms. "Then I'll carry it."

"Be careful," she warns me. "Don't bump it into anything."

A fissure of awareness goes through me like a bolt of lightning. "Okay."

She darts ahead of me, bag banging against her back. "Let me get the door."

I follow behind her at a slower pace, careful not to jostle the package on the railing. I brush up against her as I pass her, causing her breath to catch. The combustible burn we sated only the night before is already flaring up between us, demanding to be satisfied again. "Where do you want this?" My words hold a blatant double meaning.

I'll give her whatever she wants, wherever she wants it—no sex in common areas be damned.

Kelsey doesn't respond. When I look over to see if I've stunned her, I find her rooting around in her purse for something. Triumphantly, she holds a bag of Sharpies aloft. "I need to borrow your desk, if that's okay?"

Mutely, I nod before picking up the awkward box and following her.

Entering the sanctuary of my study, I kick the door shut behind me. Kelsey sets the bag down in the center of my desk with a little laugh. "You're rough on doors."

I set the box on the sofa and make my way over to her. She's leaning against my desk, her fingers clasped in front of her. Her posture is riddled with anxiety. "What is it, Kels?"

"I wanted you to know what last night—no, yesterday—meant to me. And there was only one way I could think of to show you that." Closing her eyes briefly, she fights an internal war with herself before she reaches into the bag. "When I looked around yesterday, I realized you were missing something on your shelves. Something I'd like for you to have. Something you helped inspire."

My heart pumps furiously in my chest as she pulls out a book—one of her own. The name Kee Long is emblazoned on it in large enough lettering that I can spot it even from the distance between us.

She caresses the cover. "Val could never understand why I wrote the dedication the way I did. I guess deep down, maybe I always knew I'd be handing it to you myself." She hands me a copy of a book titled *Betrayal*. I clutch it tightly, hardly able to think.

Once again, Kelsey's giving me her words. The significance isn't lost on me. I open my mouth to thank her. Before I can, she cracks my heart into a million pieces by reciting the dedication aloud without opening the cover.

"The truth about betrayals is that they happen for a reason. Sooner or later, you'll understand the reason behind them. This book is dedicated to Val and Ben. May you each find the moment of happiness that gives you the strength to conquer any harm thrown at you, much as the lessons you taught me did."

I can't stop the tears falling down my face. Even when she thought I'd betrayed her, believing I'd deliberately left her broken, she still rose above it to give her heart to the millions of children who needed her compassion.

A crooked smile crosses her face as she informs me, "They're all here. All the Pilar Martell series."

Flinging the book to land safely on the couch, I rush her. Burying my head into her shoulder, I inhale the light floral scent of her perfume.

We stand together, holding each other and letting the hurts of the past go, allowing our hearts to heal.

I don't know how many minutes go by before Kelsey draws back. Pressing a kiss to the underside of my chin, she sighs, "Go open the package, Ben."

I don't want to move out of her arms, but I sense the importance of this to her, judging by the stiffness in her posture. Sliding an arm around her waist, I tug her along with me as we make our way to the sofa. Spotting the book I tossed there, I tease, "Are you going to sign them?"

Her stoic face morphs into one of humor. "I'll autograph them now. When you read them, I'll leave your inscription in them."

"Fair enough." Carefully placing the book on the side table, I sit down, pulling Kelsey close next to me. I lift the package on my lap. "So, let me guess. It's a frame."

She hauls off and punches me in the arm. "Are you going to be like this around your birthday? Christmas? Speaking of which, when is your birthday?"

"August tenth," I tell her, my mouth dry. Because what she said implies she plans on being around for both of those events. "Yours?"

"December fifteenth." I make a mental note to spoil the living crap out of her starting around Thanksgiving for the entire month as I tear into the paper holding the frame.

And then every thought leaves my head except one.

Adoration.

"Where did you get this?" I trace over the black-and-white photo of Kelsey and me studying. A picture I never knew existed but one she obviously did. As soon as I see it, I'm transported back to that moment. Every feeling comes rushing to the surface as if we were right back in Mrs. Wiley's class.

We'd just laughed over my high-pitched imitation of my mother scolding Lisa for breaking curfew. Kelsey was trying to tell me that kind of humor was what that week's creative writing assignment lacked. Someone captured us with our heads tilted toward one another, laughing. Even overweight, her smile was dazzling. And mine . . . I squint harder, looking at myself. I was holding a piece of Kelsey's dark hair back so I could grin at her. My heart stutters when I realize I probably give her the same adoring look when I watch her now.

Tracing her finger over the photo, she answers my unasked question. "Mrs. Wiley contacted my publisher a few years ago after I dedicated a book to her. President Adams hoped I'd come back to speak at Forsyth at a graduation ceremony." My head whirls around in shock at the audacity. She shrugs as if it's something she's had to deal with a million times since her writing made her a household name. Angrily, I realize it likely has. "Even though I declined, we've kept up corresponding. She passed along this photo and a few more." Her fingertips trace the masculine filigree along the frame's edge. Her lips tip up with a small smile. "I see the picture surprised you from reading the plaques beneath it."

In confusion, I scan the frame again, searching to find . . .

Oh. My. God.

Side by side are two carefully stamped plaques. Beneath Kelsey's image are the words I'd had etched into glass years before.

But what has me frozen in shock is the plaque next to it. They're my words —ones I'd completely forgotten about, but the woman next to me didn't. My heart pounding, I read aloud, "In the cool blue of the water, nothing can touch me here. Not pain or shame, not hate, nor fear. All that can be felt is comfort and confidence."

My hands begin to shake.

She rests hers atop of mine. "You left a part of yourself behind with me as well, Ben. A big part."

Carefully, I lay the frame on the floor in front of us before gathering her against me. We both were hurt, we're both broken, but underneath it all is a foundation of understanding that's going to carry us through.

I'm sure of it.

"You know, I've got just the spot to put this. I had some unexpected housecleaning done. Good thing too," I tease softly.

Kelsey lets out a watery laugh.

With the knuckles of one hand, I nudge her chin to meet her eyes. "Thank you, sweetheart."

Hand against my cheek, she brushes a kiss on the underside of my jaw. "Thank you for being the kind of man who can stop a woman from coming apart, help put her back together, and still be able to reach the corners of her heart."

Pressing Kelsey gently back, I cover her body with mine as I can't answer her comment with words.

But there are other ways to show her how hers affect me.

Besides, mine aren't as good as hers are anyway.

CHAPTER FORTY-SIX

Benedict

If I stay in the water longer, maybe they'll give up.

Maybe it won't happen.

Maybe.

So, I keep swimming lap after lap until a shrill sound yanks me from the cool blue.

Nothing and no one can touch me here.

Certainly not fear.

All I feel is the cool slickness as the water passes over my body.

Thankfully I was reminded it wasn't swimming that caused me pain.

I frown in my sleep when I hear Coach's whistle yanking me from the pool. No, I can't. I want to just sink beneath the waves. For a minute, I debate holding my breath beneath the surface.

Letting the blue wash me away.

But the whistle sounds wrong.

My eyes jerk open and my arms tighten instinctively. Instead of my pillow, it's Kelsey I'm pulling back against my body. *Thank God I didn't cry out.* I bury my face into her shoulder as the aftereffects of the nightmare clear from my subconscious.

Then, I slide from the bed and head for the shower so I'm not late for my meeting at work.

CHAPTER FORTY-SEVEN

Kelsey

"Jilly!" I exclaim, answering my phone on the way back from Benedict's.

"It's about time I reached you. I was beginning to think you'd forgotten all about your life here in Collyer," she grumbles good-naturedly.

"No chance of that."

"What are you up to? Time to talk?"

"Absolutely. I was . . . up anyway."

"Really? Working?"

"No." Quickly, I add, "I miss you and our breakfasts. Trust me, today we'd have a lot to talk about."

There's an infectious giggle on the other end of the line. "I'm sure we would. After all, it's seven-thirty in the morning your time and I'm not dragging every word out of you in between the clattering of your keyboard."

I scramble for an answer. Jillian chuckles. "There's no way you're missing me."

Emotions I didn't even realize I was holding in come flooding out. "But I am. It's so sudden, Jilly."

"You mean like it was with me and Brett?" she recalls.

"You and Brett were meant to be," I dismiss her comment.

"And you—as well as the entire town—had vetted him." Amusement is rife in her voice.

"It didn't hurt." Both of us laugh as I pass a bakery. I debate whether I should hang up with Jillian to call Val and see if she wants to hit up Café Du Monde when I recall she's on schedule for Le Cadeau this morning.

Crap. I really need to pour my heart out to my best friend.

As if Jillian can read my thoughts, she asks, "What does Val think about you taking the plunge?"

I pull into the Macando's driveway and manage to put the car in Park. "I haven't fallen." *Yet.*

"And if I were to text Val and ask?"

I grumble, "I should never have introduced you two. All you are is mean to me."

Jillian hoots. "That's what you get for having people love you, Kelsey. Speaking of that . . ."

"La, la, la, la. I'm not talking about Benedict." I sound like I'm fourteen but considering that's how old I was when I met Jillian, I can pull it off.

"Benedict, hmm? Isn't that reunion guy?"

Laying my head on my steering wheel, I manage, "Yes," and wait for the explosion.

It doesn't come. Instead, she says, "You should bring him up to Collyer when you come for your bridesmaid dress fitting so I can check him out."

Automatically, I jeer, "You mean so Brett can have one of his police buddies run . . ." Then my words get stuck. A loving silence fills the vehicle. I repeat, "Bridesmaid?"

"Did you think I was getting married without you?"

I burst into tears. "Oh, Jilly."

"Emily's already designed your dress. Come home. Bring Benedict. Be prepared for torture."

I sniffle, completely overwhelmed. "Let me get him through meeting Val and Darin first."

"Let me get this straight. Val—your very pregnant best friend—hasn't met him yet?"

"No!" I wail.

That's when Jillian gives me very serious advice. "I'd get on that before she goes into labor due to the hissy fit she's likely to throw."

I lift my head and agree wholeheartedly. "Right, but first, I have to prepare Benedict."

Jillian uses my predicament to her advantage. "Then come get your dress fitted before setting up their first meeting. Val is going to have to be tied down to wait for the man who changed your life when you were seventeen. But she might forgive you if you're not in choking distance."

I stare off in the distance. "I'll book a flight."

Her laughter is still ringing in my ears as I disconnect the call.

CHAPTER FORTY-EIGHT

Kelsey

I'M LOUNGING IN A GRAY WINGBACK IN EMILY FREEMAN'S STUDIO waiting for her to finish up with another appointment. I'm in Collyer for the fitting of my custom-made bridesmaid dress when the door behind me cracks open. My head whirls around and I'm met with the rueful smile of the CEO of Amaryllis Events—Cassidy Freeman-Lockwood. "Oops. I didn't realize Em had a client.

"It was a last-minute favor. Emily's created a magnificent bridesmaid dress for me . . ."."

The eyes of the older woman light with recognition after studying my face. "It's good to see you, Kee. It's been too long."

"You as well, Cassidy."

Cassidy's soft drawl breaks into my musings. I tune back into our conversation. "I apologize. I didn't catch what you were saying."

"More an observation. I was merely saying I agreed with my brother-in-law when he described you as lovely." Then her smile curves up with a devilish cast before she tacks on, "Though I'd have paid good money to have been there for you dressing him down at his own office. Not many dare."

I groan. "Ryan." Amaryllis, Freemans, Lockwoods. Their branches are entangled like the tree growing outside the window at Commander's Palace. Immediately thinking that, my mind wanders to Benedict—not that it's been far from him since I left him in the early dawn hours to catch my flight to New England.

Cassidy offers, "If it makes you feel better, Caleb fell out of his chair laughing at the way you knocked Ryan down a few pegs."

My hand rubs my forehead. "Not really. Despite what Benedict said after, I was so embarrassed. I mean, Ryan's his boss."

Cassidy moves over to where I'm sitting and joins me. Up close, eyes I'd seen from across many a gala, and I'd always determined to be blue are clearly aqua. Her hair, a luxurious mink heavily threaded with silver, is the opposite of Emily's blond curls. No two women look less like sisters than maybe if you add in their younger siblings—the famed photographer, Holly, and celebrity baker, Corinna. "Now you have me more curious about this Benedict than what Ryan dished out about him." At my raised brow, Cassidy grins. "You've known us for years, Kee. You didn't pick up we're notorious meddlers when it comes to our extended family?"

I'm astonished at her outrageous assertion. "And you think I'm a part of that?"

She holds up her fingers and ticks off, "You to Jillian to Brett to Joe to Holly?"

My silent laughter causes my shoulders to shake.

Cassidy takes it in stride. "If that connection doesn't work for you, then there's a more direct one—you to Ava and Matt to me."

The air between us deepens with significant poignancy. "What do my cousin and her husband have to do with you?"

"Matt Barlow helped put the pieces of my life back together years ago, Kee," Cassidy acknowledges.

The strong, self-confident woman sitting next to me is admitting to her world being out of control. Unable to picture it, I question, "Truly?"

"I wouldn't have the blessings in my life without his support." Her voice is resolute.

Her words are like a key sliding into a lock, smoothly pinging the tumblers inside. "I feel like I can't talk to anyone; they're all too close to the situation."

Cassidy crosses her legs. "I'm happy to lend an ear while we're killing some time."

Words begin to bubble out of me—about how horribly I was bullied in high school, the emotional scars I still carry, my feelings for Benedict, Jillian's reprieve by asking me to come get my dress fit. Finally, I circle back to, "Does it diminish what I felt all those years?"

"Falling for a man who deliberately did something he knew would hurt you? No. In the end, reasons matter." Her lips curve into a private smile as if she knows something I don't.

I want to probe deeper at that nugget of knowledge, but she goes on before I can. "Forgiving him for a single act doesn't diminish what happened to you."

"Then why can't I trust easily?" I recant the entire experience with Ryan for her—how her brother-in-law played Benedict and me that morning.

Her aqua eyes flash with reassurance. "Trust is earned. You wrote, 'If life were meant to be easy, I'd have already won the game.' I've found the most important part of my life is the love I've been blessed with. It will never be easy, and it certainly isn't a game."

"There is no right or wrong in falling for Benedict because we're not the same people we were then."

"And even if you were, the only people who have to accept your relationship are those in it." Cassidy speaks the conclusion I'd already come to.

I slant a sideways glance in her direction. "Thank you for listening."

She wraps an arm around my shoulder and gives it a squeeze. "I regret not spending more time with you before you moved. Something called me to you. I mentioned it to Ava when she told me you were coming to town for your . . . oops." She stops when my head swivels in her direction. Then a cheeky grin lights her face. "Busted."

"Didn't know Emily had an appointment?" I now question, amused.

"Kee—"

"Kelsey," I correct her quietly. After all, what's the point of hiding? Since she doesn't react, I remark, "But I suspect you knew that."

Her eyes fixate on a place so far away, I wonder if my imagination could even travel there. "I'm an excellent secret keeper, Kelsey." Then she returns and brightness lights her eyes from within when she confides, "Just ask any of the sisters about how I met Caleb. It resulted in putting our older brother on a leash."

"A leash?" This conversation reminds me vaguely of Lisa accusing me and Val of playing games at Café Du Monde. And my heart flips because I miss him all over again.

Cassidy laughs. "An electronic one."

"Uh-huh." My tone is laden with doubt.

Biting back a smile, she divulges, "I assumed my husband was the groom of a wedding I was planning because my brother didn't give me the right details."

Pleasantly, I ask, "How did you not kill him—them?"

"Thus, why I know everything that goes on under this roof," Cassidy concludes.

Our mingled laughter peals out in the pale gray room. I make my own confession, "It wasn't that you all didn't make overtures. I kept to myself deliberately while I lived here. I was afraid of living, of giving."

Cassidy nods, completely understanding. "Sometimes, happiness can be found in a place. I've found it's the people who make the feeling blossom. Is Benedict your home? Ask yourself if that's what you feel when you're with him?"

I deliberate what I feel when I'm with Benedict. In such a short time, he's shown me ways I've hungered to be loved. His words show me I matter. He anticipates my hurts. He wraps me close to his heart in the middle of the night. He's become my home. Cassidy's right. But then a thought pops into my head. I demand, "Is Ava going to get a play-by-play about this conversation?"

Just as Cassidy's about to answer, Emily opens the door with my dress—a gorgeous silver column of lace and feathers. "What do you think, Kee?"

Cassidy winks before bumping my shoulder. "I'll leave you both to it."

Something feels off, something I need to correct. "Emily, don't you think we've known each other long enough for you to call me Kelsey? After all," I continue as Em trips over her own feet, "your sister was quick enough to remind me we're family."

Emily's eyes dart back and forth between the two of us. "Did you work a little magic, Cass?"

Cassidy murmurs, "Not me, Matt. He constantly encouraged me to see myself as others saw me."

Emily shakes the dress, snatching my and Cassidy's attention to the real reason I've been in Emily's studio. "Let's see you in a whole new look."

That's when I get a full view of the vision Emily's holding. "Wow!"

Emily's talking about the design, but I can only think about Benedict being with me at Jillian's wedding and seeing me in that gown.

By my side.

Now.

Always.

A soft chuckle escapes my lips when I realize I'm hiding none of my feelings from the two older women. But as I've already worked out, there's nothing wrong with what I'm feeling.

The emotions behind it belong to me and Benedict.

CHAPTER FORTY-NINE

Benedict

"Am I ever going to be forgiven for not knowing how to cook until I met you?" Kelsey grumbles good-naturedly to Val. A few weeks after Kelsey gave me the frame and made a trip back to Collyer for an unexpected bridesmaid dress fitting, we're gathered in the Macondo's backyard for an impromptu barbecue after I get off work.

After returning from Collyer, Kelsey's been working on her newest book while I've returned to my minimum ten-hour days. Every night when I'm on the way home, I call her to see if she's in a good stopping place. If so, she meets me at my house where we may spend quiet time together or crawl all over each other like it's been years since we've touched each other's skin.

Either is perfect as long as I'm with her.

Today, I made sure I finished early so I wouldn't arrive late. As I strode down the corridor, I made certain my team reaped the rewards of their hard work on the Larruscain deal, declaring, "Knock off early. Consider it a summer Friday."

War whoops followed me as I walked up and down the corridor to ensure everyone got the message. Once I got back up to my office, I called to see if there was anything I needed to bring.

"Bring anything? I don't think so," Kelsey mused.

But Val screamed through the phone, "Get your fine ass over here for the bestie inquisition, Benedict. It's time! Bring hamburger rolls."

I snorted when Kelsey shrieked at her best friend and said, "I'll be there in an hour." Which gave me time to change out of my suit into something more comfortable as well as pick up the hamburger rolls. I dared not show up without them.

I have a finely honed sense of self-protection

When I arrived, Kelsey opened the door red-faced. I handed her the bag from Whole Foods before yanking her into my arms for a kiss that lasted until Val bellowed about the burgers over-cooking and, "I'm too damn pregnant to wait for food!"

Now, we're gathering around the patio table. Kelsey sets down a platter of fixings before dropping into the seat next to me and mouths off at Val, "Now dig in before you deprive my niece of nutrients."

Val shudders before reaching for a bun, burger, and piles of lettuce. I notice Kelsey skips the bun. "Not a fan of bread?"

"I can eat more if I forgo bread. It fills my stomach up too fast. And I know what we're having for dessert," she says smugly.

"Is it something decadent?" Darin asks eagerly.

"It will taste that way. Courtesy of that one." She nods at Val, who has a hamburger wedged in her mouth like she's just been gagged with it. "I can cook delicious food that's healthy. Everything Nana cooked was fried in both butter and oil. Or glazed in sugar." Thoughtfully, she forks up a bite of her burger and chews. She swallows before adding with a slightly dreamy look, "I have to admit, I love when I go home and indulge in her chocolate pecan pie."

I glance over at Darin, who is openly drooling before remarking, "That sounds . . ."

"Fucking delicious. Do you know what I'd do to have Kelsey's grandmother cook for me again? Jesus, she came out to visit in California, and I swear, half the basketball team was ready to propose," Darin moans.

I raise a brow before taking a bite of my overloaded burger. "To her grandmother?"

"Hell no, man. To Kelsey. The guys figured they'd get her grandmother as a bonus," Darin states.

I choke on the perfectly charred meat.

Kelsey rolls her eyes as she whacks me on the back. Setting down the burger, I loop an arm over her shoulder. I question her curiously, "You weren't interested?" Surely by then, her self-confidence would have begun to repair itself from the machinations at Forsyth.

Blushing, she darts a look at me before glaring at Val, who's hooting louder than the barn owls you can spot in the predawn at City Park. "I had a thing for swimmers."

"Still do, sister," Val singsongs as she wipes her eyes against her sleeve.

My hand squeezes her shoulder in reflex at the apparent slip of her best friend's tongue.

Kelsey narrows her eyes before turning to Darin. Her smile is nothing short of evil. I observe the look and note, "Why do I have a feeling retribution is delivered swiftly around here?"

"Because you're a smart man. So, Darin, tell me you made your extra-special margaritas since we have company."

Val sobers up quickly. "Now that's just mean. Mean, I say. I'm pregnant for another million years . . ."

"Four more months," both Darin and Kelsey correct her in unison. I lean back against the bench seat, amused at the byplay.

"Fine. Four more months. And here you all are talking about Darin's miracle margaritas? That's low, sister. Even if I gave you up to your man."

"Oh, for Christ's sake!" Kelsey exclaims. She's laughing so hard at her best friend, she's dropped her utensils.

"Um, for those of us not in the know, what's a miracle margarita?" I ask, hoping my lawyer skills might help diffuse whatever situation might be brewing.

"It's a Kool-Aid margarita! Tell me you wouldn't miss them if you were pregnant," Val challenges.

"Now, see, that's where your logic goes completely off the rails, my friend." Kelsey picks up her water to take a small sip.

"Why's that?" Val throws back.

"First, because you're presuming Ben loves tequila. Second, you're assuming he likes Kool-Aid. And third, that he'd combine the two together."

Val gives Kelsey a *pshaw* gesture as if anyone wouldn't want to drink that sickening-sounding concoction. "And?"

"And finally, he'll never be pregnant, so"—Kelsey shrugs—"there's no chance he'll ever feel your pain. Even if he was a tequila savant. Even if he lusted for the taste of green apple and Patrón mixed over ice with sugar . . ."

Val picks up half of a fresh bun and throws it at Kelsey's head. Kelsey ducks, and it flies harmlessly into the grass. "I hate you."

"You love me," Kelsey counters.

"I do. But right now, I want a Jolly Rancher to make up for you taunting me, and those things are nothing but crap."

"So are Darin's margaritas, but you want one of those," Kelsey points out.

"You both realize that you're giving Benedict a terrible impression," Darin informs them. He's rewarded for his sensibility by his pregnant wife chucking the other half of the bun at his head. Scowling, he demands, "What was that for?"

"For being logical. For making magical margaritas. For being so damn hot I want to carry your baby," Val lists.

"I'll show you how hot I am," Darin mumbles around another bite of his burger, unconcerned about his wife's outburst.

Kelsey peals into laughter. Turning to face me, her smile is brighter than the setting sun. "Do you see why I need to find a place to live?"

I pick up my burger and take a hefty bite. Swallowing, I grin at her. "Just think of all the fodder you have for future books."

"Hmm," she answers noncommittally.

Val's head snaps up. Her face is comically horrified. "You wouldn't dare."

Darin splutters after taking a pull from his beer.

"Any resemblance to actual persons . . ." Kelsey begins to recite, but Val interrupts.

"Oh, come on! There's like a sacred rule between besties. You have to make me superhot and have mad sex with a gazillionaire."

Darin coughs loudly. "Excuse me?"

Val flicks a hand at him. "She can make him look like you. Jesus, get over it."

At this point, I can't control my laughter any longer. "Is every conversation like this?"

It's Kelsey who answers. "If by 'like this' you mean Val being a lunatic, then yes. Once she's claimed you as hers, she has no boundaries—emotional or physical."

"Listen, just because I like seeing your hot body all wet in the shower . . ." Damn her! Val times that comment just as I take a drink of my own beer. It ends up all down the front of my shirt and across my plate of food.

"God help me," I wheeze out.

"He can't, but if you haven't seen her wet and naked yet, I can give you a verbal description," Val offers.

Luckily, Darin decides at that moment to place his fingers over his wife's lips, giving me time to recover. "Sweetheart, if you don't stop torturing Benedict, I really will go make margaritas for the rest of us."

Val glares at him before yanking her head away and picking up her burger. "Fine. I'll behave. So, Ben, I hear you're a lawyer. Do you chase after ambulances?" Val flutters her eyelashes at me innocently.

Looking down at my slightly soggy burger, I shrug before picking it up, deciding the topic is safe enough for me to eat. "I work for Lockwood Industries."

"Does that mean you can support my girl and her addiction to clothes?"

Immediately, the burger slips out of my fingers and lands in a splat on my plate.

Kelsey's head thunks against the table as she groans aloud. "Dare, control her, for Christ's sake!"

"I haven't had much luck in ten years, Kels. What makes you think I can start now?" he replies with a note of despair in his voice. Giving me a wink, he takes another bite to show me that he finds the antics of these two friends —no, sisters—utterly hysterical.

I follow his lead. I shift the burger back into a manageable pile before lifting it to my lips for another bite. As Kelsey and Val trade quip for quip, I don't bother to hold back my smile. *Now I understand what she meant. We were both meant to grow and change. She needed these people in her life to become the Kelsey Kennedy who has stolen my heart.*

As we devour our meal, my ears pick up the song I set for Kelsey's ringtone as it plays softly through the speakers on the deck. Not that she has any idea. Dave Matthews's song about finding your one person and hanging on to them through ups and downs became Kelsey's as I walked away from her at the gym. Sliding out of the chair, I offer her my hand. "Care to dance?"

"What? Here?"

"Right now." I'm already standing. Her hand slides into mine, and I pull her to her feet.

Kelsey's joy in tonight makes me want to show off a little. I spin her out to the hoots and hollers of our audience before yanking her back into my arms. Pulling her close, I sing the refrain in her ear. "You've made me a better person since the day we met. Every single day."

Kelsey's body molds to mine as she tugs my head toward her. Obliging her by leaning down, I accept her kiss, but when I taste her words against my lips, it's then I know I'll never be the same.

"I've been alone and still had you with me. I'm strong enough to survive that. It's being with you and worrying you want this to head in the same direction I do that scares the hell out of me, Ben." Pulling back slightly, her full lips quirk upward before she brushes a kiss against mine.

I'm shell-shocked standing in place as she returns to the dinner table because in such a short time, she's becoming everything.

We've known each other in all the worst ways. Now, we're getting to experience the other in the best ones. Kelsey used to be enveloped by sadness and pain; now, that's been replaced with determination, will, and strength. By her own admission, she's quick to ire when someone she cares for has been hurt. I know she'll be the first to apologize if she's wrong. She's brilliant. She's beautiful. And she cares about the hearts of everyone around her. I'm utterly besotted, captivated.

Time isn't going to change what I feel.

It isn't going to take much more before I'm ready to accept the fact I've fallen in love with her.

Rubbing a hand over my chest, I try to alleviate the pressure settling there. I don't even realize Darin's come to stand next to me until a fresh beer's shoved into my hand. "So, based on the look on your face, I'm assuming I should stall on finding Kelsey a new house?"

My head jerks up a bit to meet the dark black eyes of the six-foot-six former college ballplayer. "You're her realtor?"

He shrugs. "She's the best and worst client ever. She has an unlimited budget but no idea what she wants other than to live close to us. Oh, and an enormous closet."

I think about the two unused ones in my master suite, and a satisfied "Hmm" comes out of my mouth.

Darin shakes his head. "Any idea how long it's going to take before I can scratch her off my client list?"

Without thinking, I blurt out, "I'm going to have to get her on a plane back to Savannah."

"The hell you are," he rumbles. He takes a step forward to get into my space.

I hold up both hands. "I want to take her outside the city to meet my parents." *And I need to ask my father to give me my grandmother's engagement ring*, but I keep that last part to myself.

"Oh." The lean giant settles back. "Well, shit, man. She swore that she was never heading back to that damn city even before that reunion."

"Might be kind of tough for her to accept. If I can't talk her into it, I don't know what I'm going to do. Maybe fly my parents out?" I mutter more to myself than Darin.

He claps a hand down on my shoulder. "Let's see how dinner with Val's family goes. If you survive that, I'm certain you'll be able to get her to do anything."

"What are you talking about?"

"Since Kels only has grandparents, Val's family pretty much adopted her. If you think she"—he nods toward his wife, who's holding on to her stomach as she laughs at something Kelsey says—"is bad, wait till you get them all together. *Madre Dios*." He makes the sign of the cross. "They're all crazy as shit and have ears like bats." The last he says softly, but from the sudden stillness of the two women, they hear him.

Fuck. "Do you think they heard what I said to you?"

"Nah, Val woulda been screechin' . . . Hey, baby." He offers her a winsome smile as his very pregnant wife waddles up.

"What are you two plottin' over here?" she demands.

"Nothing," we both answer.

Kelsey sidles up next to me and snags my beer out of my hand. She takes a pull and gives it back before warning us, "You know she's homing in on her mama bear skills."

I shudder in fear. "You're going to make an excellent mother, Val." I try to charm my way out of disclosing what Darin and I were discussing.

"Uh-huh. You"—Val points her finger in my direction—"have to deal with her. He . . .""—the finger moves toward her husband, who pales slightly beneath his caramel-colored skin as Val chastises him in Spanish.

I lean down and whisper in Kelsey's ear, which is hard to do since her shoulders are shaking so hard. "What's she saying?" I whisper.

"Do you want the edited version?"

It takes me less than a half a second to decide. "Yes."

"That she hopes he enjoyed having her this morning because if he's helping to sell me out, it would be the last time he got any until the doctor gave her the 'all clear' after the baby." Kelsey starts laughing harder. She says something in Spanish back to Val, who glares at her before giving her the middle finger.

"Thanks, Kels," Darin says gratefully. Swooping in, he bends down and kisses his temperamental wife.

"What did you say?" I'm both astounded to learn Kelsey speaks Spanish and enchanted by her ease with this dynamic couple.

"That Val liked riding his cock even more now that her hormones are out of whack with being pregnant with Lucy." I gape at her. She shrugs. "Remember? I live here. The walls aren't that thick."

Val giggles in her husband's embrace as he nuzzles her neck. Without thinking, I declare, "I like them."

Kelsey snuggles against me. "I'm glad. I can count the number of people I'm this close to on one hand."

Startled, because this is another area of our lives where we're the same, I rear back. "Really?"

"My grandparents, my cousin and her husband, and a childhood friend from Connecticut." Then her breath hitches. "Actually, I'm wrong."

"You are?" I expect her to include her editor or someone from her writing life. That's when she sweeps away any thought she hasn't captured the pieces of my shattered heart.

She pieces them back together when she holds up a single finger of one hand and places over my chest. "Now, there's you."

Even as my heart stutters over the idea she's feeling the same emotion I am, I feel panicked about confronting her family. Kelsey still doesn't know what happened between me and her grandfather. I stroke the hair back from her face. "I hope to expand that circle soon."

She cocks her head to the side before questioning, "Oh yeah? Who?"

"Cade, who you haven't met yet."

She nods sagely. "After this, it wouldn't surprise me if you arranged for us to go out in the swamps gator watching or something."

"That writer's imagination is going to get you in trouble." But I continue, seriously. "Lisa."

Her smile lights up the dark places in my soul. "She's already earning her own place, Ben. She's a special woman."

I take a deep breath, laying the groundwork for what's to come. "And my parents."

She stills in my arms, not saying a word. Her lips part, but no sound comes out.

"If it's too soon, I'll understand. But I need for you to appreciate . . ." She stops me from talking by placing her fingers over my lips.

"Give me just a moment."

My heart twists as a wrenching look of pain is chased away by one of serenity. "I thought for so long life was just wearing me down. I didn't realize it was getting rid of all the bad parts for happiness to move in."

"Kelsey," I groan. I can't stop myself from kissing her, not caring who's watching or if Val shrieks the whole neighborhood down.

All I know is that we're finally on the same page of the same story. And for once, it's not one filled with horror.

CHAPTER FIFTY

Benedict

"Hey, Dad."

"Hi, son. Not with Kelsey tonight?"

"She and Val are working down at the shelter."

"Your sister with them?" I hear the familiar whine and creak of my father's office chair as he leans back.

"If it weren't for the fact the three of them are being chaperoned by twenty kids, I'd be terrified," I joke.

The chair makes wheezes as my father leans forward. "This is the kind of night that separates the men from the boys, Ben."

This is what separates the men from the boys, Perrault. The phrase triggers a long-ago memory of a hot breath against my ear. My breath whooshes out even as my muscles freeze.

"Ben? Benedict? Son?" My father calls through the phone. His grumble, "Darn thing. I always lose signal in the house," unlocks something inside me.

It's my dad.

It is just words. It isn't anything I can't handle.

I'm not the boy I was. I'm a man.

I reach for the tumbler of water, ignoring the fact my hand is causing the water to splash over the side. "Yeah, Dad. Must be your phone. Or maybe the booster. You should have the cable guy check it out."

"I will. Now, talk to your old man. What's new? How's Cade?"

Grateful for the reprieve, I dive headfirst explaining the change in my sister and Cade's relationship. My father's, "Took long enough," makes me seek out the photo Kelsey gave me.

Yeah, Dad. It sure did. Refocusing my attention back on my father, I manage a laugh when he asks if Cade's lost the panicked horse expression around Lisa yet.

CHAPTER FIFTY-ONE

Kelsey

A WEEK LATER, I'VE CONVINCED BENEDICT HE WILL NOT BE ON THE menu at Val's family's home for Sunday dinner. Though, after forced family karaoke began and I jumped in with both feet, I'm certain he's rethinking our relationship if the terrified expression on his face is any indicator.

Forced family karaoke Sundays became a tradition when Val and her brothers scattered in a million different directions as they grew older. Mama Maria laid down the law about her children being home for one meal a week when they were in town to spend some *maldito tiempo en familia* together. When Val and I used to come back from college to visit, we'd be breaking it down in the kitchen while helping Maria with dinner—much to her younger brother's amusement. It eventually led to Carlos challenging his sister to a boys versus girls sing-off.

What a mistake that was. Not once in eleven years have the boys won. I grin as I swivel my hips. Benedict chokes on his beer as I belt out how I refuse to be played.

Maria's selection comes up, and soon the three of us are harmonizing with Fleetwood Mac. By the end, I stop mimicking Christine McVie and stare at "Stevie" in concern when she moans, "God help this child. She's going to be on my teat learning to sing. Right out of the womb."

"Classic rock runs through your blood, that's for sure," I agree, watching through narrowed eyes as Val rubs a hand over Lucy before she collapses against Darin. "You okay over there?"

"She just gets active when . . ."

"When her mama is shakin' it like she used to at college," Darin pipes in.

Val glares at him. "You keep scaring Ben," she chastises her husband.

"No, sweetheart, I think you managed that all on your own," he retorts. Facing Benedict, he gripes, "The trouble I used to have to keep these two out of was ridiculous."

"Really?" Benedict asks. I've dropped down on the floor in front of him. As he's talking, I feel his fingers run through my hair. "Even Kels?"

Darin snorts. I gasp, affronted. "I was a model . . ."

I can't even get the rest of the sentence out before Darin barrels over me. "Of how to be corrupted. Yes, you were."

"I—"

"Resemble that remark. Don't even try to wiggle your fine ass out of it, Kels. You have no idea how many guys I warned off when you'd jump up next to this one"—he squeezes Val—"on a table to dance."

"Pshaw. I think your memory is screwy."

Carlos laughs from across the room where he's been conspiring with Luis for the guys' songs. "Not hardly, Kels. The first time you came home, I swore I'd figure out a way to get you to notice me."

"You sure did that," Luis pipes up. The shyest of the Riviera family, he often sits in the background letting the conversation flow around him. "How many times did you steal her bra and parade it through the house?" Even as shock courses through my body, I feel Ben's fingers clench in my hair.

"He was fourteen," I quickly say, justifying it to the entire room. "He did what every punk at that age did—teasing the overweight girl." I shrug off another memory that, at the time burned a little.

Carlos's face takes on a comical cast. "Is that what you thought?"

Luis smirks. "I told you, you don't have as much game as you thought you did."

His brother hits him. "Asshole," he says before turning to me somewhat abashed. "Kels, I had a huge crush on you for years. I finally gave up when I put it together you weren't interested."

Heart racing, I glance around at everyone with consternation. "Um . . ." Benedict's body is rigid against me, at the perceived slight? At the competition? I slide my hand along his leg to reassure him, even though I don't know why. The tension in Benedict releases slightly. "I hope I didn't hurt your feelings, Carlos," I finally say.

I speak no less than the truth. Having lived my version of hell, I don't want anyone else feeling less because of my tunnel vision. Cassidy's—well, Matt's—words flit through my brain—the way I saw myself versus how others saw me. I have to forgive myself for not understanding. I was trying to escape from myself. But I hope God's still ready to forgive me because I still relish the thought of jabbing a heel in the hearts of a few of my former classmates on both Benedict's and my behalf, but that's different.

"Trust me, I'm more than content being your 'brother.' " Carlos's words nudge me from my reverie. His dark brown eyes crinkle at the corners when I collapse in visible relief. "Is that because you can't handle all this?" he teases as he gestures up and down his body.

"No. I'm just thrilled I don't have to feel guilty for having waited half my life for this"—I jerk my head back at Benedict, who's gone still again where our bodies meet—"and I don't have to feel guilty about bringing it home with me."

Before anyone can say a word, I'm being lifted off the floor and onto Benedict's lap. Before I can fully process the sudden change of position, his lips are devouring mine. Twining my arms around his neck, I fall into his kiss completely, forgetting where we are and who we're with.

Moments later, his lips gently brush against my still-closed eyes when he lets me up for air. "Waited half your life for? I'd swear, Kels, I'd wait not only for this life, but the next one to be right where I am right now with you."

My heart sighs with happiness. I lean my head forward to rest it against his.

The moment is perfect until Luis declares, "Now see? Benedict's got the kind of game to get a woman like Kelsey."

"Shut up, Luis!" is shouted from several different locations, the loudest being Maria as she smacks her youngest child upside the head.

I feel a hard male chest shaking beneath me. Pulling back just a little, Benedict grins before pointing a thumb at himself and saying, "I've got game, all right."

It's a measure of how far we've come that instead of stirring up our painful past, all I do is toss my head back and laugh—right before I slug him in the arm for his arrogance.

I couldn't be more thrilled with how our lives seem to blend seamlessly.

We're driving back to Benedict's after a delicious meal. Maria went all out with my favorite dishes when she found out I was bringing someone with me. "I'm stuffed," I declare.

"So am I," Benedict groans. Lifting my fingers to his lips, he rubs them back and forth before letting my hand go to return his hand to the wheel. "That was quite an experience. No wonder Darin warned me."

"I should hurt him for that," I grumble.

"You would have led me into forced family karaoke without warning? For shame, Kelsey." His lips are twisted in a smirk. I laugh at his next statement. "Val came about her brand of crazy naturally, I see."

"You have no idea." Shifting in the seat slightly, I'm regaling Benedict with tales of a much younger Val when my cell phone rings. Pulling it out of my purse, I chirp, "Oh! It's my grandfather." Turning away, I answer. "Hey, Pop-pop! What's up?" I beam over at Benedict only to find his hands tense on the steering wheel. My smile dims a little, but I don't have time to cover the phone to ask what's wrong.

"Nothing, sugar. Nana and I just wanted to check in on how you're doin'." My Pop-pop's sweet voice rings through my ear.

"Well, I'm stuffed with all kinds of Riviera deliciousness," I tease him.

He groans in agony and delight. "Save me, child. I don't think this stomach of mine can handle that kind of spice anymore."

I chuckle. "It was one time that Val cooked for you, Pop-pop. Once, and she toned it down. Maybe it was the fact you went back for thirds that caused indigestion, not the spice level." I smack my lips in my grandfather's ear to remind him just how good it was when I say, "There was cornbread today."

He groans. "I don't suppose it can be mailed?"

"You've asked me that before, Pop-pop." I hazard a glance over at Benedict, whose lips are twitching at my end of the conversation. "And I'll remind you once again, the last time I brought some home, you tried to hide it from Nana. That was just wrong."

"Your Nana was trying to ration it out . . ."

"And you tried to lock it in your safe!" I exclaim. Benedict barks out a laugh before he controls himself. He shakes his head in disbelief at the antics.

"Unbelievable," Benedict says softly. Turning his head briefly, he gives me a wicked grin. "Now I understand where you get your sass from."

"I'm sorry, Kelsey," Pop-pop says contritely. "I didn't realize you were out with a gentleman caller."

I love how my grandfather refers to any date I've ever been on like that. "Actually, it's someone I've reconnected with since the reunion." To my shock, Benedict begins shaking his head vehemently.

"Oh? Was it someone you met at the hotel? Someone on the plane?" Confusion fills my grandfather's voice.

"Kelsey," Benedict warns. But there's an underlying note of sadness in his voice I don't quite understand.

"Benedict?" I wonder aloud. I didn't expect the reaction I got on the phone.

"Benedict? Benedict Perrault? Do you mean to tell me you and that boy who hurt you . . . no! I won't have it, Kelsey Isabelle Kennedy!" Pop-pop shouts so loudly.

Benedict flinches. I know he heard.

"No, what I won't have is you talkin' without understandin'!" My Southern accent, normally a fluid ribbon, is cut to shreds. "You just stop!"

"Watch that tone. Respect your elders," he retorts in my ear.

"I will when they show some for the people I care for. What happened back then is between Benedict and me, Pop-pop. He explained, and I accepted."

"I don't know how you could."

"Because if I hold on to what I felt for Ben at that moment, then I should hate myself still, shouldn't I?" Silence greets my declaration in both ears.

"Kelsey." Benedict breaks it first as he reaches for my hand. "Sweetheart, you have nothing to hate yourself for. We talked about this."

"My self-hatred caused a vicious circle, Ben. I fed on it—and food—to silence those fears. I was so afraid of the world. You never gave me any reason to doubt you, but when it mattered most, I didn't trust." I give his hand a quick squeeze as the tension in me dissipates. "If I'd realized that, maybe I'd have been able to stop sabotaging the happiness in my life. Who knows whether our lives would have intersected at a reunion five years ago? Ah . . ." I've forgotten I'm on the phone at all. I squeeze the hand I'm holding tighter. "You went back for me."

He nods. We pull into the driveway at his house. Putting the car into park, he unclips his seat belt and faces me. "Every five years. In my mind, I couldn't erase the pain on your face. I needed to know you were happy."

My lip trembles. "I wasn't then."

"And I'm the one who gets to bask in it now."

"Ben . . ."

"It's going to take your grandfather time to trust me, Kels. Don't begrudge him the chance to do that when he spent so many years nurturing the heart that I've dreamed about."

Lifting the phone to my ear, I ask, "Did you hear all that, Pop-pop?"

"I . . . I don't know what to say, sugar. Maybe your nana and I will try to make a trip to visit you once you've settled in your new home."

I nod, and it's a moment before I realize he can't see me. I offer, "Or we'll come to you."

Ben's head jerks in shock. Then he leans down and places his forehead against mine before whispering, "Anytime you want, sweetheart."

Leaning against him, I whisper, "Love you, Pop-pop. Tell Nana I said to send you to quilting class."

The groan in my ear causes my lips to curve as Benedict brushes my nose with his. "I'll know if you don't."

"I know, sugar. I know." My grandfather swallows audibly. His voice is raspy when he says, "I love you, Kelsey. You be careful. And tell that boy to take better care of your heart this time."

"I love you too, Pop-pop." I hang up. The phone clatters to the console between the two of us. The air is thick with emotion. "What is it?"

"I realized I could have been okay without you, but I'd never have been this . . ." Benedict shakes his head as if he's in a daze and he needs to clear it.

"What?"

"Happy. I'm just happy." And the kiss he gives me reinforces that.

CHAPTER FIFTY-TWO

Benedict

"Son, you tried." My father's hand clasps down on my shoulder as I stare at nothing.

I don't flinch. I don't alter my position. I've been sitting here in the same spot for hours since he drove me back from the Barron's home.

For a long time, there's silence between us. Then my father whispers, "I would never have you hurt—emotionally or physically." He lifts my right hand and traces over the scar there.

I flinch as flashback after flashback races through my mind but no physical torture I endured was as devastating as standing above Kelsey in that stadium and being the person to hurl a boulder at her fragile contentment.

He lets my hand drop. "I want you to listen to. Look at me."

Exhausted, I do as he asks.

"I'm proud of you, Benedict—who and what you tried to stand up for. It won't be soon, but one day, you will be too."

Doubting anything but the pain filling every cell of my being, I look back over the marsh and continue to mourn the loss of the only real person I had at Forsyth.

Kelsey.

CHAPTER FIFTY-THREE

Kelsey

"I'm nervous," I admit.

"Why?" Benedict squeezes my hand as he eases me from the passenger seat of his car.

"Gee, I don't know. Maybe because I'm about to meet your best friend?" I quip sarcastically.

Lisa breezes by me as she walks around the back of the car. "Nothing to worry about. Cade's just like any other guy." I can tell she's lying as a blush crawls up her cheeks and she checks out her outfit in the reflection of the car's immaculate wax job.

"And that means?" I wonder aloud as the three of us cross the street to a slick restaurant down on the waterfront.

"Just like every other man, he's got something between his legs he likes to have played with, but sometimes the mass between his ears isn't all that bright," Lisa declares resolutely.

"Considering he's a damn doctor, I'd say he's got quite a brain on him."

I jump in, recalling our earlier discussions about his best friend, "Tulane Medical Center, right?"

"Yes. He's a resident there."

"Whoop-dee-do." Is Lisa's response, causing me to choke on the air I swallow at Benedict's fulminating glare.

His voice is arctic. "Lisa, I'd say he's a little smarter than the average guy."

In response, Lisa gives a nonchalant shrug, but she surreptitiously sends me a wink. She knows exactly how smart Cade Miller is, but she's just enjoying ribbing her brother.

"Why do I get the impression this is more than a simple double date?" I say softly to Ben as we follow Lisa, who's still fidgeting anxiously with her hemline, her hair, her clutch.

"Should I be concerned you can read me that easily?"

"It's not like either of you are hiding your anxiety," I point out.

Benedict sucks in a breath between his teeth. "Cade and I were roommates in college. He's the brother I never had. And I'm getting accustomed to the fact he's had feelings for Lisa for a long while."

Oh boy. He extends his hand to me, and we catch up with an impatient Lisa, who's tapping her foot in agitation.

Benedict's right. This isn't just my meeting his best friend, it's a coming-out dinner for everyone involved. It's admitting the baby sister he'd do anything for and the best friend whose antics he'd heard the unedited version of for years are a couple. Offering him my physical as well as moral support, I smile at the younger girl. "Are we all checked in?"

"Ben will check in. I'm sure they'll seat us as soon as . . ." Her voice trails off as the door to the restaurant opens behind me.

"Cade," Benedict calls out. "Over here, man."

In front of me, Lisa's body locks, her eyes slightly unfocused.

Shit. What kind of man can cause that kind of reaction in one of the most levelheaded women I've ever met? I turn around before every cell in my body freezes.

Holy hotness.

"What the hell did they inject into the water at that school?" I hiss at Lisa, immediately understanding her surface attraction to her brother's best friend.

Forcing her gaze away from the black-haired man, she says, "I'm so glad I don't have to suffer through another meal with them alone."

Recalling some of the more obnoxious meals with the basketball players at Pepperdine, I drawl, "Let me guess, random women approaching, snide comments in the washroom, your order coming out wrong . . ."

"Every damn time!" Before I can stop her, Lisa leans over and grabs my cheeks. She presses her lips against mine firmly. "Finally, finally, someone understands!"

A dark shadow blocks out the light. "I think I just got a little turned on by that. Want to go for it again?"

Benedict's sharp "No!" causes Cade to give me a head to toe perusal. Which, in turn, sets Lisa and me off sniggering again.

"Well, Ben, I've been interested in meeting your girlfriend for a while. After this little display"—Cade's eyes scorch over Lisa—"by my own woman, I'm more than a little intrigued."

I'm about to hold out my hand to introduce myself when Lisa—the imp—whispers, "I'll give you the details later. I've been dying to share, and Ben definitely does not want to know." Benedict groans before he slips away to check us in.

Instead of being calm and composed, I'm fighting back the need to snicker in Cade's face when I hold out my hand. "Kel . . ." I stammer before regaining my composure. "Kelsey Kennedy."

Cade lifts my hand to his mouth. "It's a pleasure to meet you after all these years, Kelsey." Jesus, this man is potent. His dark eyes burn like coals even as his breath whispers over my fingers. I'm like a lovesick puppy worshipping him before I focus on what he said. It still takes me a second to unscramble my thoughts.

"Years?"

Cade doesn't respond to my blatant probing. Instead, he slips an arm around Lisa, tugging her close to his side. Knowing I'm not going to get any information out of his decadent lips, I inform him, "I'm afraid you have me at a complete disadvantage. I only started getting the scoop on your antics a short time ago. But truly, Ben's done nothing but sing your praises."

A smile that I'm sure has done its fair share of melting the panties off plenty of women curves his lips. "Good. Then I don't have to redeem myself with you. I've spent the better part of a month explaining away years of my life to this one."

Lisa makes a face even as she settles deeper into his embrace. A look of pure contentment flashes across her waiflike features. "The problem was I knew you, Cade. There was no using that sexy voice to talk yourself out of the truth." Beneath her exasperated tone is someone who's taken a dive off the deep end and doesn't regret it.

I understand the feeling completely. Judging by the possessive way Ben's arm wraps around my waist after he rejoins us, he's feeling the same way. I'm floating on a cloud of joy so sublime, I can't express it. I let my smile speak for me.

Cade winks before dropping a kiss on the top of Lisa's head. "Should we head to the bar while we're waiting for our table?"

Lisa and I agree when a young gentleman approaches us. "Mr. Perrault? Your table is ready. If you and your party will follow me?"

Cade raises a brow in surprise. "Well, that was fast."

I'm about to concur, but then I see the young man give Benedict a thorough once over. I can't control the giggle that escapes. I hazard a glance at Lisa, whose hand has slapped across her mouth to cover her mirth. "I think I might know why," I offer.

"Shit, not you too," Cade rumbles grumpily, with a mock glare down at Lisa. "I see Lisa's been sharing her accounts of dinners out with us."

Her amusement waifs over us all as we follow behind the host to our table.

I've regained my composure, but I'm barely able to retain my straight face as the host offers to seat both Ben and Cade first before scurrying in retreat when Ben growls, "I think we'll be okay after we seat our *dates*." His emphasis on the last word only adds to the disappointment on the host's face. I want to tell him I understand—Benedict Perrault is pure heartbreak mixed with simple lust. Really, he should come with a hazard label.

"You think so?" Benedict murmurs in my ear when I realize I said the words aloud.

Blushing, I catch Cade's eye as Benedict slides my chair under the table. The approving smile he sends me does much to calm my nerves.

Then Lisa pipes up, "So, this is kind of late to make dinner and a show."

"It's called dinner theater, Lisa," Benedict says patiently.

Our waiter comes up behind us. "What a lovely way of phrasing it. Hello, darlings. I'm Zach. I'll be your server this evening. Let me get you started with some water while you have an opportunity to look over the drink menu." Zach hands Cade the bar menu with a hungry smile, but when he faces Benedict head-on, he stops dead in his tracks.

I bite my lip. Benedict squeezes my leg warningly under the table.

"And the wine list for you, sir." Zach's voice is a touch raspier than it was a moment ago.

"Thank you," Benedict's deep voice answers cordially. I'm positive Zach just joined me on Cloud Ben and doesn't plan on coming down all night.

Almost in unison, the heavy drink menus are opened by the men. There's a dark flush riding Benedict's cheeks. And I can no more hold in the splutter of laugher that escapes than Lisa can.

"I don't know why I'm laughing anymore," I gasp to Lisa. "Is it because of the puppy eyes Ben just received or . . ."

Lisa's laughing so hard her mascara is running down her face. "The fact they tried to seat Cade first?"

Benedict's blatantly ignoring us. He's flipping the pages of the wine menu without reading a word while Cade glares at the bar menu. I ask Lisa while I'm fiddling with the stem of my water glass. "I'm guessing this is a first?"

Her shoulders are shaking uncontrollably, which naturally set mine in motion. Blood rushes to my face. I'm certain it's a lovely color to complement my black strapless dress. But Lisa? Soon she's panting in and out in an effort not to succumb to the hilarity of it all.

"Who chose this place?" Lisa manages to gasp. Before either Ben or Cade can answer, the most stunning woman I've ever seen comes up to our table wearing a silver low-cut gown with a high slit along the side. Her platinum-blond hair is impeccably in place, pulled back with a diamond clip in the shape of a flower.

"Sugars, I'm Madame Magnolia," she drawls. "Welcome to Belle la Mer." My eyes go wide when I hear the restaurant's name. Even as a New Orleans newbie, I've heard of this place. Now, I'm excited. I crane my neck back and forth, trying to look for the person I know who works here. *Oh, I can't wait to tell Val.*

Magnolia continues, "Are you celebrating a special occasion with us?" Her attention drifts to Benedict, and her lips curve into a beautiful red smile.

"No," I say, somewhat disappointed, not only that I don't spy Raul, but that we're not celebrating something because I've heard the staff goes all out. Fascinated by this woman before me, I wonder what she does to apply her makeup so perfectly. "I almost wish we were. I've heard wonderful things about your place from my best friend. Her cousin works here."

Madame Magnolia's attention turns from Benedict to me. "Honey, I stole my cook from Antoine's. There ain't anything you can't get here you aren't gonna enjoy better than that. Now tell me, who's this friend?"

"Raul Riviera." With a sidelong glance at my companions, I impishly add, "But his stage name is Raquel Rivers. Will he be performing tonight?"

"Not tonight, sugar," Magnolia says, her red lips parting in pleased surprise. "Raquel's a big draw, so I save her for weekends and special shows."

"I'll have to tease him about that the next time he tries to raid his cousin Val's closet." I hold out my hand. "Kee."

Before I know what's happening, I'm being pulled from my seat and engulfed in a huge hug. "Oh, sugar. It took me a minute, but I recognize you from your photo. Raquel comes in with your books each time a new one is released." Then in his real voice, Magnolia says, "Your books give the child inside of us hope, Ms. Long."

Gently pulling back, I'm overwhelmed by the bright emotion flashing in her eyes.

She claps her hands together. "Enough. Now, do y'all have any allergies?"

Mutely, the four of us exchange glances before shaking our heads no. Madame Magnolia just smiles. "Then you let ole Mad Mags here order for you while you enjoy the show."

Suddenly, Cade's coughing savagely into his napkin.

Lisa reaches over and cups the side of his face. "Babe? You okay?"

"Fine. Water went down the wrong pipe."

"That happens a lot for first-timers," Magnolia clucks with false sympathy. Brushing her hand over my shoulder, she says, "I'll take your menus. Zach will be back for your drink order shortly."

There's a pregnant pause before Benedict turns to Cade. "You're the damn doctor. Am I wrong, or was there an Adam's apple . . ."?"

"Yep," Cade agrees.

Just then, Zach returns, no longer focused on Benedict but on me. "Ms. Long, it's an honor to have you here. Madame would like to let you know your evening meal is complimentary, and she hopes you enjoy the show."

"Oh, but I . . . we couldn't."

He chuckles before lowering his voice. "It'll take an argument much stronger than that to change Mad Mags's mind."

Again, at the nickname, Cade chokes on his drink.

Zach offers him a wide smile before straightening. "Since your companion seems to have difficulty with water, why don't we get him something else to drink? Sir? Something from the bar?"

"Bourbon," Cade declares immediately. Turning to Lisa, he gives her a pleading look. "Please tell me you'll drive home."

"Boy, are you going to owe me," she mutters. "I'll take a glass of pinot."

"The same for me," I tack on, knowing instinctively Benedict's going to go drink for drink with Cade.

He searches my eyes. I touch his leg and smile. "You can't let him suffer your sister alone," I tell him teasingly.

Without losing my gaze, he orders, "Bourbon for me as well." Then he leans down and says, "In case I forget to tell you later, you are a good girlfriend."

Brushing my nose against his, I say honestly, "I'm just following my guy's example. He makes it easy."

Slinging his arm around my chair, Benedict proves immediately why he's been friends with Cade for years when he asks, "So, who did you piss off at the hospital? I'm assuming they're the ones who recommended we bring our girlfriends to a drag show for a date?"

Cade growls, "Do you have to ask? The chief of staff. I refused to do unscheduled Botox on his girlfriend."

Benedict's eyes wing upward. "Isn't he married?"

Cade lifts his water glass in salute. "My point exactly."

"Well, I, for one, can't wait. I think you sheltered me too much as a kid, Ben," says Lisa. I feel the rigid tension surge through Benedict before the comment bounces off him the way it should.

"Look who your date is. I should have convinced Mom and Dad to lock you in a convent."

"Whoa, man. Let's not get nasty," Cade holds up his hands in surrender.

Amused, I ask Cade, "Is a night out with them always like this?"

"No. Normally I'm torn between plying Ben with liquor to loosen up and tying Lisa down."

Lisa pipes in, "Ah, if I only knew that."

Benedict snags Zach's arm as he hurries by. "Make mine a double," he says causing us all to devolve into hysterics.

Very little time passes before we have shed any inhibitions and are having a blast. Magnolia sends over an exceptional dancer to entertain Lisa and me during the show. Benedict and Cade have gotten into the spirit enough to join us when we pose for pictures with the ladies later.

"That was so much fun," I tell Benedict as I drive us home afterward. "I'm even more amazed now by the transformation Raul goes through for his performances! I mean, I've seen photos, but watching it live is completely different. You'd never know without his stage makeup; he's practically Carlos's twin!"

Ben's hand is resting warmly on my thigh. He squeezes it. "You're the amazing one." His voice is contemplative.

Pulling up to the gate protecting the back of the house, I glance over at him. The expression is filled with tenderness. I face forward as I drive his Mercedes through the gate. "What do you mean?" After pulling into the garage, I put the car in park, turn it off, and face him.

He runs his hand through my hair lazily. "Sweetheart, everywhere we go, people are astounded to get to meet you because of the way your gift has influenced their lives. As horrific as what you endured was, you turned it into something beautiful. You relate to them here." He lays his hand gently over my heart. "Do you see how you make people stronger, braver by having broken your silence?"

I'm unable to reconcile purging my emotions and simply being a compassionate human with what Benedict's saying.

"You celebrate the victories of the survivors, my love. You give people courage, power, and strength to do what should come naturally but may not. Through here"—he touches my head—"from here"—his fingers graze my heart—"using these." He grips my hands. "Even if you don't feel the same way, loving you is the best thing that will ever happen to me." He leans in and his lips brush mine gently.

"It wasn't supposed to happen here." The tears clogging my voice make it almost impossible to understand.

"Huh?" He pulls back so he can smile down at me. "I didn't think there was a wrong place to . . ."

I smush my fingers over his mouth and jump out of the car. Benedict gets out of the passenger side to find me walking toward the brick patio at a fast clip.

Spinning around, I face him. "Love is supposed to be patient and kind, but I've found it to be neither of those things." His face clouds over. Stepping into his space, I slide my arms around his neck and pull my body close. "Not when it's real."

He swallows audibly. Sliding his arms around me, he nods. "Go on."

"If it's real, it's messy and demanding. It's about learning about the person every single day—what makes them happy or what irritates them. It's full of pain and tragedy because you can't imagine a day without that person." I inhale so loud I think I'm going to pass out when I admit, "And that's why I think the crush I had morphed into love. Because it might have taken all these years for us to reunite, I understand it's not about me being perfect or you being that way. It's about our imperfections being right for each other." Taking a deep breath, I open my mouth, but Benedict lays his finger on my lips, stopping me.

"I love you, Kelsey," Ben murmurs as he lowers his head. "In some fashion, I can't remember a day I haven't felt this way. I can't imagine a day in my life where I won't."

"I love you too," I whisper, my lips grazing his.

Then I can't say another word because, under the three-quarter moon, I'm being kissed by a man who has part of me.

And this time, I trust he'll treat it with the care it deserves.

CHAPTER FIFTY-FOUR

Benedict

"TELL ME ABOUT IT," CADE ENCOURAGES ON A SLUR.

"You're a sick fuck if you want to hear about what they did to me," I growl, reaching for the bottle of scotch between us. It's about halfway filled. And if Cade wants a blow-by-blow of the agony I endured so we can compare it to the ones he similarly lived through, "We're going to need more booze. Who's making the run?"

He shoves so hard that I tip over the camp chair I'm slouched in. I hit the floor with a crash. Precious drops of whiskey start to spill. For a moment, I debate lapping it up like a dog—something they didn't make me do—when Cade's words freeze me. "Tell me about what it was like knowing she believed you to be the biggest asshole in the universe."

From my prone position on the ground, I divulge a secret I'd share with no one else. After all, no one else could appreciate the conviction in my words. "Betraying Kelsey was like they raped me all over again."

Cade stares off into space. Whether it's the scotch pumping through both of our veins, I don't know, but he slurs, "Sometimes you've got to lose the thing you hold most precious to regain it, Ben." Then he falls out of his chair to join me on the ground.

I shift awake, holding the most precious part of my life close to my heart. "I love you, Kelsey," I murmur into her fragrant tresses.

She just snuggles closer.

I was right earlier tonight. Cade's a smart bastard.

CHAPTER FIFTY-FIVE

Kelsey

Everything feels right, I muse as I climb the steps to Le Cadeau. A dreamy smile graces my lips as I wander down the hall toward the welcoming raucous noise.

For the last few days, I feel like the corner Benedict and I turned has flowed into every area of my life. I'm already chapters into my next book, and Pilar's showing the strength the title indicates after a summer away from the bullying. The understanding Benedict gave to me about his actions so long ago has removed the enormous burden of resentment and pain I didn't realize I was carrying, and it's not only changing my life but my character's as well.

Even Val commented on it the other morning. "This is the you I always prayed you would become," she said, right before she burst into tears.

"Stop crying," I demanded.

"I can't," she blubbered into her smoothie. "I just hate it's taken so long for your sparkle to appear."

"I'd thought I'd lost my will until I met you. Even my friendship with Jillian wasn't enough for me to hold on. Family certainly wasn't." I reached over and wrapped my arms around her, even as my brutal words stunned her. "If Ben's brought something else into my life, well, maybe it was always his to have."

By the time Darin came into the kitchen, we were both a wreck. "Jesus, do I need to be happy or kill someone?" He was aghast.

"The first, babe," Val assured him as she tipped her head back for a kiss.

Shaking my head at the memory, I push the door outside open when I catch someone in the shadows out of the corner of my eye. Startled, I take an involuntary step back. Max emerges partially, his face mostly hidden, still clutching my book like a lifeline. Clasping my chest, I admit, "You surprised me."

"I apologize, Ms. Kee." His voice is subdued.

I start to step in his direction, but he slams up the book like a shield warding off evil. "Please, don't come any closer." There's a break in his voice I relate to all too well.

"Is there something you want to talk about?" I ask carefully. I'm not a trained counselor, but if this boy is willing to open up, maybe I can guide him to the person he needs most—Morgan.

"Does Pilar ever heal?" he asks me almost desperately. "After everything done to her in this, how can she?"

The book in Max's hands is forever burned in my brain. Staring down at it, I remember the criticism I received because it was too dark for a first release for a young adult novel. I had no other way to start to let go of the pain. I remember purging a variation of what truly happened to me through Pilar's eyes to set myself free because my memories were too heavy for me to handle alone any longer.

But now, since that first night at Benedict's, when I learned there can be motivation behind contemptible behavior, I realize not everything is as black and white as words on a page. Even as I think back to what I wrote, I intuitively knew that—for both myself and my character —there was hope to be found in the pages of *Betrayal*. Love, too, if you looked past the obvious to find it.

Softly, I quote the words I wrote when I was a little older than Max is now —the words Ben had etched in glass before they fell out of my fingers in shock. "The worst thing that's happening to you is the best thing that will ever happen to someone else. All you can do is move past it. After all, if life were meant to be easy, I'd have already won the game."

"I know. It's right here." He flips to the exact page and points at my words, underlined. "I just have a hard time believing it."

"Why?" I tread cautiously.

"Because they hurt me. Right now, I can't believe anyone could hurt more," he snarls.

I inch forward to get a read on Max. At that moment, a stream of light brightens the shadows. I see the bruises along the side of his face. "Who did this to you?" I whisper. Stretching a hand out, I reach for his book, but he jerks away.

"Don't touch me," he hisses. My heart thumps in my chest.

"I wasn't. I wanted to look for a passage in the book." At his doubtful look. I hold up my hand. "That's it. I swear it to you."

Tentatively, Max hands me his battered copy of my book with just his thumb and fingertip. Taking it gently, I flip toward the end of the book for the page I'm looking for. "I have a responsibility to you to help you. And you know what drives that? Not my job, but my heart." Closing the book, I hold it back out to him. "If you don't feel comfortable with me because you don't know me, I appreciate that. But please," I whisper in the hallway that has shrunk down to just the two of us, where the loudest noise is his harsh breath. "Talk to Morgan, Lisa, Val . . . someone."

His fingers close over the top before he shifts back into the darkness. I can't let him go without reminding him of something. "Morgan named the center Le Cadeau because she knows—just like I do—you're a gift. Remember, Max. You told me that. You're a gift." Knowing I've pushed enough, I move to open the door.

"Ms. Kee?" The dark whisper stops me in my tracks.

"Yes?"

"I just can't—not today. Maybe tomorrow, but not today," he chokes out.

Turning, I let my eyes bore into the area where I know he's still standing. "Will you promise me one thing? If you need medical help, you'll come to one of us, no questions asked."

There's a long pause before he quietly concedes, "I promise."

"Then you know where to find us." Though it's the last thing I want to do, I start down the hall. I stop when Max calls out my name.

As I face him again, his whispered "Thank you" finishes the job of shattering my heart into a million pieces.

I wish Benedict were around to hold me together, but I know later he'll understand.

He always seems to.

Later that night, his body tenses next to mine when I explain what happened. "What did you do?" Benedict's arms are like steel bands around me. His voice is harsh next to my ear.

I twist around to face him. His grip is so tight it almost chafes my skin even to turn in his arms. "I made him promise to come to me if he needed medical help."

If anything, Benedict's arms get tighter. "You don't think bruises up and down the side of his face necessitated medical help?"

I drag my arm from between us. Uncertain, I touch his face. Caressing his clenched jaw, I whisper, "Ben, this isn't a page from a story. I don't know what I'm doing," I admit. "He was already so anxious and so angry. What if I said the wrong thing? I don't have any trust built with him other than my words. I told Morgan the minute I found her." I continue when it looks like he's about to protest, "She went in search of him, but he was already gone.

Her only hope is he comes back in the next few days so she can find out what happened."

He goes to open his mouth but then snaps it shut. Letting out a shuddering breath, he loosens his arms before burying his head in the crook of my neck. "You're right. You handled it perfectly. I'm . . . infuriated that . . . in this day and age, a child can be harmed."

Nuzzling my face against him, I whisper, "Not everyone has a person like you to save them, Ben, but maybe they learn the person strong enough to save them is looking at them in the mirror."

As soon as the words are out of my mouth, I'm rolled over to my back. Something I can't name crosses his face, but it causes my heart to lurch in my chest. It's gone in between one heartbeat and the next, which is all the time it takes for him to press his lips gently to mine. Giving myself up to the pure pleasure of his kiss, I put his anger about Max down as reminder of the disgusting things that mark us from Forsyth.

Things we'd both rather forget ever happened.

CHAPTER FIFTY-SIX

Benedict

"WHAT'S WRONG?" I HEAR MY DAD CALL OUT AS I RACE UP THE STAIRS to my bedroom.

Stripping out of my clothes, I drop them wherever they land and run as quickly as possible into the shower and turn on the water full blast. Grabbing the sponge and shower gel, I begin vigorously scrubbing my body as hard as I can. I reach up to turn down the blast because there's water that's pooling in my eyes, leaking out.

It's making me unable to see where I need to wash.

I'm not sure if it's the wetness on my pillow or Kelsey shaking me that wakes me up from my nightmare.

I twist away and sit up in bed. "I'm fine," I struggle to get out.

Her hand moves up and down my back. "Ben, you're shaking." Kelsey's voice is low in deference to either the late hour or my destroyed nerves. "Was it a nightmare?"

I don't answer, my body still trapped in the memories that rarely make a reappearance. "Talk to me," she pleads.

I'm unable to form words. *Jesus, how am I supposed to tell her everything that I've buried inside me?* Instead, I capture her hand as it smooths over the joint of my shoulder. "I'll be okay," I choke out.

She lets out a sigh that's both terrified and relieved. Pulling her around the tangled covers while I twist to face her, I make a promise to both of us, willing it to be so. "It will be okay, Kels. It was just a nightmare."

She bites down on her lower lip so hard that through the moonlit window, I can see the blood drain from it. Using my thumb, I pull it out. "Baby, I swear." I'm just not telling her everything about the past because I have it under control.

I have to. I refuse to let what happened to me in the past affect my future.

With a sigh, she lets it out as a shaky smile forms. "I want to be there for you, Ben. The same way you were always there for me."

"The same way I'll always be," I vow before lowering my head to hers to capture her tender lower lip between my teeth.

As I roll her onto her back, I give her something she should have already known. "Even back then, I knew you cared. These eyes of yours"—I kiss each lid closed. They remain shut for a moment before opening languidly, shining with an ethereal glow—"were mirrors into your heart, Kels. And knowing I had a place in your heart kept me from sinking. My true regret is losing you before I could beg you for forgiveness. I lost a part of myself that's been yours since you put honor and pride above fear." I swipe at the tears flowing from her eyes. "I wish I'd been able to do the same."

She reaches up and grips my wrists tightly. "Never apologize to me for what happened again," she says fiercely. "I understand. And who's to say if I weren't threatened with something to do with my family or Val, I wouldn't have done the same thing. Love causes us to do things we'd never believe we were capable of otherwise." Her voice is so adamant, I know she's trying to tell me something. My breathing is harsh in the room.

"Like what?" She squirms beneath me. I pin her slightly beneath me. "Kels?"

Her hands are shaking against my wrists. Slowly she lifts one to touch my brow, my cheek, and my lips before her words cement our reunion into a permanent reconciliation. "I'd never believe I could look in the mirror and see my beauty—until I saw myself through your eyes. Because the hurt of yesterday is never going to come back and haunt me. You'd never let it." What's left of my nightmare dissipates when she clasps my face and pulls my lips down before murmuring, "Isn't it beautiful the way love causes us to see ourselves?" right before her lips meet mine.

As I'm pulled under the gentle onslaught of her kiss, a small part of my mind shrieks in panic.

After all, what will she say if she ever truly sees all of me?

Slowly, I kiss her until my racing heart calms, but where before I would have pulled her body beneath mine and loved it back to sleep, I just can't.

I feel too tainted by the past to touch my future.

CHAPTER FIFTY-SEVEN

Benedict

THE END OF A QUARTER DRAINS ME. BETWEEN EACH DEPARTMENT head sending summaries of their open contracts, procurements, and pending awards as well as trying to put my seal of approval on the ones that pass through the C-suite, it's usually a week where I practically eat, sleep, and breathe Lockwood Industries. But this one is made even worse because every time I close my eyes, all I feel is despair.

The last three nights, I've crawled into bed well after eleven only to find Kelsey wrapped around my pillow. A plate of cookies and a Yeti filled with sweet tea sat on my nightstand. But the simple note she left with them burned through me the most as I stared down at her sleeping form.

I love you. ~K

What the hell is wrong with me? I wonder. Shoving away from my desk, I wander over to the windows overlooking the bold city I've lived in for years

—a city whose dark side is so eloquently depicted by the Mardi Gras masks you can find by any street vendor. Play, hide, but never entirely reveal your true self. Sounds familiar. My fist clenches at my side.

The soft sound of my intercom interrupts my introspection. "Yes?" I call out.

"Mr. Houde to see you, sir," Vince, who's covering for my assistant while she's at lunch, announces.

"Send him in."

A tinge of amusement laces his voice when he asks, "Do you want to know which one it is?"

I bark out a laugh. "It's not going to stop me from telling you to send them in."

Seconds later, Simon Houde and his wife, Bristol Todd– affectionately known as the "Queen of Wall Street"—come through my door. "True, but at least you know it's more of a social call than dealing with my big brother."

I come out from around my desk to greet them. "Now, this is a pleasant surprise. I was working on some end of quarter reports when Vince interrupted me. I keep expecting Ryan . . ."

My intercom beeps again. Vince's voice is much more anxious. "I hate to interrupt, Ben, but Mr. Lockwood—Ryan—just called to ask when he can expect the combined quarterly contract summary."

"Well, I see my dropping Alex in his office didn't improve his disposition," Simon grumbles good-naturedly.

I shrug. "It's always like this at the end of the quarter."

"I understand perfectly. We won't take up much of your time," Bristol says.

"What can I help you with?" I lean against my desk.

"I'm not certain if you heard the rumors about Redemption?" Simon begins.

"What about it?" Simon's older brother Marco runs the most successful nightclub on the East Coast.

"Marco and his partner Louie are considering expanding," Bristol adds.

I whistle. "Good luck with finding real estate big enough in New York."

Simon explains. "That's just it. With their daughter, Marco and Lynne want to get out of New York. Lynne loves it here in New Orleans but is concerned about her job. Bristol decided to make it fait accompli by presenting her and Marco with a home to rent for the next year."

The idea of Ryan's long term financial sage growing her career with someone who cares for her just as much as he did brings a smile to my face. "What do you need my help with?"

Bristol is blunt and to the point. "Names. I'm not well-versed in Louisiana law. I need someone to review the contract we're expecting to receive tomorrow from the agent to give it their stamp of approval."

I'm about to ask a few questions just as Ryan struggles through the door, bent in half by a toddler leading him around by his tie. He tries for a look of austereness and completely fails as Alex smashes him against his father's thigh. With a swoop, Ryan lifts him up before blowing a raspberry on his stomach. "You both realize this is a place of business."

"Obviously," Simon says dryly. He tries to extract his son from Ryan's clutches, but it's hard to choose who puts up more of a protest. Meanwhile, Bristol—bulldog she is—loftily informs Ryan, "We're trying to ask Benedict for some legal advice to help Lynne and Marco. It won't be a minute, and then we'll let you get back to sacrificing your employees for sport."

Ryan narrows his eyes at his financier for the dig. "Is something wrong?" he demands.

"No, and if you'd let me answer their question, I can evict all of you from my office," I begin, but no one listens to me except the youngest invader of my sanctum.

Alex shrieks his agreement. When I meet his gap-toothed smile head-on, I mentally agree. *You're right, kid. Adulting can be hard.*

While the byplay continues, I pull up a standard rental agreement template we keep on file and scan the clauses to see if there's anything I'd remove. "Bristol, can you let me know if you plan on executing the agreement for a set duration or month-to-month?" I call out amid the friendly repartee.

There's a dead pause before she offers, "Six months with an option to buy."

I mutter, "Good to know. What's the address?"

Simon rattles it off, and I begin typing. A blessed quiet descends on my office other than the clicking of my keyboard. A few minutes later, my printer's whirling as I lean back in my chair. "Truthfully, there's no real reason we can't do it here in the office. Neither you nor Simon are employees of Lockwood, and therefore the company holds no vested interest if your renters trash the place . . ."

"Hey, I do!" Simon objects.

Both Ryan and Bristol hit him simultaneously in the arm.

"A legal vested interest, Simon. Neither you nor Bristol are family, neither are Lynne and Marco, so unless you want to spend a fortune on legal representation"—I shove a handful of papers in their direction—"go back to the landlord with these. Come here, have the papers notarized in front of Vince and Carol. All that can done in a few hours. Plus, they have to be mailed in."

Ryan smiles wickedly. "I'll pay for the stamp."

We all start to laugh. "So generous of you, Ben. That wasn't what I expected when we came in to ask. Truly, Simon and I were hoping for the name of someone you trusted," Bristol says.

"I trust me." Pushing out of my chair, I extend my hand to shake hers. "See if lunch tomorrow works with the landlord to get this settled. Then I can pawn off Ryan on Lynne when he comes to town. He's so needy." Especially now that I have Kelsey in my life.

"Hey, I resemble that remark," Ryan jokes.

"Great. We'll see you tomorrow then." Bristol smiles at me brilliantly. It makes my heart ache because I haven't seen Kelsey smile at me in days. It doesn't help I haven't been home, and when I have, I've been doing my damnedest to avoid her since the nightmare the other night.

Simon comes around to clap me on the shoulder. "Thanks, man. It is a huge lift knowing someone we all trust can help."

I wave him off. "It's nothing," I start, but Ryan interrupts. "It's not nothing, Ben. It's family. Once again, you've come through for us. We appreciate it."

My lips quirk. "Good. Now get out of my office. My boss has been a jackass calling and asking when I'm going to give him reports."

Ryan growls. "When is marketing going to get their head out of their ass and get their reports to you on time?"

"Who said it was marketing?" I ask mildly just as Carol bursts through the door.

"Jesus, Ben, thanks for covering. Here they are. Don't tell . . ." She stops in her tracks when she sees Ryan there. "Shit, caught." Strolling over, Carol drops the hard copies of the quarterly reports in my hand I know are now waiting in my email.

I shake my head. "Thanks, Carol."

"No problem. I hope you don't have to stay too late." She turns as if she didn't just get visually skinned alive by her boss.

Simon wraps an arm around Bristol's shoulders. "Now you know one of the many reasons I don't work in business."

"That and the world would be missing an artistic genius," she agrees, snuggling close.

"There's that. Thanks again, Ben." The two of them wave as they depart, leaving Ryan fuming.

"A man puts down rules so employees aren't struggling at the eleventh hour . . ."

"And something always goes wrong." I drop back in my chair with the inch-thick folder Carol handed me. "Don't worry about it."

"Except you have your own life you need to go home to. You should send Kelsey flowers. This is her first time going through the quarter end with us."

"That idea holds merit. Look at you being all romantic."

He strolls to the door. "Open or closed?"

"Closed. Otherwise, I won't get a thing done."

Just before he shuts it, Ryan grins. "Next time you two are together, ask Jared how I wooed him if you don't believe I can be romantic."

"Don't think I won't!" I yell through the door before focusing on the billions of dollars of contracts in front of me. Losing all track of time, I forget to send Kelsey flowers. I forget to call her to tell her I won't be home for dinner.

In fact, the next time I see her, she's curled into a ball on her side of the bed, looking so small and defeated, my whole heart shrivels in my chest.

The next day, a happy silence steals over the room when Vince rises from where he was leaning over the conference room table.

"All set." He holds out his hand first to Bristol and then to Simon. "Congratulations."

"Thanks for your help."

"Not a problem. Is it inappropriate to admit that I'm a huge fan of yours? I can't wait to see what you're staring in next on Broadway."

Simon leans forward and gives Vince the thrill of a lifetime when he shares, "I can't say much other than Evangeline Brogan and I will be starring in it together."

Vince swoons. "Be still my heart." He turns to me to say, "I'm requesting time off now to go to New York."

We all laugh. Handshakes are exchanged around the room before Bristol wraps up our meeting, thanking everyone. "Who knows? Maybe you'll see more of me around here?"

I'm about to retort when my cell buzzes in my pocket. Pulling it out, I frown when I see it's Kelsey. Pressing Accept, I answer, "Hey, Kels. Problem?" *Other than the fact I hate that my behavior is leaving you looking so broken in our bed by the time I get home*, I think.

Her soft voice is both a balm and a whip when she says, "Other than missing you, things are perfect. I don't suppose you're free for lunch?"

With a long, drawn-out sigh, I spy the stack of work that's come in from overseas since last night that I only scratched at before Bristol and Simon came into my office. "I really can't, sweetheart. My office looks like a poorly filed archives storage."

Her soft expulsion of breath forgives me again for being distant. I'm going to have to make up my behavior somehow soon, but how do I explain that something she wasn't the cause of has sent me into an emotional tailspin? Instead, I offer, "When this craziness is over, I will plan something special for us." I don't know where that promise came from, but down to my soul, I mean it.

"As long as I get to spend time holding you, Ben, I don't need anything." And just like that, she destroys me.

Avidly aware of the people still in my office, I gently tell her, "I have people in here."

"And that's my cue to let you go before I turn a brighter shade of pink. Good thing I didn't drop by."

The laughter that follows abruptly dies when I say, "Yeah, this is a crap week for unannounced guests."

Kelsey's "Oh" seems to reverberate over and over in my head. "Well, I'll let you get back to it."

"Kelsey . . ." But before I can tell her I love her and I'll see her later, she's hung up. As I lower the phone, I replay what I said to her. God, I sounded like such a detached jackass. I need to find time to truly reconnect with her, but then what?

Cade's words haunt me. *"Though if this goes the distance, I suspect you'll end up telling her everything."*

After everyone clears the room, I make my way over to the wall of glass. Laying my head against it, I watch the movement on the street floors below.

I can't seem to stop the inevitable from occurring. I've never cared much about the end of a relationship before, until now. I just know once certain words are spoken, there's no taking them back.

CHAPTER FIFTY-EIGHT

Kelsey

"WHAT DID HE SAY?" VAL ASKS WHEN I HANG UP THE PHONE.

"He's too busy." I force a lightness into my voice I don't feel.

Val curses in Spanish, but I hold up a hand. "Stop. Okay?"

She waddles over to me and takes my hands in both of hers. "Not that I don't love you, but I've seen your face more—between here and at Le Cadeau—than when you and he first started dating. That's not how it's supposed to be, Kels."

"Maybe it's just these crazy hours. He did warn me the end of each quarter is a nightmare."

Benedict warned me that the end of the quarter is always a crazy time around the office as everyone tries to finalize last-minute contracts, which ultimately pass through his office in some way. Whether he's scouring over high-level summarizations or writing modifications to billion-dollar agreements, he's exhausted when he stumbles home late each night after going in before I wake each day.

If I didn't feel the soft press of his kiss against my cheek, then my collar, each morning before he whispers, "I love you, sweetheart," I might feel more than just a knot of anxiety at the distance growing between us. We haven't joined together physically since the night I returned from Collyer, and our sleep was once again disturbed by his soft moaning.

I'm afraid and don't know who to go to or what this means. Instead, I reaffirm to Val and myself, "It will be over soon, and things will get back to normal."

She opens up her mouth and then closes it.

Yeah, I'm not fooling either of us. No matter how much I want to.

It's about nine when I hear the back door unlock. I'm sitting on the sofa in Benedict's office, waiting for him to come home so we can talk.

All I want is for him to talk to me.

I've been over every moment and conversation in my mind since I left Val's. Did he understand I understood what he sacrificed for Lisa? We've talked about Forsyth since then—he knows I don't lump him in with my opinions of the other students. Right? But maybe my words didn't penetrate.

What's happening between us?

Rubbing my hands up and down arms covered in a thick sweatshirt, I'm chilled despite the brutal temperatures swamping the city. I need, no, I deserve, to understand what's wedging itself between us. Hearing his footsteps on the hardwood before the carpet runners muffle them, my anxiety kicks up a notch.

"Jesus, Kelsey, you scared the crap out of me. What are you doing sitting here in the dark?"

"Missing you," I admit softly. For a moment, his face softens before the bland look drops back down. God, I hate that expression. Does he even realize he's been giving it to me? "I was hoping we'd have a chance to catch up since I haven't seen you all week."

He sighs as if he's been confronted with a sullen child irritated they couldn't get a treat. "Kelsey, not all of us have your ability to set our hours. Every quarter end I have to be in the office for ungodly hours to ensure people keep their jobs."

"You don't get a break? At all?" Is it these brutal hours causing the tension between us?

"No. I was working the entire day. I still have a few hours of work to finish up."

His eyes flicker to the side as he answers, and a memory slams into my memory bank.

"Why didn't you do your assignment this week, Ben? Are you trying to fail this class?"

His eyes flicker to the side. "I just forgot, Kelsey."

Unwilling to let him lie to me, I jab him squarely in the chest. His eyes flash to mine. There's a blankness I don't know how to breach in them. "It's due tomorrow. You're on your own."

He's lying. I know it as surely as I know my name, and it's like I've been smacked in the chest with a full broadside. The truth can hurt, but lies are more devastating because they exist between you forever. "I'll leave you to it, then."

I make for the door as fast as I can. His bag drops against the desk just before he calls out my name. I pause but don't turn around lest he glimpse the tears welling in my eyes. "Yes?"

"Are you feeling okay? It's a million degrees out, and you're dressed like it's winter."

He notices the fucking sweatshirt, I think with wild amusement. "Don't worry about it. You're busy. Remember? Good night, Ben." I start to make my way out of the doors of the study, wondering if it's worth it to have a conversation with him when he calls my name again. Frustrated, I whirl around exasperated. "What? You said you have work to do."

His face is shocked when I lash out at him. "I . . . I'm worried. If you're not feeling well, that is."

I bark out a sharp laugh. "Don't worry. It's nothing you can catch." After all, broken hearts are entirely one-sided, aren't they?

As if in slow motion, he drops the folder he's holding to the desk. "You were waiting to talk to me."

"And you don't have time right now. It will keep." We're ten feet from each other, but it feels greater than that. "Good night, Benedict."

"Good night, sweetheart," he whispers.

And with that, I charge down the hall like the fires of hell are licking at my heels. Quickly I dash into his room, even as I flick tears from my eyes. I grab my purse, intent on leaving. I need to write. This pain has to be poured out somehow.

And I refuse to punish myself because, after all I've endured to regain my sense of self-worth, a man is beginning to take it away.

I'm dashing through the house when I come up short in the kitchen. Benedict's standing there with his head bent forward, arms braced on the kitchen counter. "You were just waiting in my study to tell me that you planned on leaving?" He doesn't bother to look at me.

Moving around him, I say, "I was planning on staying, but if you're going to be working all night, then I'll go home and do the same." He cringes at my emphasis on the word home.

"Why don't you get your computer and come back here?" His jaw tics. As if it's taking everything in the world to make the offer.

Because you don't seem to want me here. I almost say the words out loud. But suddenly, my desire to confront Benedict drains out of me. I can't drive while I'm sobbing out my heartbreak. I need to leave while I still have a chance. "If you want to see me tomorrow, just call me."

"Want?" he asks, as if confused. Lifting his head, there's exhaustion and more written all over his face. "Kels, I always want you here. I . . ." His head drops down again.

"Yes?" My voice is hopeful.

He shakes his head, and my spirit plummets. Pulling out my keys, they jangle a little in my hands. "Good night, Ben."

My hand's on the doorknob when I feel the warmth of his body heat me better than the sweatshirt I wear ever possibly could. My head crashes against the jamb. "You have to work," I protest because although I hate myself for my weakness, I can't help but love the gentle way he turns my body around in his arms.

"No, what I have to do is take care of the woman I love," he declares. Yanking my bag off my shoulder, he drops it to the floor. He pulls the keys out of my hand and drops them as well. "Come with me."

"Ben." I dig in my heels, but he tugs a little harder, so I stumble against his warmth. I've been so cold all night that it's like setting my skin on fire.

"Come on, sweetheart. Let's go to bed for a little while. Once I know you're resting, I'll work." And true to his word, Benedict walks both of us to the master suite.

"Just let me go," I whisper.

Benedict stops dead in his tracks. For just a moment there's naked longing on his face, the kind I haven't seen since the first night we came together. Slowly, he brushes his lips against mine, letting them linger for just a moment before he straightens, giving me the barest of smiles. "Never willingly." Turning away, he pulls down the covers before motioning for me to climb in.

Later, as I stare out the window at the moon with Benedict's soft breath fanning my ear, I wonder if I've survived one level of bullying only to endure another. Last time, I feared the cruelty of hundreds of people.

This time, I fear the heartache of a single one.

I'm not sure which is worse.

CHAPTER FIFTY-NINE

Benedict

I'm trying to finish reviewing a new contract that landed on my desk this morning so I can head home early. All I want to do is spend as much time with Kelsey as I can before I change our lives by giving her my truth. Cade is right. I have to tell her. Even though my nightmares have eased off, there's something else happening I can't quite put my finger on. Kelsey's changing, and it's making me feel more anxious as I work up the courage to tell her.

I know I started it by pulling away, but since she confronted me in my office that night, she's becoming more detached. Pounding my fist on the desk, I'm startled out of my frustration by the phone ringing. Hoping that's her, I snatch it up quickly. "Perrault." I can't keep the hope out of my voice.

"Son? Are you working on something important?" My father's voice comes through the line with an undercurrent of something that has fear skating up my spine.

"There's nothing you can't interrupt, Dad. What's up? Don't tell me you threw out your back again," I joke despite the mixed feelings of disappointment and foreboding that wash over me. My father never calls me at the office to chat, that's more my mother's style. But even then, she usually waits until after typical business hours. Not—I glance at my watch —at a quarter to eleven in the morning.

"I was at the golf club—"

"I thought your doctor said no golf until your back healed from trying to change the tire," I interrupt.

"I wasn't trying to play, Ben." A note of exasperation enters his voice before it's quickly subdued. "I was having breakfast when the police came in."

Jumping to my feet, I shout, "What the fuck, Dad? What happened? Do you need me to come home to represent you? Tell me I'm not your only phone call."

My wild thoughts are pondering who I know who can get my dad out on bail until he croaks, "Ben, tell me you're sitting."

Heart pounding, I reach for my chair that I shoved away. Pulling it up behind me, I fall back into it. Succinctly, I ask, "Dad. What. Happened?"

"The police came in to arrest Tom Balboni on charges of reckless conduct, hazing, and"—there's a pause while he takes a deep breath—"sexual assault."

Immediately, the room begins to spin faster than an out-of-control carousel. "Would you mind repeating that?" I ask. Tom Balboni graduated Forsyth a few years before me. He's the assistant coach of one of the local high schools in the area, but back then, he was the ringleader behind my hazing and subsequent brooming when I was a sophomore on the boys' varsity swim team. I still vividly recall the ring of witnesses switching from jeering to an eerie silence as Balboni used the painted stick to mimic the sexual act before demanding we all drop our suits.

As if the one wasn't bad enough.

I begin to sweat as the memories of being pinned up against the metal locker come back full force. I shove my right hand into my mouth as I let out a scream around the teeth marks I made in my hand seventeen years ago as I endured the kind of physical and mental torture no one should.

Forsyth wasn't as much a prep school as it was a sentence in purgatory, no matter who attended.

Feeling nauseous, I reach for my trash can. My father would never bring this up unless there was a reason. "Why are you telling me this?"

My carefully constructed walls begin to crumble as my father finds his words—words I struggled with the day after I graduated from high school. Beads of sweat break out across my forehead. "It was John's grandson." John has been my father's lifelong best friend. They met when they attended Forsyth over fifty years earlier.

"How old is he, Dad?" I wipe my brow with the back of my sleeve.

"Fifteen."

"Goddamn it!" I roar.

My office door inches open. Vince pokes his head in. "Is everything . . ."

"Get the fuck out!" I lash out. His eyes widen enormously before he quickly snaps the door shut behind him. I grip the phone in my hand so tightly I'm afraid it's going to crack. Hell, it might shatter when I throw it against the wall when I'm done anyway. "What do you need me to do?"

"No one knows who violated you, son."

My body lurches at hearing those words said aloud. He's never said it that plainly. And it can't be true. Hurt, yes. But it is Kelsey who was violated day after day. Lisa is the one who was threatened. And then the world crashes down on me while I'm thirty-three years old, sitting in an office that overlooks the city it dominates.

I'm a victim. Just like the kids in the stories Kelsey tells, just like the kids my sister wants to help.

This is the reason I've been instinctively pulling back from Kelsey. I never wanted her to know what happened to me because of the shame. I've hidden this because I never wanted to face the pity, the odd looks, or maybe the woman I love walking away after she realizes I'm not the man she thought I was.

The collision of my thoughts leaves me sick at heart, but one terrifying thing keeps surging to the forefront over and over, even as my father continues talking.

I'm going to have to tell her I am a casualty of the same war she fought. Only while she rose triumphantly, I'm still just a victim.

"I should have known better than to believe a reunion between us would be so smooth and easy. But I thought it was a reward for both of our lives being so fouled by Forsyth. What a joke."

"Damn it, Ben, are you listening to me?" my father bellows.

"Not really," I admit.

His ragged sigh is just a mirror of the pieces of my heart.

"What do you need me to do?" I ask him again, trying desperately to focus on something other than the fact that my world is crumbling around me.

"If you think you're capable . . ." And my father goes on to talk about how he'd like me to come home. Before I get there, he'll break a vow he swore to me he'd take to the grave. It would mean talking to a young man who thinks his life is over because he was abused by someone he was supposed to be able to trust.

This time there's no controlling my response. I grab the trash can and begin hurling the breakfast I ate before I left for work inside it. In my ear, I vaguely hear my father's tears as the sobs he's likely been hiding from my mother cut loose.

That's all right. They mingle with those sliding down my face.

CHAPTER SIXTY

Benedict

A FEW HOURS LATER, I DRAFT MY LETTER OF RESIGNATION AFTER preparing notes on all my open tasks. I've asked Ryan's secretary for the last appointment of the day. Resting my hand on the door, I wish there was some other way, but didn't I learn that doing what's right involves sacrifice? Even if it means hurting the people you care about.

Knocking on his door, I wait for him to call out, "Come in," before I push the door inward. Ryan leans back in his chair, crossing an ankle over the opposite knee, steepling his fingers. "What can I help you with, Ben?"

I cross the large office with my hand holding the sealed envelope behind my back, suddenly as anxious as I was when my father and I walked into President Adams's office the day after graduation. It's as if Ryan already knows what I'm about to say.

Swallowing convulsively, I stand in front of my friend, despising how my past has collided with my present. I'd give anything to change this part of my life. But even as that wayward thought sneaks in, thunder claps outside, grabbing my attention. Now I hurt even more because the floor-to-ceiling windows in Ryan's office show me the stormy skies that are like drowning in Kelsey's eyes. Desperately, I try to figure out a way to avoid doing this, but I have no idea how long I'll be gone. "I need to hand you this." I pull the letter out from around my back.

Ryan doesn't react. He doesn't even look away from my face. "You don't appear to be pleased by it."

Pleased? By giving up a job I love? Knowing I'm going to end up losing the only woman I'll ever love in the process? Not hardly. Instead of answering his question, I walk forward and lay the letter on his perfectly organized desk. His face remains implacable. "Ahmed will make an excellent replacement," I state. My assistant general counsel has a CV almost as impressive as my own.

Ryan waves his hand as if he can't be bothered with that. "Tell me why." The first edge of bitterness slides into a voice that's usually precisely cultured.

"As your general counsel, it's my duty to protect Lockwood Industries from all known threats."

"Since when did you become one?"

Wearily, I run my hand over my head. "I guess I've always been one."

Ryan surges to his feet. "Excuse me?" A few inches taller than me and broader, his anger is usually impressive. Today, it does nothing but bounce off. It can't touch me.

Nothing can.

"I'll be going home for an indeterminate amount of time."

Ryan makes his way around the desk, eyes narrowing. "And there's something there you think can hurt us? This company?"

"I'm certain of it. If anything about what happened were to come out, the media coverage would . . ." Fuck. I didn't mean to go there. "Just forget I said anything."

"Not hardly," Ryan scoffs. Coming around his desk, he gestures to a chair.

I shake my head.

Silence hangs between us. "We can do this standing, but you look like you're about to collapse." Ryan motions again to the black chair behind me.

Exhaustion, the kind I've only felt two other times in my life—the first after telling my father what happened to me and the second after explaining why I hurt Kelsey to President Adams—settles over my shoulders like a yoke weighed down by anvils. "You're not going to change my mind." I drop into the chair behind me.

"We'll see about that by the time we're done talking. Now"—he folds his long body into the chair facing me—"will that letter tell me you're going to work for another company?"

"Don't be an ass," I grumble. I rub my hand over my forehead back and forth. When I finish, I get a glimpse of Ryan's face. He's trying to put the pieces of the puzzle together. *Good luck, buddy*, I think with a flicker of amusement that's gone as quickly as it appears. "Listen, I don't know how long I will be gone. None of the reasons I'd be taking a leave of absence fall within company policy—" I begin, but Ryan cuts me off.

"That's bullshit, and you know it. I'm not an asshole, Ben. Though I'm beginning to think I might be looking at one," he says pointedly. "I'm a demanding employer, yes. I'd also like to think I care about my employees—"

"You do." I cut him off this time because the guilt is killing me. There's no way for me to win. I'm going to walk out of here having lost it all. Why wasn't I brave enough to do something about this when I was just a kid?

My hand clenches on the arm of the chair, nails digging into the leather, when Ryan murmurs, "I see." Pushing himself to his feet, he walks to the cabinet in his office that holds the bar. Pouring a few fingers of rich amber liquid into two tumblers, he carries them back and hands me one. I'm nauseated after I swallow a sip when Ryan says, "I've always kept your secrets, Ben. All of them. So, why would you think I'd ever believe the crap you're trying to hand me right now about being a threat to the company?" The knowing look he flashes me is like the shock from a defibrillator.

He knows, my mind whispers. "How?" I croak out.

Ryan nods down at the drink in my hand. "It was the same night you told me about Kelsey. I asked one question that night. Why? I couldn't understand why you wouldn't fly out to apologize to the girl who held your heart back then. And in your inebriated state, you told me why you didn't feel worthy enough of doing just that." He lowers his eyes to his shoes, not giving me any chance to read him until he pulls the rug out from beneath my feet. "I suppose now I can thank you though. Knowing you'd trust me with that without knowing my background? Able to see the kind of man you turned out to be helped me see myself differently." He spins the tumbler around in his hands.

"You?" I can't stop the word from popping out of my mouth.

"We are more than what we appear on the surface, Ben. Somewhere inside all of us are demons we've either conquered or are preparing to." The crystal stops moving. "In my case, it was my mother."

"And your family didn't stop it?" I can't prevent myself from asking the question.

"They didn't know. When I managed to escape—and yes, that's the correct word—I met someone who saved me."

"Jared," I guess.

Ryan shakes his head. "His name is Dr. Jason Ross. He wasn't married then, but shortly thereafter, he met his husband—Phillip Freeman."

My jaw must have bounced to the floor and back because I feel my teeth snap together. "As in your now brother-in-law through marriage?"

"Small world, isn't it? Jason showed me basic humanity and gave me the tools to find my inner strength."

I want to ask him a million questions, but Ryan's smile is crooked. "And that's where my story ends, and Caleb's begins."

I nod because he's right. As he so often is, much to my annoyance. "You understand then. I have to go, and I can't leave Lockwood without its lead counsel for an indeterminate amount of time." The words are torn from my soul. I don't want to leave, but I need to do what's best.

Ryan's face gets hard. "Fuck no. If you need time off to do something, I'll rely on your team, but I expect your ass back in the chair when you're ready to return." Turning, he stalks over to his desk. Slamming the tumbler down, he snatches up my letter of resignation. "Do you want to destroy this, or should I?"

"Jesus, Ryan. It's not that easy." But I feel myself caving.

A ghost of a smile crosses his face. "Nothing worth having ever is. But, Ben, you've earned the life you have now—your job, Kelsey, happiness. Don't throw it away because you think you're a victim of anything. *That's* what Jared convinced me of. That's how I found the strength to come back and take over my inheritance."

Putting my glass aside, I push to my feet. I hold out my hand and Ryan slaps the letter into it. Tearing it in half and half again, I ask him curiously, "What would you have done if I'd insisted?"

The corners of his lips tip up. Picking up his drink, he knocks half of it back before turning to reach for a file on his desk. Lifting it, he faces me with a wicked smile on his face. A face, I think with some amusement, I've heard more than one legal assistant sigh over when they believe they are not being overheard. He fans himself with it. Amused, despite myself, I ask, "What's that?"

"Your contract. I figured you needed a reminder that unless I fire your ass or you're leaving for medical reasons, you're under one hell of a noncompete for the next decade. By the way, I asked Sam to pull this up for me since I didn't want to trip any alarms. When he did, he did a little snooping in your drive." Ryan shrugs as my shoulders begin to shake with suppressed laughter. "What the fuck is going on with the terms on the Enclave deal? Did you forget we like to make money in this company?" Yanking out sheaves of paper, he waves them in my face.

I snatch them right out of his hand and point to the words at the top. "You and Sam need to look at the headers and footers more carefully, my friend. D-R-A-F-T—it's there for a reason. This is a template, you ass."

Ryan mutters, "Right. I knew that."

Sobering, I whisper, "I don't know what's going to happen when I tell her."

He tosses the file back onto his desk. His hand comes up to clasp me on my shoulder. "If she's half the woman I know she is, she's going to have your back, Ben."

Ryan's reassurance goes a long way, but it still doesn't altogether remove the fears that when I tell Kelsey the truth about the kind of man I am, the kind of person who hid from his own pain and fears rather than stand up against what was wrong before it was too late, that she's going to turn away.

And there's a part of me that understands if she does, since isn't that what I've been doing?

CHAPTER SIXTY-ONE

Benedict

I PULL MY CAR BENEATH THE OPENING GARAGE DOOR WITH SMOOTH precision born only of long practice. Kelsey's BMW is parked outside, and it suddenly strikes me as wrong. Lisa's spending more time at Cade's than at home lately. I frown, wondering why tonight, when I expect Kelsey to run and never look back, is the night I'd notice I should have adjusted the parking situation.

Sighing, I slide from my vehicle. Chalk it up to yet another way I didn't protect her. Though this transgression is so minor, I doubt she'll hold it against me, not when she has so many others she can hurl at me, especially after tonight. I grab my briefcase from the back seat and make my way toward the house. Lost in my misery, I don't feel her presence until I'm almost on top of her.

"Hey," Kelsey says softly from where she's waiting at the back door.

I flinch away from the warmth of the lights from the kitchen shining behind her. "Hey," I say as I climb the stairs slowly, putting off the inevitable as long as possible.

She reaches out a hand, and I pretend not to notice, just like I ignore the flash of hurt that crosses her face when I do. Upon entering the kitchen, I'm punched with a one-two to the heart because not only has she been waiting on me, but Kelsey also has something delicious-smelling cooking on the stove. The aroma drifting toward me reminds me of everything I'm about to lose. I wonder if I can do a lap outside before coming back in. I wonder if I can beg her forgiveness for being an ass before talking to her about so much more.

"Another lap around the room. And this time, you'd better shake those asses like the tadpoles you fucking are," Balboni jeers. The three of us, naked after being ordered to strip off our suits, prance around the locker room to the snickering catcalls of the seniors. I shudder as memories I've been suppressing for far too long start to bombard what they never should be able to touch.

The woman I love.

"Long day?" Kelsey's voice is uncommonly neutral. I pause for a moment, surprised she's letting me get away with the slight I delivered a moment ago, before shrugging out of my jacket. Instead of tossing it and my briefcase on the nearest surface, I hold them both in my arms like centuries-old armor.

"That's an understatement," I reply. Pain lances through me as Kelsey holds her place, her countenance becoming more uncertain until she finally retreats behind the stove.

"I don't know why I had the urge, but I felt like making stew despite the heat." She lifts the lid, and the smells that were tantalizing before wrap around me in the best and worst of ways.

An unexpected burn pricks the back of my eyes. *If she doesn't accept what I'm about to tell her, how the hell am I supposed to survive? It will be like having my heart ripped from my chest while I'm still living.* "That sounds . . ." I clear my throat. "Amazing. Do you think it will hold?" I watch her closely for her reaction.

Her body visibly locks. She squares her shoulders before turning to face me. Her voice is careful. "What's wrong?"

I open my mouth and realize I need to be in the one place where I'll feel her presence after she's gone—my study. After all, it's where we began, so why shouldn't it be where we end?

"Do you mind coming with me for a moment?" I don't even recognize the sound of my voice. "I need to talk to you about something that's happened."

Kelsey spins around, a dripping ladle clenched in her hand. Her breath is coming out uneven as she flings it to the side. "Tell me." Her tone is harsh.

Tell her.

"I don't know how to begin," I start slowly.

"Tell me why you're ending things between us," Kelsey asks bitterly, wrapping her arms around herself.

"What?" What the fuck is she talking about? I take a step toward her, but she backs away.

She begins to tick off reasons. "There's more going on than just your quarter end. I can't remember the last time you touched me, and you sure as hell can't look at me. Let's not mention you practically attack me when I want to have a simple conversation, but won't let me leave when I try to give you your space. I would rather go back to being a footnote in your life than being skimmed over as if I don't matter. I matter."

I fall back against the island in shock, inadvertently blocking her in. "How could you think you don't?" I demand angrily, the shields of my jacket and briefcase falling helplessly to the floor. My hands clench into fists as I prepare to defend myself against these insane accusations. "Jesus Christ, Kels, you're all I think about." *At least how you're going to react to this*, I think wearily.

"That expression when you look at me. Right there. What did I do to put it on your face?"

Maybe I'm not as good at hiding things from Kelsey as I thought.

She puts her hand on her forehead and shakes it, almost as if she's awoken from a crazy dream. "Has whatever you're hiding been there since the beginning? Did I just finally clue in to realizing it?"

"Kelsey, if you'll just . . ."

Her voice becomes more accusatory. "Then it must be something about me. Something I did that you're offended by. Was it the way I handled Max?"

"What? No," I rasp out.

What she's saying isn't possible. Is it? Frantically, I think back. I know I've lain next to her every night. Have I held her in my arms? There's no way I'd have been able to sleep without her. She's become such a part of me.

"It's more than possible, Ben." Kelsey's answering the questions I didn't realize I voiced aloud. She flings her arm out to encompass the table I never even noticed was set for an intimate dinner for two. "All this was to try to get you to talk to me. I feel like I've been lying next to a stranger for the last two weeks."

"Nothing could ever change what you mean to me," I breathe, barely able to stop myself from reaching for her to reassure her.

"Then maybe you can explain why you're over there looking like we're coming to an end and I'm over here praying I just have an overactive imagination," she whispers.

I close my eyes, tortured, and hear her say despondently, "That's what I thought. Give me a few minutes, and I'll get out of your way."

I open them just as she's about to pass me. I reach out and hook my arm around her waist.

"Let me go." She struggles as I angle her to face mine.

"It's not what you're thinking. I swear."

Shoving out of my arms, she races out of the kitchen. I follow on her heels, bellowing her name, "Kelsey!"

"Just let me go!" she cries out wildly. Her head swivels to the left, to the right, before she bolts to the place I need her the most.

I follow at a much slower pace. Even if she tears out of the study after hearing the truth, I need to repair what I broke between us long before tonight. Crossing the threshold, I find her standing in front of the frame she gave me, which hangs in a place of pride behind my desk. I can't see her face in the dim light, and she might prefer it that way, but I need her to see mine.

I quietly close the door before flicking the switch that turns on the lamps by the sofa.

"Just tell me why?" Grief is etched on her face. "I deserve that."

I nod. She's right, she does. "It started at Forsyth."

Confusion washes away her grief. "What about Forsyth?"

I try to get a sentence out, but I can't.

"Don't blame our past if you don't love me," she says as she walks around the desk to storm out, but my next words stop her in her tracks.

"I was fifteen the first time it happened."

Her lips tremble, but she firms them up. Stoically, she waits for a blow like the kind she endured at Forsyth. Like the one she forgave from me.

I march right up to her and drag my fingers down her face. Her eyes meet mine and swirling in the storm is agony. "I didn't realize I'd shut you out, love. Which is crazy because my mind can't think past loving you and how everything that's ever happened to me or I've ever done will send you running for the door," I admit.

"Then tell me. Trust me," she pleads.

I shudder. "I'm so afraid you're going to turn away when I do."

"Ben?" A million questions are swirling in her gray eyes. And I don't want to answer a single one, but I know I have to. Before I do, I brush my nose against hers to seek permission for the kiss I need so desperately.

Tipping her head back, she presses her lips delicately against mine—a sip of water in the barren desert. "There's nothing you could do to drive me away. Well, unless it was another woman . . ." She chews her lip vulnerably.

I shake my head. "Never."

"Oh." Kelsey tries to shift back, but I clutch her close. I need her goodness nearby when I ask the next question. Ryan's words from earlier come back to me. *Don't throw it away because you think you're a victim of anything.*

Taking a deep breath, I ask, "Do you remember Tom Balboni?"

With a pained gasp, she reels back. "Remember him? I'll never forget him since I was one of his favorite targets. Why?"

"Because you weren't his only one." Aching, I reach up to touch her cheek again. This time, her hand reaches up to hold mine in place.

Hesitantly, she asks, "What . . . what do you mean, Ben?"

I tell her brutal truth. "Though you were the one Balboni played with publicly, for those of us he had a crack at privately, he dubbed it hazing. And let me assure you, the sick pleasure that bastard found in torturing the people he 'liked' almost makes me wish I was someone he despised."

"No." She shakes her head back and forth.

"It always started the same," I continue, as if she hasn't spoken. "In our graduating class, there were three of us . . ." And for long minutes after, I describe in detail what we endured behind closed doors.

I can honestly admit that I've lived our entire relationship in fear of this very moment. But now the time has come. The truth of my past pours out of me, one helpless episode at a time.

I realize she's not saying anything, nor is she moving. But a fire in her eyes sparks an odd caution in me. Maybe in all the bitter despair that's been darkening my soul, I found the glimmer of hope I need to light it.

CHAPTER SIXTY-TWO

Benedict

"Why are you telling me this now?" To my shock, Kelsey hasn't moved an inch. I've lost all track of time, and I'm taking it as a good sign she didn't bolt for the door during my explanation.

"If it were my choice, I never would have told you," I admit honestly. She flinches, her head whipping away as if I've struck her. "Do you think I want to admit to my biggest shame?"

"What do you have to be ashamed of?" Hearing that makes my heart ache. I rub a hand over my chest, trying to ease the pressure while she rails on, beautiful in her fury. "You did nothing shameful, Benedict." Her hands land on her hips as she squares off against me.

"What about what I did to you?"

"What about it?" I draw back in confusion. She steps forward. "What's changed except the level of hatred I hold for the people who hurt you, hurt me, the same ones who threatened your sister?"

"It can't be that easy, can it?"

"Yes, Ben." Then she confuses me by saying calmly, "So, what you're telling me is that it was Max's fault he's been bullied at school."

"The fuck it is!"

"Are you sure? It's not his fault for not taking the jeering about his sexuality better," she pushes.

Her taunting words register, and my temper rises. "What's wrong with you? Of course it isn't!" I explode. I take a step to put myself back into her space when she wraps her arms around my waist, surprising the hell out of me.

"Then how could I blame you for the same thing? What would ever make you think I'd blame you for being harmed and exploited?" A lone tear rolls down her cheek.

"Don't cry," I rasp out. I know I can't handle her tears.

"I can't help it. I always tear up when the hero shows up." A second follows the first. Automatically, my hand reaches up so my thumb can brush it away. Instead of letting my hand go when it would have moved away, she grabs hold of it. Turning, she presses a kiss on the center of my palm. Leaving her lips there, she whispers, "I will always wish this never happened to you, but I think you forgot something after you got that call from your father today."

My head swimming, I barely manage to rasp, "What's that?"

"I'm not the same girl who left her demons behind fifteen years ago. I'm the woman who went back to face them. And I'm strong enough to help you do the same." Reaching up, she cups my face. "Don't you dare forget it again."

I'm sure there must be some prayer I'm supposed to say to thank God for the woman in front of me, but I don't know what it is at the moment. When I do, I'll be on my knees saying it over and over. Right now, all I can do is lean my head down against hers.

If I didn't feel so weak, I'd feel selfish absorbing the strength she's pouring into me. I don't know how long we stand there in the shadows of our past.

Each time her mouth opens, it's to whisper words of encouragement and love. The first few times, I freeze, almost panic at the idea that would be the moment Kelsey would finally walk away.

Eventually, a shudder runs through me. Her arms hold on tighter. "When do you leave?" she asks me quietly. During my explanation, I told her about my father's call and what is happening back in Savannah.

"I have a flight out tomorrow night." I'd give anything to not have to go, but not because I'm selfish, simply because I wish this had never happened. Even though I feel like I'm reliving what happened to me so long ago, the pain John's grandson is feeling is fresh. It should never have happened. "Maybe, if I'd been stronger . . ." I don't finish the sentence because Kelsey grabs my face.

"You can't feel guilty about those you weren't able to save." Her voice is scratchy.

"If I'd have come forward—" I try again, but she cuts me off.

"You can what-if all you want, my love. You saved two special people by being as brave as you were—you and your sister. And back then, were the right laws in place to protect you?" I rack my brain, trying to remember when hazing laws went into effect, when Kelsey asks me something completely unexpected. "Why did you stay on the swim team, Ben?"

Surprisingly, a smile crosses my face. I move us both to the sofa and drop down onto it. Pulling her into my lap, I answer simply, "You."

A look of confusion crosses her face. "You took part in a team you hated?"

"Because you made me remember why I loved the sport, Kelsey." Clarity replaces the confusion and along with it, a rather becoming blush. "That's right. When you asked me what I felt while I was in the water, you forced me to remember why I loved it." Lowering my head down to hers again, I admit, "And as you began to mean more to me, it gave me the leverage to protect you."

"And who again did you think you didn't protect? Because right now, I've counted three," she persists.

I open and close my mouth, unable to say a word, which is good because she proceeds to blow my mind.

"You do what you need to, Ben, but don't you dare apologize to me or anyone else about the decisions you made. They're what make you . . . you. The man I love." While I'm falling in love all over again, she causes me to do something I never imagined I'd ever be able to do when I told her about what happened in that dark locker room all those years ago.

Laugh.

"All I ask is don't lose yourself in that godforsaken state." She gives a mock shudder in my arms, which causes me to roar before her words sober me with the fierceness they're spoken. "If I have to go back there without you by my side, someone's going to wish I hadn't."

All humor's wiped from my face when I lean toward her upturned one. Kelsey's jaw is so tight it might break. I smile at her tenderly before I brush my lips gently against hers.

Leaving her is going to be the hardest thing I've ever done, even if it's for the right reasons. "Now that I know I no longer have to fear the truth damaging our love, I'll do everything in my power to get back here as soon as I can." The thought of even one night without holding her is more painful than not knowing where she was for fifteen years.

"Come on." I slide Kelsey off my lap before standing. Reaching down, I take her hand and pull her to her feet. "I want to spend time with you before I leave."

"That sounds perfect." We make our way out of the study, turning lights off along the way, briefly pausing in the kitchen to put dinner in the refrigerator. After our conversation, neither of us is hungry. Well, not hungry for food. On the way to our bedroom—I *really need to ask her to move in when I get back,* I think ruefully—Kelsey stops in her tracks.

"Ben?"

"Yes, love?" I lean down and kiss her shoulder just as we're about to cross the threshold into the master.

"I learned a long time ago that grief and pain don't ever let you go." Turning to face me, she says seriously, "I want you to talk to someone about how to cope with all this when you get back. Time only helps if you have the right tools. Otherwise, you'll be yanked back every time something like this happens."

While my stomach lurches at the idea, my mind knows she's right. My heart, exhausted over the day's emotional roller coaster I put myself through, merely forces me to nod.

"Promise me." Her head collides with my heart as she leans forward.

My hand comes up to press her closer, if that's even possible. I'd imprint myself on her soul if I could. "I promise."

A shudder runs through her. "I wish I could remain calm enough to be the person who carries all your burden, but I fear that if you give it all to just me that I'm going to go back and kill them all. Painfully." Her eyes lift to mine, and I see a barely banked fury that oddly sends a wave of tenderness through me and kicks up a lick of fire through my veins when I didn't think that was possible tonight.

Then, for the second time this evening, she surprises me when she declares, "Besides, despite looking good in red, I don't want to wear the color for the rest of my life when I'm considered a high-risk inmate. I'm just sayin'."

Because on a night when I expected to be desperately trying to forget who I was, I'm grinning as I hold on to the best part of who I am. "So noted."

"Ben?" Her soft voice burns through me, scoring my heart in a million ways.

"Yes, my love?" We approach the bed like two shipwrecked sailors and fall onto it fully clothed. Kicking off my shoes, I pull her practically on top of me. "I don't want to let go all night," I murmur when she squawks before settling against my chest.

There's a moment of silence before she asks, "Maybe I should have pushed things between us sooner?"

Rolling us to our sides, I pull her tightly against me. "Loving is new for both of us. I was afraid of losing you by telling you the truth, and you were afraid to ask for it."

"What happened to you will never stop me from loving the person you are."

I groan as my lips capture hers briefly. We're both too drained for more than this simple reaffirmation of our love. "I think we've both learned something important," I conclude.

Kelsey laughs softly. "Yeah, when you ignore me, pick a fight. It seems to get you talking more easily than asking if anything's wrong. Hey, do you think that's the lawyer in you?"

I snicker before turning serious. "I found out losing you would gut me, Kels," I admit.

"Me too. I think we also learned that it's safe to be vulnerable with each other."

"And I know you're my safe place, no matter what. I can talk to you about anything." The wonderment of that echoes in my voice.

Her hand squeezes me where it's worked its way under my dress shirt to rest against my skin. "You would think you would have learned that after the first time we made love here, but I get it." She silences me with a quick kiss when I protest. "As you're much more of a linear thinker, being a lawyer and all, I'll explain it to you." Rising on an elbow in the dark, she softly says the words that first fascinated me when written by a sad girl with gray eyes. "The worst thing that's happening to you is the best thing that will ever happen to someone else. All you can do is move past it. After all, if life were meant to be easy, I'd have already won the game. What you don't realize is that you already won, Ben. And now, you're about to coach someone else to win." Brushing my lips once more, she snuggles deep in my arms while I contemplate the darkness for a while.

Her breathing evens out when I realize something profound I want to share with her. I whisper it into the dark of the night instead. "We both won."

Her sleepy "I know" makes me hold her closer against my heart with the knowledge this is forever.

Kelsey's going to have me on my knees soon, I damn well know it. I don't have to kiss my days as a bachelor goodbye. I'm sending them off with a bon voyage party. If it wasn't for what I'm about to face, I'd already be planning the most expedient way to tie her life to mine.

And somehow, I'm blessed because I know that when I go back tomorrow to face my past, my future will be waiting right here for me.

CHAPTER SIXTY-THREE

Kelsey

THE EXPRESSION ON HIS FACE IS LIKE NOTHING I'D EVER WITNESSED. The tenderness, gratitude, and love shine brighter than the fatigue I can read beneath his eyes. Running my thumb gently under one, my voice is raspy when I ask, "Did you sleep?"

The angles and planes of his bared upper chest catch the morning light as it filters through the windows. Ben shakes his head. "I didn't want to miss a single moment with you."

"Ben," I protest, but the graze of his lips against mine stops my words.

"Overnight, I realized you were right. I won. You can't imagine the pleasure I get from holding you while you sleep, but touching you? Ah, Kels, that makes every moment of pain worth the price." He glides his hand down over the sleeveless arm of the rumpled dress I slept in, sending goose bumps up and down my skin. Slowly, he inches the hem upward.

"Nothing was worth that price," I counter even as my body begins to react to his.

"Your love is," he corrects me, just before he captures my lips in a kiss so fierce my head is forced back against the pillows, as if he needs to prove to himself I'm still here. As if there's anywhere else I'd be knowing he hasn't walked away from me in his heart. I slide my hands up his bare chest and hold on. Tearing up, he pants out, "I'll do anything to protect you, Kels. Anything—know that."

I barely get the chance to nod before he's fused his lips back to mine like our kiss is a lifeline, because maybe it is. I can feel the wet heat of Ben's tears mingling with my own against my cheeks. The searing agony he'd held inside for so long, too long, finally open. Exposed.

Love and pain swirl up and settle over us like the humid summer air, full of weight and heat. *How had he been carrying this burden for so long?* I wonder before his hands wander down to the curve of my hip, lifting me flush against the hardness of his body and taking away thought by driving pleasure in its place. "Ben," I moan out his name.

Warmth pools between my legs as his bare thigh—when did he strip off his clothes?—slips between mine. Tangling my fingers into the hair at the nape of his neck, I pull his head back just enough to breathe into his mouth the words I need him to understand down to the core of his soul. "I love you, Benedict Perrault. Always," I say before I fuse our lips together. Wrapping my arms tightly around his neck, I open myself up for whatever he needs to take.

Because that's what I need to give.

And even though I wish I could do more, right now, he needs this. Needs me. I might wish I could go back in time and stand up for him the way he stood up for Lisa. I'd bear the burden of being humiliated a thousand times, a million times, if I could have spared him an ounce of the agony he endured. But that's not what he needs.

Twisting to free myself from the force that he's clasping me to him, I growl and push him to his back. He rolls, allowing me to smooth my hands over his shoulders, trying to replace the memories I know are burned into his skin with new ones. Maybe the memories we create will eventually ease the ones festering there for what seems like a lifetime. I know nothing can wipe them from his mind, just like nothing can take away mine.

My lips tear away, leaving nothing but our harsh breathing in the room. "Kels," he moans. His hands clench on my ass as I rock against him.

"Shh," I whisper. My lips brush his lightly before traveling over his jaw, down his neck, and onto the wide expanse of his chest. I'm making love to every inch of skin I can touch. I'm branding Ben with tenderness instead of terror. My lips and fingers are doing what words will never be able to, attempting to heal wounds I never inflicted, but ones that need to be cauterized for us to move on.

Slowly, my lips trail across his collarbone until I'm just above his heart. There they linger. "This is the part of you I fell in love with." My eyes well with tears. "The man who would sacrifice his soul for those he loves is worthy of more eloquent words than that, but there's a beauty in their simplicity. There's a beauty in you, Ben."

He shakes his head vociferously. I reach up to capture one of his hands to hold it against my heart. He stills, feeling the rapid beat against his palm. "Yes, my love." As much as I try, I can't prevent the wetness from falling down my cheeks. "I wish you could understand I would endure anything to take this pain from you." My voice cracks. "But it doesn't make you less of a man. It makes you one of the most courageous ones I know."

"I never wanted you to look at me differently," he chokes out.

"How could I not?" He turns his head away, but I pull it around. "Ben? You are so much more than the man I fell in love with. Your strength and honor humble me. And every day for the rest of my life, I pray you'll give me more reasons to look at you in a new way," I whisper as I lean down until my lips press against his bare chest. Leaving a firm kiss there, I sit up so he can read the truth in my eyes.

I'm hurting for the boy who endured a hazing that was pure physical abuse, but the man doesn't want my pity. He'll always have my compassion and understanding.

And my love.

Blindly through my tears, I find his lips. They're wet and salty beneath mine. He presses his to mine hesitantly, still on an emotional roller coaster after what he shared. All these years, he's been living with his pain and torment while trying to save everyone from theirs. Now, it's my time to show him there are no words to right the wrongs.

There's only love.

For a long time, I brush my lips against Ben's chin, his cheek, his chest. In comfort. "Let me show you how to love yourself as much as I do."

A bittersweet laugh escapes his chiseled lips. "I don't know if that's possible."

"I do," I assure him with the utmost confidence.

A glimmer lightens Ben's eyes, making them shimmer like the deepest water of the ocean. "How?" he murmurs. His hand, balled in the material of my dress, comes up to brush the matted hair tangled in the wet of my cheek.

With a tender smile, I lay my lips gently against his when I whisper, "Because you turned my life inside out. You helped me conquer my fears to understand I was always worthy of love—your love."

Ben groans as his arms wrap around me. "I don't know what I did to deserve you," he whispers into the top of my hair.

"You were you," I tell him. Tipping my head back, I give him my whole heart. "Then and now."

Beneath the morning sky, I hold on as Ben lowers his head and plucks random kisses from my lips, knowing this won't solve everything buried in his soul. But maybe, just maybe, he'll take it with him to remember during the nights when he's away from me.

"I love you, Kels." His voice is hoarse. "But I think it's time for you to lose this dress." My breath catches as Ben smooths his hands up my hips, over my ribs, lifting my dress with him. Within seconds, he whips my dress away from my body, leaving me clad in only a gray lace demi-bra and matching thong.

Pulling back just a bit, Ben moves his hand down my arm and catches the edge of the strap beneath his finger. Dragging the strap down as far as it will go, the cup barely stays up, only by the swirling lace along the edges, catching against my taut nipple. "Pretty. If you want to keep it that way, take it off," Ben rasps.

My nipples tighten even further at the veiled threat. Reaching behind me, I flick the clasp before slowly letting the other strap slide off my shoulder. My lips part as I hear the low growl from the back of his throat.

"Let me see."

I thrust my shoulders back even as I roll them to force the cups from clinging to nipples now aching for Ben's touch, his lips. Without breaking his gaze, I pull it off one arm before casually tossing it to the side of the bed. "Anything else you want gone?"

Snap. Stunned, I helplessly glance down at the matching thong Ben's torn as he pulls it from between my spread thighs. "I don't want to waste precious time, not when I've been doing that for weeks," he explains.

I feel my breath escape me as I catch the bold, unapologetic expression on his face. "If there were a way for you to repeat that move on less-expensive underwear, I'd appreciate it. You tend to tear apart the most expensive pairs," I tell him tartly, not at all upset.

Judging by the bland tone he uses to reply, he doesn't give a damn. "So noted," he says, right before he pulls one of my nipples deep into his mouth. He lashes the firm tip with his tongue, back and forth.

I hold his head close, but not too close. I don't ever want him to feel trapped where he can't break away. *Have I ever done that before?* I think in a panic.

Suddenly I'm on my back, and he's on top of me, pushing his hips against mine. The feel of his cock nestling against my pussy just makes it ready. I'm incoherent with pleasure when a hoarse scream is torn from me as Ben sheaths himself fully inside me. The full, heavy length of his cock enters me in one thrust, triggering all my inner muscles to clamp down on him. "Oh God."

"Don't you dare think about anything else when I'm loving you." He angles his hips back and pushes back into me again. And again. "Only this." He pushes against me, grinding against my clit.

I don't reply. I can't. I'm too busy thrashing beneath the sexual onslaught. Over and over again, Ben pistons into me, erasing weeks of doubt and replacing it with pleasure. But I don't go over until Ben's lips cover mine.

We're fighting to breathe, our eyes firmly locked on each other, when the overwhelming pleasure begins to race over my skin. It burns throughout every inch of me that's connected to Ben. From the hair he's pulling to the tips of my toes that are digging into the back of his thighs, everything is on fire.

Slowly, we sip at each other's lips as we both come down from the high we flew to. "The only thing I want is you. Nothing will cause that to change, Kelsey." He swallows before ducking his head and brushing a kiss against my shoulder. "Knowing you're here with me means I can go do what has to be done and come back whole."

"Ben," I begin, hesitant to bring up the promise I wrung from him from last night, but knowing we don't have much time.

It turns out I don't have to. Pushing his lips against the pulse in my neck, he whispers, "I promised, baby. Just . . . bear with me. There's going to be days I'm going to come home after laying things out and not be able to see through the exhaustion of doing so."

Tears prick my closed lids, but I refuse to let them escape. Turning my head, I stare into the glorious sunlight as it streams into the windows. I'm blind, but at least the rapid blinking has dried my eyes, so my face is smooth when I face the man I love beyond a shadow of a doubt. "As long as you promise that if you need me for any reason, you'll ask me to be with you. Anywhere."

"Even Savannah?" he asks with a touch of amusement. But I don't have it in me to joke.

"I'd walk there if I had to," I tell him in all seriousness. "I'd march down Calhoun Square and up the steps of Forsyth to get to you if need be."

And somehow I know I would find the strength to do so when he rolls to his back, buries his head in my shoulder, and finally cries.

Hours later in bed, Ben's clinging to me as he dozes. Nightmares chase him where I can't go. This is precisely what I fear.

My mind is too full to relax, even though it might be the last time I get any real rest until he comes home. Instead, it's my turn to stare up at the coffered ceiling. I need to take my pain and anger out on my characters, but only the realization that I'll wake Ben keeps me from slipping from bed to do just that. I'm practically vibrating with my fury, but harnessing my energy to heal Ben? That's what matters now, I think firmly.

The real challenge is going to be transforming his perspective about himself. Because if he doesn't understand that none of this was his fault, I fear he'll never be free from the pain licking at his soul.

CHAPTER SIXTY-FOUR

Benedict

Ding dong.

The imposing sound of my family's front doorbell rings just as I descend the grand staircase. I lean over and push a button on the intercom. "I'll get it."

My mother's voice answers, "Thanks, sweetie. I've got my hands full of cinnamon roll dough."

"Keep them there," I plead. Disconnecting the intercom, I jog the last few steps to the impressive doors. Opening them, I find a dark-haired man wearing a lightweight suit. His head is tipped back, admiring the oak trees. Praying he's not a salesman, I ask politely, "May I help you?"

His head whips around before his soothing voice says, "Actually, I believe I was sent here to help you. That is if you're Benedict."

Warily, I start to slam the door in his face. The dark-haired stranger surprises me with his next words. "Ryan sent me."

"Pardon me for asking this, but who the hell are you?"

His warm chuckle is somehow soothing, though I don't quite know why. He whips off his sunglasses, and I'm met with candid green eyes. "I'm Jason. Well, Dr. Jason Ross—a close friend of Ryan and Jared's. He flew me down to see if there was any way I could help with your current situation."

I pinch my fingers in the corner of my eyes. "Of course he did."

"I hope we'd have a chance to speak, Benedict."

Resigned, I throw the door open to get my full impression of the man who helped rescue Ryan. "The meddlesome bastard just couldn't let me work through things on my own."

"He's not very patient when it comes to helping family, no," Jason admits cheerfully.

Before I correct Jason's comment about my being family, my father's voice booms across the hall, "Son? Is everything all right?"

I lift my hand in Jason's direction and let it drop. "My boss sent a gift."

"Ben, that's not a gift, that's a person."

"I'm well aware of that, Dad.

"I'm a doctor, Mr. Perrault." Jason extends his hand. My father crosses the hall and takes it. "I specialize in trauma and emergency surgery at NYU Medical Center in New York."

Despite being impressed with Dr. Ross's credentials, "I'm not certain there's much for you to do down here, Doc. Physically, the patient is fine."

Jason corrects my misconception. "Ryan didn't send me here to talk with anyone else but you, Benedict."

"Well, I'll be damned," my father bursts out.

"So will I."

"Ryan thought you might feel like that." Jason reaches into his pocket and pulls out a sealed envelope with my name scrawled on it.

I tear into it.

Ben,

I know you're asking yourself what the hell am I doing? Just keep reading.

Jason found me almost unconscious in an alley outside of a bar. I was a bleeding, sobbing catastrophe. I didn't know who to reach out to for help because the only person I trusted—Caleb—was stationed overseas.

The man standing in front of you took me in, got me immediate medical attention, and that's before he used his good name as a physical barrier to protect me because I didn't feel safe returning home.

You see, I understand what it's like to survive hell. The one lesson I'll never forget after climbing out is you need a hand to help you escape it.

Take hold of the one I'm offering you. Talk to Jason.

Then get your ass back to work. You're missed.

Ryan

I fold the letter before slipping it back into the envelope. I begin, "Dr. Ross . . ."

"Jason," he corrects.

"Jason, my mother's making homemade cinnamon rolls for breakfast. Would you care for some before we find a place to talk?"

"That sounds perfect."

My father gapes at me. I walk straight over to him and grab his shoulder. "It's okay, Dad. Really."

"You're certain."

Light sparkles off the ring on the third finger of Jason Ross's left hand. I know without a shadow of a doubt for me to get to the place where I'm ready to for my future to be permanently entwined with Kelsey's without fear, I need to keep my promise to her.

"Yes. I'm certain. Ryan just precipitated what I'd planned on doing anyway."

I stride over to the older man. “How does coffee sound?”

“Like we’re going to become very good friends.”

I bark out a laugh before guiding Jason into the kitchen.

CHAPTER SIXTY-FIVE

Kelsey

I've been struggling with a scene all morning. I'm grateful for the distraction when my cell phone rings. I'm surprised to find it's Morgan. "Hi, Morgan. How can I help you?"

Morgan gets right to the point. "Max just came into the center. He's asking for you."

Without hesitation, I save the work on my laptop and toss it to the side. I could lose the entire manuscript and it wouldn't mean as much as this phone call does. "I'll be there in fifteen minutes."

"I'll let him know you're on your way." Morgan disconnects.

I'm already searching amid the boxes around my room for a pair of sneakers, sandals, something to throw on. Fashion doesn't matter.

Finding out the status of a young man's broken heart does.

Max's face has some remnants of yellowing bruises, but I'm grateful not to see any fresh ones.

My anger reignites as I recall first our furtive meeting in the hall at Le Cadeau and later the stilted way Max confessed to Morgan about what led to him being beaten on the streets of his neighborhood. Seeking a confidant with whom to discuss his confusion about the emotional conflict he was experiencing about sexual orientation, Max did the right thing—he turned to a school counselor. The problem being a punk at school overheard the conversation.

"The brutality of the words flung at him during the attack may have scarred him more than the physical blows," Morgan warned me.

That was weeks ago, before I knew what happened in Benedict's past—long before I found I could hate as fiercely as I can love. Twisting away, I agreed. "There are many ghosts he's going to have to face."

"And the help he needs is out of our hands," Morgan concluded grimly.

All because a door wasn't closed properly. Then again, so many critical moments of our lives are affected by the smallest chance—a car wreck, a failing grade, an apology or lack thereof. But despite the chaos swirling around Max between school, his home, and the state becoming involved with his living situation, one thing happened when word eventually spread to the kids at Le Cadeau.

Those who attend the same school as Max became his sword and shield, defending him. Morgan credited me with the change in a staff meeting. Her vivid eyes bright, she reminded us all, "Sometimes the words that make the most impact don't have to be written."

My heart shattered and reformed even as I struggled with Ben being gone. I kept praying Max was okay. Morgan couldn't say much, and Val, Lisa, and I all wondered about his welfare because Max never came back to the center.

Until now.

Now, at Le Cadeau, Max's multicolored eyes are filled with something I've never seen in them during our brief acquaintance—peace. "I have news."

I lean forward, eagerly awaiting his update.

"I'm moving to Lafayette."

"What? With whom?" I'm shocked.

Morgan interjects, "With his paternal grandmother, Kee. It's taken social services some time to finalize the arrangements. In the meantime, Max hasn't been able to come to the center because he hasn't been living close enough to get here on his own. He also . . ." She pauses, stopping herself from telling the whole story.

Max takes over but starts farther back than where Morgan began. "I took your advice, Ms. Kee. I spoke to Ms. Morgan about things—a lot of things. She pointed out that I had choices. Then, before I could decide what I wanted to do next, I still had questions about the kind of person I was becoming inside. I thought it might be easier to discuss those things with my school counselor."

"Was it?"

"Yes, ma'am. He was patient and kind." I let out a breath I wasn't aware I was holding. Almost urgently, he says haltingly, "Don't, please don't."

"Don't what, Max?"

"Don't be . . . angry. There's too much anger. What Mr. Ferguson did was an accident. He feels horrible. And he's been an advocate for me—just like Ms. Morgan, Ms. Val, Ms. Lisa. And you."

It's kind of hard to swallow around the watermelon that's lodged itself inside my throat, but I manage to. "How are you physically?" I ask.

"The pain is mostly gone. Gran gave me some of her special . . . what's it called again, Ms. Morgan?"

"A poultice. Max's gran made it for him when she saw the bruising." Her lips curve but not in pleasure. I can't deduce why until Max tacks on with a snap of his fingers, "That's right! She said she used them when she had her own 'incidents.' Did she ever explain what she meant by that, Ms. Morgan?"

Morgan clenches her teeth behind her smile. "I'm certain if she wants you to know, she'll explain over time."

Steering the conversation, I probe, "Are you content with how things turned out? How do you feel about moving away from New Orleans?"

Max sends me a look filled with such profound gratitude I want to cry before he begins to speak, "I need to fly away to change. Who knows, maybe I can soar. Maybe I'll shed the burden that weighs me down during the day —and I don't just mean physically."

Max quotes my words from my second book *Change* and not for the first time do I appreciate the impact my words have had on this young man. With a note of disbelief, he confides, "My gran has the same color eyes as me."

I let out a sigh that some prayers have been answered. *Now, if you can just help Ben,* I think furtively.

"It's almost time for the social worker to pick you up. Is there anything else you wanted to let Ms. Kee know?" Morgan prompts.

Max stands and moves directly in front of me. Instinctively, I surge to my feet as well. For a long moment he does nothing but stare into my eyes. Then he heals another piece of my heart—a piece that's reserved just for him. "Ms. Kee, I'd like to ask . . ."

"Anything." And I mean that without reservation.

"You held out your hand to me. You weren't the first who did"—his eyes drift to Morgan before meeting mine—"but so many times you pulled me from the darkness."

At this point, I can no sooner prevent the tears from sliding down my face than I can move. Either are completely impossible. I whisper, "It was my honor."

"Can I . . . is it allowed . . . ? What I'm trying to ask is . . ."

"Max, trust your instincts," Morgan murmurs.

He rushes his words together. "Can I give you a hug goodbye?"

I step back. "No." Max is crestfallen. I make my way to Morgan's desk, pull over her notepad and quickly scratch out something. Tearing off the paper, I walk back and extend it to him. "I refuse to say goodbye."

Max reaches for the scrap. His head cocks to the side when he sees what's written. "What is this?"

"How to keep in touch. That's what friends do, right? That's why I refuse to give you a hug goodbye, Max. Because we're not saying goodbye, we're saying see you later."

"Ms. . . . Kelsey? This is your real name?"

"Drop the 'Ms.' and you've got it right."

"You want me to write to you?"

"Letters, email, phone. However you want." This time I'm the one who asks, "Now, friend, can I have a see you later hug?"

My arms are soon wrapped tightly around Max. I murmur, "If you get scared or lonely, come back here."

His laugh is watery. "I can't drive, Kelsey."

"Come back to this hug. Then reach out. We're not letting you go." It's a promise.

There's a knock at the door. Max pulls back, folding the paper carefully and placing it in his copy of *Change*. He makes his way to the door, stopping to hug Morgan briefly. Before he opens it to depart, he promises, "I'll be in touch."

Long minutes after Max leaves, Morgan holds a cup of coffee. "The hardest part is not knowing what happens next."

"That's why I write books, Morgan. I get to decide on the ending."

She barks out a laugh. "And if you were writing this one?"

I think a moment before I reach for her notepad. I write long handed, just the way I used to when I wrote in my journals as I daydreamed about Ben all those years ago.

And look how that turned out.

I flip the notepad to her before I walk over to the window. She reads aloud, " 'Under the twinkling stars, Max danced, having just released his lover's lips from a tender kiss. He closed his magical eyes, having made a wish on every single one. It was disconcerting to know the person in his arms would be the person who would stand by his side for eternity—both elusive and courageous. Until that magic moment where they began their journey, he was content to have the sweet music wash over them as night fell. And they danced the night away.' I hope like hell you're right."

Spying Max as he climbs into the back of the social worker's car, I murmur, "So do I."

CHAPTER SIXTY-SIX

Kelsey

"Have you heard from Ben today?" Lisa asks me as we're standing in the kitchen.

"Not today. Have you?"

She shakes her head. "With today being the day the movers were bringing in the big items, I expected him to call or text you."

I did too, but Lisa also doesn't know how hard Benedict's been working to overcome the past—from talking to Jason Ross about his guilt to facing Logan, John's grandson. I can hear the weariness and the struggle growing every night when we talk. A large part of our conversations center around him unburdening himself by telling me in detail about the progress they've each made, which in Logan's case is little.

Just before the car came to pick him up for the airport three weeks ago, he pulled the key off his ring and pressed it into my hand.

"I love you. And if the mistakes I've made over the last few weeks have taught me anything, it's that I can't live without you in my life." Leaning down, he laid his lips on mine. "You may have to be patient with me, Kels, but I need to know you're here, in my life, my home, my heart, when I get back." Without giving me a chance to throw my arms around him to give him my unequivocal "Yes," he brushed his lips over mine once more before racing out the door.

And our conversations since haven't offered the right moment to bring up the fact that with his sister's help and Val's amused supervision, my life has stopped spanning two homes and has fully settled into one.

Lisa and I went to my storage unit last weekend to look at my furniture to see what should be kept and what I could save to donate to Le Cadeau's annual fundraiser. "Oh my god, this desk. We've got to find a way to get this back to the house," Lisa whispered as she stripped the plastic off my custom-built mahogany desk. "It would look perfect in the loft upstairs." Then she turned to me and begged, "Tell me this is where you wrote *Betrayal*."

I smirked before shaking my head. "Do you think I had the money for this desk when I wrote *Betrayal*? I wrote it while sitting at my dining room table, thinking about your brother. Disappointed?"

"Only if you tell me that table isn't in here."

"It's in the back."

"Thank God." We both laugh before I tell her, "I did write *Forgotten* at it though."

"Save me. I might bring Cade over to kiss me on it."

"Ew." I raised a brow at her as her fingers trailed over the scrolling inlay reverently. "But speaking of that, won't having this monster around impede your living space?"

Lisa blushed hard. "Not when I tell you that Cade asked me to move in with him."

I reached for her and hugged her hard. "Holy crap, Lisa. I take it you said yes."

"It took him a while to convince me," she said almost proudly.

"When did he first ask you?"

"About a week after we started dating." Simultaneously, we both burst into laughter. Wiping her eyes with the ends of her shirt, she looked up at me and asked, "Why do you think you and Ben had so much privacy at the house? Cade called it a test run."

"So, you're ready."

"Beyond. I knew there were secrets he was keeping from me. Now? I know everything I need to. And judging by the fact we're in here picking out furniture, I'm guessing you know what I'm referring to."

I opened my mouth and closed it. The extent of her brother's secrets are his to tell or share. Diplomatically, I replied, "I guess homes have a way of letting people know when they're ready for them."

"And so do men's hearts."

Now, the movers have just left, and we're both trying to find space for duplicate kitchen gadgets. "If Ben were to walk in the door right now, he'd have a coronary that his kitchen isn't in perfect order," I mutter as I bend over, trying to find a spot for my nifty Rachel Ray box mandolin.

When I stand, it's to find the feminine version of the eyes I love smiling at me. "No, he wouldn't. He'd be grateful."

God, I hope so, I think to myself. "Is it too much to wish that kitchens have magical powers to absorb all your gadgets and spit them out when you need them?"

Lisa is still laughing at me when I hear my phone ring amid the mess on the counter with Ben's distinctive Dave Matthews ringtone. "Shit. I can't find it! Can you get to it on your side?"

Lisa scans the counter before snatching it up. Quickly answering before it goes to voice mail, she says, "Hey, big brother. Nope, we're rearranging things in the kitchen. Ask Kelsey. Here." She holds out the phone to me with a smirk. "Someone tall, dark, and, dare I say handsome since we look alike wants to talk with you."

Snatching my phone out of her hands, I breathlessly greet him. "Hey."

"What's this about the kitchen? What was wrong with it before?" He sounds bewildered and lost.

Twirling a thick strand of hair around my finger, I turn away from Lisa. "Well, I decided to put all my energy from missing you to good use."

I hear him sink back into the chair he said on an earlier call was in his room. "Really? How's that?"

Slightly anxious, I bite my lip. "Maybe I misunderstood . . ."

"You didn't," Lisa calls out. I wave my hand to hush her.

"But you did say you wanted me in your home when you got back, right."

There's silence on the other end of the line. "I meant to be waiting for me," he starts.

"Oh." Crap. "I can . . ."

"Because I was going to do something more than act like a complete jackass before I asked you to move in. Now, how am I supposed to top you reading my mind?" His voice is filled with tenderness as he continues to talk right over me.

"I'm sure you'll figure out a way," I blurt out.

"I'm going to have to. Kels?"

"Yeah?"

"I don't give a crap what the house looks like as long as you're in it. But tell me you're not lifting any heavy furniture, or I will get pissed."

After I reassure him that no backs were injured in the course of moving me in, Ben turns into his new quiet self while I prattle on about where things are in the kitchen. It isn't until I mention my desk being upstairs that he asks, "What about Lisa?"

That's when I take great delight in sharing, "Well, the movers were great about moving her to Cade's."

Ben spews whatever he's drinking on the other end of the line. "Jesus. A little warning?"

"I only heard about it the other day. I would have thought he would have told you." The dirty look I shoot Lisa is positively worthless in the face of her glow.

"That might explain the eight or so voicemails I haven't listened to yet. I suppose I should call him back if only to warn him about her cooking."

"Somehow, I don't think he asked her to move in for her cooking ability."

Lisa concurs, "Or lack thereof. I have other . . . skills he's more interested in."

Ben groans in my ear. "I did not need to hear about that."

I let out a throaty laugh. He sighs. "Prettiest sound in the world, sweetheart."

Trying to be as circumspect as possible, I turn my back and lower my voice. "How are things there?"

"Slow, Kels. Logan is where I was when everything first happened."

"Oh, Ben." My heart is in shambles for so many reasons.

Benedict's voice is tired. "After speaking with Jason, I know I should have trusted my support system—sought out help whether that was my parents or even the administration at Forsyth. Logan was violated by the institution that was supposed to protect him."

"Has Jason being there helped?" Benedict shared Ryan's "gift" with me.

"Yes? He isn't mature enough to separate trusting the need to see a psychologist—which he desperately needs."

"It will be a long time before he trusts again," I murmur sadly.

"The things he's shared? Let's say what I told you was nothing compared to what this boy went through."

A soundless whistle escapes through my clenched teeth. "Do you feel like being there is helping?"

"It's helping John," he tells me honestly.

"And you? Is the hurt letting up any?"

Ben whispers, "The only thing that's going to ease the ache inside me is having you by my side, my love."

I inhale deeply. "Ben."

"No one warned me love would be like this," he says almost conversationally.

"Like what?" I try to keep them at bay, but the stinging tears are like little pins behind my closed lids.

"A bond that can never be severed. I love you, Kelsey."

The stinging has resulted in salty liquid sliding down my cheeks at a hot, furious pace. So, I'm not surprised when my breath hitches when I whisper, "I love you too."

"Thank you for being patient with me."

"Always."

And before I can say another word, Benedict's hung up the phone. Slowly, I pull mine from my ear before turning to Lisa, who's unabashedly listening in. "I have a favor to ask."

"Anything."

"Think you'd mind cleaning up the kitchen on your own? I have to call and book a flight before I pack a bag to get to Ben."

Lisa comes around the counter to wrap her arms around me. "That's not a favor, that's my honor."

And suddenly, all I can think about as I race down the hall to Benedict's— no, our— room is that I need to get to him as soon as possible. Maybe I should have been with him from the beginning, but I thought he needed the time to sort through this part of his past on his own.

After quickly booking a flight on my phone and calling out the details to Lisa, I grab a suitcase I recently unpacked and begin to throw clothes back into it.

I ask Lisa, "Do you have time to drive me, or should I call a car?"

A tall figure appears in the doorway, startling me. "Is that all you're bringing?" Cade asks.

"No," I tell him tartly. "I need to get another bag and my computer."

"Right. I'll just put this one in the car. Lisa's . . ."

"Right here. I just got off the phone with my dad. He had to know you were coming so he could call the gate to let your cab in. Apparently, he chewed them out pretty well when they let Dr. Ross in without calling first," Lisa tells me apologetically.

I nod distractedly as I toss shoes into a weekender.

"Dad said to pack a dress, Kels. You can't get into the club for dinner without one."

"You pick." I straighten from the floor of the closet. "I need to get my laptop."

"Right," she agrees. "I'll finish in here."

Cade checks his watch. "We only have a few minutes before we have to leave if you want to make that flight."

Right. Without warning, I dash out of the room, leaving Lisa to finish throwing anything resembling clothes in my bag. The laptop is a priority since I can purchase anything else I need.

The most important thing is to get to Ben.

CHAPTER SIXTY-SEVEN

Benedict

Hanging up the phone, I rub my fingers across my lips. So many things haunt me, including how much my heart aches for the woman on the other end of the line. "Soon, I'll come home to you, my love," I whisper.

I think about the changes I've helped guide John and his family through with Jason's assistance. There were none as significant as when Logan, anxious as fuck and backed by his grandparents, held out a shaking hand to me, saying, "Thank you. I wouldn't have known where to start to try to make them understand."

I shook his hand firmly, but released it quickly so he could retreat to the safety of his grandfather's arms. "If we're fortunate, they'll never be able to understand, only to support us with all their unconditional love."

A weary maturity settled on Logan's face—the very look I used to see in the mirror until a victim of a different sort showed me how to search my soul for the freeing words. She taught me to describe the love of something that wasn't theirs to take—though none of it was—and by forcing me to dig deep, I took it back and found a pathway to a future I might never have traveled down otherwise.

A knock startles me. I give my father a semblance of a smile. "What's up, Dad?"

"Your mother's in a tizzy." My bark of laughter surprises me, and he takes it as an invite to join me in my suite of rooms.

"Why?" I ask curiously.

"Something about an unexpected dinner guest." He waves his hand, dismissing the topic. Knowing my mother, that could be a neighbor to the governor of the state of Georgia, so I dismiss my father's words. He continues, "I just came to see how you're holding up after today."

"With Logan?" He nods. I take a deep breath. "I can't say seeing his devastation isn't bringing up more bad memories I tried to move past."

"And nightmares." At my startled jerk, he shakes his head. "Son, despite your age, I wouldn't be your father if I didn't check on you every night. Right now, you're sleeping under my roof. One day when you're a parent, you'll understand."

"Understand?" I parrot back almost automatically as my mind thinks of Kelsey's beautiful body ripe with our child. A million feelings rip through me, none of which is fear.

"You'll get it if you ever have children," he assures me with a grin.

Still in a state of shock, I stumble when I tell him, "If you'd have asked me a year ago—hell, six months ago—I'd have said I might find the right woman when hell freezes over."

"And now?"

"Now, I ache because I can't hold her." Sitting back, I wonder, "How is it possible for me to love her so quickly?"

"Maybe, son, because you started to fall when you were seventeen. Life's natural roadblocks only slowed the fall, but it never stopped," my father tells me sagely.

I think in the comfortable silence for a few minutes before nodding. "You're right."

"Want to say that again?" he jokes. I toss a throw pillow his way. "Better get this room cleaned up before your mother sees it."

I groan. Since I no longer live here, my parents transformed the shrine of my teenage years into a well-appointed suite. I take pleasure in teasing my mother about how there's no basket awaiting my dirty clothes. She retorts, "It's a guest suite, not your permanent residence."

My response is to pile them up in a corner and bring them down to wash when I'm close to running out. I grumble good-naturedly, "There are times when being at home makes me feel about twelve."

My father shrugs, all sympathy erased from eyes as blue as my own. "I just figured you'd want to not look like a slob by the time Kelsey gets here later." Pushing away from the door, he disappears from view.

I shove myself out of the chair. I must be hearing things. "Dad?" I call out as I dash out on bare feet to catch up with him. He's already made it to the stairwell. "Did you just say Kelsey?"

"If her flight lands on time, I expect her here before dinner, son." Giving me a critical once-over, he tacks on, "A shower wouldn't be remiss in this situation either."

"She's coming?" I feel like I barely breathe the words. She swore she'd never come back to this place that left such scars on her soul.

"From what your sister said when she asked me to let her into the gates, she's hell-bent on getting to your side."

The warmth I've been missing since I left New Orleans—no, even before that—starts to fill me up. She's coming to me. She isn't leaving me alone to deal with this pain, wondering if everything will be okay when I return.

She's making sure it will be.

Somehow, I didn't just find the love of my life, I found the person who will willingly follow me into hell to save me. And she'd better know I'd do the same for her. "Hey, Dad?"

"Yes, Ben?"

"While Mom's spinning around in a dither, do you think you can do me a favor?"

"Anything, son. Just ask."

"Can you get Grandmother's ring out of the safe? I want to bring it back with me." The solitaire my grandmother wore for more than fifty years on her hand was passed down to me to give to the woman I love when I propose. While we're not ready for that, I want it with me so I know there's no delay when the time is right.

A lot of shit happens in life. We both know that it isn't always the perfect memories that get you through marriage, but the strength of your partner who holds you up when you can't handle anymore. For him to know I found that in Kelsey. "I'll leave it in the top drawer of my desk. Grab it when you're ready. Now"—the bittersweet tone of his voice changes to amused—"I think I'll try to convince your mother not to call the cleaning crew out at four p.m. on a Thursday for an emergency touch-up."

"Remind her that Kelsey's practically been living with me."

"Practically? What's taken you so long?" he teases as he descends the steps into the kitchen. There's a peaceful silence before I hear him call out, "Roberta, will you please put down the phone? The house looks fine."

I race back to my room and strip my bed, tossing weeks' worth of dirty laundry in the center of the sheets and tying them up like an enormous bundle that would hang off a runaway's stick. *If they could manage to lift it,* I think with a touch of humor. Thank God my father spoiled what I suspect was supposed to be a surprise. I might have spent the first hour trying to clean up rather than holding Kelsey in my arms, which is precisely what I intend to do,

Racing for the bath and turning on the shower, I debate shaving when I get a hard look at my face. I don't remember the last time I did this. Sure, I've had to use a mirror to shave, but when have I really looked at myself?

Not since the day after I was first violated.

I thought I had an amazing life when what I had was the pieces of one clinging to me by tightly held bandages. Now that the wounds are all exposed, and everyone I care about knows what happened in my past, I can take pride in the invisible scars.

The worst thing that's happening to you is the best thing that will ever happen to someone else. All you can do is move past it. After all, if life were meant to be easy, I'd have already won the game.

Kelsey's prophetic words flood my head. The pain of what happened to either of us isn't going to disappear, but it makes us who we are, standing on top of the podium holding the most important trophy in our arms—each other.

And with that thought, I reach for my shaving kit. I want to greet the woman I love with everything that she deserves.

Me.

And it's been too long since I gave her that.

CHAPTER SIXTY-EIGHT

Kelsey

"I love him," I mutter as I step off the plane onto the jetway where my plane landed at Savannah-Hilton Head International airport later that same day. "I swore I'd never come back to this city, yet here I am."

Wheeling my carry-on bag quickly through the airport, I make my way to baggage claim. With a sense of déjà vu, I scan the crowd for the driver holding the device with my name on it.

I approach him, and we're soon on our way toward Skidaway Island.

Where I can see for myself the damage this city truly caused not just to my life but to that of the man I love.

Pulling up to the gatehouse, I pull out my identification and hand it over. "Kelsey Kennedy here to see the Perrault family, please."

"One moment." I'm grateful now for Lisa calling her father when my ID is handed back seconds later. "Follow the street straight until you reach your first left. The Perrault residence is straight back, Ms. Kennedy."

"Thank you." Something is driving me to get to Benedict quickly. Rolling up the blacked-out window, I relay the instructions to my driver.

Within minutes, the car pulls up to a four-story brick home that gives the impression of warmth despite the enormous size. I wait for the driver to come around and open my door before sliding out. Holding one hand to my forehead, I tip my neck back as far as it will go as I take in the house that nurtured Benedict to become the man he is, all while holding his secrets with such a grip that he's never healed.

I'm so absorbed in my study I don't hear the footsteps on the flagstone next to me. It isn't until I hear a deep voice say, "I was hoping we'd have a chance to meet before Ben came rushing out here," that I whirl around and get shocked to the core.

If I want to know what Benedict will look like in thirty years, all I need to do is stare at the man in front of me. His father is an older, more distinguished copy of him, even down to the blue of his eyes. "Ben's told me a great deal about you, Kelsey. I'd always hoped to meet the girl who inspired my son fifteen years ago," he continues, oblivious to my shock. "I'm thrilled I get to meet the woman he loves instead."

"I'm not so certain I should be here. I ran out of the house without thinking." My voice comes out in a tight rasp.

"What on earth makes you believe that?" Pierre Perrault tips his head to the side in a way that reminds me so much of Benedict's that my heart aches.

I open my mouth to respond, but before I can, I hear, "Maybe you should let me take it from here, Dad." I turn, and there he is. The fall breeze ruffles his overlong hair. His lips are curved softly, but it's his eyes that make me want to burst into tears. His blue eyes are missing the clouds that have overshadowed them since he told me exactly what happened. Benedict's father slips away to give us privacy.

"Surprise," I whisper weakly.

He shakes his head. "I can't believe you're here."

"There was no choice."

"What do you mean?" Confusion starts to edge in.

Here's where I risk it all. Everything. Taking a deep breath, I rush my words. "You left because you needed to face your pain alone. I came because I thought you needed me, but what if you don't? What if I misunderstood everything you said? What if—"

Cutting me off, he growls, "Get over here."

"I'm afraid to move," I admit.

"You're afraid of nothing, nobody. You're unconquerable."

I shake my head because I know that's not the truth. Benedict's face softens. "Well, that's true when you're with me, because I feel the same way when I'm with you."

A hiccuping sob escapes my throat as I move forward. He meets me partway. "How long are you here for?" he whispers against my hair.

"As long as you want me." I burrow against his neck. I can smell the soft scent of his aftershave next to the still-damp strands of his hair.

His arms squeeze. "Then you're not going anywhere." His voice holds a note of satisfaction.

I nod blindly. "I'm certain the driver was cursing my name when he hefted my bag. I don't know how much I threw in there," I admit.

Benedict pulls back, staring at me for a moment before he bursts out laughing. He swings me around in circles in his family's front yard amid the enormous oak trees whose leaves are just starting to change color.

Clutching him as tightly as I can, I give thanks for time, strength, perseverance, and miracles. I figure you need all of those to get not only through life, to find love, but to withstand a high school reunion.

All of which we both seem to have done brilliantly.

Lowering me back to my feet, Benedict keeps an arm around me. "Come on. Let's go inside. I think Mom's going to burst something if she doesn't get a chance to meet you."

"Wait!" I exclaim just before he drags me toward the house. "There's something I need to do first." I let go of his hand and step back. "I figured out the name of the next book," I declare.

His face softens. "Already? Have you been writing twenty-four seven since I've been gone?"

"Pretty much," I admit. Unable to break away from the intensity of his gaze after being so long without that powerful connection, I blurt out, "It's called *Courage*. After all, I think it's time for Pilar to see there's more than her own pain swirling around her."

I no sooner get the words out of my mouth before I'm swept up in Benedict's arms, and he's pressing my back against a tree. His hold on my neck is firm, ensuring his lips can possess mine as his head descends. Over and over for long minutes, our teeth, our tongues, our souls clash in that kiss. His hands holding my head tighten in my hair, sending sizzling sensations to places that have long been denied his touch.

I whimper when I'm finally let up for air, the world spinning around me where the only thing making sense is to hang on to Benedict. So I do.

"I missed you, sweetheart. I missed your brilliant mind, your generous heart, and your beautiful face."

And with those words, weeks of wondering and worry disappear. I aim a cocky grin up at him. "Then don't you think we should go meet your mother? If I were her, I'd be rating the show you just put on."

The red color riding Benedict's cheekbones disappears as he shakes his head desperately. "No. She wouldn't. I'm a grown man, for Christ's sake." His voice is rising.

I lay my finger on his lips and murmur, "If my son brought home a woman, you can damn well believe I'd be doing the same thing."

Lowering his head, his next words start my heart beating in triple time. "And imagine when it's our daughter? Forget about it." Without any indication that he's just shaken my world to its very foundation, he steps back and holds out his hand. "Come on, love. Let's introduce you to my mom."

Twining my fingers in his, I walk alongside him, thinking silently for a few moments before asking, "Where should I tell Nana and Pop-pop to come for Thanksgiving?"

Just as the front door opens to reveal Benedict's mother, who has a beaming smile of welcome on her face, he answers, "Tell them to come to New Orleans. If they don't feel up to it, we'll all"—he nods at his mother to indicate his family as well—"fly to Jacksonville to celebrate a day meant for family."

"A day to give thanks for all of our blessings," I add and squeeze his hand. "I do that every day."

"Me too, sweetheart." Helping me up the stone steps, he presents me to his mother. "Mom, I'd like to introduce you to—"

Benedict doesn't get to say my name before I'm engulfed in a mother's hug. It's different than Nana's and Val's mother's but no less warm and welcoming. "You hug just like him," I blurt out.

A warm laugh washes over me. "I hope so, Kelsey. I've been doing it almost thirty-four years," Roberta Perrault says warmly. "Welcome to our home."

And as I'm ushered inside with Benedict, I realize that's exactly what it is. Home.

"So, Mom, if Kelsey's grandparents are up to it, Thanksgiving at my house this year?" Benedict tosses out casually over dinner.

"Sure, honey. Will it be just the five of us, or is Cade going to show now that he's finally admitted he's in love with Lisa?" Roberta asks calmly, the news about her children clearly not surprising her.

I choke on the bite of olive I've just swallowed. Two sets of male hands come out to whack me on the back. "I'm okay," I wheeze out.

Roberta looks on in concern. "Are you sure?"

I flap my hand. "Fine. It's just I thought she would have told you they moved in together."

There's a silence around the table before Pierre bursts out into laughter. "Well, that explains the twenty-seven voicemails she left," he muses.

"It's how we got my desk into the loft," I explain before clamping my hand over my mouth as all the attention focuses on me.

"So, you moved in with him?" Roberta's face holds dreams of weddings and grandchildren. My eyes dart to Benedict, whose expression clearly states, *You're on your own.*

Fine. I can more than handle this.

"He kinda asked." I shrug as Roberta gapes at me.

"Kinda? Did I raise you in a barn?" She turns to glare at her son.

"I asked," Benedict defends himself. Then his brow lowers to a *V*. "The morning I left. At least I'm pretty sure I did. That's what you said."

"His words were, 'But I need to know you're here, in my life, my home, my heart, when I get back.' It sounded like he wanted me to move in, so I took a gamble. I guess I got it right."

There's a pregnant pause around the table before laughter rules. "I've learned an incredible lesson being in love with a writer, Dad." Ben recovers to address his father.

"What's that, son?"

"Never argue over words. She's always going to win." Winking at me, he picks up my hand and kisses the back of it. "You're right. I bungled it, but you knew what was in my heart. Does this mean I still get to pick on Cade?"

Even though I'm melting over his words, I look out for Lisa. "No."

Three of us chortle again over Benedict's obvious disappointment. We spend the rest of the night talking about Ben and Lisa as kids while I'm tucked against Ben's side. Soon, the clock strikes midnight, and Pierre holds out a hand for his sleepy wife. "Good night, Ben, Kelsey. We'll see you both in the morning."

They disappear down a hallway and behind a door. I tilt my head in question. "Is the master suite on the first floor?"

Ben stands and tugs me to my feet. "Elevator to the upper levels. Their suite is on the third floor. They had it put in a few years ago."

An elevator in a house. Even as the wonder of it sets in, and before I can ask to ride in it tomorrow, Ben's tugging me up the stairs to the second level. "My suite is up here." Wandering hand in hand down the carpeted hallway, we don't make a sound until we reach a dark-paneled door. Swinging it inward, I spy my suitcases when Ben says, "Your things were brought up earlier."

Whirling around, I ask, "Is it right that we . . ."

The slamming of the door behind him as he pulls the shirt off over his head is answer enough. "I guess so," I murmur as I hold up my hands only to find his warm flesh beneath them.

"What are you feeling?" Ben asks as he smooths his hands over my back.

"The happiest I've been in so long, I feel like I'm going to burst. All I can feel is you, and I'm so in love with you, my heart forgot for just a moment what that kind of breathlessness was like," I admit.

He moves his hands from my back to cup my face. "Good." Lowering his head, he sips from my lips briefly before he pulls back. "I want to make love to you, but . . ."

I tip my head. "But?"

"But more than that, I want to talk while I can hold you against my heart." Tugging me across the room, he drops into a chair, pulls me into his lap, and begins to tell me everything he's already said over the phone. Only now I can feel his pain. I can wipe away the tears. I can soothe his hurt. This is more intimate than the physical connection of our bodies because the trust that's built by something like this is what will carry us through life as passion fades.

Eventually, though, our needs change. He spears his fingers through my hair, holding my head against his heart. In the distance, I can hear the grandfather clock ring out two chimes, but we're too wired to sleep. It's then he drags my face up, and his lips land on mine with a hunger born of our need for each other after being apart for so long.

We shed the rest of our clothes quickly in between kisses and nips of each other's skin. Hard, heated kisses intermingle with slow-burning ones as we relearn each other's body with fingers that have a direct connection to our souls.

When Ben slides into me, it's equal parts hunger and branding. There's a thickness to the air when Ben pants out, "I love you, Kelsey. Forever," as he works his cock inside me.

I toss my head back as I grip his shoulders. "I love you, Benedict." After he's fully seated, I move my hands to clasp his face. My hips involuntarily rock, ripping a groan out of him. "I've loved you and will love you always." Then I begin to move.

Soon, we're both lost to the sensations of his cock throbbing inside me as it releases. It's an indescribable pleasure and pain and chaos that echoes our relationship.

CHAPTER SIXTY-NINE

ONE MONTH LATER

Kelsey

"OH MY GOD, THEY'RE INSANE," BENEDICT WHISPERS IN MY EAR. NOT one to lose the moment, he presses a soft kiss to my neck.

I shiver. It takes me a second to be able to think coherently. When I do, I joke, "You mean when you get married, you don't expect to have a bucket of water dumped all over you?"

Still with his face buried against the curve of my shoulder, Benedict murmurs, "Sweetheart, when we get married, if anyone pulls a stunt like that I'd likely be in jail for decking them." He leans back a bit and his eyes are a caress up and down my dress. "Especially if you're wearing anything like this. Christ, you're beautiful."

Just then, Emily dances by with a handsome blond man. "You two having fun?"

I grin. "Ben was admiring the dress you made for me."

"Glad you like it, Benedict." Emily wiggles her fingers before they spin off.

Benedict tugs me closer. "Wasn't she dancing with a different man earlier?"

I nod toward the stage where a man is playing the guitar and singing. "That's Em's husband. The man she's dancing with now is her brother Phil —Jason's husband."

Benedict cranes his neck. "I thought I saw Jason before. Where's he at now?"

I catch sight of him and grin. "Dancing with Ava. Matt's likely hiding behind the food. Ah, see? There he is." I point to where my cousin-in-law is checking the catering table, despite nothing being needed.

Benedict's eyes are serious on mine when he asks, "How did you ever leave this place, all these people who obviously care for you?"

My eyes circle the room and touch on all the connections I left behind—Ava and Matt, Jillian and Brett—glowing despite being soaked to the skin since Brett was baptized by the men and women at his station. Emily, Cassidy, who is tucked next to her husband, Caleb. "Collyer will always be here, Ben. But—"

"But what?"

"But I needed to go south to find my heart. That means my home is with you wherever we are. Even if that means we end up in"—I mock shudder—"Savannah."

I'm rewarded for my words with a scorching kiss in the middle of the dance floor. When it's done, he loftily informs me, "Now that's the kind of happy ending Pilar needs."

I let out a laborious sigh. "Someone's always a critic. How about you let me write the books, and you stick to keeping Ryan's business out of trouble?"

His uproarious laughter has a few heads swiveling in our direction. "Why do I think your job sounds like more fun?"

"Because it is."

Later that night, after Benedict's loved me over and over, we're snuggled together.

A trickle of knowledge dances up my spine. Now that *Courage* is finished, my writer's sense tells me there's only one name for the title of Pilar's last book.

Reunion.

Then it's time to move on to the next chapter of all our lives.

EPILOGUE

TWO WEEKS AGO

Kelsey

"There are times when I reflect on my life and am in awe over the transformation of what was, what is, and what will be. Martha Beck said, Any transition serious enough to alter your definition of self will require not just small adjustments in your way of living and thinking, but a full-on metamorphosis." Turning my head away from the teleprompter, my gaze roams the graduating class, who are eagerly listening to my words.

"It's been twenty years since I stood on this very stage. The last time I was here, I believed I was broken. Instead, it was a gateway to my journey to become the woman I am today. That has very little to do with my physical appearance and everything to do with the strength I've built inside of me.

"The night my parents died, I was in the car with them. But long before the freak accident that cost them their lives, life was already changing. I remember my father clearly shaming my mother for her weight, blaming her for having me, and stating my life was the deterioration of their marriage. It was then I started feeling guilt over my body issues because I can recall the emotional pain of those words." You can hear the wind whispering through the microphone in front of me. The silence is so loud.

"In that split second before the car crashed, I was left with a final life lesson from my father—not all people loved one another. But even at the age of thirteen, I realized, shouldn't we respect each other? Particularly our children?"

There's a smattering of applause before I go on. "The next thing I remember, I was awake, hurt, and crying. My grandparents were trying to assure me my injuries would heal, but how does one go about healing the wounds of a child's heart?

"There's nothing I can do about the absolute resentment I felt toward my father for his utter selfishness other than say I coped. There's nothing I can express about my emotions for my mother other than share my devastating pity. I detest that, as a mature adult, I will never be able to confront them for the emotional burden they left me to carry. Like it or not, my father was my first bully. And he got away with it.

"I will be forever grateful to my grandparents for giving me the opportunity to fulfill my dreams. They did this by sending me to the best academic institution in the state of Georgia." A loud cheer goes up from the audience, students, parents, and faculty alike. "To fulfill my dreams, I endured hell every single day in these hallowed halls." A deathly silence again descends over the crowd. "The boys shoved me up against walls. Girls would call me names or make fun of me in class because I weighed more than they did. I didn't have friends—after all, who would be willing to risk the wrath of the most popular cliques in school? I had no means with which to stand up for myself.

"I'd be lying to all of you if I didn't admit to the fact I considered ending my life," I admit brutally. With a shaking hand, I reach for a glass of water to my left and take a sip before continuing, "One thing stopped me—the agony my grandparents would endure. So, instead of joining clubs or participating in sports, I buried myself in books where I could pretend to be anyone or do anything. In my world, I was the most popular girl in school, the prettiest, and the most adored. My reality was far from that. Day-to-day life found me exceptionally insecure. I dreamed of becoming the person everyone said I should have been, not the person I really was."

Taking a deep breath, I look down at the audience. There's a sea of royal blue. That was part of my deal with Forsyth. I'd speak if the students were permitted to decorate their mortarboards in blue, breaking the century-long tradition of no enhancements to the black-and-white attire at graduation. This way, I could look out across the sea of blue and garner my strength for the speech on anti-bullying and anti-hazing I was delivering to the students who would help shape the future.

"Standing where I am now, it must be hard to imagine all of this. Forsyth now has such a strong stance against bullying and hazing. In part, it's because of what happened to so many of us all those years ago." With a quick glance to the side, I see Benedict nod slowly before mouthing, "I love you." He's holding our baby daughter in his arms. Just seeing them there settles the butterflies swirling inside my stomach.

About a year after we got back to New Orleans from Benedict's trip to help young Logan, Jillian's wedding, and keeping his promise to work with a counselor, Benedict proposed with his grandmother's ring. "Here's to knowing that with you by my side, I'll win every single day," he whispered right before he slid the antique diamond on my finger.

When he asked, we were lying in the backyard of our house, looking up at the stars through the leaf-covered branches of the summer trees. I sobbed out, "Yes."

Our wedding, held at Commander's Palace six months later, was everything I dreamed of as Pop-pop walked me under the overhang of the beautiful tree in the courtyard into Ben's waiting arms. My cheeks hurt from smiling so much as Val and Jillian danced with Pierre and Pop-pop. Nana cut a rug with Vince. Ryan Lockwood and his husband Jared Dalton deliberately bumped into his brother Caleb and Cassidy. My cousin Ava was twirled around by her husband, shocking everyone from the Collyer contingent. Emily Freeman—who designed my wedding gown—boogied with Darin as her husband crooned onstage with his cousin-in-law, country music legend Brendan Blake. It was a huge surprise Em and I managed to keep to ourselves until the mad shrieking began from all the kids at Le Cadeau—an appearance Em arranged with Brendan to make while he was on his way to a concert in Alabama.

Dancing under the twinkling lights in my husband's arms, Benedict whispered in my ear something that cemented the night as perfect. "Is it just me, or is Logan hitting on Max? Aren't they a bit young?"

Tipping my head to the side, I met Morgan's watchful eye. She mouthed, "Nice ending." I laughed before brushing my lips against Ben's lightly and whispering, "How old were we when you almost kissed me?"

"Point taken," he said before he took control of our kiss. Our guests got into the spirit of it by clinking cutlery against their glasses with enthusiasm. And the kiss, much like the magic of our night, went on and on.

"I ate to mask the agony of my parents' death. I ate to control the pain of what was happening at school. I was eating to camouflage the pain I couldn't work out on my own but didn't know how to reach out for help. And even as I was enduring that, there were others dealing with physical torments who didn't know how to reach out to end their pain. We were all wondering the same thing—had we asked for it? Did God think this was what we deserved? In my subconscious, I was filling in the gaps of my life with food, wedged in every cheek and jowl.

"But there was one light in the hell I endured here at Forsyth. I hoped that maybe God was listening to my heartbreak after all. Maybe he was sending me a response to my prayers.

"I was horribly wrong." A huge gasp arises from the crowd. My eyes dart to the side. Benedict is wiping the tears falling down his face. A serene smile that's meant for him alone lightens my face. "Then."

Facing the crowd, I plow on. "I ran from this very stage after being subjected to what I believed was brutality, but was really a desperate cry for help. I was devastated in ways I know some of you understand. Right here." I lay my fist across my heart. "I didn't understand at the time that pain isn't limited to one person. It isn't limited to a person because of what they look like, where they live, or even who their friends are. The light I mentioned a few moments ago? He was bullied—more accurately, criminally hazed—himself. And in an attempt to protect someone else from suffering the same fate, he was forced into doing something harmful to me.

"Even though it devastated me then, it set me on a path of necessary healing. Would we both give so much to have found the love we now share without that in our past? Absolutely. But trust me, I don't think it's possible to love my husband more for standing up for his family. Then and now." I turn to face him, and even though he's holding precious cargo in front of him, Benedict and I are openly swiping tears off our faces. I take another drink of water before facing forward and continuing.

Fiercely, I bite out, "I want to point out that if you think the victims of bullying are limited to those to whom the words are said, who deal with the physical abuse, I'll vehemently disagree. Not long after my graduation, my grandparents moved away from this city they loved because I swore I'd never come back again. My husband's father suffered the knowledge of what he endured. These people lived our pain right along with us—victims of the monsters that brutalized our lives. Don't let others rob you of life's precious moments." I wipe my eyes, the next part the hardest for me to admit.

"I left for college scared but hopeful, and that hope was rewarded when I was given a gift of strength from God—my roommate, Valeria. My senior year of college, Val—a nutritional science major—found me a job working for a wildly famous bariatric surgeon. Let me state, this was not what I spent four years of study to be doing in my life." There's a titter through the crowd. I lean against the podium in a manner of negligence as if I'm sharing a secret. "Let's be frank, you're all going to need to call a doctor's office to schedule an appointment eventually. Please—for all that's good in the world —be kind to the person on the other end of the phone. And while you're at it, most customer service people have it pretty tough. Cut them some slack," I add jokingly.

The room laughs like I was hoping they would. Because what I'm about to say is about to get very real.

"I worked in a job I never dreamed of doing for two years because I wanted my mind to stop being bullied. You see, just because I left here didn't mean I left the words behind." The room goes eerily silent. "I worked for Dr. Toli to save up enough money after insurance coverage to have gastric bypass surgery. I slaved away during the day, being abused by callers who assumed I must be fat to work there, only to go home and write like a demon every night. But that wasn't the worst of it.

"I had to weigh in before surgery. I weighed almost a half ton—458 pounds. I was a size 6X. I could not walk from one side of a room to another without feeling as if I was going to collapse. Yet, I remember proudly stripping naked and climbing onto an operating table so a surgical team of doctors could work on me for nine hours to hopefully give me life.

"I remember asking the anesthesiologist to make me beautiful right before the mask was lowered onto my face. And do you know what he said? He told me I already was." Closing the folio in front of me, I work solely off the prompter. "Of course, I thought it was just talk. After all, who could believe I was anything special? After all, who was I but King Kong?"

This time, it's my voice bouncing the dreaded name off the walls of Forsyth. It still echoes back at me. I hear clothing shift as people move uncomfortably in their seats. "When it came time to choose my pen name, I was transported back to the place that inspired me to write *Betrayal*. Here. Forsyth. King Kong"—I pause for effect—"became Kee Long. There was a hope that people would relate to my characters because, as much as I am Kee Long, I'm also Pilar Martell. And I'm finally proud to admit it.

"After selling *Betrayal* to my publisher, hitting bestseller lists, and securing three more book deals, I started faking beauty. In becoming obsessed with ensuring no one would ever be able to point at me again and call me King Kong, I shelved the girl who desperately wanted just to be loved. And that's where true beauty comes from. That's the woman who is laying her soul before you.

"You need to understand what I didn't appreciate back then. You are already beautiful." One girl, whose hair is a gorgeous shade of blond, is shaking her head back and forth. I grab the mic and walk down the steps on the side of the stage until I'm right in front of her. "Yes, you. All of you. Do you realize you are the next generation of honesty, trust, faith, and loyalty that Forsyth has been trying to instill in you the last four years?" People start twisting as I walk around the graduating class of 2022. "Right now, you have the most important tool you'll need to make the changes in the world that will be evolutionary. You have a heart."

I make my way back onto the stage. As I pass by Benedict on my way up the steps, his hand reaches out to snag mine. I grip it tightly even though the connection is brief. A million words and a thousand heartbeats pass through us in that single touch. His love for me, mine for him, exchanged in a brief touch.

I'd endure everything I went through all over again just to have this feeling every day for the rest of our lives.

I speak into the mic before my heel even hits the stage. "Matthew 7 says, 'Ask, and it shall be given you; Seek, and ye shall find; Knock, and it shall be opened unto you.' I didn't ask for help and almost lost everything. The same with so many of us. We kept our silence. Instead of opening up our hearts and trusting family, grandparents, teachers, or maybe someone who genuinely wanted to be a friend, lives were almost ruined. If you get nothing out of what I say today, find the person you trust with everything so they can listen to you with an open heart." I give the nod to the AV guys just off to the left. "I'd like everyone to listen to this song. It says more than my words possibly can. The lyrics are printed in the back of today's graduation booklet with permission by the artist."

"Grey Street" by the Dave Matthews Band begins to play. Thinking back to my class reunion five years ago, I feel like everything in my life was gray before Ben walked back into my life. There was no color.

And I'm so glad I tired of it the minute I looked up into his startling blue eyes.

In the time we spent on Skidaway Island after Benedict went to be with Logan, I will never forget the night he framed my face with his hands, leaned down, and told me, "Our pasts aren't going to be given a chance to ruin our future. Not anymore. While what happened mattered, it won't define us, Kelsey. It can't break us. Nothing will."

Thank you, God, for the miracle of insight you sent us both. After all, look at what we gained by taking the leap and holding onto the only thing that matters—each other.

The song winds down. My nerves start to make my stomach churn. "Before I wrap up, I'd like you all to take a stand with me against bullying and hazing. Right here, right now. It's okay if you can't, I understand. But know I'm standing right with you, and there is support from me, and from your now former administration, if you need it. Students, parents, administrators, family, and friends, if you are or have ever been a victim of bullying or hazing, please stand. I want this cycle to end here for the people in this room. Now. Let's go forward with the promise we will be kind. We will stand up for those who need us. We will be the leaders of the future." I step out from behind the podium in a black graduation gown with the blue shoes I bought so long ago at Easy On Me when Benedict and I were just a possibility.

Behind me, I hear the slap of chairs hitting their seats as members of the administration start to stand. Including, to my surprise, President Adams. Then the sound is like the popping of balloons. Chairs from sections all around the outdoor amphitheater start slamming as people stand.

More than half of the people are standing, including to my shock Chad Zhang. His tear-streaked eyes meet mine, and his head bobs in acknowledgment of the words I've spoken. My hand flies to my mouth as a sob erupts. I cry passionately into the microphone, "I am here for all of you. Do not believe you are alone ever again! Do not think you don't deserve life, happiness, love—in whatever form that takes.

"My name is Kee Long. I was bullied, have had loved ones hazed, but we're united in standing for this cause. Whether it's through my words or organizations such as Stomp Out Bullying, there are people ready to stand by your side. Now, let's talk about reunions. In a few years, you're going to be invited to one. Promise me this. In ten years, I want to be invited back to yours. I want you to share your stories with me because I know reunions aren't easy." I flash a huge smile at Benedict. "But, boy, do they have their rewards."

His magnetic smile lights up my life as I wrap up the speech I've agonized over for a month.

"I'd like to leave you with another quote by Maya Angelou. 'I can be changed by what happens to me, but I cannot be defined by it.' Life will test your faith. You may feel like it's going to let you go, but trust me, it won't. Somewhere along the way, there will be people who will catch you when you stumble. They'll love you just for being who you are. Nothing more, nothing less." My hand reaches up to frame my neck. "Just keep your hearts open and find the courage to go on. Thank you."

Turning off the microphone, I'm almost knocked off my feet with the overwhelming applause I receive. Lips parted, I turn slightly to find Benedict cupping his hands over Hope's head, trying to muffle the noise against her delicate ears. The love and pride on his face are like a gravitational pull. But before I can take the first step in his direction, President Adams is at my side. "I have never been more honored to call someone a graduate of Forsyth Academy than I am right now, Kelsey," he murmurs.

My throat feels tight, but I still manage to say, "If I succeeded in getting through to even one of them, it was worth it."

"I think you did more than that. Look," he encourages me.

And I do.

The blond-haired girl has lifted her head. She has a scar on her face that she'd likely been ridiculed for. A group of teens is surrounding her, urgently saying something. She turns her head to hide that side of her face until a tall, dark-haired boy walks up behind her and lays his hand on her shoulder. We watch as he tucks her hair behind her ear, showing off the flush in her cheeks. Glaring at the others, he leads her away.

"So, it won't be perfect in a day." Miracles are just that, and they're reserved for the right moment at the right time.

"But at least you got them talking," President Adams reminds me. He leans over and hugs me before turning me in the direction of my family.

Maybe, just maybe, by the time Hope's in school, all students will have a chance for a better future—one where people are accepted for who and what they are.

Inside their hearts.

In the meantime, I wonder what Benedict's going to think later about the fact I arranged for our family to watch Hope for us tonight. Since we'll be celebrating the speech at the Perrault family compound with Ava, Matt, Val, Darin, and Lucy, Cade and Lisa, Nana and Pop-pop, and Pierre and Roberta, there are plenty of volunteers willing to look out for our little girl.

I already have a reservation at the Westin, where our personal reconciliation occurred. With a sidelong glance in my husband's direction, I catch the way his eyes rake over me before they meet mine.

Then again, he may already know.

While tonight may start out the same way as the last one, I already know it will end differently. After all, Benedict and I are already reunited.

WHERE TO GET HELP

AS WELL AS A FEW PERSONAL TRUTHS

When I brought Kelsey and Benedict into Amaryllis, I knew I'd fall deeper into their story and tell more than a bit of my own. As much as we've seen and heard about fat shaming in the media, there's also been worldwide coverage about sports hazing.

Yet, some will say these individuals don't deserve a happily ever after.

I beg to differ.

I have a tattoo that spans my shoulders. If you see it, it might give you insight into my life. Smack dab in the center is a line from a song that spoke to me after enduring years of being persistently bullied.

Helplessness is not a feeling I expected to find myself in lockstep with. Despondency is worse. And yet, I still gave the impression of strength.

Sound familiar?

Now, tell me I don't deserve the love I fought for with my husband and son.

Here's my truth. I was bullied. I had loved ones hazed. I stand against bullying.

Whether through my words or organizations such as Stomp Out Bullying, there are people ready to be your advocate. Another resource is Stand Up to

Bullying (an official website of the United States Government). From there, you can find specifics about school bullying, cyberbullying, laws, and more information to get help.

Don't let others rob you of life's precious moments.

Especially love.

ACKNOWLEDGMENTS

Nathan, two words. Grey Street. I love you.

To my son, Your eyes are blue for a reason. I just know it. As handsome as you are, it's your heart that's the most beautiful part of you. I love you.

Mom, I love you. Thank you for fighting for being my sword and shield before I knew I needed one. Dad, I wish you could read this. I hope you know how much I love you and I appreciate why.

Jen, you inspired this story sixteen years ago when you asked me to give a "talk." You forced me to confront emotions I wasn't ready to. Then. Now? Thank God. I love you.

Anne and Jim, for grounding me for a $538 phone bill. Listen, that first month at college was hard. Thank you for always leaving your self-service sign up for me and for bouquets of peach roses.

My Meows, when you're shopping for your wedding dress to the man of your dreams, there's nothing like your friends offering to expand your budget if you fell in love with a different dress. I didn't need the dress; I just needed all of you. I love you. Always.

To my missing butterfly, Susan Henn. You were the first to read this story; hell, any of my words. There isn't a day that goes by where I don't feel the loss of you.

Amy, Kristin, and Dawn, you make me shine and give me strength. Thank you for being my friends as well as so much more.

To Missy Borucki, I'm so grateful you've entered my life, Queen of T... I can't write it here. You know what I'm want to say.

To Holly Malgieri, my twin. Thank you for saving everything—including my heart.

To my cover designer, Deborah Bradseth, Absolutely astonishing. This cover, this series, is Amaryllis. XOXO

To Wander Aguiar, Andrey Bahia, Jenny Flores, and Donna Lathan. One of these days we're all going to be in the same place so I can hug you all properly. XOXO

To Gel, at Tempting Illustrations, holy hotness! I love every thing about your art and you!

To the team at Foreword PR, thank you for all the big and little things you do.

Linda Russell, thank you for your faith and continual kick in my pants. Thank you for looking out for coincidences and always being someone I can trust to have my best interests at heart.

My Musketeers, every day I'm grateful we don't have the burden of long-distance phone charges. We'd be screwed. I love you.

And finally, the most important dedication. To you, my readers. I am overwhelmed by your emails, your comments, and reviews. I love hearing from each and every one of you. Thank you for your support and for choosing to read my words.

ABOUT THE AUTHOR

Tracey Jerald knew she was meant to be a writer when she would re-write the ending of books in her head when she was a young girl growing up in southern Connecticut. It wasn't long before she was typing alternate endings and extended epilogues "just for fun".

After college in Florida, where she obtained a degree in Criminal Justice, Tracey traded the world of law and order for IT. Her work for a world-wide internet startup transferred her to Northern Virginia where she met her husband in what many call their own happily ever after. They have one son.

When she's not busy with her family or writing, Tracey can be found in her home in north Florida drinking coffee, reading, training for a runDisney event, or feeding her addiction to HGTV.